ROADKILL

AJ PELAYO

CONTENTS

To my family for always believing in me

PROLOGUE

THE TARP LINING HIS TRUNK FLAPPED IN THE BREEZE, THE STENCH of death sliding off it and cutting through the fresh morning air.

James Finn sat on the curb between his dark gray sedan and the black and white cruiser with his head in his hands, his dark brown hair clasped between his fingers. Lights from the police car flashed across his face in the dim morning light.

His thoughts were on his daughter Elizabeth, named after his mother, but everyone calls her Ellie. She was his baby girl, although, in all honesty, she wasn't much of a baby anymore at twenty-two years old. But whenever he looked into her bright blue eyes, he felt the same rush of emotions that he had looking down on her in the hospital bassinet for the first time and knew that he would die for her.

There wasn't a thing he wouldn't do for her, so he was sitting here waiting for the police officers to decide on his fate while they stared, puzzled, into the trunk of his car.

He was turning fifty this year, and this morning was

making him feel old. Sitting on this curb made his legs and back ache. He should have taken Eric up on his offer to take this morning's shift, and he could have just stayed in bed.

James flinched and lifted his head when he heard the trunk slam shut. The two police officers were talking in hushed tones, and James strained his ears to try to make out what they were saying. He hoped he wouldn't hear any words like "arrest" or "jail," and he could tell from their stern looks that they also wished he had stayed in bed that morning.

How was he supposed to know that picking roadkill up off the side of the road was suspicious activity? He had always thought of it as a public service. Maybe they would thank him. Although from the looks on their faces, it didn't seem likely.

The first officer - the one obviously in charge - was going over the legalities of the situation with his partner; he was a solid man with a bit of extra padding under his utility belt. He slid his well-seasoned, no-nonsense cop look at James as he was talking, a look that assured James that a thank you would not be a part of this particular exchange.

The second officer was shifting on his feet, a rookie for sure. He was tall and lean, with youth written all over his angled face. He was trying to grow a mustache like his part-ner, but he wasn't having much luck because it was coming in patchy and only added to his boyish appearance.

It suddenly struck James that if they arrested him, he wouldn't be able to finish checking this last stretch of road before Ellie went to work, which would be an absolute disaster.

"Sir," the first officer stood over him, hands on his hips, relaxed but ready for anything. James looked up but didn't say anything, waiting to see what the officer would say about the contents of his trunk before he spilled his guts.

"Can you tell me why you have dead animals in your trunk?" The officer had his most understanding face on, looking down at James with what almost looked like concern. Maybe he thought he was mentally unstable.

James was sure that the officer thought he was nuts - hell, sometimes he felt he was too - but he was just trying to be a good father. He ran his hand through his hair and sighed before looking back up at the two officers, deciding to lay it all out and see where the chips fell.

"Officer, do you have kids?" James shielded his eyes from the pulsing red and blue lights as he looked up at the officer.

"Three."

"Well, you know how it feels to want to protect them, right?"

The officer looked at James, stone-faced and quiet. Several times, the rookie looked between his partner and James before landing on James with a practiced brow furrow. The officer sighed and finally gave James a slight nod.

"My daughter Ellie has anxiety, bad... and if she sees anything dead on the side of the road, she doesn't always make it to work. She has panic attacks, and the last time she saw a dead rabbit on the side of this road, she crashed her car into that street sign over there," James stopped to take a breath and pointed at the sign. The two officers looked over at the sign as well as if the sign mattered in all this.

"So, my son or I clean the roads every morning before she heads to work. And then again in the afternoon before she gets off." James stopped. Surely the officer wouldn't want to know more than that. He waited and hoped it was enough to get him sent on his way.

"Alright, sir, here's the deal. It isn't illegal for a citizen to pick dead things up off the road as long as you aren't blocking traffic or breaking any other laws," he looked down at James and gave a slight shake of his head as he thought the situation over. "However, you should look into a long-term solution to this problem. You can't pick up roadkill forever."

He wasn't saying anything that James hadn't thought before; the officer sounded like James' wife, Sarah. He nodded to the officer and assured him he would think of a permanent solution. He knew this situation wouldn't work forever, but they had been doing this routine for almost four years, and it was working fine.

James stood up when the officer stepped back and indicated that he was free to go with an open-hand gesture toward his car.

"Just out of curiosity," the rookie said, looking at James after a glance at his partner. "What do you do with all of them?"

James was hoping they wouldn't ask that question. He looked at the first officer, hoping he would tell the rookie to mind his own business, but he was also looking expectantly at James, probably thinking it would be good to know.

"I have an account with the local pet crematory." James grimaced and gave a small wave as he climbed into his car and took off to finish his route. He had less than an hour before Ellie would leave the house for work and needed to be home before then.

She didn't know the lengths her family went to keep her from facing the hidden monsters in her mind, and James planned to keep it that way.

CHAPTER
ONE

ELLIE SPLASHED WATER ONTO HER FACE TRYING TO WAKE UP AFTER a rough night. She had nightmares about being trapped in her room. She would open the door to her bedroom and walk right into her room again. She was on a loop track and couldn't get out. She wasn't sure what made it scary because she loved her room, but she still panicked, and that told her it was a nightmare.

It had been her room her entire life. Her parents, James, and Sarah Finn, bought the house before she was born, and she started sleeping in the light green room the night she came home from the hospital.

Not that she could remember that, but somebody had told her.

Her room had changed throughout the years, as children's spaces often do, but it still felt the same. She was twenty-two now, and it still had touches of her childhood, like the light switch plates with the little pink flowers that matched the worn comforter on her bed and the few well-loved stuffed animals that still peeked around her pillows.

The walls were covered with bookshelves, prompting

her parents and her brother Eric to joke that she lived in a library, fitting since she worked at one.

Looking at her reflection in the mirror, Ellie tried to put on her most confident smile. She was average height with ghostly pale skin, brown hair, and ice blue eyes. She thought she looked like Plain Jane, but realistically she was nothing close to plain.

She could hear her parents talking with Eric in the kitchen. He lived in his own place about ten minutes away from home, but he was at the house so often she wasn't sure why he wasted his money on rent.

He had gone to college straight out of high school and received his bachelor's in science two years ago, right on time. Eric did everything in the timeline that society and their family expected. He grew and bloomed into a fully functioning adult as if it was the easiest thing to do. If Ellie had followed in his footsteps, she would have completed her degree this year. But Ellie was stuck.

They had accomplished every life milestone two years apart from the time she was born until she came running home from college after the first three days.

Two years after Eric went to college, Ellie moved into her dorm room. The first day she went to her first class for the first hour without hearing a word the teacher said, then ran out to find a bathroom to throw up.

She tried the second day to go to her second class, and she only lasted twenty minutes before she ran out with sweat dripping down the back of her neck and pooling in her bra cups.

She didn't make it to her class on the third day. She called Eric instead, but she couldn't even speak, and by the time he got there, her dorm roommate had called the campus police.

Eric found her crouched in the corner of the room shaking, tears silently streaming down her face as she gasped for air. She didn't remember Eric getting there that day, but when she could pull herself out of the grips of her mind, she was in his truck, wrapped under his arm, driving back home.

After that, she gave up on the idea of school and started to look for work instead.

Luckily for her, she was able to find a job quickly at the local public library. When she saw the ad, she knew it was the perfect job for her. Working in a library meant limited interaction with people; they had to be quiet because it was a library. It was just what Ellie needed, a calm environment with clear and reliable expectations.

She sighed and stepped out of the bathroom. It was six thirty a.m., meaning she needed to grab her standard breakfast muffin and head out for work. Every day she left her house at precisely six forty-five a.m. and arrived at work at six fifty-five a.m., which was the perfect amount of time to clock in, put her lunch in the break room fridge, and be at her little desk surrounded by stacks of books right when the clock struck the hour.

She was about to step onto the stairs when she heard her name and stopped with her foot hovering above the first hardwood step. She brought her foot back over the carpet and leaned forward to listen to what they said about her.

"Dad, you could have gotten into trouble this morning... we need to figure out something better." It was Eric. She could tell by his tone that he was upset with their father, but that didn't explain why her name had come up.

"It ended up alright, Eric. And you know that if we could figure out a better way to fix the issue, we would."

Ellie crouched down next to the railing while her father was talking. She had sat here often as a child with Eric, listening to private conversations between her parents.

Except now, her brother was a part of them, and she wasn't. Maybe this was another one of those life milestones that she hadn't reached yet.

Then again, since she was the youngest, she might never be on the other side of this particular milestone.

"We are making it impossible for Ellie to be independent. She needs to start figuring out who she is, Dad, and you need to let her."

Ellie frowned; she was independent; she had a job and drove herself to and from work. She didn't like the idea of Eric thinking of her as some baby who couldn't care for herself.

Eavesdropping on her parents used to be fun, but she didn't want to listen anymore. It wasn't the same with Eric on the other side.

Pulling herself off the floor, Ellie stomped down the stairs to ensure everyone heard her coming.

Walking into the now silent kitchen, Ellie tried to look oblivious. Her parents were standing side by side drinking coffee, and Eric was leaning against the wood counter of the kitchen island. They were all watching her. Ellie wondered if they knew that she was listening in. They looked guilty, making Ellie feel bad even though she didn't know why. They should feel bad, not her. She would just get her muffin, leave, and not look at them. Or was that just more obvious?

"I'm going out with Dane after work," Ellie said. *How's that for not being independent; would someone that wasn't independent have a boyfriend?* She didn't think so.

"Is he picking you up?" Her dad asked, showing a hint

of concern. He had always been such a worrier. Ellie frowned, wondering if that was the case.

"He's going to come to the library, and we'll walk over to Sally's Creamery. I'll be home after."

"Okay, just let us know if you are going anywhere else." Her dad smiled and gave her a wink as she closed the front door behind her.

She hadn't had time to eat in the house since she spent so much time listening at the stairs, so she would have to eat as she drove, and she was already five minutes behind on her schedule. She felt the first tendrils of anxiety snake down her arms as she held the steering wheel with one hand and her homemade banana muffin with the other.

Focus on the road, she thought, trying to steady her breathing. She could feel the tightness in her chest, and she opened her mouth to breathe deeply. Her watch pulsed, and she knew the "Breathe" icon would appear if she looked at it, but she couldn't stop to do that right now.

As she wound down the road, she was once again thankful that she didn't work far from home and would soon be back at her familiar desk chair that squeaked when you scooted it in and out from the smooth wood desk. The desk would have books stacked on it from the book return cart.

Her boss Ana would have opened the return bin outside this morning when she arrived at six thirty and took all the books in to be processed by Ellie, which was her favorite task of the day. Any job that required zero human contact was a plus to Ellie, people made her feel nervous, and she always over-thought even the most trivial conversation and picked it apart for inaccuracies and stupidity.

Thankfully, the library didn't open until nine a.m., so she had plenty of time in the morning to adjust.

As she turned into the parking lot, Ellie felt the breath she had held for the last couple of blocks release in her chest. She hadn't noticed that she was holding her breath until she felt the relief that washed over her when she let it go.

"Good morning Ellie!" Ana called out to her as she walked through the large glass doors at the front of the building. Ellie flipped the lock behind her and walked through the quiet lobby. Ana had a few necessary lights on, and the dim light streaming in from the windows mixed with the books' dust gave peace to the space. Ellie took a deep breath, and the library hugged her.

"Morning," Ellie said as she walked back to her desk. She saw the stack of books waiting for her and the tightness she had felt in her chest during her drive finally uncoiled—five piles waited for her, two on the desk and three on the floor surrounding her chair.

She loved when there were a lot of books to check in because work could be slow, and the longer she was checking in and processing the books, the less time she had to spend at the check-out desk. She was happy to leave that job to Ana.

Ellie's desk was behind the checkout counter in the corner and tucked against the wall. It felt secluded because she could sit with her back to the public at the counter, and sometimes she would forget that they could still see her. Ellie sat and began looking through the books.

She needed to check every book that came back in for damages before she could scan it as returned and then put it on her cart for someone to put away. Any books that had damages had to be assessed and, if necessary, repaired before returning to their home on the shelf. She hated to see the books come in damaged, but she loved spending more time with them, so it wasn't always such a bad thing.

It took her over an hour to go through all of the books, and only one had come back with damages; some unsupervised child had scribbled their giant crayon across every page of *Are You My Mother*, it might be a lost cause, but Ellie would try her best to save the classic.

She was so focused on the repair that she barely noticed when the library opened. The rest of her day would go to shelving and finding books for people less educated on the Dewey decimal system.

"Excuse me?" asked a small, shy voice.

Ellie looked up and saw a young girl standing at the counter, barely tall enough to see over.

"Yes, may I help you?" Ellie politely asked as she groaned internally.

"Can you recommend a book for me?" The girl looked about ten years old and seemed nervous to be talking to Ellie, which immediately helped her feel more relaxed. She loved being asked for a recommendation and had a list of questions to decide what book would be right.

"Sure. What types of books do you like to read?"

The little girl gave Ellie her list of likes and dislikes and was now following behind her as she walked through the stacks picking out a book every so often and placing it in a book tote. After she had found a bag full of books for the girl, she handed them over, and the girl left with her mom smiling and excited about her new books.

Ellie returned to her desk and was immediately worried that she had picked the wrong books. What if she had chosen a book that was too scary or hard for the girl to read? She always felt like this after giving a recommendation. It was too much pressure.

The rest of the day went by quickly, with only a couple more book recommendations given and covering the front desk while Ana went on her lunch break.

The next time Ellie looked at the clock on her desk, it was already two forty-five, which meant it was almost time for Dane.

Dane made Ellie anxious in a whole new way. He sent flutters down her body, and she felt heat flush through her when he was close. Two things that she had never felt before.

She met Dane at the library a little over two months ago when he came in to check out a book on dinosaurs for his nephew.

He was 6 '1 with jet black hair that fell onto his forehead in a shaggy mess but was kept short on the sides, so it was tight behind his ears and against his head.

His eyes were so dark brown that they were almost black, and he had a dimple on his right cheek but not the left, which made his smile appear crooked and devastatingly charming.

Dane was the first boy to ever ask Ellie out on a date. This wasn't because she wasn't a pretty girl; she would be somewhat striking if she only cared a little.

In high school, the boys noticed her often, and a few might have even gotten up the courage to ask her out, but her pretty face failed to distract from her awkward and extreme introversion.

She was trying to become what the world thought a young woman should be, and the day Dane came through the door, she felt fearless. She had given herself a pep talk in the mirror that morning and told herself that she would talk to someone about more than just books, anyone.

And that anyone just happened to be the first guy that walked in.

Lost in thought, Ellie wondered how she could snag the attention of a guy like Dane and keep it going for this long. She constantly worried and obsessed over things and thought she must be pretty annoying.

When she finally looked up again, Dane stood outside the glass library door, giving her his best crooked smolder.

The clock overhead showed that he was right on time. Ellie quickly gathered up her things and turned the light out on her desk lamp before waving to Ana and joining Dane on the sidewalk outside.

"Hey baby," Dane said as he grabbed and pulled her into his arms.

"Hey, how was your day?" Ellie peeked out from under Dane's arm. They turned together and started walking towards Sally's Creamery.

"It was excellent. I put in for a promotion at work, so fingers crossed that I get that."

Dane worked down the road at Harry and Son's, a small family-owned hardware store he had been with since college. There wasn't much room for growth, but Dane had somehow gotten closer to Harry than his sons, so he hoped to edge out at least one son.

"I am sure you will get it! But just in case..." Ellie said, crossing her fingers and holding them up so he could see. Maybe she could move up in her job if she put in for a promotion, which would make her brother see her as independent.

"We'll see next week if those fingers did their job." He winked at her, and she felt heat rush to her cheeks.

"Maybe I should put in for a promotion too," Ellie said,

glancing sideways at Dane to try and read his expression when she suggested it. He frowned.

"Sure, babe. What would that be?"

Now it was Ellie's turn to frown. The next step up at the library would be a supervisor and then she would have to be in charge of others as part of her new responsibilities, which sent tendrils of panic crawling through her veins instantly.

Dane was still watching her as the panic started to leave her fingertips, so she muttered quietly, "Uh, I'm not sure."

"Well, it's something to think about. How was your day?" Dane asked while pulling open the door to the creamery.

"It was good. I recommended some books to a young girl."

"You don't sound so happy about that," Dane said.

"I'm worried that I didn't pick the right ones. What if she doesn't like them?" Ellie knew she probably shouldn't be discussing this conversation with Dane again.

"Honey, I'm sure she'll be fine. If she's ever seen any Disney movie, you are definitely golden."

Ellie swallowed down her worry and smiled, "You're right."

When it was their turn to order, Ellie stepped up to the counter and asked the girl with the ice cream cone hat for two scoops of mint chocolate chip.

"Didn't you get that flavor last time?" Dane asked while he scrutinized the options under the foggy glass.

"Yeah. It's my favorite." Ellie said.

"Don't you want to try something new? They have a Halloween special."

Ellie made a face and shook her head. She couldn't

imagine ordering something new, and Dane did it every time they went out.

"I'm gonna get it. Two scoops of the Halloween special, please." He paid, and they stepped to the side to wait.

"What if you don't like it?"

"That's what taste spoons are for, babe!" He said with a laugh.

"But you didn't ask for a tasting spoon. You just got it."

"I like to live dangerously. If you want to join me, I might be willing to share a bite." He grinned at her and leaned in to give her a light kiss.

They got their ice cream and found a table towards the back. Ellie could still feel Dane's lips, and she wanted more. They had been dating for a couple of months but hadn't gone further than kissing. She had never gone further than kissing, period.

"I think you should come over to my place tonight," Dane said, putting another spoonful of black and orange Halloween ice cream in his mouth.

"For dinner?"

"Yea, dinner. And maybe a movie. I am sure we can find something good on Netflix."

Ellie had heard her brother talking about having girls over to "Netflix and chill," which meant something more than the literal words defined. She wasn't sure she was ready, but the idea of being more grown-up was still growing in her mind.

"There are a couple of movies that I have been wanting to watch," Ellie said with what she hoped was a confident smile.

"Well, if we are going to make it a marathon, maybe you should just plan on spending the night." Dane reached over and squeezed her knee, which sent a shiver up her leg, and a squeak escaped her lips.

"Uh, yeah. I think that would be okay." Ellie picked up her phone to check it with her mom and hesitated.

Dane read her mind, "You don't need to check it with your mom, babe. You're an adult."

Shit. She was an adult. Maybe this was the reason Eric didn't see her as an adult. She did a mental head slap and smiled back at Dane.

"I was just checking the time. I need to go home and get some stuff before spending the night." She set the phone down, even more determined to prove Eric wrong.

"Yeah, I was thinking you could pick up some things while I start making dinner."

Concentrating hard, Ellie was able to keep her face neutral, but her mind went into hyperdrive. This was it; she was going to spend the night with a man and away from home, finally! She was terrified but maybe also a little excited. It was weird.

"Your place at five?"

"That sounds great," he said as he leaned in to kiss her. Knowing what the night probably had in store caused heat to rush from Dane's lips straight to her stomach.

Standing up, Dane once again draped his arm across Ellie's shoulders and steered her toward the lot behind the library. He walked her to her little blue Sentra and retraced his steps to his Silverado.

———

ELLIE SAT in her car for a moment and fought off the darkness closing in on her mind; you're *okay; it will all be okay*. Breathing in through her nose Ellie held it to the count of four before slowly letting it out through her mouth. She felt a little dizzy and did this a few more times.

Okay, mental inventory, she thought to herself, hoping that she could gain control over the situation with clarity. She had just accepted an invite to Dane's house to spend the night, which obviously meant sex, well it didn't have to mean that, but Ellie kind of hoped it did, and she was going to have to tell her parents where she was going and staying for the night which meant they were going to know she was having sex. Gag. *Get it together, Ellie. Most girls your age have already had sex with a bunch of guys. Mom and Dad can't expect you to stay alone and celibate forever.*

Ellie pulled up in front of her house and sat there waiting for the courage to go inside and talk to her parents. She thought she would speak to her mom first because she was the safe bet for support and understanding. She looked at the house that she had grown up in. It was a two-story beige house with an even darker beige trim. It had curtains instead of shutters, and they were all hanging open to allow the sun to warm the house. It was Spring, so - in California - that didn't mean cold, but it was chilly enough to create the need to seek out the sun inside a closed space, away from the winds.

Ellie took one last calming breath before climbing out of the car and walking up the pathway to the front door. She could see her mom cooking dinner in the kitchen through the window. The smell of pot roast night filled her nose as she opened the door and covered her like a blanket. Her shoulders relaxed as the safety of home overpowered her fears.

"Hey, Mom," Ellie said, walking into the kitchen.

"Hey, honey. How was work?"

"Good, pretty quiet."

"How was your ice cream date with Dane?"

"It was good. He asked me to come over tonight for dinner and a movie."

Her mom stopped chopping the vegetables she was working on and looked at her, "Oh really?"

"Yeah, and I was thinking that the movie might end late, and I should probably just stay over there so that I don't have to drive late at night." Ellie thought this sounded like a reasonable explanation that didn't scream sleepover with a man.

"You are going to spend the night at Dane's apartment?" Her mom had wholly forgotten the veggies, turning her back to them to face Ellie.

"Well, it would just be easier to stay there and not have to worry about driving late at night when it is dark. If you don't want me to, I don't have to, but I will probably be really late."

Her mom was thinking things over, not saying anything.

"I just figured since he lives closer to the library anyway, and I will be tired...So that is probably the safest idea." She hated the silence. Her mom was still just looking at her, and Ellie could feel her wheels turning, but she couldn't stand the silence.

Finally, her mom answered, "Okay, sweetie, if that is what you want to do. I will let your dad know." She smiled at Ellie and turned back to her veggies.

Ellie sighed in relief that that was done, and she didn't even have to tell her dad. She had been banking on that when she decided to talk with her mom first. Quickly before somebody could make any questions about sleeping arrangements, she turned and ran up the stairs to her room.

She closed the door behind her and flopped onto her

bed. It was almost four thirty, and she told Dane she would be there at five, so she should pack her things. The trouble was she didn't know what she should pack. A toothbrush was a given, but did she need to bring toothpaste, shampoo, and conditioner? She wished she had some little shampoo bottles because packing her mega bottle with a pump nozzle didn't feel right.

She decided just to bring a change of clothes and her toothbrush. She would borrow shampoo and toothpaste from Dane. That seemed like a regular relationship-y choice.

Ellie shoved all her stuff into her "I Like Big Books" tote bag and was ready to go. Not really. She had everything tangible that she needed, but she could use more confidence and courage.

As Ellie walked down the stairs, she heard her parents in the kitchen whispering again. She paused before the doorway, and they hadn't noticed her, so she decided to listen in.

"Eric is taking care of it. I called him right away," Her mother said.

"Okay, well, maybe I should call him real quick to make sure he's done." Her dad looked flustered, and he had his phone in his hand as she paused in the doorway.

He turned to leave the room; he looked stressed and didn't notice Ellie until he almost bumped into her in the doorway.

"Oh, sorry, sweetie, I didn't see you there. I'm going to call Eric, and then I will say goodbye. Don't leave yet." He smiled at her and went to his office.

Ellie looked at the clock and saw that it was already ten to five, and she needed to leave. She was going to be late as it was, and she didn't want to wait around.

"I told Dane that I would be there at five, so I think I should go," she told her mom. "Will you tell Dad that I had to leave and that I said bye?"

"He won't be long, Ellie. Just give him a minute." She gave Ellie a strained smile and opened the door to the oven to check on the roast, but Ellie knew she didn't need to check it. Her mom had roasting time down to a science. It was in the oven for exactly four hours and fifteen minutes. A minute more, and it was dry.

"Before you go, I thought we should talk," her mom said, peeking out of the kitchen to ensure no one was there. "You've never spent the night with a boy before, and I just want to make sure that you understand what will probably be expected of you tonight. By Dane, you know...."

"Uh, Mom, I'm not a child."

"Oh, I know," Sarah blushed. "I know that. I just assumed that you might not know. Since you haven't dated anyone before, I don't want you to rush into anything."

"Mom, please. I know about sex, and just because I stay over there doesn't mean that we need to do anything or that we need to talk about anything, please." Ellie was horrified. And she knew her mom was, too, by how she wrung her hands around.

"I know, Ellie. I just want you to be safe." The painfully earnest look that passed over her mom's face made Ellie cringe.

"I'll be safe, Mom. Dane is a good guy."

Ellie took a step to go into the foyer and saw her dad coming out of his office. Sarah followed behind as they all met in front of the door. James slipped his phone into his pocket and hugged Ellie.

"Bye, sweetheart. Have a good night." He had a hint of

sadness behind the smile in his eyes, and Ellie felt a pang of guilt.

"See, I told you it wouldn't take long," her mom said. "We love you. Drive safe."

"I will," Ellie said as she walked out the door with a weak smile back at her parents.

Once the door was closed, Sarah sighed.

"Eric said everything was good. Did you talk to her about, you know?" Typical dad that he was, James was nowhere near comfortable talking about his little girl's sex life.

"Yes. It was awful."

CHAPTER
TWO

ELLIE ARRIVED AT DANE'S APARTMENT COMPLEX FIVE MINUTES late and rushed to the stairwell. Dane's apartment was on the second floor in the three-story brown stucco building off Lincoln Ave, and the elevator was usually on the fritz, so it wasn't worth bothering with. Also, it was a tight fit, and the walls always felt like they were closing in on her.

Ellie took a few nervous breaths outside of Dane's door. She was fiddling with her tote handles, trying to smooth the edges that were starting to wrinkle from use. Taking a quick breath in, she knocked and stepped back.

Dane opened the door with a spatula in one hand and a glass of wine in one hand. He kissed her quickly on the cheek as she stepped into the foyer.

"Hey, you made it," Dane said with a smile. "Let me grab your bag."

Ellie reluctantly handed over her bag. She wasn't sure what to do with her hands after he took the weight from her fingers. After a hesitant and slightly awkward moment, she let them drift down to her sides. Too bad the weight on her chest hadn't gone with it. She wished he had offered her a glass of wine, and she wondered if it would be rude to get it herself.

She had been to the apartment once just to drop off groceries before they went out to dinner.

She followed Dane into the small entryway of the apartment that opened up into a space between the living room and kitchen. The rest of the apartment was just a single bedroom and bathroom.

The bathroom was technically inside the bedroom, but it also had an additional door off to the side of the hall near the opposite side of the living room so guests could use it too.

Dane put her tote next to the door to his room and went directly back to the stove to tend to dinner.

"What are you making?"

"I am making chicken parmesan with angel hair pasta for my angel." He smiled at her with his crooked grin, and Ellie felt like she was melting.

Maybe it wasn't that scary to be here and away from home. She felt some weight lift as she thought about the butterflies floating in her stomach. They fluttered their wings whenever Dane gave her that smile. The change was hard, and it took some getting used to, but Dane seemed worth the time.

"It smells delicious. Is there anything I can help with?"

"I think I have it all under control. Do you want to put your things in the room? When you come out, I will pour you some wine, and you can relax."

"Sure," Ellie said, trying to be peppy to hide her nerves.

Ellie looked at her bag, and the tendrils came crawling back. The whispers of doubt that she should have brought her shampoo. What if she had forgotten something?

She grabbed the bag, walked into the room, and stopped in the middle. Now what?

She looked at the bed; it was simply made with gray striped sheets and a matching comforter. Ellie put her toothbrush in the bathroom but left her clothes in the tote beside the bed.

That seemed like enough. Now what?

Ellie looked around at the rest of the room. After looking at each wall, it became shockingly clear that Dane didn't have a single bookcase. Which was weird because who didn't have a bookcase? She stalked slowly around the room, looking for someplace else that could be used to store books and was disappointed to find nothing but a stack of magazines on Dane's nightstand.

She picked up the top magazine, Sports Illustrated—swimsuit edition.

Ellie frowned and looked desperately around the rest of the room, but there was little else to look at. A weight machine in the corner with clothes hanging off it, a dresser with odds and ends cluttered over the top. And a laundry basket with clothes piled in the corner next to it.

Ellie had seen enough. She wasn't sure why she was disappointed, but the feeling washed away when she came out of the room. Dane was lighting a candle on his small dining table. He pulled a chair out and gestured for her to sit in front of an already-filled plate of food, complete with garlic bread.

"This looks amazing, Dane."

"I hope you like it." He waited for her to take the first bite, watching her avidly.

"Mmmm, this is so good," Ellie said with a quick smile. She hated when people watched her with expectation. Expectations made her feel like she could fail.

After eating, Dane cleared and washed the dishes while he tasked Ellie with picking a movie on Netflix. She was slipping through trailers stopping every so often, but the horror of having to pick was blinding her to anything she landed on.

"How's it going, babe?" Dane called from the kitchen. He could see her over the counter and smirked as he scrubbed the dish in his hand.

"Uh, I am not sure what to pick. Do you have any suggestions? There are too many good ones to pick from."

"Whatever you want. Didn't you say earlier that you had a couple of movies that you wanted to watch? Just pick one of those. I am almost done here."

Now she was panicking. She said that comment about movies she wanted to watch just to sound confident and like someone who likes to watch movies, but honestly, she hadn't watched a movie in months.

She scrolled down and found the Netflix top ten, a new feature she hadn't seen before. The first thing listed was a show, so she skipped it, but the second one was a movie, and the guys on the front looked like they were running from danger. An action movie seemed right up Dane's alley, so she clicked on that and settled into the couch to wait for him.

"Alright, what we got?" Dane slid onto the sofa, taking care not to leave room for anything between them.

"Action? Something about a guy that has to save the world, I think. But to be honest, I watched a bunch of trailers, so I could be confusing it with one of the million other movies that require the guy to save the girl and everything else."

Dane chuckled deep in his throat, and Ellie could feel

the vibrations from his chest which was now tucked slightly behind her shoulder.

"Sounds about right, babe. Hit play."

They cuddled throughout the movie, which had an explosion every other scene, and any scene that didn't include blood included a half-naked girl. When the credits started to roll, Ellie finally felt like she could relax.

Dane leaned in closer, pressing light kisses against Ellie's neck and up her cheek until his lips closed around hers. She sighed with the pleasure that flowed through her, and she couldn't remember why she had been so worried about tonight.

He slid his hand up her thigh, and she remembered. Dane was Ellie's first everything. When he kissed her for the first time, and she almost passed out from nerves, it became glaringly apparent to Dane that she was inexperienced. To say the least.

Dane was so sweet about taking it slow at first. So far, they had only kissed a lot, and once or twice Dane had let his hands explore under Ellie's top, but he had been careful not to push her.

Now his hand was going places it had never been.

"Is this okay? If you aren't ready, I understand," Dane whispered huskily against her lips between kisses. "But I hope you are... Cause I have never wanted anyone more."

His lips were back on hers without even letting her answer, and he shifted his body to cover hers as they seemed to melt into the couch.

Panic and pleasure warred in Ellie's body.

Her brain was telling her that she had waited long enough, and she didn't want to make Dane upset. She knew that wasn't a reason to give in, but the pressure was there, and she hated the pressure.

Her chest was constricting with nerves. She felt the claws of panic climbing up her throat. *What if it hurts?* She knew from movies and books that it could.

But there was a very convincing location of her lower body that felt hot and hungry for something more. Ellie didn't know how, but she knew pleasure would win out when Dane's hand reached her breast.

———

ELLIE WOKE up in the middle of the night and couldn't breathe. She got out of bed and went to the bathroom, trying to talk herself into thinking she was okay.

You are okay.

You can breathe.

Stop freaking out.

She sat down and put her head between her legs, but her chest was tight. She opened the window and stuck her face close to it, breathing in through her mouth because her nose felt stuffed. She tried to relax and breathe through her mouth but couldn't get a deep enough breath.

What happened?

She was asleep. Did she have a bad dream?

The last thing she remembered was falling asleep next to Dane after having sex for the first time. She frowned; it was pretty disappointing.

Maybe the first time is never good for the girl.

Even though Ellie was a virgin before last night, she still knew a thing or two. She had been exploring her body since she was fourteen, and the other eighth-grade girls started talking about their shower heads like they were magical.

Plus, she had read plenty of books that her mom would consider smut, the kind that had *those* scenes that made you feel tingles and twitches and clench in places you didn't know you had.

The men in those stories did things a lot differently than Dane had. Ellie sighed.

The women in those stories always fell asleep happy, warm, and satisfied. She had fallen asleep, questioning why it wasn't the same for her, and now she was panicking.

Maybe it will be better next time?

She wasn't sure, but she was convinced she couldn't breathe right now and felt like she was dying.

Maybe I should wake up Dane.

No, come on, Ellie, this is ridiculous. You can breathe fine. It's all in your head.

You must have had a nightmare.

What if I am allergic to Dane's sheets? The detergent?

Should I take some Benadryl?

She opened the medicine cabinet to see if Dane had Benadryl, but he didn't. Who doesn't have Benadryl on hand at all times? What would he do if he had an allergic reaction? Ellie had Benadryl in her purse, but she didn't want to go out into the hall and possibly wake Dane.

The pressure of having good manners was enough to let her accept death on Dane's bathroom floor.

Ellie stayed on the floor for a while, laying her cheek against the cool porcelain tub.

She had decided when she sat down not to wake Dane. She didn't want to bother him, and even more importantly, she thought he might not like her as much if he knew. He would think she was crazy.

If he could see inside her head, he would break up with her for sure. No guy wanted to be saddled with a drama queen.

She finally crawled back into the bed an hour later,

unnoticed. She didn't think she was dying anymore, at least not currently. She cuddled up to him and focused on her breathing until she fell back to sleep.

In the morning, Ellie woke up with Dane's arm resting on her back and his leg against her thigh. She blinked at the light streaming in through the single curtain-less window.

She looked at her watch and was relieved that she still had plenty of time to shower and get ready for work, but she had forgotten to pack her banana muffin for breakfast, and she didn't have anything to bring for lunch either. She knew she was going to forget something.

Dane joined her in the shower, and her time went down the drain along with his shampoo.

"Babe, you are so amazing," Dane said as he kissed her again. Their bodies were still tangled together, but he was getting ready to pull away.

Ellie smiled at him and rinsed her face instead of answering.

"I was thinking. Maybe I could clear out a drawer for you in my dresser? And I can make room in the closet. That way, if you want to stay the night more often, you could have some space for your stuff."

"Really? You want me to stay over more?"

"I think you should stay over all the time. A drawer is the least I could do." Dane switched positions with her so that he could rinse himself off one last time.

Ellie looked up at the shower head, noting that it was not a handheld, and sighed internally.

"That would be great." She smiled up at him and thought about how she could tell Eric she was so independent now that she was getting a drawer at her boyfriend's house.

"Alright, then, it's settled. One drawer coming up!" He

flashed his dimple at her, making her heart rate pick up, and reminded her that she did feel things for Dane. She just needed a little more from him to get her there when her mind was busy distracting her while they made love.

Dane got out first, toweled off, and walked out to get dressed in his bedroom.

Ellie had brought her clothes in with her, and by the time she was dressed and ready to go, Dane was in the kitchen with a pop tart and a bag of leftovers for Ellie to take for lunch.

She didn't know what to say, but it was the sweetest gesture she could have imagined. No one other than her family had ever worried about caring for her, and it felt amazing. She swallowed the pop tart in a few bites, kissed Dane, and ran out the door for work.

ELLIE WAS SITTING at her desk a couple of hours later, repairing books, when her brother came into the library.

"Hey, sis," Eric said, smiling at her from across the counter.

The swinging door that met where the counter ended had a sign that said Employees Only, and Eric was playfully pushing it with his foot. Knowing that the swinging motion and perceived threat of Eric entering a space he wasn't allowed would drive his sister crazy.

"Hey, what are you doing here?" Ellie stopped working on the book she was repairing and walked over to give him her attention. She put her leg next to the swinging door to keep it closed and looked around for Ana. She didn't want to waste too much time talking, not that anyone would care.

"I just wanted to stop in and say hi. Dad said you stayed at Dane's last night." He was looking at Ellie, assessing her reaction, typical big brother.

"Yep."

"So, things are getting serious with this guy?"

"I think so," Ellie hoped Eric wouldn't go all protective big brother on her and make her feel bad about last night.

"Really? Well, that's good, Ellie. I want you to be happy."

Ellie was surprised that Eric didn't have any warnings about moving too fast with Dane, and he wasn't telling her that she shouldn't be staying the night there yet.

She was glad he wasn't upset. Since she could remember, she had always looked to him for guidance and respected his opinion so much that she would do anything to make him proud of her.

"Thank you." Ellie smiled at him, and she felt like she was truly happy. Maybe if she could hold onto this feeling, she wouldn't feel the dreaded panic creep through her so often. Maybe it would go away altogether. That seemed unlikely, but she was holding out hope.

"Yeah, but you need to be careful too. I mean, how well do you know this guy? Has he had a chance to show you his true character yet? He could be one of those possessive control freaks that barely grasps the English language other than to tell you what to do to make him happy."

There it was. Ellie rolled her eyes and gave her brother a give-me-a-break frown.

"You never know. I mean, I have never met a guy like that, but I have seen movies."

"I don't watch movies, so I guess I wouldn't know," Ellie said nervously.

"Yeah, you wouldn't. See? And I know that all the guys

in your books are written all sexy and confident and with the ability to grow and shit, but this is the real world. Boys may be better in books, but you can't date those ones."

Now they were both laughing. Ellie smiled at her brother and leaned in when he did for a hug.

"I'm going to be home for dinner tonight, so I'll see you at home, okay?" Eric asked. This was probably his whole purpose in coming to the library and trying to find out if she was spending another night with her boyfriend.

"Yeah, see you at home." Ellie thought about giving him another hug, but she didn't want to seem needy either.

It was hard constantly worrying about what others wanted from her.

Eric left, and Ellie returned to work on the book she was repairing. Someone broke the spine on a copy of *Little Women*, and she was trying to reinforce what was now flopping.

She loved the story, and as she worked, she thought about how hard it was for her to make friends. She had a work friend a while ago, but she was transferred to a sister branch of the library, and they had lost touch over time.

Now Ellie didn't really have any friends.

She talked with Ana a little when things were really slow, but the two others on the library staff held different hours, and they stayed out on the floor. She knew their names but not much else.

———

As Ellie walked into the house hours later, she smelled marinara sauce simmering in the kitchen and garlic bread under the broiler, spaghetti night. Eric and her dad were watching a game on television, waiting for Mom to call them to the table. Typical. Ellie chose to go into the kitchen with her mom instead of joining the men of the family to watch whatever sport it was that had their attention.

"Hey, Ellie," her mom was stirring the sauce that was bubbling on the stove. "How was your night?"

"It was good. Dane made chicken parmesan, and we watched a movie."

"That sounds nice," her mom said, still focused on her sauce.

"I think I am going to start staying at Dane's more often."

"Really?" This got her mom's attention. She stopped stirring the sauce briefly to narrow her eyes at Ellie.

"Yeah, Dane and I talked about it, and he said I can even have a drawer for when I want to stay over." She paused to give her mom time to digest that information. "I think it is a good way for me to be more independent."

"Well, Ellie, being independent isn't just about staying the night away from home." She was stirring again, but she was watching Ellie, and her eyes kept flicking to the living room, probably hoping that Eric or James would come in.

"I know that, Mom," Ellie said. She thought that staying with Dane was absolutely what being independent was because she wasn't home depending on her parents. She was in an adult relationship and making adult decisions.

Ellie suddenly couldn't handle talking anymore. She needed a space break. While her mom was busy with dinner, she turned and slipped out of the kitchen. She decided now was the perfect time to put her stuff away in her room.

After putting the contents of her small tote away, she turned to her bookcase to pick a new book to read. Her TBR list had taken over the entire second and third shelves, and she was still tempted to buy a new book off Amazon rather than read one.

She was on her second perusal of the books when her phone started to ring. Knowing it was probably Dane calling her after getting home from work, she flew to the phone and answered on the third ring.

Ellie panted as she answered the phone. And she could hear Dane's deep chuckle coming through the line so clearly she could almost feel the vibrations.

"Excited to hear from me, babe?" Dane asked. She could hear him moving around, putting his keys on the counter, and shuffling through the mail.

"You don't know that. Maybe I was exercising."

"Yeah, cause that sounds like you. Are you at home?"

"Yeah," Ellie wasn't sure what to say anymore. She felt so awkward on the phone.

"Do you want me to pick you up for dinner? I'm feeling like sushi."

"Oh, I can't tonight," Ellie bit her lip, hoping he wouldn't be too disappointed. "I already promised my family that I would eat dinner here." ,

"Oh, okay, well maybe tomorrow night."

"Do you want to come over here for dinner? It's not sushi but it should still be pretty good." The invitation just popped out of Ellie's mouth and she immediately regretted it.

"Okay, yeah that would be nice." Dane sounded genuinely happy about coming to her parents' house for dinner. He had met them before but only in an awkward set of minutes when he picked her up for their first date.

"Okay, great," Ellie said even though she was thinking, *oh shit*. "I'll let my mom know you're coming!"

"See you soon," Dane said with another small chuckle

at her enthusiasm, and he hung up before Ellie could say anything else.

Here came the spiral of dread. Dane was going to have dinner with her parents. What if her dad asked Dane a million questions and scared him away? What if she couldn't think of anything to talk about and everyone just sat in awkward silence? What if her family told embarrassing stories about her?

The what ifs kept coming as Ellie made her way downstairs to tell her mom Dane was coming for dinner. The last what if being, what if her mom got mad at her for inviting Dane without asking first? That one was important, and she didn't even think of it until her foot hit the ground level.

CHAPTER THREE

Dane arrived right on time for six o'clock dinner. The Finn family always had dinner on the table at six and not a minute later. Mom said that "stability in schedule gave stability in life," and this had been the mantra since before Ellie could remember.

Her mom was fine with her inviting Dane. In fact, she seemed excited to set another place at the table. Ellie knew her mom would have enough food, but she also knew she didn't like surprises, so she was glad it wasn't an issue.

Ellie's dad and Eric also seemed happy to hear that Dane was coming over, and her dad even said he was "looking forward to getting to know him," which was a little problematic since Ellie didn't want her dad playing twenty-one questions with her new boyfriend. Still, it was better than him being upset and grumpy about sharing his baby girl with a new guy.

That left Eric as the wildcard. He knew everything about Ellie, and the two were more than just siblings; they were best friends. Or rather, he was Ellie's best friend. Eric had plenty of other friends. Unlike Ellie, he probably considered one of them his best friend, not his little sister.

Eric was a good sport. He let Ellie tag along with him and his friend group. The years they weren't at the same school were the worst for Ellie. It was hard when Eric went to Middle school, and Ellie was still in elementary school. She was never able to find a new place to belong.

The worst was when she was in Middle school without him. She only had him with her for her first year at Oak Hills Middle School; the next two were her worst school years. Kids bullied her relentlessly, her hormones were all over the place, and she had absolutely no friends.

When Eric graduated from high school, it wasn't as bad. Ellie was barely at school anyway. She made sure to take as many classes as possible to get credits the first two years, and in the last two, she could leave early in the day and avoid her peers altogether.

Eric would never do anything to hurt Ellie, but he could be ruthlessly protective, which she was worried might drive Dane away. Not that she had much experience dating, but she read books and watched some TV, and the guys in those didn't seem to like having to deal with protective brothers or fathers when it came to women they wanted to be with.

It was some innate primitive function that screamed from the long past evolutionary gene pool, the need to be the top male or some bullshit like that.

Dane sat beside Ellie and across from Eric, with Mom and Dad at either end of the table, taking up the head positions. They passed the food around so everyone could fill their plates with spaghetti, marinara sauce, meatballs, garlic bread, and salad.

"Everything looks delicious, Mrs. Finn," Dane said, smiling at Ellie's mom.

"Thank you, Dane," Ellie's mom smiled. "Please call me Sarah."

The minutes dragged on without much more than chewing, smiling, and nodding. Ellie couldn't stand it.

"Dane is up for a promotion at work," Ellie blurted out. That definitely wasn't smooth, but it was the first thing that came to mind.

"Congratulations Dane," Ellie's dad chimed in. He was always good at taking a hint, subtle or otherwise. "What's the new position?"

"It's a manager position, sir," Dane smiled easily and didn't seem flustered. Ellie was always impressed with how calm and put-together Dane seemed. She would have been a rambling mess.

"I thought you had to be a son to be a manager at that place," Eric said, observing Dane.

"I guess Harry considers me like a son," Dane replied with an easy smile, and his hand reached over to squeeze Ellie's thigh. Electricity sparked up her thigh, making her clench thinking about how Dane had touched her last night.

"Careful, if he thinks of you too much like a son, you will be stuck like one." Eric's eyes sparked, and Ellie thought he could see Dane's hand on her thigh through the wood table.

"Dane likes his job, Eric. He doesn't feel stuck." Ellie frowned at Eric. She mentally sent a "be nice" signal which he smirked at.

"Well, I don't know that I want to be there forever, but I definitely don't feel stuck. I have been working there for a while now, and I have been taking business classes. I wouldn't be against running the place for Harry down the road. If he needed me, that is." Dane shoveled more spaghetti in his mouth and sopped up some sauce with his garlic bread.

Ellie envied how at ease he looked. He didn't seem worried about what Eric thought of him at all. Ellie wished she could feel that at ease with the judgment of others.

The conversation flowed well after that, but Ellie was still glad when it was over. She wasn't sure how her family felt about Dane, and she really liked him, so she didn't want them to ruin this for her.

After dinner, Ellie helped her mom wash dishes in the kitchen while Dane went into the living room with her dad and Eric to watch a sports game of some kind.

"So, Dane, I'm glad you came over tonight," James said, looking over at Dane. He was judging his next words carefully. He didn't want to scare this guy away from his daughter, but he would need to bring him in on things if she stayed at his house.

"Well, it was nice of you to have me on such short notice," Dane said.

"Yeah, listen, we need to talk while Ellie isn't around."

Eric walked over to the door and looked out. Then he shut the door a little so there was only a sliver opening, giving them more privacy.

The game was forgotten, but the noises droned on in the background. Dane looked between James and Eric, but neither said anything else.

"Do I need to guess what this is about? Cause Ellie is a grown woman, and I don't-"

James put his hand up to cut Dane off and grimaced as

if he was in pain hearing Dane mention his daughter in that way.

"Ellie is an extraordinary girl, but... she struggles with her emotions when it comes to certain things."

"Okay...." Dane's brow furrowed, but he didn't hint that he understood what James was talking about, so Eric jumped in.

"She gets nervous about things," he supplied.

"Yeah, I've noticed that," Dane said. He had been dating Ellie for a couple of months, and she worried more than any other woman he'd been with.

"Okay, good," James said, relieved. "Well, one thing she has an issue with is roadkill."

"Roadkill?"

"Yeah, actually, anything that has to do with death is a terrible trigger for her, but roadkill is the one that has been causing trouble."

"Last year, she saw a dead rabbit on the side of the road and crashed her car into a street sign," Eric said.

"Wow, really?" Dane was looking between Eric and James, and he was obviously wondering where this was going.

"Yeah, it was pretty bad. Ellie was okay, but when the police arrived, she was gasping for air like she couldn't breathe."

"I had no idea."

"It all started four years ago when she came home from college and started learning to drive. She was driving with Sarah, and she saw a coyote hit by a car, and a little way later was a pup hobbling down the road injured." Eric stopped. He looked at James for reassurance that he was on the right track, but James was lost in his thoughts.

"And that is what triggered her fears?" Dane asked. He

was trying to understand, but his face showed he was struggling.

James was paying attention now. A look of guilt washed over him, and he cleared his throat.

"That one was bad. She refused to drive for a month and cried for days. She wouldn't even talk after they passed the pup, and our mom refused to let her stop to try and get it. Since then, driving has been a problem if she even sees animals on the side of the road. But roadkill is the real problem right now." Eric would have kept talking, but James finally looked ready to join the conversation again.

"Yeah, but we have been taking care of the issue," James jumped back in to steer the conversation away from more stories about Ellie.

"How are you doing that?" Dane asked, confused.

"Since then, Eric and I have been cleaning roadkill up off the roads that Ellie will be driving on before she goes out. We missed one time last year... scheduling mishap." James cringed a little. Having it out in the open for Dane to judge was nerve-wracking.

"You go out and clean roadkill off the street? How do you know where she is driving?" Dane's eyebrows were so furrowed that they were beginning to look like one.

"She tells us what her plans are, and we make sure that we go out before her and check the roads. It is pretty simple because animals are usually hit at night, and we go out and check early morning before a lot of people are out driving and clean it up. After that, during the day, less roadkill happens."

"Okay," Dane said. He was processing the information slowly. "So, what do you need from me?"

"Well, if Ellie is going to be staying with you, we might need you to help occasionally."

"Wouldn't she know that I left the apartment?"

"We don't want you to go out on the first shift. That would be noticeable. Just let us know if something changes in her schedule, and if you can help with the after-work shifts sometimes, that would be great."

"Or you can just drive her to work. That would help, too," Eric chimed in.

"I'll help out however I can." Dane sounded willing, but his face was a war of confusion, and James thought a little judgment.

They were all silent for a few moments. Slowly each turned back to the Lakers game that was on.

"Can I ask a question, though," Dane said suddenly. "What do you do with all the roadkill?"

Eric burst into laughter. James shook his head at his son. He looked at Dane and cursed him a little for asking that question. He hated that question.

"I've got an account at the local pet crematory."

"Yeah, we're on a first-name basis with Dead Fred." Eric snorted and leaned back in his chair, trying not to laugh.

"Dead Fred is a pretty good name for someone that cremates animals," Dane laughed. "What does he call you guys?"

James shook his head at Eric again, but he couldn't help but smile a little. Eric was practically vibrating, trying to keep in the laughter.

"He calls me 'James Lector,' and he calls Eric 'Reaper.'" And with that, they were all laughing at the absurdity.

The men finished watching the game as Ellie and her mom finished the dishes, and James felt like things were looking pretty good.

He was able to talk to Dane about Ellie and include him in helping to take care of his little girl. That alone gave him reason to like the guy. Even though he would rather keep her safe all on his own, he knew that wasn't possible, and eventually, she would move out, and he would have to relinquish even more of his role.

His wife wasn't as supportive of his protective work as he thought she would be, but he knew deep down she understood why he did what he did. It was all for Ellie.

LATER THAT NIGHT, Sarah asked James about his conversation with Dane. They sat in bed together, Sarah reading a novel and James filling out a crossword puzzle. James sighed at his wife's question.

"He seemed a little judgmental, but I guess that's understandable," James said as he scratched a line through the clue he just completed.

"You are lucky he didn't run out of here."

"Nah, he likes Ellie. I could tell he would be able to handle it. Besides, his running out of here wouldn't have been a negative in my book. That would have fixed the issue just as well."

"The issue? James, the issue is not Dane. Or Ellie wanting to go out and be an adult..."

"Here we go." James lowered his crossword and slammed the pencil down with it.

"Yes, here we go. I have been telling you for years that we need to confront the real issue. Get Ellie some therapy and stop acting like picking up roadkill daily is sustainable." Sarah closed a bookmark between the pages of her book and set it on the stained oak nightstand.

"We've talked about this, Sarah. I don't want her to hurt. We bring up all these issues and trauma, and she will be hurt. And we tried the therapy, remember? It wasn't working."

"Maybe she just needed more time."

"Yeah, and maybe, it would just make everything worse."

"James, I think ignoring the problem is just going to make it worse." Sarah huffed and got up out of bed, heading to the bathroom. She always did this when she was tired of a conversation. She moved away.

"What we are doing is working. Ellie is growing up and becoming more independent. As things progress with Dane and she gets more friends, I am sure she will grow out of it on her own."

"I hope you are right. Because otherwise, YOU are just delaying her chance to get real help."

And with that, Sarah closed the door to the bathroom and the conversation, leaving James with his thoughts. He was just trying to do what was best for Ellie, and this was working. Why change the system if it was working?

James hoped he was right about this. Sarah would never let him hear the end of it if he wasn't.

CHAPTER
FOUR

Early the following Saturday morning, Ellie was at home on the family couch reading a book when Eric walked in.

"Hey, sis," Eric said as he shut the door behind him. "How's it going?"

"Good. Just reading. What are you doing here?"

"I just came to hang out a bit. Dad and I have plans later." Eric sat near Ellie on the couch and grabbed the remote. He started channel surfing. After a thorough search, he settled for cartoons. Ellie thought he must be feeling nostalgic for childhood. But after a few minutes, the weird yellow characters that hadn't been part of their childhood were not holding his interest, and he went back to flipping.

"What are you looking for?" Ellie asked.

"I don't know... Don't they have anything good on anymore?"

"Define good?"

Eric stopped when he got to a rerun of *Fresh Prince*.

"Perfect! So, Ellie, I liked Dane." Eric said. Ellie could tell he was fishing for something. He gave her a quick sideways glance.

"I do too." She decided to go simple and see what Eric was looking for.

"Do you think you will be spending more time with him?"

"What do you mean?"

"I mean, are you going to be staying at his place more and doing more stuff with him?"

"Yeah, I guess so." Ellie wasn't sure why Eric was interested in her spending more time with Dane. She didn't even know who he spent time with outside his family and friends. He was twenty-four and had been out of the house for the last six years, but he had never brought home a girl in all that time.

"That's good." Eric went back to watching Carlton do the Carlton, and it was driving Ellie a little crazy. Why didn't he explain himself? Did she have to ask him why he wanted to know? She probably shouldn't be worried about it. Maybe he was just curious about her life. Maybe she should be asking him questions about his life.... Was she a bad sister?

She didn't know the answer to that one.

"Why do you ask?" Ellie finally broke.

"Oh, no reason. I just like that you finally have someone. Hopefully, he will help you be more independent."

"I *am* independent." Ellie frowned. She hated that he thought of her as such a baby.

"Come on, El. You never do anything on your own other than go to work."

"That's not true." She was starting to get angry. First, he told her parents she wasn't independent, and now he was telling her. Now she felt like she had to defend herself and hated doing that, especially with Eric.

"Okay, when was the last time you drove anywhere other than the library by yourself?"

"I go to the store by myself all the time."

"You walk there and back. It's not far enough to count. I'm talking about driving. When was the last time you drove anywhere other than the library?" Eric turned on the couch and gave Ellie a soft look. She could tell he wasn't trying to be mean, but she felt judged nonetheless.

"Okay, so I don't like to drive places alone, so what?"

"Ellie, you are twenty-two years old. You should be able to drive places alone. You should be going out and hanging out with friends, shopping at the mall alone or with girl-friends."

Ellie knew he was right. She had no friends to go out with, and she panicked whenever she drove anywhere. The only place she had mastered driving alone was her job, which was out of necessity.

Plus, her parents and even Eric had given her a ride the first three weeks she had her job before she would go on her own. Why was she like this?

Driving terrified her. She never wanted to learn, but once she quit college and moved home, she knew it was the only way to get to work and not be a total burden on her parents. When her mom first started taking her driving, she had watched a coyote pup limp away from its dead mother in the middle of the road, and she had never felt so helpless and heartbroken.

That was the first time she had a panic attack while driving. Her mom made her pull over, and she had to take over. Ellie didn't drive for weeks after that and even tried to think of a different way to get around town.

Now she could make it to and from work, but she still

really hated having to drive, especially on roads she didn't know.

"So, if I drive somewhere new by myself, will I be independent? Is that what I need to do to be an adult in your eyes?"

"Ellie, that's not what I'm saying. I just think you'd be happier if you got out of the house more and stopped being afraid of living."

"I'm not afraid of living!" Ellie was taking everything that Eric was saying and twisting it into anger in her mind, even though she knew that it was true and that he was only trying to help.

She stood up, feeling her stubborn side boiling up, and headed for the door.

"Where are you going?" Eric jumped up from his spot on the couch when he realized that Ellie was heading for the door, and he was following after her.

"I'm going out! How's that for independence!?" Ellie grabbed her purse and slammed the door behind her.

She ran to her car to get there before Eric came out to try and stop her. He made it out just as she was angling out of the drive.

He was yelling something at her, waving his arms, but she wasn't listening. She was going to prove to him that she was independent.

Just because she still lived at home and didn't like to drive didn't mean she was a baby or something.

SHE DROVE down the street with no direction in mind. Where does one go when they want to prove that they are a free independent woman? She hated the freeway, so she decided that a back road would be best for her first show of independence.

I'll show him.

She was trying to pay attention to the road but wasn't quite sure where to go. She turned down a road that she knew led to the beach. That seemed like a good place. It wasn't too close, but it wasn't too far, and she was pretty sure she remembered the way from all the family trips they had taken when she was a kid.

The wind kicked up out of nowhere and pushed against Ellie's car. She felt like she had to grip the wheel tighter as the wind shifted her around on the road.

It suddenly hit Ellie that no other cars were on this back road. This was good and bad.

Good, because she didn't like too many cars around her, it triggered her anxiety. She couldn't control them and whether they would crash into her out of their own negligence.

Bad, because that meant she was alone on the road.

The road was snaking close to the mountainside with trees and a forested area on either side, and she was starting to think this wasn't the way to the beach. She hadn't been in a while, but she couldn't remember there being so many trees.

As she made the next turn, a deer came out of the trees next to her passenger side and jumped into the road right in front of her car. She slammed on the brakes, and as the deer hit the front of her car, she felt the front end of her sedan spin to the left. Her head smacked against the window and bounced back, coming to a stop on the airbag that had whooshed into existence in the small space.

When the world stopped spinning, and her car came to a jarring halt, Ellie sat stunned—trying to breathe.

Shaking, Ellie twisted to try and open her car door. It fell open with the help of gravity, and she realized that the car had run up the side of the mountain a little so that she was on an incline with her side of the car tilted down. She unbuckled her seatbelt and tumbled out of the vehicle, landing in shards of her broken headlights. Pulling herself up on the dangling door, she looked around at the damage. She felt something tickling her cheek and put her hand to her face. She pulled her hand back and stared at the sticky red blood sliding through her fingers. She had cuts and scrapes on her arms and legs but had nothing to bandage the wounds. She stepped away from her car and looked back at the deer.

The deer was on the side of the road near her, and she moved toward it with tears in her eyes. She reached out to touch it but pulled her trembling hand back before it felt the deer's smooth fur. Looking into the face of the deer, she could see it was as stunned as she was, probably more since it was on the outside of the car, but they were both gasping for air in the same panicked, mouth-gaping way.

Ellie let out a sob as she thought about watching this poor creature die because of her carelessness. Maybe she could save it.

She turned back to the car and searched for her cell phone. Was there a 911 for animals?

She didn't think so, but she felt like there should be.

When she finally found her phone, she was relieved that at least she could call for some kind of help, but the feeling didn't last as she quickly realized she had no bars. No service.

Was that even a thing nowadays?

She thought the guy in the cell phone commercials said

the service was worldwide, so why didn't she have service? She tried again and again, but she couldn't get a signal.

She walked back to the animal that was no longer struggling to breathe and collapsed on the road next to it. She killed a deer. It was dead because of her.

Tears were streaming down her cheeks as panic streamed through her mind. No one knew where she was. She had no service. She had no idea when someone would come along.

And she had just killed a deer.

She choked on her emotions, coughing and gagging as she tried to breathe. Her stomach churned, and she ran a little into the brush to throw up.

She was still sitting on the side of the road hours later. She was still staring at the dead deer with tears flowing, making it hard for her to see, and her body vibrating with feelings she couldn't even name.

A face flashed in her mind. It was a girl's face that had replaced the deer's unseeing eyes. The girl was young, elementary age, with the same blank eyes as the deer. Ellie blinked hard to make the face go away, but it was still there when she opened her eyes.

The face was vaguely familiar, and Ellie squinted to see it better. The squinting didn't help, but she had another flash of the girl's face gasping in pain and reaching out to her for help.

Recoiling, Ellie moved higher onto the mountainside, away from the deer and her car. She still had no service when her phone died maybe an hour earlier, and she knew it had to be getting late in the afternoon.

She wanted to be at home and hoped her family or someone would find her soon. The sunlight drifted down through the leaves over her head, and she felt her eyes get heavy with the rays' comforting warmth on her cheeks.

Her heart was pounding, and she could hear the twisting screech of metal. Ellie heard voices, and she looked around. She was on the side of the road, but this was a different road. The twisted metal next to her was not her car. She turned around in a circle, trying to figure out where she was. She started walking toward the people and saw the girl she kept seeing in place of the deer. The girl was lying on the side of the road, trapped under a car or metal or something, but Ellie couldn't make it out. The young girl was gasping for air and reaching for Ellie to take her hand.

"Ellie," the girl cried. "Ellie, save me."

Ellie bent down and reached for the girl's arm but couldn't pull her out from under the metal. She was breathing hard, pulling on the girl's arm and pushing her feet against the metal for traction. The girl cried louder and screamed for her to stop. Ellie fell back on the road next to the girl.

"Ellie, I don't want to die." The girl was trying to breathe, but her breath was becoming shallow. Her eyes opened wide, and she was staring at Ellie with tears drying on her cheeks.

Ellie started to gasp for air; she felt like she was choking. She scrambled away from the girl, wrapped her legs in her arms, put her face down inside her body's circle, and started to rock. She heard voices again, but they were far away.

Ellie's eyes snapped open, and she was back on the mountainside. She had fallen asleep.

"Are you okay?" a woman was asking. She had beach-tossed blonde hair, wore a polka-dot bikini, and smelled like the ocean. Behind her stood a man on a phone. Apparently, he had phone service because he was talking to someone on the other line, and two young boys were peeking out of their car on the other side of the road.

"My husband is calling for help," the woman said. "My name is Sue; can you tell me your name?"

"Ellie."

"Okay, Ellie, I have some clean towels in the car that I will grab. I will be right back." Sue ran across the street and talked to her husband for a minute before returning with the towels.

"Let's put this one to your head because it looks like it is still bleeding." She placed the towel on Ellie's head and applied a little pressure while she continued to talk. "We are heading back from the beach. Do you know how long you have been out here?"

"What time is it?" Ellie asked. She didn't know how long she had been asleep and lost track of time when her phone died.

Sue looked down at her watch, "It's two forty-three."

"I crashed my car a little before eleven."

Sue frowned, "That's quite a while."

Sue's husband crossed the street with a water bottle and handed it to Ellie. "I found a fresh bottle of water and thought you might need it."

"Thank you," Ellie said. She drank half the bottle and closed her eyes.

"Ellie?" Sue put her hand on Ellie's shoulder. "I don't think you should be sleeping right now. You might have a concussion."

A siren screamed in the distance, and they all watched together as first a firetruck and then an ambulance turned the corner. Two police cars with their lights flashing followed shortly behind them. The rescue vehicles pulled to the side of the mountain, and the firefighters and para-medics emerged with bags full of equipment. The police cars blocked the road, and the officers inside started pulling out traffic cones and placing them around Ellie's car.

The firefighters and paramedics surrounded Ellie, and before she knew it, they had her on a gurney and strapped in for the ride back up the mountain. The paramedics checked her pulse and listened to her chest. They placed an oxygen mask on her and walked her back to their rig, asking her questions: "Where does it hurt, ma'am?" "Can you tell us your name?" "Do you have any dizziness or shortness of breath?"

Ellie was so overwhelmed by all the activity that she only managed to whisper her name, and she nodded to all the other questions. She saw Sue and her husband back on the side of the road, talking to a police officer. Their two children were wide-eyed, with their faces still plastered to the window of their car.

The ride back to town was longer than Ellie remembered. She thought about her family and asked the paramedics if they could contact them, but they told her the hospital would have to do that.

At the hospital, there was even more activity and people surrounding her. They brought her into the emergency triage room through the ambulance bay.

"Hello, Ellie. My name is Dr. Parker." He was a middle-aged man with graying hair and a white mustache. He had friendly wrinkles around his eyes and mouth, and he was looking at the chart that magically appeared at Ellie's bed's foot.

"Can you call my parents?" Ellie asked. She knew they would be worried about her, and she wanted someone to get them here so she wasn't alone.

You don't have to be independent when you are in a hospital. There has to be a rule about that.

"Absolutely. The paramedics grabbed your purse and phone, but it seemed dead. If you can write down their number, I will give them a call while we get you cleaned up." He smiled at Ellie, his wrinkles working overtime, and handed her a clipboard with paper and a pen.

She wrote down her parent's number, and Dr. Parker gave the nurses some orders and walked out of the curtained room to make the call.

"Alright, Ellie, we will take you to CT now." One of the nurses told her as she snapped up the rails on the bed and clicked off the brakes.

"What about my parents?"

"Dr. Parker is talking to them in the waiting room, and after your CT, we will bring them in to see you."

Ellie had never had a CT before, and she felt fear bloom in her stomach as the nurse wheeled her down the hall and into an elevator. She started to breathe harder as the elevator doors closed. She hated being closed in spaces.

You are going to be okay. The doors will open soon, and you will be out of this metal death trap. What if it gets stuck? It will be okay. The nurse is with you. Don't worry. Breathe.

They made it out of the elevator and down to the CT machine, which was scary but not as frightening as Ellie thought it would be. She thought it would be a tube-like on TV, but it was open on both sides and just slid back and forth around her.

As she lay there listening to the whirl of the machine, she started thinking about the girl again.

She saw the girl's face on the dead deer, and she saw her in her dream too. That had to mean something, right? She looked familiar, but Ellie couldn't remember how she knew the young girl. Maybe it was an old classmate or someone she met at work. Either way, she didn't think it meant much. She thought it must have just been due to the stress and trauma of the accident.

She should probably stop trying to figure it out.

She thought they would be wheeling her back to the small, curtained room in the emergency bay after her CT, but instead, they wheeled her down the hall and into a private hospital suite.

The room had a window and a chair that could pull out into a bed on one side and a computer with a rolling stool on the other. It was painted a pale blue with a strange beige trim with multicolored diamonds patterned inside it. It was glaring and didn't go well together.

There was a space where the bed would fit, and on one wall was a cabinet holding a computer. Oxygen tubes lined the wall behind the bed along with an I.V. stand and one of those things that take your blood pressure. There were emergency lights and buttons near where the head of her bed would go, and she didn't want to see them in action.

She didn't want to stay in the hospital overnight, and she thought this might indicate that they would try to keep her. The smell of the hospital squeezed her lungs and made it harder for her to breathe. She hated this feeling. She knew it was her anxiety but couldn't hide the emotions that invaded her body and soul.

Another nurse joined the one that had been with her, Tammy, and they started systematically cleaning the many cuts and scrapes on her arms, legs, and face. They started stitching up the deep gashes, and Ellie regretted her stubborn show of independence with each poke.

Just as she started to feel like a baby that needed her mommy, in came her parents, Eric and Dane. And just like that, the room felt better. She had her people and could distract herself for the time being.

She pushed the fears of the hospital and any thoughts of the girl's face into the far reaches of her mind, and she smiled at her family. Her mom's eyes were red-rimmed, and her lips were trembling. She sat down on the side of the hospital bed, grabbed Ellie's hand, and held on tight.

"Oh, Ellie," her mom said. She looked at all the stitches in Ellie's face, arms, and legs.

No one spoke as Tammy and the other nurse continued to stitch her many wounds. They all watched the process, and Ellie was surprised to see her brother turn a little green before turning away to look out the window.

Dane joined him a few minutes later, and James also decided that the room needed inspecting.

Sarah was the only one brave enough to sit with her through the rest of the pokes.

After she was stitched and bandaged, Tammy adjusted Ellie's I.V. and hooked the bag onto the stand in the room. Then she patted Ellie on the arm and told her she would be back to check on her soon.

Ellie's dad came back to stand at the foot of the bed watching her, and it was starting to weird her out that no one was talking. It didn't surprise her that Eric was the first to say something.

"Ellie, you scared the shit out of us," Eric said.

"Eric," her dad warned. He was obviously following the "she is fragile and not to be upset" routine.

Eric was telling it how it was.

"No, Dad, she did. And she needs to know not to run off like that again without telling anyone where she is going." Eric was hiding his fear with anger, and Ellie knew it. It made her feel worse than if he acted sad because she knew she had scared him.

"I'm sorry, Eric. I don't know what I was thinking."

"Don't be sorry. It was my fault. I shouldn't have said all that stuff. I'm sorry." Ellie had never seen Eric so distraught. His shoulders sagged, and he seemed to sigh heavily with each phrase. His hair was sticking out in all directions, and she knew why when he ran his hands through it again.

Her mom choked on a sob, which was all Ellie needed to start her tears. Her dad walked over to her mom and put his arm around her shoulders.

"It's all okay now, honey." He was not one for emotional displays, and he was beyond his comfort level with both the women in his life crying.

Dane looked shell-shocked. He was on her right, sitting quietly, eyes wide and unblinking. When he realized Ellie had reined in her tears and was watching him, he blinked a few times and tried to smile.

"Hey, babe," he said.

"Hey," Ellie replied. She tried to smile, but when she did, the girl's face popped back into her mind, and the smile disappeared.

She went pale, and everyone came to attention, watching her carefully.

"I'm okay. I just had a bad day." Ellie closed her eyes and tried again to push back the image of the girl's face.

If I say anything about this girl's face, everyone will think I am crazy. I don't want Dane to think I'm crazy. But what if I am?

Dr. Parker came in a few moments later to talk to Ellie.

"Hey Ellie, how are you feeling?"

"Tired," Ellie said as she struggled to keep her eyes open.

"Well, you had a tough day, so that is understandable. Your CT results look good. Just a small concussion, nothing

I am too worried about. You were a little dehydrated when you came in, so those fluids we have you hooked up to should be helping with that," he gestured to the I.V. bag. "I don't think you need to stay the night, but I want to keep you for observation. I don't expect your concussion to worsen, but I would like you to be here if it does."

"I don't want to stay here," Ellie's voice started to rise at the thought of spending the night alone in the hospital. Dr. Parker must have seen the fear in her eyes because he jumped right back in to reassure her.

"Someone can stay with you, of course. And I will release you tomorrow afternoon. Is that okay?"

Ellie looked around at her family, and they were all nodding. Her mom gave her the "you are doing what the doctor says" look, which pretty much settled that.

"Okay, as long as someone stays with me," she wasn't happy, but she was conceding.

"Great, and then I want you home from work for a week, I will get you a note for your employer."

Ellie blinked. She hated to miss work. She knew it was no use arguing, so she managed to nod.

"Any other questions for me?" Dr. Parker looked at Ellie and looked to her parents to give everyone an equal opportunity to ask him questions about her health and well-being.

"How many stitches does she have?" Of course, Eric would ask that, Ellie thought.

"I believe the nurse said the final count was thirty-eight." Dr. Parker replaced his signature smile with a grimmer version. "If you have any other questions, don't hesitate to call me at this number." He handed her dad a card with his name and information and waved as he ducked out of the room.

Ellie's mom planned to stay the night, so the Finn family left Dane and Ellie alone while they went back to the house to pick up some things. All was quiet but the faint beeping of machines that carried down the hall and into the room.

"I was so worried, Ellie," Dane said once her parents were gone. "Your dad called me to ask if you were at my apartment, and we all started looking for you immediately. Why did you go off like that?"

"Eric thinks that I'm not independent. He said I never go anywhere or do anything alone. I was trying to prove him wrong."

"I don't think it worked, babe." Dane leaned closer and kissed her gently on the lips. He deepened the kiss and hovered one hand near her face so that she could feel the heat radiating off his palm. He would have rested his hand on her face and run his fingers into her hair if it wasn't for the stitches.

There were a lot of things that he would have done if there wasn't a rail between them.

A nurse broke up their tender moment to insist that Ellie use the restroom, which was a good idea because she couldn't remember the last time she had.

The nurse helped her to the small sterile bathroom and told her to call for help when she was ready to return to bed. Ellie didn't like attention, so she agreed but had no intentions of calling the nurse back.

She quickly used the bathroom and peeked to see if the coast was clear. She didn't want the nurse to come back and scold her. She didn't want to cause any trouble, but she was sure she could walk from the bathroom to her hospital bed.

Ellie saw Dane watching her from across the room as she carefully started the walk back to her bed. Her mom wasn't back yet, and he seemed to be thinking hard about something because his eyebrows had the slightest crease.

"You should move in with me," Dane said. Ellie stopped walking and stared at him. So, he continued, "I know that we have only been together for a couple of months, and that might seem fast, but it would be awesome to have you around all the time. And that way, you could prove to your brother that you are independent. You could get your place or a roommate, but I would rather have you with me. If you want to be, that is. I understand if you don't want–"

"Okay." Ellie blurted out, deciding quickly not to think about it too long. She wanted to be more independent, and this was better than her choice this morning.

Plus, she knew that she would talk herself out of it if she thought about it too much.

"Okay?" Dane was smiling from his dimple to his eyes, and he jumped up and crossed the room to stand in front of her.

"Yes," Ellie said. She smiled back, and Dane pulled her in for another toe-curling kiss.

"I better get you behind that bar before I get too excited." Dane winked at her, kept his arm around her as she finished the walk across the room, and half lifted her into the awkward hospital bed.

She seemed to sink instantly into the middle, and she couldn't imagine getting any sleep in this horrible excuse for a bed.

"Alright, so when do you want to move in?" Dane leaned in close and whispered so it felt like their little secret. They were conspiring together.

"Now." Ellie teased with a smile that threatened to split her dry lips.

"Today?" Dane's eye sparkled mischievously.

"This moment."

"So desperate for a repeat of the other night that you are willing to break hospital rules?" Dane feigned a shocked gasp and put his hand to his chest.

Ellie giggled. She really did wish she could move in right now instead of staying in this smelling hospital.

"Hmmm, I guess that would be frowned upon."

"Especially by your mother." Dane chuckled. They were still whispering as if they might actually break Ellie out.

"Alright, when do you think I should move in?" Ellie asked more seriously but still quietly in case her mother came back.

"How about next weekend?"

Ellie would have thought he was joking since that was still really soon, but Dane's face was completely earnest. And she was glad because she couldn't wait.

"It's a date." Ellie smiled. And Dane leaned forward to plant another knock-your-hospital-grippy-socks-off kiss on her lips. Which was just what she needed to chase her nerves away.

That gave Ellie a week to tell her parents and pack her things. She was excited to be out of her parent's house, and she knew this would be the step she needed to take to be seen as an adult in her family's eyes.

She failed the last time she tried to move out, and she would make sure that didn't happen this time.

CHAPTER FIVE

THE NIGHT BEFORE ELLIE MOVED IN WITH DANE, SHE WAS PACKING and panicking but happy.

She had spun her worries around so many times that she started feeling better. Nothing could be as bad as the spider web of nightmares in her brain. Her parents were shocked when she told them the news the night she got home from the hospital, and Eric magically showed up the next day to try and talk her out of it.

She knew her parents would be supportive and then have Eric do their dirty work and try to convince her to change her mind.

That had been their play since Ellie was a little girl trying to bring home a stray cat, and her parents sent Eric to talk to her about the fleas and possible mites that the stray cat might bring home. Ellie was an early start germaphobe, and she almost immediately agreed to take the cat to the animal shelter instead.

Ellie loved animals, but her family was a cat family, and dogs were strictly to be loved from afar.

Eric had a different approach this time because rather

than trying to talk her out of moving, like she knew her parents wanted him to do, instead he told her that they didn't want her to move, but he thought it was a great idea and he was glad she was doing it.

Eric was good at pep talks when she needed them, and he reminded her that he was closer to Dane's apartment than to Mom and Dad's, so if she needed him, he would come right over.

When she didn't change her mind and instead started packing up her things, her mom finally came to talk to her about her decision and brought up some of the things that could go wrong.

"What if you have an anxiety attack, Ellie? Has Dane seen you have one of your big ones?" Her mom gave her a concerned and knowing look as if to say; *you don't want that* and implied he wouldn't like her anymore.

Ellie had been thinking about that same thing since Dane asked her to move in, but she was trying to push it down and ignore it along with the girl's face.

Since the accident, she had seen the girl's face in her dreams every night, and she had to concentrate on not thinking about the girl all day.

What if she did have an anxiety attack around Dane?

He had seen her have minor anxiety attacks or what she liked to think of as worry attacks. She knew she worried a lot and was notorious for overthinking every little thing, but she tried not to vocalize everything.

Ellie couldn't bring herself out of her thoughts, and her mom sighed in frustration. She was obviously tired of waiting for Ellie to respond to her question.

"Ellie, you have never even lived alone, and now you are going to move in with a man?"

"Dane is a great guy, mom. He loves me."

"Those are not reasons to move in with him after only four months?"

"I'm an adult. How's that for a reason?"

"Ellie, you are an adult whether you move in with Dane or not. I think you are making this move for the wrong reasons."

"No matter what my reasons, you know you would find a way to find fault in them. I haven't been allowed to make any major decisions since quitting college."

"Can you blame me for trying to steer you in the right direction? Quitting college was a big enough mistake. I don't want to watch you throw your life away for a guy."

"Wow. I will never live that down. I will always be the child that dropped out of college."

"Yes. And the child that will come running home after running away to her boyfriend's to playhouse." Sarah said as she stalked out of the room and slammed the door behind her.

Ellie shook her head, thinking about how uncomfortable things had been around the house since their talk.

It probably wasn't close to how uncomfortable Dane must feel right now. Her dad had asked Dane for a private talk, and the two were meeting at a coffee and donut shop down the street. Yet another thing for her to worry about.

———

JAMES WASN'T ready to let go of his little girl. She still needed him. She couldn't even make it to work without him cleaning roadkill up. And now that she was moving out right after another terrible accident involving even more trauma.

He was sure her anxiety and panic attacks would only

worsen. James was sure she wouldn't be doing this if it wasn't for Dane, and the thought filled his veins with dread.

Ellie still wouldn't talk about the accident, and he was afraid that if she kept bottling up what happened, she would eventually crack, and all the emotions she was damming up would spill out.

Dane was sitting across from him at the sticky brown laminate table. They were toward the back of the little coffee shop, and Dane was looking longingly at the front door.

"Dane, I'm worried that you won't be able to protect Ellie." James thought it was best just to say it straight.

They had done the awkward small talk thing, and then they did the uncomfortable not speaking while sipping their coffee thing, so this was the next step.

Dane twitched a little and shifted his attention from the freedom of the door to James.

"I don't think Ellie needs to be protected as much as you think."

"Oh, you don't?" This was the problem in James' mind. He shook his head and ran his fingers through his hair in frustration. "She has thirty-eight stitches because she tried to go off alone. She has extreme anxiety, and she doesn't cope well. She's not like other girls you have dated."

"She has thirty-eight stitches because she hit a freaking deer. It could have happened to anyone."

"You aren't getting it. A year ago, Eric and I messed up our road clean-up schedule, we weren't on top of things, and she crashed her car into a street sign over a dead rabbit. That's not normal. I need to know that you are going to protect her. If you want her to live with you, you have to take the night schedule. Eric and I will still handle the mornings, but you have after work."

"That's fine. I'll take care of it." Dane finished his coffee, set his mug down, and pushed back from the table a little to emphasize that he was done.

James took the hint and finished his coffee too. He stood up and thanked Dane for meeting with him before he pushed his chair in and headed for the door.

───────

IT WAS FINALLY MOVING DAY, and Ellie was ready. Well, she was packed at least, and Eric was there helping to carry boxes down to Dane's truck.

Her dad was helping too, and her mom was making sandwiches for everyone in the kitchen. Moving builds an appetite, she said.

Ellie wasn't taking much furniture because Dane's apartment was already filled with furniture, but she was bringing a bookshelf and most of her books, clothes, pictures, toiletries, and a few other odd items.

Eric was carrying a big box down the stairs huffing and puffing under the weight. "Jeez, El, what do you have in here, rocks?"

"Those are my classic hardbacks. Be careful with them." Ellie moved out of the way to let Eric pass. She was carrying a lamp, so it was the least she could do.

"Well, next time you move, spread the books around. They're too heavy all in one box. I'll be surprised if I don't herniate a disk."

Dane came in while Eric was still complaining about the book box, and Ellie saw him trying to hide a smile. He had just told Ellie the same thing when he came down the stairs with his last box.

"I'm going to grab a box that says clothes on it next," Dane whispered to Ellie, giving her a wink as he trotted back up the stairs.

Ellie loved that he could find the humor even though she knew he was still feeling uncomfortable about his talk with her dad.

Dane hadn't told her everything the two of them had talked about, but when she saw him later that day for a dinner and movie date, he was unusually quiet and only said he had a lot on his mind.

Her dad had put a lot on her boyfriend's mind, and she was worried that it would be enough to make him change his mind about moving in together, but here they were making a move.

Ellie was glad it was finally here so she could get it over with. She was so tired of worrying and creating lists in her mind about why she should or shouldn't back out of the move.

Her mom finally came around just the day before, and Ellie was glad she was trying to be nice and friendly about moving out, even though it took her a while.

Ellie helped load a few more things in the back of the truck and then decided to grab the mail on her way back into the house.

She lifted the mail from the mailbox and felt something move against her left hand. She switched the mail to her right hand and shook her hand off. A spider fell to the ground in front of her, and she jumped back with a squeal.

"You good over there, Hun?" James was walking out the door with another box and paused to watch her.

"Yeah. I just gotta talk to mom. Don't worry." Quickly

she walked into the house and into the kitchen, where her mom was now cutting a watermelon into bite-size chunks.

Her hand and finger started to tingle, and she looked at it to see if it was swelling. It might have bitten her hand.

"Mom, I think I got bit by a spider," Ellie said, trying to squelch the panic.

She didn't know exactly why because she knew that if she did get bit, it probably wasn't by a spider that mattered. She was allergic to several things, though, and she was always afraid that she would have a reaction.

"Did you feel a bite?" Ellie's mom kept cutting watermelon inside the rind and then dumping the chunks into her bowl, which was painted to look like half a watermelon.

"No, but look, it's swelling up right here." Ellie pointed to a spot on her hand that she thought looked puffy.

"Looks fine to me," Ellie's mom glanced at the spot before she started cleaning up the watermelon's remains.

"I know. I just can't help thinking...." Ellie decided to stop. She started talking to herself instead and decided to make herself busy by going to find Dane.

She checked her finger a few more times while helping Dane. It must have been noticeable because Dane even looked at her finger once.

Ellie had moved on to other worries by the time everyone sat down to lunch, one of which being the fact that after they finished eating, they would be leaving and heading to Dane's apartment to unload her things.

———

As THEY DROVE to the apartment building, she thought about the elevator they would need to use to get her stuff to Dane's apartment.

There was no way she could convince her brother and father to carry every load up two flights of stairs. They knew she was terrified of elevators, but that wouldn't win out over their desire to save their backs.

She knew the elevator would be faster, so she understood its necessity, but she still managed to skip it. Ellie held the door open as Dane, Eric, and her dad loaded as much as possible onto the elevator, and then as they rode the elevator up, she ran up the stairs to meet them at the top and held the doors open as they did the same thing in reverse on the apartment floor.

It only took two trips for the four of them to move Ellie's things into the apartment; the rest was on her and Dane. Eric and her dad left shortly after the last box hit the floor, and it was just the two of them.

Dane started pushing boxes aside while he was on the phone ordering a pizza for dinner.

Watching him reminded Ellie that she had to return to work the next day. She was worried about going in with stitches in her head. She didn't want people to stare at her, but she was also excited to return to her desk and books.

Dane got off the phone and walked up behind Ellie. He wrapped his arms around her waist and kissed the space between her neck and shoulder, which sent shivers down her spine.

All thoughts about work fled her mind, and she leaned back into him and breathed him in. He smelled like Cedar and sweat from a hard day's work, and it was intoxicating.

"We can get to the unpacking slowly during the week. Let's just put some of your clothes away, and then we can relax." Dane whispered against her neck. His lips brushed the sensitive skin.

"Good idea," Ellie smiled. She turned and waited for

Dane to take possession of her lips. He obliged immediately, as she knew he would. A small groan of appreciation escaped her lips, and he deepened the kiss.

Dane pulled away from her with a sigh and turned his head to look at all the boxes. She looked at them, too, and echoed his sigh of exhaustion. There was still more to do, and they silently agreed that it should be done sooner rather than later.

"I wanted to talk to you about something else too." Dane opened a box marked clothes, pulled out shirts, and handed them to Ellie. "I think we should carpool to work this week. I can drop you off before I go to work."

"I go in at the same time as you, though."

"I know, but Harry won't mind if I am just a few minutes late."

"If you think it will be okay with Harry..."

"At least for the first week, and then we can see what we want to do afterward. I just thought it would save gas and help you out."

This was perfect for Ellie because she hated driving and was especially worried about having to drive since the accident.

Her dad was the one that picked her car up from the shop when it was fixed, and he was the one that drove the newly painted blue Sentra over to Dane's apartment so that he could drive back with Eric.

She hadn't been looking forward to driving to work, so this fixed that for her, and if Dane didn't want to drive her after this week, she was already thinking of alternative ways to get to and from work.

CHAPTER
SIX

A couple of weeks after moving into the apartment, Ellie was still roller skating home. She wanted to use a bike but decided she would be more comfortable on roller skates.

She had been using roller skates since childhood and was better on wheels when she was closer to the ground.

Her stitches were finally out, but her scars were still bright pink, and she felt like Frankenstein's monster. She had always identified with the creature in the novel because he was alone and isolated in his feelings, but now that she had the scars, she felt like she understood him even better.

She was running behind after stopping to talk to Ana on her way out of work. Since her accident, Ana and the other girls, Jean and Nancy, had started talking to her more, and she liked being able to talk about books with women that loved them as much as she did.

But now she was paying for the distraction. She was trying to get home to start dinner before Dane came home from work. Today was Dane's first day working as a manager, and she wanted to make a special congratulatory dinner.

She took her skates off at the bottom of the stairs and ran up the steps taking them two at a time. She was rounding the flight between floors when she crashed into a girl on her way down. The two hit and fell apart in a stunned heap.

"Woah, what the fuck!" The girl rolled to her side and held her elbow where she landed.

"I'm so sorry!" Ellie pulled herself up and reached down to help the girl she had mowed down.

"Girl, you need to slow down. You could have hurt me. And you. Lucky you hit me on the floor and not on the steps." The girl stood before Ellie, looking down at herself and brushing invisible dirt off her pants.

"You're right. I should have been paying attention."

"Well, that's alright, I guess. I haven't seen you around before. You must've just moved in. I'm Clara." Clara held out her hand for Ellie to shake. She was the same height as Ellie, maybe an inch shorter. Her hair was short spiky blonde. She had piercing blue eyes, and four little gold hoops pierced each ear. She was shamelessly wearing a *Friends* t-shirt and low-cut jeans showing off the area between the bottom of her shirt and the top of her pants.

Ellie would never have the confidence to show any skin on her stomach. She was barely able to wear shorts because she hated her legs, Eric teased her that her legs never saw the light of day, and when she did wear shorts or a swimsuit, he would pretend to go blind from the light reflecting off her stark white legs.

"My name is Ellie. I just moved in with my boyfriend last week." Ellie shook Clara's hand and bent to pick up the skates she dropped in the collision.

"Awesome, so we are neighbors. I am in apartment 3A, the one at the top of the stairs all the way up."

"We are in 2C," Ellie replied.

"Well, seeing as you nearly broke my arm, I think that means we should hang out sometime. There aren't many girls our age in the apartment building." Clara winked as if the fact that they were close in age and girls meant they had a special connection. Ellie thought it took a little more than that, but it would be a good idea to start making friends, so she smiled back and agreed that they should get together.

"Alright, cool," Clara said. "Well, I'm off to work."

Clara waved to Ellie and started walking down the stairs again. She called back, "Don't run into anyone else!" And her laughter floated up the stairs after her.

ELLIE WAS STILL SMILING when Dane walked in the door, and she had succeeded in making dinner. It was a doubly good day.

"You look happy," Dane kissed Ellie on the top of her head when he walked into the kitchen. "This looks delicious, babe!"

"Penne with pancetta and a vodka sauce to celebrate your big day!" Ellie opened the oven and pulled out a sheet of fresh garlic bread.

"And garlic bread, this is great. I thought we could go out to eat, but this is even better."

"How was your first day as a manager?"

"It was terrific! We had a shipment come in, and I caught an error. We were supposed to get nine boxes of Ladies Fix-it kits, but they only sent us six, so I got to call about the order. And I get to do an interview tomorrow!" Dane was helping move dishes and plates to the small dining table while Ellie grabbed wine and napkins. "How was your day, babe?"

"I talked with Ana after work, and then I ran into a neighbor on my way home. I think she wants to be my friend."

Dane grabbed the bread and dipped it into his pasta sauce before taking a bite. "That's awesome. I'm glad you are making friends in the building. What was she like?"

"She was running down the stairs as I was running up, and we literally ran into each other. Well, I mostly ran into her cause I wasn't looking, but she was nice about it. She didn't make me feel like an idiot, which was good enough for me. Her name is Clara, and she lives upstairs. She must like scary-looking Frankenstein monsters since she is willing to be friends with me." Ellie laughed at her joke, and a little snort slipped out. Dane wasn't laughing, though.

"You're not scary at all, babes. You're beautiful. The scars will fade, so don't make your new identity focus on something temporary."

Ellie was only trying to make light of her situation, but she didn't want Dane to think she was beating herself up internally over her scars. Yeah, they bothered her, but they were nothing compared to the other monsters she dealt with.

Dane leaned over and kissed her on the scar that ran down her cheek. Tingles erupted on her skin, and she hoped that maybe tonight would be the night things shifted in the bedroom.

So far, it had been all about Dane when they went to bed. He would start with a few kisses and some roaming hands, but before long, he was grunting out his own pleasure and falling back on his side of the bed while she was left aching.

Maybe tonight, that would change.

"You are so beautiful, Ellie," he said huskily. He brushed her hair away from her neck and made a trail down to her collarbone. "And haven't you heard? Scars are sexy."

He leaned back and smiled wolfishly at her as he picked up his fork and took another bite of food while devouring her with his eyes.

"I think the "scars are sexy" saying usually refers to men, babe." Ellie laughed, but she did feel a little better. Maybe she will look like one of those badass adventurous girls who risk their pretty faces for a good story. Right now, her scars were pinched and angry red lumpy lines, not sexy whispers of stories.

"Well, you are sexy, so it works. Now hurry up and eat 'cause I want you for dessert."

Ellie's heart jumped, and her thighs clenched.

SEVEN

ELLIE WAS IN A PANIC. IT WAS SATURDAY AFTERNOON, AND SHE was waiting for a knock on the door.

She had made plans to hang out with Clara, and the time they scheduled was fast approaching.

She thought of a few excuses to cancel the plans. She could say she was sick. She could say her mom needed her help with something. She could say there was an emergency at the library, and she had to go in.

Okay, so that one wasn't very believable. What kind of an emergency happens at a library that would require her to be there?

Not all of them were winning excuses, but usually, people don't question you too much when you send an excuse. Still, she couldn't bring herself to type the message with an excuse because she felt canceling at the last minute would be rude. And thinking about being rude made her worry that Clara wouldn't want to be friends anymore.

Would that be so bad?

Yes, Ellie, stop it. You want to have a friend.

She saw Dane watching her from the kitchen and gave

him a weak smile. She was dressed up, as best as she could, in a mint green sundress. Dane said green looked good on her because it brought out her eyes. She looked down at her dress and saw her ghost legs sticking out. Ugh! She closed her eyes again and focused on her breathing.

"So, what are you girls going to do?" Dane asked. He was trying to distract Ellie from her panic but talking about it would only make it worse.

She grimaced and wished she didn't have to talk. She just wanted to sit in her personal dread and try not to think about it.

"I don't know. She said, 'The Mall.' That's it. She didn't tell me what at the mall."

"Well, she is probably thinking, shopping. Don't girls like shopping?"

"Sure," Ellie said. "Shopping is fun."

Ellie preferred shopping online, where she could take her time with a purchase decision, leave it in her cart for a day or two, and deliberate. Online there weren't a bunch of people crowded all into the same space. Plus, there were reviews online, and she could see what other people thought of the product.

In the store, there were people everywhere, and when you were with someone else, you felt the pressure of having to make a decision and stay with it. The last time she went shopping at the mall with her mom, she bought something at a store, and then before they reached the door, she was hit with buyer's remorse. She had to turn back and return it.

That wasn't so bad with her mom, but with someone else, it was embarrassing.

There was a knock at the door, and Ellie jumped up. She

was going to power through. She grabbed her purse and kissed Dane on her way to the door.

Clara was dressed for shopping in jeans and a stretchy white T-shirt. She had her hair smooth instead of spikey and a giant tote slung over her shoulder. Ellie didn't know what she could keep in there, but there was so much room that she wouldn't be too surprised by what came out.

She thought about how many books she could carry in a bag that size.

"Ready?" Clara asked. She oozed excitement, and Ellie wasn't sure she had ever come close to the enthusiasm level that Clara was at right now.

"Yep!" Ellie tried adding extra emphasis, but it still came out flat.

"Awesome! Your car or mine?"

"The mall is close. You don't want just to walk?"

"No way. When I go to the mall, I need to drive so that I have a way to get all the stuff I buy back to my apartment." She laughed and gave Ellie a playful shove.

"Let's take yours." Ellie grimaced; she still hadn't driven her car since the accident three weeks ago. She was avoiding driving like the plague. Although, she never understood that saying.

You couldn't avoid the plague.

"WHAT STORE SHOULD WE HIT FIRST?" Clara was practically bouncing next to Ellie as they walked into the mall.

She reminded Ellie of their old dog Pogo, he was a border collie mix, and he was named for a fairly obvious reason.

"It doesn't matter to me." Ellie didn't care what store

they went to because she was still mentally focusing on not having a panic attack over the number of people that would soon be swarming around in packs throughout the mall.

"Okay, cool! I think we should go this way first," Clara grabbed Ellie's hand and pulled her to the left side of the mall. "We will hit the stores down here and then go upstairs, loop around, and then hit all the downstairs stores on the way back."

Ellie's eyes bugged out as she listened to Clara. It sounded like she wanted to hit every store in the mall.

That couldn't be possible. We would be here all day.

Apparently, it was possible. They worked their way through the mall, stopping in most stores along the way.

Clara was carrying multiple bags from different stores as they walked the last section of the mall. She had bought several shirts, a couple of pairs of pants, a pair of high heels that she thought would go perfectly with her black flowy date night dress and more makeup than Ellie had owned in her life.

On the other hand, Ellie only had one bag, which contained a dress and a t-shirt that Clara told her would be perfect with jeans for casual Friday, but she wasn't sure now that she was carrying it through the mall.

Up ahead of them was the mall bookstore, and it was probably the only store Ellie wanted to go to, but she didn't know if Clara was interested in books. So far, Ellie knew Clara was obsessed with the tv show *Friends*. She talked a lot about boys and was trying to get into acting.

"Look, the bookstore!" Clara grabbed Ellie and pulled her forward. They browsed through the books. Clara grabbed a book off the shelf and then another one handing it to Ellie.

"They have *Someday, Someday Maybe* by Lauren

Graham. I heard this is a really good book! We should read it!"

"We could do like a little book club!" Ellie finally felt like she could match Clara's enthusiasm level.

She was starting to feel relaxed with Clara and felt like she could have a friend. She spent so much time keeping people at a distance and not getting close to anyone that she didn't realize what she was missing out on.

And even better, she hadn't thought about the little girl's face since making plans with Clara.

Ellie started sifting through the books in the Fiction section while Clara headed to the Romance shelves across the aisle. Ellie didn't read a lot of romance because she didn't relate to the characters.

Do real people ever fall in love as they do in those stories? She doubted it.

"I love Romance novels. They might be cheesy and unrealistic, but I still swoon!" Clara added three more books to her arm stack.

"That's why I don't read many romance novels," Ellie laughed. She felt like Clara had just read her mind.

"Well, but that is part of the fun. Since we are reading a book together, we should also read a recommendation from each other. I will pick a book for you, and you can pick one for me. What do you think?" Clara looked over at her while shaking a book that she had grabbed while explaining her plan.

"That sounds fun! What did you pick for me?" Ellie grabbed the book Clara held out and almost forgot not to frown at the cartoony couple on the front.

"One of my favorite tropes, Enemies to Lovers! You are gonna love it. Now, pick something for me!" Clara was back to bouncing.

This was a lot of pressure for Ellie. She hated the thought of picking a book that Clara might hate. What if she picked something Clara hated and ruined the game?

"Okay, but I like Classics. Have you read many?"

"I only read the classics I had to read in school, but I can handle whatever you throw my way. Lay it on me."

Ellie searched the shelves for the novel she had in mind. When she came to it, she sighed and hoped she made the right choice. She handed the book to Clara and waited for her to read the title.

"*Pride and Prejudice.* I think I saw this movie. Isn't this a romance?"

"Yeah, but it is a classic. So, it is a little different."

"What's the difference?"

"Mostly, the language. And any dancing is on the dance floor. If you know what I mean." Ellie smiled at her joke, and Clara's head fell back as she laughed.

Everyone looked at them, but Ellie didn't even care. She had a friend. A friend that laughed at her jokes and took her book recommendations.

They bought their books and decided to get lunch at the mall food court.

The food court was a circle with food vendors surrounding the eating area, and the food smells were over-whelming. You couldn't determine whether you were smelling fried food, pizza, or Chinese, which confused your stomach. It was hard to pick one thing with all the conflict in the air, but the two finally decided on a small sandwich place in the far-right corner.

They picked up their food, and Ellie steered them away from the crowd and over to a table close to a window. Ellie was trying to cut down on her people anxiety by being away from the crowd, but the noise was crushing her.

"So, how did you meet Dane?" Clara shouted over the roar of a hundred people getting lunch simultaneously.

"We met at my work. He came in to check out a book for his nephew."

"Aw. That is so sweet! How long have you guys been together?"

"Almost five months."

"Oh, wow, you moved in fast. The last guy I lived with took us a year to move in and about three months for me to kick him out."

They both laughed, and Ellie loved how easy it was becoming between them.

"Well, I wanted to get out of my parents' house, and Dane asked me to move in."

"Is this your first time not living at home? That's wild!"

"I never had a reason to move out before." Ellie was starting to feel a little defensive; she didn't want Clara to think of her the way that Eric seemed to.

"What about college? I moved out for college and never looked back. I need my freedom. I moved here from Washington to get sun and space." Clara seemed to laugh while she talked, as if her joy bounced the words from her mouth.

She also seemed to have zero filter, and Ellie wasn't sure if that was a plus or a minus towards her personality.

"I tried to move out for college, but it wasn't for me, and I went back home."

"What do you mean it wasn't for you? College is the best. I learned more about myself and life in the three years I attended college than any other time."

"Three years?"

"Yeah, I didn't finish because I decided to pursue acting, but my college didn't offer theater arts, so I went off on my own."

"I just didn't like it. College was stressful."

"Well, everything worth doing in life is at least a little stressful."

Ellie didn't know what to say to that. Everything in her life was more than a little stressful, and she hated it. Clara was still smiling, and Ellie thought she must be missing some social cues that should make her feel like she wasn't being judged. She sat quietly long enough that Clara noticed she must have said something wrong.

"Sorry, I just meant life is stressful. I would get it if college weren't your thing. I mean, I quit, too; it just took me longer. And I might go back so that I can finish my degree. You can always go back if you want."

"You're right. Life is stressful. I don't know if I will go back, but that's cool that you might. What would you get a degree in?"

"I want to go somewhere with theater arts to get my degree in that. I have been looking into it more because I think it might help me get into the acting scene."

"Have you done any acting yet?"

"Just small theater acts and I did one commercial, but it never even aired," Clara sighed and rolled her eyes at the ceiling as if asking the magic man in the sky, 'Why?'

"That's still pretty good."

"Yeah, well... What would you go back for if you went?"

"Library science," Ellie said without thinking. She loved working with the books, and if she was a proper librarian, she could have an even more significant role at the library with more pay.

"Wow, you answered that quickly. I guess you *have* thought about it."

"Yeah, but I don't think I could do it."

"I think you could do anything you put your mind to.

Stop doubting yourself." Clara finished her sandwich and crumpled up the wrapper. She leaned back in her seat and patted her stomach to show how full she was.

"So, you never told me what happened to your face and arm? Those look like fresh scars."

"I was in a car accident a few weeks ago. I am hoping they will fade." Ellie put her hand to the side of her face where the scar ran from her forehead to the bottom of her cheekbone.

"It will totally fade. That must have been a nasty accident."

"I was driving to the beach, and I hit a deer. It was awful. I was on the side of the road for hours all alone."

"Shit. That's wild. I'm glad you are okay."

"Yeah, I'm alright now. It was a bad day. I have repressed it pretty well, though." It might have sounded like a joke, and they both laughed, but it was more accurate than anything else. Ellie was an expert at repressing upsetting thoughts and memories.

They threw away their trash and walked out of the mall well past noon. Ellie was surprised at how fast the time had gone, she thought she would be miserable, but she was having fun. Ellie had never spent so long at the mall before, and while it wasn't her favorite place, it was better than she remembered.

"I'm so glad you ran into me last week," Clara said with a laugh as they walked up the stairs in their apartment building. She gave Ellie a teasing smile and a friendly nudge.

"I am too. We should get together again soon." Ellie smiled and immediately regretted letting those words fall out of her mouth, but she wasn't sure why since she had just had a wonderful time. Ellie liked Clara and was glad they met, but the social pressure was still a little much.

"Yeah, we definitely should! I work most mornings and some weekends at the coffee shop, but I will text you when I'm free, and we can figure it out!" They reached the second floor, and Clara hugged Ellie before continuing up to her apartment on the third floor.

"How was your day, babe?" Dane called out when Ellie walked in. She could hear Dane in the bedroom, and she moved toward the sound of his voice.

"It was better than I thought it would be. A lot better." Ellie dropped her purse on the table in the hallway and brought her two shopping bags into the living room with her.

"I knew you would have fun! Girls always need girl-friends." Dane came up behind her, wrapped his arms around her waist, and subtly peeked over her shoulder into the bags. "What'd you get?"

"I got this dress," Ellie held up the blue and cream striped dress that was a form-fitting cotton material but had a good amount of stretch. Then she pulled out the t-shirt that she still had second thoughts about. If she was the type of person that liked going to the mall, she might have taken it back and returned it, but now that she was all the way home, she figured it was easier just to keep it. "And this t-shirt."

"I like the T-shirt. It looks short." He kissed her neck as he continued to press against her. She knew he would like the shirt. He always seemed to enjoy the things that made her most uncomfortable.

"I think it is a little too short for me." She held it out farther so she could look at it better. It was a mid-length red cotton tee. She thought it would probably only show a little of her stomach, but that was enough to be worrisome. Clara talked her into it by telling her that she had "a cute little waist and she should show it off." Ellie thought that was a terrifying idea.

"No way, babe, you can pull this off."

"Well, I'll try it out, probably just around the house."

Dane chuckled, "Okay, at least I will benefit. What else did you get?"

"A couple of books. Clara got one of the same ones I did, and we are going to read it together, kind of like a little book club."

"Fun."

Ellie didn't think he thought it was fun. But honestly, it was the best part of shopping with Clara. That and the talking, she never really talked to Dane the way she spoke with Clara.

In fact, the only other person she felt comfortable talking to was Eric, but recently she felt different about sharing with him.

Ellie had always wanted to be in a book club, and you would think she would have plenty of opportunities since she worked at a library, but she was always too afraid to sign up when the flyers were put up on the library information wall.

She was so excited that she went and put her clothes away in the closet so she could start reading right away.

"Can we order in tonight? I am tired from shopping." Ellie sat on the couch next to Dane, giving him her most exhausted look.

She wasn't too tired to go out physically but was mentally overloaded. She needed to detox from the large crowds at the mall and all the human interaction from the day.

"Yeah, of course. I can go pick up some Chinese if you want?"

"Yeah, that sounds good." Ellie leaned over and kissed him before sitting back into the plush gray cushions of the couch and opening her new book. She read a lot of books, but because she knew that Clara might be opening the book and reading it at the same time, she felt a new tingle of excitement that had never accompanied reading before.

Dane left the apartment to get food, and Ellie sighed in relief. It felt so nice to be alone in peace.

She was only on page five of the book when her phone started to ring in her purse and tore her out of the story.

She jumped up to get it thinking it would be Dane calling to ask her if she wanted to add or change anything to her regular order, but Clara's name lit up on her phone screen.

She was surprised to be getting a call and not a text, most people her age were constantly texting, and she couldn't remember the last time she had an entire conversation on the phone other than with her mom.

"Hello?"

"Did you start reading the book?" Clara didn't bother with the formality of saying hello back. She just jumped right in like everything else she did in life.

CHAPTER

EIGHT

PART OF ELLIE'S JOB WAS ANSWERING PHONE CALLS FROM THE public if Ana wasn't there and not often, but once in a while, a library patron would call in a tiff about their account.

Unfortunately, this Monday morning Ellie got a call from a man who started yelling at her about his account charges. Before she finished answering the phone, she got through "Oak Valley Library. How may I..."

"Hey! I don't have time for this shit. I got charged for damages to a book on my account, and I didn't damage any book! You can't charge me for this shit when I didn't do it. You know how many people check out those damn books? I'm not the first person to touch that book, and you can't prove that I damaged it. You better take these charges off my account!"

"I'm sorry, sir; may I get your name to look into the charges?"

Ellie tried to keep her voice calm, but she would never get used to this harsh treatment. Usually, she would put the person on hold and get Ana. After all, as senior librarian, that is why she got paid the big bucks.

But Ana was out at a meeting, so she was on her own.

"Name is Adam Houser. You gonna take these charges off or do I have to come down there?" The man continued yelling.

"Okay, Mr. Houser, let me look at your account. Hold on a moment."

"I told you I don't have time for this shit! I don't want to sit on hold while you pretend to give a damn and come back to tell me there is nothing you can do. Just take the charges off!"

Ellie looked at the account screen and saw the charges she had put in the week before. She remembered the book and had a tough time repairing its damage. Sand was in-between all the pages as if it had been left open at the beach. It might be winter but it was never really too cold for the beach in California. The charge was only a dollar fifty, though, and she didn't want to have this man yelling at her.

She knew she shouldn't back down from such a bully, but she didn't have Ana to back her up.

"Okay, sir, I will take the charges off."

"You better! I don't want to get another bill from you, or I will come down there and deal with you in person!" He slammed the phone down, and the dial tone droned lazily over the line.

"Jerk," Ellie said as she placed the phone back on the cradle. She gave him what he wanted, and he still couldn't bring it down a notch to say thank you. She looked up, and Jean stood there watching her with a Cheshire cat smile.

"Nice guy?"

"He was the worst. He yelled at me until I agreed to take

the charges off his account, and then he didn't even say thank you." Ellie realized her hands were shaking as she talked, and her heart felt like it was racing.

"Why don't you take a break for a minute, and I'll cover the phones if anyone else calls?" Jean parked the cart of books she was pushing to shelve and came behind the desk with Ellie.

She touched Ellie's shoulder, "Don't listen to that guy. He is a jerk."

Ellie walked to the back and into the small break-room to the left. It was deep into the building, so it was quiet and much cooler than behind her desk. Still, she felt flushed, and her heart was beating like she just ran a race.

She paced around the small room, trying to burn off the extra energy that came from the confrontation, she hated stress, and she hated being treated as less. She stopped at the fridge, opened the door, and stuck her head in. The cool air brushed her face, and she leaned further into it.

She took a deep breath, and the smell of peanuts hit her nose.

She pulled her head back quickly and shut the door. She breathed out and blew her nose but could still smell peanuts. Ellie was allergic to peanuts, and their smell freaked her out. She knew that smelling peanuts wasn't going to hurt her, she wasn't that allergic she only reacted severely when she ingested it, but the smell triggered the fear, and there wasn't enough logic in the world to stop the anxiety once the fear woke it up.

Ellie's heart stuttered, and she felt her throat thickening. A dingy brown sofa was in the corner, and she sank into the overused plush.

Her mother always told her to sit and put her head

between her legs, so she did that first, but she still felt like she couldn't breathe, and her brain was screaming at her. Her hands went up to her throat to stop the feeling of her lungs clawing for air.

She needed air.

She jumped up and quickly walked further back into the building and out the back door.

Just as she walked out, Ana stepped out of her car. There were only two parking spots in the back of the building that the library could use, and they were kept open for Ana and any techs or special guests.

Ana saw Ellie outside in the back as she walked toward the door, and her eyebrows pulled so closely together they were practically touching.

"Ellie, are you okay?"

Ellie hated having to explain her anxiety because people often misunderstood.

People thought that an anxiety attack meant an emergency, that you would be shaking, screaming, crying, hysterical, convulsing, pulling your hair out, or all of the above, which it can be, but more often, anxiety is silent and goes unnoticed because it is internalized and unspoken, but that didn't make it any less accurate.

"Yeah, just getting some air. I had a nasty client on the phone."

"What was the problem?"

"He didn't like being charged for a damaged book."

"Who was it?"

"Adam Houser."

"Oh! He is such a jerk. I hope you didn't let him off the hook."

"Um," Ellie looked down at her hands, twisting them together, and she tried to stop the nervous tick. "Well, I didn't know what else to do. He wouldn't stop yelling at me."

"Ellie, he always tries to get out of paying his fees. You can't let him get his way when you know he is in the wrong. Stand up for yourself and the books. That's your job."

"I'm sorry, Ana." Ellie felt awful that she hadn't held her ground. It made her feel like she wasn't good at her job. And she already felt like she wasn't good at much else either.

"Next time, don't back down. Take a minute and pull yourself back together and then get back to work." Ana opened the back door and disappeared into the brick building.

Ellie stood there for a minute, unsure what to do next.

She was panicking about peanuts when she got out here, and before that, she was panicking about the guy on the phone. Now she wasn't sure if she was back to panicking about the guy on the phone or if this was a completely new and unnamed panic.

Panic that she could get fired if she couldn't stand up to people. And she knew she couldn't stand up to people because she hated confrontation. Ellie was sure she had been a horse in a previous life because she was solidly a flight animal when it came down to fight or flight.

After taking a few more deep breaths and giving herself a mini pep talk, *You got this, Ellie, you are going to be okay. Just breathe.*

Ellie went back inside. She walked back down the long hall and into the library, then back behind her desk and thanked Jean for watching her station. The rest of the day, Ellie worked in her corner desk repairing books, and thankfully since Ana was back, she didn't have to answer any more phone calls.

ELLIE SAT on a small metal bench out front and removed her shoes to replace them with her roller skates. It had been almost two months since she moved in with Dane, and her dad still called her every night to ask if she was driving the car yet and how she was getting to work.

She sometimes felt like a big baby, but she just couldn't bring herself to drive the car. It just sat in one of the apartment's two designated parking spots waiting for her, but every time she thought about driving, the deer popped into her mind and was quickly followed by the image of the little girl.

Ellie started skating home, watched for cars as always, and obeyed all traffic laws but was distracted.

She was just stepping off into the crosswalk on the corner before her apartment building, and a bike turning right onto the street slammed into her. She landed on her back with the bike and the guy riding it on top of her, and the air rushed out of her lungs.

"Fuck!" The guy said as he tried to pull himself off Ellie, which was difficult because his leg was trapped between her body and the bike, giving him little range of movement. A car stopped next to the curb, and a man jumped out to help pull him off, Ellie. Another vehicle pulled around them and stopped as well. When the woman in that car got out, she was already on the phone with 911 calling for help.

Ellie was working on getting her lungs to work again, but she didn't think paramedics were necessary. She didn't want a fuss over something so minor. The guy that hit her and the man that stopped were both looking down at her and offering her help.

"Are you okay, miss?" The man asked.

"I'm so sorry I hit you. I didn't see you and just made the turn. Does anything hurt?" The guy that hit her was talking to her too. But she couldn't focus on anything being said because his arm was hanging at an angle she knew wasn't right.

"Your arm." Was all Ellie could manage.

"Oh, shit, yeah, I think I broke it."

When she finally bothered to look up at his face, Ellie lost her breath again. He was incredibly handsome. His eyes were the color of melted caramel and dripped with kindness. His light brown hair was cut short and styled in a soft spike. He had a strong jaw and a five o'clock shadow that Ellie wanted to run her hand over.

The thought shocked her, and she bit her bottom lip, which drew his still-watching eyes down, and she saw his pupils dilate.

"I called for help," the woman said as she joined the group and crouched near Ellie. "Are you okay, honey?"

All three had now asked if she was okay, so she started thinking about a reply. And stop thinking about the butterflies warring in her stomach and what they meant.

She didn't feel like she had broken anything, and when she looked at her limbs, none of them were dangling in the wrong direction.

She thought she was doing alright, but she felt a trickle on her arm and burning on her leg and the small of her back. She lifted her arm to take a look and saw the blood.

"Yeah, I think I'm okay. Just scraped up."

"Oh honey, your arm is cut open pretty bad." The woman looked at Ellie's right arm with concern, but it was nothing compared to the twisted mess of the guy beside her.

They were sitting on the curb listening to the sirens

approach, and Ellie was starting to get nervous. Another paramedic encounter, and it hadn't even been a month. What if it was the same paramedics, and they thought something was wrong with her?

"I'm Nick, by the way." The guy said as they watched the paramedics and firefighters park on the street next to the corner.

"I'm Ellie," she reached out to shake his hand and then remembered it was not up for being involved in a handshake. She pulled her hand back and gave him an awkward smile instead.

He laughed and tried to reach for her hand with his good arm. But reaching forward with any arm must have been painful cause he winced and let it drop.

"I'm sorry I crashed into you. I don't know. I guess my mind was somewhere else." He said with an apologetic smile. His eyes flicked down to the lip she was biting again.

"You got it worse than I did, so don't worry about it," Ellie said.

The paramedics approached Nick first and started to assess his arm.

"Can you check her out first? I am okay. It's just a broken arm."

"Yeah, but my buddy Joe here is going to check on her already, so I am good here with you." The paramedic, whose name tag read Sam, gestured to the fireman behind him, walking over to Ellie before he looked back at Nick's arm.

"Okay, I just wanted to make sure she was okay before you took me away." He gave the paramedic a pointed look and tried to convey something, but Ellie couldn't figure out what, even though she hadn't stopped watching him even while the fireman was assessing her injuries.

"You have a pretty good gash here that will need some stitches. Do you have pain anywhere else?" Joe said.

"She hit her head," Nick said as he tried to lean closer to Ellie.

Another paramedic walked over, pulled a splint out of his bag, and placed it under Nick's arm. He was attaching it with some type of wrap. At the same time, Sam walked over to join Ellie and Joe.

"Hi, ma'am, my name is Sam. Can you tell me, is your head hurting?"

"No, I have a helmet on, so I don't think I hit it too hard."

"Okay, well, just to be sure, can I have you follow my finger?" He held his finger up in front of her face and asked her to follow it with only her eyes.

"Where were you headed?"

"I was skating home," Ellie pointed down the street at the brown stucco buildings. "I live in the apartments right there. I can just walk from here."

He asked her to take his hands, squeeze his fingers, pull on his hands, and try to push him away. When she could do everything he asked, he made a note in his chart and swung it around for her to sign.

"Okay, I think you are okay to drive yourself to the hospital for stitches. Just sign here acknowledging that we gave you care, and you will follow our recommendation to get medical attention on your own." He smiled at her and held out his hand to help her stand up. She had taken her skates off and put her shoes on while they waited for the paramedics to arrive, but this was her first time standing up. She took a step and yelped in pain. She stumbled forward a little, and Sam reached out and caught her before she fell.

"What happened?" He looked down at her legs to see what caused her to stumble.

"My ankle hurts." Ellie looked too.

Sam crouched down and looked at her ankles. "Which one was it?"

"My right."

He picked up her right ankle and looked at it before rotating it and watching her face for a reaction. Ellie winced and sucked air through her teeth each time he moved it.

"Well, go ahead and sit back down because you aren't walking anywhere. Is there someone that can pick you up? Or do you want a ride with us?"

"I will call someone to pick me up."

Ellie pulled out her phone and dialed Dane. While she made her phone call, Sam looked over at the ambulance to act like she had some privacy.

The firefighters had left, and she noticed that the police were standing beside the good Samaritans, asking questions and writing notes on their little flip pads. Dane answered on the third ring.

"Hey babe, what's up? I thought you would be home by now."

"I got into a little accident—"

"What happened? Where are you?"

"I'm just down the street. I was in the crosswalk, and a bicyclist turned the corner and hit me. He didn't see me."

"Are you okay?"

"Yeah, I'm okay, but I need you to pick me up and take me to the ER to get some stitches and an x-ray."

She finished her conversation with Dane, and he said he was heading out the door, so he should be right there. She looked up at Sam and gave him a thumbs up.

What was that dork?

Ellie shook her head at herself, but Sam smiled.

"All set?"

"Yep, he is on his way."

"Okay, we will go ahead and take the other guy in. Are you going to be okay waiting here? The police look like they want to talk to you."

Ellie looked over at the ambulance. Nick was loaded on a stretcher with his arm all wrapped up and his bike on the side of his gurney. The bike mirrored Nick's slim figure, lying on the floor looking slightly twisted. She felt a little sad that all she knew was his first name and wondered if she would ever see him again.

Dane would not like that. He wouldn't want her thinking about another guy. And she wasn't sure why she was. Hot guilt trickled through her, and her stomach clenched at the thought of Dane finding out.

Then she looked behind her to see the police officers standing and waiting to talk to her. The man and the woman that stopped to help had left at some point while she was on the phone with Dane.

"Yeah, I will be alright." Ellie smiled at Sam. "Tell Nick I hope he is okay."

"Nick will be fine, but I will let him know."

Sam walked over to the ambulance and closed the back doors before walking around and jumping into the driver's seat. Ellie knew the police would come to talk to her now, and she was more anxious about that than she was about more stitches.

"Hi, ma'am. Can I ask you a few questions about what happened here today?" The police officer was a short, stocky man with buzz-cut hair and a five o'clock shadow about three hours past.

Sitting on the curb next to Ellie, he flipped a page in his notepad to be on a new paper.

First, he wanted the basics, name, and age, then just the story, and finally, he asked the direct questions he needed to get down for his report.

Dane showed up just a couple minutes after the officer started talking to her and was waiting off to the side, watching her. She could tell he was feeling protective of her, but he was also trying not to hover.

She knew he would fail when he started huffing and shifting from foot to foot. He looked at his watch for the hundredth time and moved closer.

"Excuse me, officer?"

The officer paused his scribbling and looked up at Dane. He didn't say anything but raised his eyebrows to indicate he was listening.

"I am sorry to interrupt, but my girlfriend needs medical attention. Do you need the answers to all these questions right now?"

Ellie admired how much he worried about her. But didn't he worry about being rude to an authority figure? She would never have the nerve, even though she was in a lot of pain. The stinging in her arm had doubled, and the bleeding wasn't heavy, but it was still trickling down her arm.

The officer looked down at his notes and shifted the pages. Once he had considered all the pages, he looked back at Ellie without answering Dane and addressed her himself.

"You look like you are hurting. How about I take your number and call you if I have any more questions?" He smiled kindly at her and poised his pen over the paper to take down her number.

Ellie gave him her number, and he helped her to her feet

before handing her off to Dane. She wasn't sure, but she thought as the officer handed her over, he scowled at Dane. Dane must have seen it, too, because he recoiled at the officer's gaze and quickly moved Ellie into his waiting car and off to the hospital.

ELLIE WAS TREATED in the emergency room for her arm laceration and a sprained ankle. They got her arm back together with thirteen stitches and gave her a boot for her ankle.

She was told to keep her ankle elevated for two days and was given another note for work. She was worried about missing more work days but was also a little relieved because she wouldn't have to deal with Mr. Houser if he called again, and she could hide in her house.

Dane called her parents while he was waiting for her to get her arm cleaned and stitched. They wanted to come to the hospital, but Ellie told them not to worry. She didn't want them to think this was her new normal.

Instead, she asked them to come over for dinner during the week, and she would cook for them. Her mom hadn't seen the apartment yet, and Ellie thought it would help her accept that she was out on her own now.

"I can't believe that jerk crashed into you," Dane said as he angled his body into her Sentra. Dane decided to pick her up in her car so she didn't have to climb into his truck.

"He just wasn't paying attention. It could have easily been the other way around."

"Don't defend him. He should have been paying attention. He could have really hurt you."

Ellie furrowed her eyebrows. Thinking that one over,

she wondered how hurt she would have had to be to qualify for being really hurt.

"I'm not defending him. I was distracted too. I could have been paying better attention. It's not all his fault."

Dane gave Ellie an exasperated look and shook his head.

She could tell that he wasn't happy with her, but she wasn't willing to put all the blame on Nick, partly because she didn't and mostly because he seemed like a nice guy. He genuinely cared that she was hurt and put her above himself even though he was obviously worse off.

She sighed, knowing she couldn't voice this to Dane once she had smiled too wide at the waiter when they were out to dinner, and Dane had accused her of liking him. That was the topic for the rest of the night, and Ellie didn't want to relive that.

Getting up the apartment stairs was difficult, and Dane half-carried Ellie up both flights. He sounded like the big bad wolf trying to blow the door down as he tried to get the key in the door.

Dane carried her through the doorway before he realized what he had done.

"Uh, I didn't mean to do that." He set her down awkwardly and took a small step back to close the door.

Ellie laughed and nudged him playfully. "I am not getting any ideas, don't worry."

He relaxed and laughed with her. "Alright, good. I just know how girls get. It's like marriage is always on your mind. Looking for signs that its fate and all that nonsense."

The laughter died in Ellie's throat as Dane walked off to the bedroom, and she was left standing in the entryway alone with her boot and thoughts of not marrying Dane.

Ellie decided to call work instead of lingering on that

depressing thought too long. She let them know that she wouldn't be there again until Thursday. Nancy was working, and she made a huge fuss when Ellie told her what had happened, but she managed to get off the phone quickly, and as soon as she pressed the end button, she felt her body relax on the couch.

CHAPTER
NINE

ELLIE WOKE UP SINKING INTO A KIDDIE SIZE POOL OF SWEAT. THE girl's face was still etched in her mind as her eyelids flew open, and she tried to blink the image away.

She sat up and tried to catch her breath. She had nightmares about the girl almost nightly, but this one was different.

Tonight, she was trapped under the car with the girl. Her cries were louder and drowned out Ellie's screams for help.

The dream began with them both trapped in the car. She couldn't breathe. The girl cried out for Ellie to help her even though she was trapped, and just when she was about to give up, Ellie felt hands grab her. They pulled her out of the car, and the last thing she saw was the girl's face, mouth gaping opening, wide blank eyes watching her leave.

That was when she woke up; now, she didn't know what to do. Her heart was pounding, and she felt her lungs constricting.

She looked at the bedside clock flashing two forty-seven at her in a neon greenish-yellow glow.

"Dane," she said, reaching out to nudge him. "Dane, wake up."

Dane didn't open his eyes, but he turned toward her and grunted. "Hmwhat?

"I- I had a nightmare." Ellie hated waking him up, but she needed him. Maybe she should finally tell him about the girl. Maybe he would be able to help.

"Sorry, babe," Dane reached his hand out and patted her on the shoulder. "You're okay. Go back to sleep."

With that, he rolled back over, and Ellie was left staring at the back of his messy hair.

She tried to lie back down and felt her pajama shirt's cold, sticky cling pressed into her back. She gave it a minute, but the feeling was too uncomfortable to get back to sleep, so she decided to get up and change.

It only took a couple of minutes to change her pajamas, but that was enough for her to be solidly awake. She didn't know what to do now that she was up, so she decided to see if a little tv would help her to fall back to sleep or at least forget the girl.

But it wasn't the girl that was bothering her tonight. It was the fact that she was in the car too.

She settled into reruns of Diners, Drive-ins, and Dives, and after three episodes, she felt her eyelids drooping.

The next time she woke up, she was lying sideways on the couch with her hurt leg and arm resting on the back of the couch in an awkward sideways butterfly. Ellie lifted her head and sucked back the drool threatening the couch's dingy beige upholstery. Dane was standing over her when she looked up.

"Why are you sleeping out here?"

"I woke up in the middle of the night and couldn't get back to sleep, so I came out to watch TV. I guess I fell asleep." Ellie looked at the tv and saw that an early morning infomercial was filling the screen, telling her that if she bought these six DVDs, she would lose weight and look fantastic. Lies.

"Okay... Well, I'm leaving for work. Are you going to be okay?"

"I'll be fine," Ellie said with a smile she didn't feel.

"Call Clara if you need help. And I will try to take a long lunch and bring you food if I have time. Don't go out by yourself. You are a magnet for fucking trouble."

"I thought you knew that," Ellie said, trying to deflect some of her defensiveness. Dane laughed and bent over the couch to kiss her.

As the door closed, Ellie felt a wave of relief wash over her. She was alone.

Ellie didn't think she had ever felt relieved to be left alone, but she didn't want to think about that too much when she had more significant problems.

For instance, she hadn't noticed how sore she felt until she started to get up from the couch and decided to flop back down. Her back and legs were aching, and she knew they would be black and blue by now.

She groaned, trying to reach for the remote, when her phone started ringing, and she moaned again because her phone was back in the bedroom.

By the time Ellie could make it into the bedroom and get her phone on the side table, she had missed the call. It was Clara. Ellie picked up the phone to call Clara back, but just as she unlocked the screen, it started to ring again.

"I ran into Dane in the hall, and he said you were hit by a bike! That's wild! Are you okay?"

"I'm fine. I sprained my ankle and cut my arm, but other than that, I'm good."

"Damn! Dane said you were really hurt, and the guy who hit you was an irresponsible jerk. Are you really going to sue him!?"

Ellie was surprised because they hadn't talked about suing Nick at all. They hadn't talked about Nick or the accident since the hospital.

"No, I don't want to sue him. He really isn't a jerk at all. He was just distracted; it could have happened to anyone."

"Girl. I'm coming over."

Clara hung up before Ellie could say anything else. She panicked for a second and quickly moved into the kitchen to ensure it was clean. She didn't know Clara enough to let her come over to a messy house, so she took a few minutes to throw the dirty dishes in the dishwasher and stuff the junk mail into the junk drawer.

She threw the laundry into the bedroom when Clara knocked on the door. She walked over and opened the door for Clara, who didn't wait for an invitation, walking right in and tossing her bag on the side table next to Ellie's.

"I thought Dane said you were supposed to be resting. Why aren't you sitting with your foot up?" Clara started for the kitchen and went straight to the freezer. She dug around until she found an ice pack, then pulled a towel out of a drawer and wrapped it in it.

"Well, I was sitting, but I had to get up to open the door for you."

"Hurry up and sit back down then. You could have just called out, and I would have let myself in." Clara gestured for Ellie to take a seat on the couch.

"I didn't know if the door was locked or not," Ellie said as she sat down and adjusted the pillows on the coffee table so that she could prop her leg up. Clara came over, placed the ice pack on her ankle, grabbed another pillow off the couch, and stuffed it under Ellie's leg.

"Well, I don't have to work today, so I can stay and help you out. We can watch movies and binge-watch *Friends*!" Clara grabbed the remote and started surfing through the HBO Max selection. She found *Friends*, and Ellie guessed that movies were off the table. They started the series from the beginning.

"Did Dane tell you to hang out with me?"

"No, he just said that you had to stay home. How many stitches did you get this time?"

"Just thirteen." Ellie lifted her arm and twisted it across her body so that Clara could see the stitches going up her arm.

"Oh, dude, that's not a good number. You should have asked for one more. They could have put it anywhere, but at least you wouldn't have thirteen stitches in your arm, making you unlucky."

Ellie laughed at that as if she could get any unluckier. She hit a deer, crashed her car, was hit by a bike, and - if that wasn't enough - for some unknown reason, she was being haunted by a little girl. "I think the number thirteen is the least of my worries now."

"I guess that's true. Never underestimate the power of luck, though." Clara was splitting her attention between Ellie and the show. When the laugh track would go, they would both stop and watch even though they had already missed the punchline.

"Are you hungry?" Clara asked Ellie when they were halfway through the second episode.

"Yeah, I haven't eaten breakfast. I think we have some cereal and stuff in the pantry." Ellie moved to get up so she could get them both some food, but Clara put her hand on her shoulder and pushed her back down.

"Nope, I will get it. You are supposed to stay off your feet. What cereal do you want?"

"Just some Frosted Flakes is good. I have almond milk in the fridge. I hope that's okay."

"Coming right up." Clara bounced into the kitchen and rummaged through cabinets until she found two bowls. She grabbed the Frosted Flakes for Ellie and chose Fruity Pebbles for herself.

After pouring cereals and milk, she did some more rummaging until she came up with two spoons. She brought it all over to the couch, and they ate their cereal and tried not to spit out milk while they laughed along with the show.

———

ELLIE WAS HALFWAY through her second day of being stuck at home and starting to feel like she would just like to stay home forever.

Her parents were coming over for dinner in only a few hours, and she had no idea what she would feed them. She was starting to panic.

She should have figured it out and asked Dane to stop at the store, but now she would have to figure it out herself.

Clara was working too, so she couldn't ask her for help either.

Ellie flipped the channel on the regular tv stations to further her procrastination and denial. Flip, Maury Povich was telling someone he wasn't the father to some kid, flip, Chip, and Jo Gaines were revealing a house, flip, Bobby Flay was doing something with a barbecue.

She watched Bobby grilling veggies and meats for thirty minutes before she had an epiphany. She could order dinner, have it delivered, and then switch the food to plates so it looked like she made it.

Okay, her parents would probably see right through that plan, but she didn't think they would say anything so that it wouldn't matter.

———

ELLIE'S PARENTS arrived right on time for six o'clock dinner, and they had Eric with them, which Ellie was not expecting.

Dane had gotten home thirty minutes before, and he laughed as he watched Ellie hobbling around trying to switch food from take-out containers to bowls and platters, then stuff the empty containers into the oven.

Now that everyone was in Dane's tiny kitchen, the apartment felt small, and Ellie longed for the afternoon when she was alone or yesterday when she was with Clara.

"So, El, how's your ankle doing?" Eric leaned against the counter next to Ellie and looked over her shoulder at the food.

"It's worse than yesterday. It's super swollen and aches, but I'm hoping tomorrow will be a turning point."

"How are you getting to work tomorrow?"

"Dane is taking me."

"Have you driven your car at all since the accident?"

"Well, I haven't needed to." Truthfully, she avoided driving her car at all costs, including the dinner she presented. She could have driven to the store and bought something to cook for her parents, but instead, she ordered it so she didn't have to drive.

"Really? How have you been getting to work every day? How do you go to the store by yourself?"

"I haven't needed to do any of that, Eric. I use my skates to get to work, and Dane and I go to the store together because it is easier that way."

"Ellie, you see what you are doing right?"

Ellie picked up a bowl and a platter and walked to the dining room table. She looked at Eric and raised her eyebrows, indicating that he could go on and tell her what she was doing. She braced herself because she was sure he would only tell her what she didn't want to hear.

"You are transferring Mom to Dane."

"What does that even mean, Eric?"

"It means that everything you used to do with Mom, you now do with Dane."

Ellie finished turning and walked the dish she had over to the table. Her parents had been talking to Dane while she was in the kitchen with Eric, but she could feel her mom's eyes on her and tell that she was sizing her up.

Her parents sat next to each other on the side of the table closest to the kitchen, and Eric sat across from them while Dane and Ellie took up the heads of the table. They passed the food around, and once everyone had stacks of food on their plates, the conversation started to do the dinner-time drone.

"Ellie, what happened this time? I'm worried about you." Ellie's mom said. She watched Ellie closely as she absently pushed her Brussels sprouts away from her salmon.

"Mom, I told you, I was stepping off the curb into the crosswalk, and a guy rounded the corner and slammed into me. We both fell. He broke his arm, which is much worse than anything that happened to me. I am fine. It's a pretty boring story." And Ellie was tired of telling it.

"What was this guy doing that he couldn't pay attention to where he was going." Ellie's dad wanted to know. He had his mouth full of salmon and potatoes.

"He was distracted. I was, too, so things could have easily gone the other way."

"Still, you can't just hit a woman with your bike and expect to get away with it," Dane said, and Ellie and Eric looked at each other. Neither of them liked how old-school Dane was being.

"I agree with Dane." Her dad said, still shoveling food into his mouth while talking.

"I don't think being a woman has anything to do with anything," Eric said. "I think we should just be glad that Ellie wasn't hurt more, and hopefully, she won't get into any more unfortunate accidents."

"This one wasn't my fault. I couldn't have prevented it."

"Well, you could be driving your car," Dane said, knowing that Ellie hadn't mentioned not driving to work to her dad, and she was avoiding that conversation. She looked at him, mouth gaping; how could he throw her under the bus like that?

"You aren't driving the car to work at all, Ellie?" Her dad looked at her now, and he didn't look happy.

Eric shifted nervously and looked between Ellie and their dad. He knew she wasn't driving the car because she had called and told him, but she also told him not to say anything to her parents.

"I haven't been driving the car to work lately, Dad. We are so close that it's easier to roller skate, and it's good exercise."

"Well, I want you to drive until your sprain heals."

"I think Dane will just drop me off for a bit. It will be hard to drive with the boot anyway." Ellie didn't look up at Dane to see if this plan was okay with him, and she hoped he wouldn't call her on it in front of her dad.

"Fine. This guy is paying for your medical bills, right?" Her dad was back to focusing on his meal. He probably wouldn't be happy when she said she wasn't worried. She figured she would let the insurance companies figure those things out.

"I'm not sure what will happen with all that yet." Noncommittal, that was good. Maybe he wouldn't question her too much more.

"He'll have to pay; the insurance companies won't let him get away without paying."

Ellie started pushing her food around on her plate. She decided she was done talking on the topic because the idea of tracking down Nick and 'making him pay' seemed a little too wild West for her.

Eric was closest to her, and he put his hand over her knee under the table and gave it a little pat.

Dinner finished smoothly after the subject of Ellie's most recent disaster passed, and once again, Ellie was in the kitchen working on dishes with her mom. The boys were all in the living room, but there wasn't as much separation in the apartment as in the family home.

"Are you happy living here with Dane?" Her mom asked quietly so that the boys wouldn't hear. She was washing dishes, and Ellie was on drying duty.

"I like it. Dane is great." If Ellie were more honest, she would say things with Dane were up and down. Some days, he was so sweet and helpful; others, he was overbearing and possessive.

"That's good, sweetie," her mom said. "Just in case, we

will keep your room exactly how you left it." She smiled at Ellie and handed her a new dish to dry.

"Thanks, Mom, but I think I'm okay here." She put the dish into the cabinet and glanced at the guys.

Eric and Dane were talking, and she wondered if it was about her. She imagined the conversation would look very different from the one she was having. Maybe Eric was telling Dane that he was a dead man if he hurt his baby sister. She smiled, thinking that might be the case.

"Ellie?" Her mom was looking at her and holding out a dish for her to dry. "Did you hear what I said?"

"Sorry, I missed it."

"I asked if you are ready to return to work tomorrow?"

"Oh, yeah, I was thinking about calling out one more day. My ankle is really sore." She had been thinking about it all day. She had plenty of sick days left but was still debating its ethics.

"Oh, I think you should go in. You've missed a lot of time recently and don't want to lose your job. You love that job."

"I know. I just think I'll have a hard time moving around, and I won't be much help on the floor."

"Didn't your doctor give you a note for work? So that you could sit more or something like that? I think you should be able to take it easy at work for a few days."

"Fine, I'll go." Ellie put the dish in her hand away and reached for another one fighting back a swell of emotion. Her blood felt hot and heavy in her veins as she thought about going back to work.

"I'm so proud of you, Ellie. Look at you, out of the house and doing well." Ellie's mom hugged her. "I can't believe my baby girl is so grown."

"Thanks, Mom," Ellie said. She was glad her mom saw

what an effort she was making. But she could do without the smothering.

"When do you think you and Dane will get married?" Her mom asked as she handed her the last dish. She dried her hands and turned to watch Ellie dry the plate. Ellie felt like an ant under a magnifying glass.

"Mom, Dane, and I haven't even talked about marriage. We've only been together for like three months."

"Yeah, but you already live together, and marriage is the next logical step. If you guys aren't going to get married, what's the point of living together?"

"I... Well, I mean..." Ellie stopped; she was trying hard to think of something that she could say to make her mom understand this was not a good subject right now. She couldn't just tell her no, they weren't getting married, and she wasn't sure she wanted to marry Dane. Her mom wouldn't understand.

She was so focused on thinking she forgot what she was doing and dropped the glass she had been working on drying.

The glass hit the linoleum floor and shattered around their feet. Dane and Eric jumped up from the couch and came to the kitchen to help while Ellie's dad walked over from the living room and leaned slightly over the kitchen counter to see the mess.

Ellie's mom had shoes on, and she stepped around the glass and out of the kitchen to make room for Dane coming in with a broom and dustpan. On the other hand, Ellie had one foot in the boot, and the other barefoot. Glass shards surrounded her, and some pieces were on the top of her foot and boot.

"Stay where you are, Ellie," Eric said as he moved up behind her.

He grabbed her around the waist and lifted her out of the glass pile, pulling her out of the kitchen as he moved back. He leaned over and looked at her feet to make sure all the shards of glass stayed in the kitchen and not in her feet. As he was looking, a few blood spots appeared on the top of her bare foot.

"Looks like you have a couple of shards stuck in the top of your foot. Maybe we should go get them checked out." Eric said as he stood back up.

"I don't want to go to the hospital again. Let me see if I can get them out with tweezers first." Ellie walked the short hall from the kitchen into the bedroom to get tweezers. She closed the door behind her and sank onto the bed to put her head in her hands.

Why is it so difficult to talk to Mom?

You are such a mess. Look at you. Another injury, and if you can't fix it, they are going to make you go to the hospital again.

Ellie brought her foot up onto the bed and picked out three pieces of glass stuck in the top of her foot. They weren't deep cuts, so she cleaned them and put bandages over them.

When she left the room, Dane was finished cleaning up the glass and huddled with her family, talking in quiet undertones. She couldn't hear what they said but figured it was about her and her newly found accident-prone self. As she got closer, Eric noticed her, and everyone stopped talking.

"Hey, Sis, how's your foot?"

"It's fine. What are you guys talking about?"

"Nothing. We were just saying that we need to get going." Eric leaned over and hugged her.

They all said good night, and her mom told her to have a good day back at work. Her dad told her to drive the car.

And then they left her and Dane standing at the door of their apartment.

Ellie sighed and turned back into the hallway. She slowly hobbled back to the living room to sit on the couch with Dane close on her heels.

She didn't want to go to work tomorrow, but she also didn't want to just sit around the apartment anymore. It was too easy for her mind to wander back to the girl's face when she was alone, with nothing to distract her from the dark crevices of her brain.

CHAPTER
TEN

ELLIE STRUGGLED THROUGH THE NEXT WEEK OF WORK. THE ONLY thing that was getting Ellie through the week was Clara.

They were still reading the book that Clara picked, and they texted each other every day to talk about the next chapter. They made sure not to go ahead of the other so that no one gave anything away, and it was the most fun Ellie could ever remember having.

Clara called her sometimes instead of texting, and if Dane were around, he would roll his eyes as Ellie laughed and chatted about the antics of Franny, the main character, and which guy she should be with.

Dane found this incredibly annoying because while Franny was dating one guy in the story, the girls were sure she should be dating another.

Dane drove her to work every day and picked her up too. They went to the store together, made dinner, and went to bed together. The only thing they didn't do together was wake up because Ellie wasn't sleeping much.

Every night the girl visited her with her arms stretched towards Ellie and her mouth gaping open like a dying fish.

Ellie would get up, go into the living room, and fall asleep on the couch to some late-night show.

After the first few days, she realized that Dane finding her on the couch always caused an argument, so she set the alarm to wake up on the couch and get back into bed with Dane to "wake up" next to him. Unfortunately, she didn't set the alarm early enough on Sunday, and Dane found her on the couch again.

"Ellie, why do you keep coming out to sleep on the couch?" Dane stood over her as she tried to open her eyes and make her brain turn on.

"I couldn't sleep again and didn't want to wake you up."

Ellie rubbed her eyes and sat up, swinging her foot still in the boot onto the floor.

"Are you still having the same nightmare? Your accident was almost over a month ago, Ellie. You need to get over it. It is time to move on."

"I'm sorry. I'm trying."

Ellie didn't want to fight with Dane, and she wasn't being completely honest with him either because her nightmares were about the girl, not the accident, but she didn't share that part of her nightmares. They still surrounded the accident, and the two seemed tied together, but she omitted the part about the girl so she didn't seem crazy.

She got up and walked into the bathroom, hoping he would let the topic go by the time she came out.

When she came out, Dane sat on the couch watching the news. She looked at the headline running across the screen, Mass Shooting in Mountain Valley, California.

"Twenty-two dead and fifty wounded. The guy was only shooting for four minutes. That is unbelievable." Dane leaned forward to focus on the tv. His face pinched in frustration.

Mountain Valley was only two towns away from them.

"A school?" Ellie asked, her voice barely above a whisper.

"A mall. The police got him already."

"Not fast enough." Ellie felt her stomach roll. She wasn't breathing, and she gasped for air and tried to steady her pounding heart.

Ellie didn't want to hear anymore, so she walked back to the room and into the walk-in closet. She stood there for a few moments breathing deeply and exhaling slowly. After several rounds of deep breathing, she sat on the floor and put her head between her knees.

After a while, she breathed easier and pushed down the fear, but she was still in the closet. She could hear her phone ringing in the other room, and she contemplated leaving the safety of the closet.

"Ellie?" Dane called from the living room. "Clara is calling you."

"I'm in the closet!" Ellie called back. Maybe he would bring her phone, and then she wouldn't have to leave the closet yet.

Dane opened the door and looked down at her, "What're you doing?"

"The news was upsetting me."

"Okay..." Dane gave her a look and handed her phone over. He closed the door and muttered something that sounded a little like 'crazy,' but Ellie wasn't sure, and she didn't want to worry about it.

The call had gone to voicemail when Dane brought the phone, so Ellie listened to the message before calling Clara back.

Clara: Hey, Ellie! What are you doing? I need to get a new outfit for a date tomorrow. Let's go to the mall! Call me back!

Ellie stared at her phone. Clara must not have heard about the shooting. She couldn't go to a mall today. She wasn't sure she would ever go to a mall again. She was starting to feel anxious all over again. She put the phone next to her on the floor and put her head between her knees again.

Deep breaths, Ellie. You are okay.

There was a knock on the door to the apartment, and Ellie heard Dane open it, and then voices floated back to her. She groaned because she already knew it was Clara, and she would come into the closet and make her leave it. Worse, she was going to make her go back to the mall.

"Ellie?" Clara knocked on the closet door. "Can I come in?"

"Yeah," Ellie mumbled.

Clara opened the door, and Ellie could feel her eyes on her even though she didn't lift her head from her knees.

Clara stepped in and shut the closet door behind her. It was a good thing it was such a large closet; otherwise, Ellie would start to get claustrophobic. Clara sat down next to Ellie and leaned over to her. Their shoulders were touching, and Ellie felt the warmth and energy coming from Clara.

"Are you okay?" Clara asked.

"All those people... and all they did was go shopping," Ellie said to her knees.

"Yeah, I heard about that. It's really sad."

"It doesn't make any sense. Why are people so horrible? Why doesn't anyone do anything to make this stop?" Ellie lifted her head to look at Clara.

"I don't know. It makes me anxious too, but I have to

bury it; otherwise, I would never leave the house." Clara laughed a little, but Ellie thought never leaving the house didn't sound like such a bad idea.

"Well, I can't go to the mall today."

"Come on. I need you to come with me and help me find an outfit. I have a date, and I really want him to like me. This guy is Ryan Reynolds hot."

"How is an outfit going to make him like you more? You are beautiful no matter what you wear."

"Aww, thanks, bestie! I just really want something 'wow' for tonight, you know? And I am just not feeling it from any of the clothes in my closet."

"What about your black flowy date night dress?"

"No, I need something better."

"Listen, I am going to level with you. I can't go to the mall today. What about that small stripe of stores across from the library?"

"With the little boutique shops, cafes, and the bookstore?"

"Yeah, they have some cute stuff over there. I have gone with my mom before."

"Okay, deal. Let's go." Clara stood up and reached a hand down to Ellie.

Ellie grabbed Clara's hand, and the two of them left the closet together.

"We are going to shop for a little bit. Do you need anything while I am out?" Ellie asked Dane.

"No, thanks. This is perfect because I was going to ask the guys over to watch the game. Do you think you can stay out with Clara until the game is over? Maybe a little later?"

Ellie looked at Dane and tried to think of the right words. She wasn't sure why she felt jilted when she was the one leaving, but she also felt like it was rude of him to tell her to stay out of the apartment until his friends left.

"Okay, that's fine." Ellie decided to just go with it. She grabbed her purse off the table in the hall and followed Clara out of the apartment and down the stairs to her red Honda Civic in the parking lot.

"Dane was kinda a jerk. He didn't need to talk to you like that." Clara said as they climbed into the car. She turned the key in the ignition, and the car purred around them.

Ellie was surprised that Clara voiced what she was already thinking.

"Aren't all guys like that?"

"I know this is your first relationship but girl... Even you should know that was fucking rude. You shouldn't let him talk to you like that." Clara reached over and patted her on the knee.

Clara was right; this was her first relationship, and now she was questioning if it was as great as she thought.

———

THE GIRLS SPENT a couple of hours searching through the small boutiques lining the main road looking for the perfect outfit for Clara's date that night.

They came out of the little shop next to the bookstore with an outfit that Clara deemed close enough to perfect. It was a red slinky dress cut low and showed off some cleavage and cut high to show off some thigh. Clara also bought a pair of black stilettos with little rhinestones trimming the sides.

They got stuck on earrings, Clara wanted dangly earrings, but Ellie thought she should go with diamond studs. Clara landed on little white gold hoops, and they called it a day on the shopping, which was a good thing because Ellie was working herself up into a panic the entire time.

She was on the lookout for angry-looking men the entire time, and she made sure that she always knew where the exits were in each store.

As they walked past the bookstore, Ellie paused to look in the window.

"Do we dare go in?" Clara asked, coming up behind her.

"We still have all the books left from our last bookstore trip," Ellie said, laughing at how Clara pressed her face as close to the window as she could to see the books inside.

"So? You can never have too many books!"

Ellie's stomach growled loudly, and Clara laughed at the embarrassed face she made.

"I think your stomach just saved you from spending a lot of money."

It was still early, and since Ellie couldn't go home because of the guys, they went out to lunch at a nearby restaurant, Alfredo's. They asked to sit outside on the patio, and they ordered artichoke dip and hummus with pita bread, avocado egg rolls, and a large Caesar salad to share, along with a glass of wine each.

"This is so much fun," Ellie said, stuffing an egg roll in her mouth. She was finally enjoying herself and feeling more relaxed.

"The food here is so good. This is our new spot."

"It's so nice to go to a real restaurant for a change. Dane always wants to order in." Ellie said as she grabbed another avocado egg roll. She looked across the patio and saw Nick, the guy that hit her with his bike. His arm was in a cast, and he was sitting with an older-looking couple who she assumed were his parents.

He looked over at her, and their eyes met. He quickly looked back at the people he was with and stood up from his table.

Crap, he is going to come over here.

Ellie didn't know what to do at first, but then she remembered that Dane wasn't there to make a scene.

"Okay, remember the guy that hit me with his bike?" Ellie started talking rapidly to Clara before Nick could reach their table. "He is walking over to us right now."

Clara looked behind her right as Nick made it to the table and was standing looking down at Ellie. He smiled, and dimples popped out to frame his perfect teeth. Clara's mouth flopped open as she looked from Nick to Ellie.

"Hi," he said. "How are you doing?" He looked at her foot that was still in the boot and frowned a little.

"I'm fine. How are you? How's your arm?"

"My arm is fine; I get the cast off in a couple more weeks. You hurt your leg?" He was concerned for her, making her heart do little skips.

"Oh, yeah, it's just a sprain. I didn't realize I hurt it until they tried to get me to stand, and you were already in the ambulance."

"Shit, I'm so sorry."

"It's alright." Ellie gave him her most reassuring smile, and Clara cleared her throat and gave Ellie a nudge with her foot under the table.

"Sorry, I should introduce you to my friend. This is Clara, Clara; this is Nick."

"Hi Clara, it's nice to meet you," Nick said.

"Hi to you too." Clara smiled at Nick and gave Ellie a look that said, 'he's cute!'

"Well, I should get back to my table. I am here with my parents."

"Yeah, of course. It was nice to see you." Ellie didn't know why, but she was disappointed that Nick was leaving.

"But hey, here's my number, just in case you need any help with medical bills or anything." Nick grabbed a napkin, wrote his number down, and handed it to her.

"Thanks," Ellie said.

"Alright, well, take care." Nick awkwardly waved to Ellie and Clara and returned to his parents. He looked back at Ellie twice on his way to the table and narrowly missed a server carrying a tray full of food.

"Oh, he is an awkward one." Clara laughed, "He reminds me of you."

"He is so cute," Ellie said before clapping her hand over her mouth. "I shouldn't say that."

"Why the hell not? He is super cute."

"He is, but Dane would get mad."

"Well, Nick seems nice."

"Dane hates him. He thinks I should sue him for medical expenses."

"I don't think you need to sue him... He said he would help. But if you ask me, he just wanted to give you his number."

"You think so?" Ellie looked at the number on the napkin and wondered what to do with it. If she kept the napkin, Dane might find it, and he would freak out, but she didn't want to lose the number.

"Give me your phone," Clara said, reading Ellie's mind. "You don't want Dane to find the napkin. He would totally overreact."

Clara put Nick's name and number in her phone, opened messages, and typed a message to Nick.

Ellie: Hey! This is Ellie. It was so nice to run into you again. *wink*

Ellie looked up at Nick, but he was busy talking to his parents, so she tried to shift her focus back to artichoke dip and avocado egg rolls.

"Clara, that is flirting!"

"Yeah. So? He is totally cute. Didn't we cover that already? And this way, he has your number."

"I already have a boyfriend, so I shouldn't be flirting with Nick." Ellie knew what she was saying was right, but it also felt wrong, and that freaked her out a little.

"Oh, calm down. It's totally innocent."

Ellie swiped her phone back out and frowned at the message. She wished she could come up with fun, flirty messages that easily. This is why it was so easy for Clara to meet guys and get dates.

"Tell me about the guy you are going out with," Ellie asked Clara to distract herself from Nick and the confusing thoughts associated with why she cared about him looking back at her.

"His name is Jesse, and he is a regular at the coffee shop. I don't know what he does for a living, but he came in and flirted with me every day for three weeks before he finally asked me out on a date. He is taking me to this fancy Italian restaurant across town."

"That sounds nice! I can't wait to hear all about it." Ellie was watching Nick in her peripheral vision, and she saw when he got up and left the restaurant, but she didn't see him look back at her after he got out onto the street.

As they walked back into the apartment building, they saw an older woman pushing the already lit-up button for the elevator. Ellie had never seen her before, and she wondered if she knew that the elevator hardly ever came when it was called.

"Hey, Lottie! Is the elevator on the fritz again?" Clara stopped next to the woman who shuffled her walker around so that she was facing them.

"They keep saying they will fix the damn thing, but I have pushed that button a dozen times, and it just won't come down." She huffed as she looked back at the door to double-check that they hadn't snuck open.

"Well, how about I help you up the stairs instead? No sense waiting." Clara stepped closer to the woman offering her arm.

"Alright, honey, that sounds nice. And tell me. Who is your friend?" Lottie looked past Clara to Ellie and gave her a warm smile.

"Oh, you haven't met? This is Ellie. Ellie, this is Charlotte. She lives in 3F on my floor but on the other end."

"Call me Lottie, dear." Charlotte reached out to shake hands with Ellie. Her smooth wrinkled hands felt fragile and comforting. They reminded her of her grandma's hands.

They all started making their way up the stairs. Clara and Ellie on either side of Lottie and Clara with her walker hooked onto her back.

When they finally made it up the stairs to Lottie's apartment Clara fished out her house keys and opened the door. A happy bark came through the door, and then a tail's slap-slap against the wall began.

"Settle down, Zeke." Lottie laughed at her dog as the massive mutt shoved his head into Clara's hands for rubs and pets. He had a medium coat with black and brown fur that swirled around in odd patterns. Ellie couldn't have told you his primary breed, but block-headed cuteness was all anyone needed to know about Zeke.

"Zeke! I have missed you too, buddy!" Clara patted him with one hand as she held Lottie's arm with the other.

Once they were past the threshold and Zeke lost interest in Clara, he moved on to Ellie, who was happy to give him all the pets he wanted. She had always had a cat with her family, but they had never had a dog. She always wanted one.

After a stressful climb, they got Lottie settled in her apartment with a rerun of Family Feud and a nice cold iced tea.

"Thank you so much, dears. Oh, and Clara, I was wondering if you could get some groceries for me tomorrow? I meant to call, but I am getting pretty low on everything."

Clara walked over to the fridge and opened it again with inventory in mind. "Damn, Lottie, all you have is iced tea, milk, pickles, condiments, and leftover pasta. You need food."

"Yeah, I know. So, the store?" Lottie chuckled as Clara checked the pantry and gave her a withering glare from the shelves that seemed only to house dust.

"Of course, I will go to the store. Make me a list! I will even drag Ellie along." Clara smiled at Ellie and gave her a nudge.

"Yeah, that would be nice." Ellie didn't know what else to say, but she was happy to spend more time with Clara.

They excused themselves and promised to return the next day to pick up a list.

"How do you know, Lottie?" Ellie asked as they started walking down the hall.

"She has been my neighbor since I moved in a couple of years ago. One day I met her in the hall as she struggled to get groceries into her apartment, she had just gained the walker, and I helped her out. We started talking, and that was that. I have helped her out and been a friend ever since."

"So that's why you have a key?"

"Yeah, that, and I help take care of Zeke when she needs me too."

After they returned to Clara's, Ellie checked in with Dane, and he still had his friends over, so Clara suggested that Ellie help her prepare for her date. This was a girl moment that Ellie had never experienced, and she had to admit she was excited.

Clara's apartment layout was precisely like Dane's as far as the floor plan went, but everything else was completely different. Dane's apartment was white and simple, with few pictures and minimal furniture. On the other hand, Clara's apartment was purple and trimmed with gray and had posters, photos, bookshelves, and mirrors on every wall, and was overflowing with mix-matched furniture. In the hallway, there was a wooden fixture: part chair, cubby, and coat rack. Clara threw her bags on it as she walked into the apartment and gestured for Ellie to sit.

Ellie chose a pink sofa with a wooden back and more pillows than cushions. She pushed aside a few pillows and sat down, letting the pillows fall back down around her. It was oddly comforting.

"Do you want anything to drink?" Clara asked from the kitchen.

"Just water. Thanks."

"Water? No girl, I need a pre-date drink, and you are walking down a flight of stairs to get home, so you can have one too. What will it be? I have beer, wine, and vodka that I can mix with cranberry juice?"

"Fine, Vodka Cranberry." Ellie wasn't much of a drinker, but from her limited drinking experience, she knew she could handle a juice-based drink.

Clara mixed two drinks and came over to sit in the living room with Ellie. She handed Ellie her glass and grabbed the remote as she flopped down on the orange loveseat closest to Ellie.

She immediately flipped to HBO and put on *Friends*. Laughter burst through the speakers, and Ellie realized that the furniture in the room was channeling Monica and Rachel's apartment. Clara read Ellie's mind as she looked from the tv to the room.

"Yeah, I know, I have a problem," Clara said.

"Not a problem so much as an obsession."

"A healthy obsession?"

"Is there any such thing as a healthy obsession?"

Clara thought about that and shrugged. "Well, I don't care. I like it."

After the episode ended, Clara got up and went into the bedroom. She took the bags from their shopping trip with her, and a few moments later, she returned fully dressed in the red slinky and the "almost slutty but not quite" heels.

"Well, what do you think?" Clara asked.

"You look great!" Ellie said, even though that was a vast understatement. Clara looked stunning, and Ellie was jealous. She never dressed up and didn't think she would look half as good even if she did. She was too plain.

"I have to do my hair. Come in the bedroom."

They entered the room, and Clara started pulling out hair curlers, clips, and a blow dryer. Ellie had no idea what Clara was going to do with all that stuff, but she watched as Clara got to work.

Clara wet her hair in sections and rolled the sections into the curlers, then clipped them up, and after she had all her hair wet and up in the curlers, she turned the hair dryer on low and started blow drying her hair.

"Normally, I would let them air dry, but I don't have time for that," Clara yelled over the dryer's noise.

Clara felt her hair and declared it done, but she didn't remove it from the curlers. Instead, she started working on her makeup. Ellie never wore makeup, probably because her mom never wore makeup, and she never learned how to use the stuff.

Clara was methodical, and the two chatted while she applied the different liquids and powders to her face. She swiped mascara across her lashes and lipstick on pursed lips before smacking them together and turning for Ellie's approval which was readily given. Once her hair was down, the effect was complete, she looked like an actress, and Ellie wondered how she had yet to be discovered.

"Jesse is going to be here any minute," Clara said once ready. "Do you just want to stay here?"

"No, I should go home. I'm sure Dane's friends have left, and if they haven't, I will just go hide in the room."

"Why doesn't Dane want you around his friends?"

"I think he just wanted to have some guy time. It's fine, really."

"You are going back to hiding in your closet, aren't you?"

Ellie smiled because Clara already knew her pretty well. There was a knock on the door, and Clara suppressed a squeal. She took one last look in the mirror twirling from one side to the other, trying desperately to see herself from all angles. She gave up after a quick second and turned to Ellie.

"This is it. I look okay?" She smiled and did a twirl for Ellie.

"You look absolutely gorgeous," Ellie said. "Movie star gorgeous."

Clara beamed at Ellie and hugged her quickly before the two walked to the door. Ellie grabbed her purse on the way. Clara quickly introduced Ellie to Jesse, and they all left the apartment. They walked down the first flight of stairs together, and Ellie split off to her apartment. She could hear loud laughter running from the apartment, and there were no more doubts that she would end up in the closet.

She waved to Clara and Jesse and put her hand on the doorknob. Ellie took a deep breath and braced herself for human interaction and possible unhappiness from Dane before she opened the door.

CHAPTER

ELEVEN

ELLIE WAS CORRECT IN THINKING THAT DANE WOULD BE UNHAPPY she was back. When she walked in, six guys crowded together on the couch that only sat three people, and Dane was right in the middle.

"Hi, babe," Dane said. "What are you doing home so early?" The tone was friendly, but the words implied that she shouldn't be back yet.

"Sorry, Clara is going on a date. I'll just stay in the room." Ellie scampered into the bedroom and then into the closet, where she shut the door and plopped down on the cream-shag carpet.

There was a space heater in the corner that she flipped on, not that it was cold, just to get it cozy. She had a book on the floor next to her dresser from earlier. She didn't know why she liked the closet so much when she hated small spaces. But for some reason, the closet felt safe and comfortable.

She was leaning back against the wall reading her book when her phone buzzed beside her, and Nick's name popped up on the screen. Excitement shot through her, and she grabbed the phone, but then panic crept in as she thought about Dane finding out.

He was jealous of Clara sometimes, so she couldn't imagine how bad he would be about another guy, especially this guy.

Ellie closed her eyes and took a deep calming breath before opening her eyes and the message.

Nick: Hey Ellie, I'm so glad I saw you today at the restaurant. I want to say I am sorry again about your ankle. If there is anything I can do to make it up to you, please let me know!

Ellie couldn't help but smile, and she didn't know why. She also didn't know what to write back and wished Clara was around to discuss it. She could say something short and vague, but then he might not write back, and she wanted to say something he would respond to.

She didn't know why she wanted the conversation to continue, but she did. She typed out seven responses and deleted every one of them because they weren't good enough, but the eighth time was the charm.

Ellie: It was great to see you too. I was worried I might never see you again. Don't worry about my ankle. It's feeling better already. How's your arm?

Ellie hadn't realized she was holding her breath until she hit send, and the phone made the bird swooping out the window noise and took her breath with it. Instantly she was rethinking her words.

I was worried I wouldn't see him again. Why?

He was going to think she was coming on to him. Maybe she was.

She thought that would be it for at least a few minutes, but right away, her phone buzzed and chirped to tell her she had a new message.

She opened this one right away and felt the excitement creeping back in.

Nick: It's totally fine. I'll be back to riding my bike in no time. I promise to watch out for beautiful girls crossing the street next time. *Tongue out emoji* *Wink Emoji*

Her stomach flipped, and she felt her pulse quicken. He was calling her beautiful. She didn't know how to respond. If she said something flirty, she would be being unfaithful to Dane. She had already toed the line. But she also really wanted him to keep texting her.

She needed Clara. Guilt was already shaking through her.

She was about to text Clara even though she was out on a date and ask her when Dane opened the closet door.

"The game is over, and the guys left," Dane said. "What do you want me to get for dinner?"

"I'm fine with whatever you want."

"Okay, fine, I'm going to order pizza then." Dane turned to leave and then looked back at Ellie, "Are you just going to stay in the closet all night?"

"No, I'll be right out." Ellie stood up to show Dane she would leave the closet.

"Okay, 'cause it's weird."

Ellie rolled her eyes at Dane's back as he walked to the kitchen. She didn't understand what was so weird about it, and even if it was weird, she didn't care because it made her feel better.

She could hear Dane ordering pizza on the phone, so she decided to write Nick back quickly.

Ellie: I was happy to break your fall. *Smile*

After she pressed send, she thought it was too flirty, but

she couldn't take it back, so she quickly copied the conversation and sent it to Clara for help.

She didn't want to mess it up, but she also didn't know what she was afraid to mess up or why she felt guilty just for smiling at a text. Maybe it was because Nick was the one that was making her smile and not Dane. And she didn't know what to do with that.

THE NEXT DAY was another workday, and Dane still drove Ellie to work. She had an appointment at the end of the week to find out if the boot could come off, and she couldn't wait.

She knew her dad didn't want her to use her roller skates anymore because of the accident, but Ellie would take an accident like that over a car accident any day of the week.

Dane pulled up along the curb and waited for Ellie to leave the car. She kissed him quickly and jumped out of the car with her book tote and lunch bag.

Dane sat and watched as Ellie walked into the building, this was routine, and once she was inside, he took off without so much as a glance in the side mirror. She walked back to the time clock at the door to the employee lounge and finally received a message from Clara; as she typed her number into the machine to tell it that she had arrived for the day.

Ellie scanned the message from Clara before walking to the fridge to put her lunch box away.

Clara: Girl! You are totally flirting! That's awesome cause he is cute. Sorry, I didn't get back to you last night! Jesse took me out dancing. It was so much fun. I

stayed the night at his house... He is perfect. I can't wait to tell you everything. Wanna meet up after work?

Ellie wrote back that she would meet Clara at Sally's, and she got to work. Ellie thought the day was so slow that three would never come, and when it finally did, she was out the door as fast as her boot would go.

Ellie walked into Sally's Creamery at three ten, and Clara was already waiting for her order at the counter.

"I hope you don't mind, but I ordered for you," Clara said. "I love this combo, and I swear you will love it, or else you can have my favorite pair of shoes."

Ellie plastered a smile on her face even though she was distraught. She did not like trying new things but didn't want to offend her new friend.

"What did you order?" She asked.

"A triple scoop with cookie dough, chocolate fudge, and mint chocolate chip. It tastes like a thin mint cookie."

The girl behind the counter handed them each a bowl of ice cream, and they walked outside and sat at a table out front to eat.

"So, tell me about your date," Ellie said.

"It was so amazing. This guy is perfect, Ellie. He's funny, handsome as hell, smart, and he is so sweet. He works as a screenwriter, which is like the coolest job ever. He said he likes you too, by the way."

"He barely met me." Ellie scooped up cookie dough and mint chocolate chip all together. It did taste a little like a thin mint cookie. It was good.

"Well, I told him all about you. He knows that he has to like you to be with me."

"And he wants to be with you?"

"Well, he wanted to be with me last night," Clara said. Her eyes twinkled in the sunlight, and Ellie could tell she was pleased. It was nice to see her friend shining.

"Clara!" Ellie said, feigning shock at her scandalous comment.

"Oh! And I forgot to tell you, I got an audition tomorrow for an actual show. It isn't a big part, but it would be on TV."

"That's amazing! What's the part?" Ellie did not doubt that Clara would make an impression and go far in the entertainment industry once she got her break.

"Thanks! It's 'Girl in Cafe,' which is perfect cause I already know how to do that." Clara finished her bowl and pushed it into the center of the table. "So, when do you get that boot off?"

"I go back to the doctor on Thursday, and I should get the all-clear after that."

"That's good, and then will you go back to roller skating, or will you start driving?"

Clara knew all about Ellie's issues with driving, and she knew that Ellie didn't want to drive but also that the pressure was on from her father and Dane.

"I'm going to go back to roller skating. It isn't far enough from the apartment for me to need to drive, and it is good exercise. Plus, it was a fluke accident. What are the chances of it happening again?"

"Well, it could happen again with a car, is what I think your dad is worried about."

"Yeah. I guess I'll just have to take my chances and be more careful. Speaking of which, will you give me a ride home? I told Dane we were meeting, and he said he would go home and start making dinner while we are here."

"Of course. Just let me know when you are ready to go."

Ellie's phone danced across the table, and they both looked at it. Her phone used to display the sender's name and a peek at the message, but the screen was blank this time.

Ellie had changed the settings so that it no longer displayed a name, and if that didn't make her feel guilty, the look Clara was giving her did. She picked it up and opened the phone to see who it was. It was Nick.

"It's Nick," Ellie said.

"What did he say?" Clara leaned forward on the ready for all the juicy details.

"He just said hi with a smiley face. What should I do?"

"What smiley face?"

"That's important?"

"Of course, that's important! Let me see it."

Ellie pushed the phone over to Clara. "Well?"

"He is flirting with you. He must like you!"

"Well, I have a boyfriend. What do I do?"

"That depends. Do you want him to stop flirting with you?"

"I don't know."

"Alright, well then, just don't answer for a bit and write back something non-flirty like What's up."

"What's up? That's it?"

"Yep, that's it. Let's get Lottie some ice cream. I still need to go by her place to get that list of stuff she needs."

They returned to the counter, and Clara ordered a double scoop of strawberry ice cream which she said was Lottie's favorite. The girl got it for them in a to-go cup and passed it over in a brown paper bag.

"Come on, let's go back to the apartment. I'm sure Dane has dinner for you, and I need to start prepping for my audition tomorrow and my second date with Jesse." Clara said, grabbing the bag.

The girls walked to the lot, and Ellie told Dane she was

on her way. He always wanted to be told when she was on her way home and any other time she did or went anywhere.

He didn't tell her when he was leaving work or coming home, but apparently, that wasn't the same.

They were back at the apartments in just five minutes. It took barely any time, and they talked about Jesse and Clara's audition the entire ride. Ellie was listening to Clara speak about the lines she was practicing, and she told her the one she remembered, but as they turned the last corner, Ellie saw a dead rabbit on the side of the road.

It was stretched out, reaching for the safety of the sidewalk and the bushes beyond, it was right in the gutter, so close but too far, and Ellie felt emotion well up in her chest. The poor little thing was just trying to cross the road, but it was too slow, judged wrong, or unlucky, like her, and it died in the street all alone.

The little girl's face flashed behind Ellie's eyes again. She was usually pretty good at keeping the girl's face out of her mind during the day, but she couldn't stop the image from flooding her mind, along with her sadness for the little animal.

"Are you okay?" Clara asked. She was looking over at Ellie, and she looked concerned.

Ellie was trembling and sucking in the air at a rapid pace. She closed her eyes and tried to focus on pushing down the thoughts and images of the girl flooding her mind, but she couldn't breathe.

The girl's face was firmly plastered behind her eyelids. She couldn't form words, so she shook her head, maybe a little too frantically, because Clara sped up and pulled into the parking lot, going fifteen mph above the speed limit.

Clara got into her spot and threw it into the park, causing the car to jolt forward before it settled back.

"Ellie, you're scaring me. What's wrong?"

Ellie gasped for air a couple of times. She choked out "nothing" and bolted out of the car and into the apartment building. She ran up the stairs taking steps two at a time, and through the door to her apartment, which Dane had luckily left unlocked. The door slammed behind her, and she dropped her bag in the middle of the hall before running into the bedroom closet. She collapsed onto the floor and shoved her head between her knees, trying to breathe.

Why am I still thinking about this girl? Am I crazy?

I must be crazy. She is driving me crazy. I don't know what to do.

She wrapped her shaking arms around her legs, hugged them into her chest, and started rocking back and forth. Dane came and knocked on the door a few minutes later.

"Ellie? Clara is at the door, and she says she won't leave until she sees that you are okay. Open the door and tell me what's going on. Now." Dane had an edge to his voice. He sounded scared but also maybe a little mad.

Ellie was feeling calmer on the outside, wasn't shaking, and was breathing easier, but her thoughts were still running wild. She leaned over and pulled the handle down to open the door, and Dane opened the door and looked down at her.

"What happened? Did you get in a fight with Clara?"

"No. Will you send her back here? I don't want to go out there yet."

"Okay." Dane turned and walked back to the front door. Ellie heard him say something to Clara, and then she heard footsteps approaching her.

Clara came into the room and to the closet where Ellie was sitting. She joined Ellie on the closet floor and closed the door.

"Okay, seriously, Ellie, what the fuck?" Clara didn't look angry, but she looked a little peeved.

"I'm so sorry, Clara. I saw a dead rabbit on the side of the road."

"You say that like that is an explanation..."

"I don't do well with death." Ellie breathed out in a pained whisper. She sounded weak.

"Girl, why didn't you tell me?" Clara leaned against the door, and having her in the closet with her made Ellie feel much better.

"I just couldn't get it out. Have you ever had a panic attack?"

"No, I haven't, but that doesn't mean I can't be understanding."

"I don't know what it is, but whenever I see something dead or hear about death, it triggers something, and I just panic. Other things do it too, but I don't always know the triggers. Thankfully there isn't usually much roadkill around here. The last time I saw a dead animal on the street was over a year ago, I was driving to work, and I freaked out and hit a street sign. It was awful."

"Have you ever talked with anyone about this, Ellie?"

"Just my mom and dad. I talked to the doctors in the hospital after my accident last year, and they talked to me again when I had my accident this year."

"I think you should think about talking with someone regularly. It might help."

They continued talking until Dane returned to the door and knocked to tell Ellie that dinner was ready, and it was then that Ellie noticed the bag of ice cream for Lottie.

"Oh crap, Lottie's ice cream."

"Eh, I am sure it is fine," Clara said. "She can put it in the freezer, and it will be alright in a couple of hours."

Clara stood up and reached down to help Ellie up too. They walked out of the closet just as they had the last time, arm in arm. Ellie didn't want Clara to leave, but she was feeling much better about her anxiety, thanks to her. She still didn't think she wanted to go and talk to someone about her issues, like a therapist.

She didn't want people to think she was crazy. She was already thinking she was crazy, and she didn't need anyone else thinking she was crazy.

After Clara left, Ellie told Dane about the dead rabbit and her panic attack over dinner. She had stuffed down her thoughts on the girl by telling herself she would look into it later.

She was starting to think this wasn't just a random face. She didn't know what the girl's face meant, and she hadn't thought about it before, but now that it was becoming more of an issue, she really couldn't force her mind to stay in denial.

Dane stayed quiet after she told him what had happened, and she couldn't know if he didn't care or if he just had nothing to say because he didn't know what to say. Maybe he thought she was crazy too. That was her worst fear. She didn't want to lose Dane because she was crazy. He did so much for her and was pretty good to her. She didn't know what she would do if she drove him away.

After dinner, Ellie washed the dishes and told Dane to relax on the couch and watch football. He got on the phone while she was working on the pots, and she couldn't hear anything, but she figured it was one of his friends.

When Dane was off the phone and she was done with

the dishes, Ellie sat close to Dane and started to rub his back. He focused on the game until she moved closer and put her legs on his.

She leaned back against the couch, and after a few minutes, he turned and ran his hand up her thigh. He kissed her lightly, tentatively, like he was testing the water to ensure she was warm.

"THAT WAS DANE," James said to Sarah. "He said Ellie saw a dead rabbit and locked herself in the closet."

"Is she alright?"

"He said she was, but I think you should call her tomorrow."

"Maybe I should call her now," Sarah said as she picked up her phone and hit the speed dial for Ellie, which gave James no time to object. The phone rang and then went to voicemail. Sarah left a vague message to Ellie.

"She might still be in the closet," James said, flipping the page in the magazine he was reading in bed beside his wife.

"Why are you not more concerned about this?"

"I am concerned. I will call Eric and put him back on the afternoon shift. Dane is obviously not doing his job."

"James, maybe we should figure out something else to do."

"I told you I'm not going to make my daughter feel like she is crazy, and if we tell her to talk to someone, they will bring up all the memories that we have worked so hard to help her forget."

"We didn't help her forget. We just didn't talk about it, and she repressed it herself. Her pediatrician said that it is common for kids to repress trauma. And you were the one that always said forcing her to relive it will only cause more trauma."

"I still think it would cause her more trauma. Ignorance is bliss is a saying for a reason, Sarah."

They considered this as they sat side by side, worrying about their daughter. James flipped the page again even though he hadn't read any of the words on the page he was on. They both jumped when the phone rang.

"Ellie, how are you, sweetie?" Sarah said when she picked up the phone and put it on speaker so that James could hear.

"I'm fine, Mom. How are you?"

"I'm good. Your father is on too."

"Hi, Dad," Ellie said.

"How is work, sweetheart?"

"It's good."

"Have you been driving the car?"

"Uh, no. Dane or Clara have been driving me because of my foot."

"Are you going to start driving the car soon?"

"I think I will go back to roller skates when I get my boot off."

"Well, I would really like you to start driving the car again. I can come over and drive with you the first few times."

"We can talk about it later, Dad. Was there something specific you called for, Mom?"

Sarah was listening to Ellie's voice carefully. If she was being honest, she missed her daughter, and she was worried about her.

"No, sweetie, I just wanted to say hi. We miss you. You

and Dane should come to dinner next Saturday. Eric is coming, and he is actually bringing a girl."

"A new girl? What's this one's name?"

"It's a J name, Jessica or Jennifer, something like that."

"Okay, I will talk to Dane about it."

"I am making stuffed shells and chocolate cake."

"We will be there." Ellie laughed a little, her mom knew stuffed shells were her favorite, and she would never turn it down.

They talked for a few minutes longer, and then they said goodnight.

James and Sarah looked at each other and let out a sigh. They had been married for long enough to be able to communicate without speaking, and right now, alarm bells were ringing in their minds. They were concerned for their daughter and everything she was leaving unsaid.

CHAPTER

TWELVE

ELLIE WOKE UP IN A COLD SWEAT AGAIN. SHE REACHED OUT TO Dane for comfort but then thought better of it. He seemed unhappy with her lately, and every time she brought up her anxiety, he shut down and treated her like she was a drama queen.

This nightmare about the girl was a little different. It started the same with the girl reaching out to her for help and gasping for air. But instead of waking up, Ellie stayed with her and watched her die. She sat next to the girl shivering in the cold of her dream until headlights blinded her, and she heard the screech of tearing metal. And someone else called her name.

That was when she woke up. What scared her the most was it felt familiar.

How could this seem so much like a memory? Her parents never talked about an accident, and something this major would have been brought up.

She got up and went to the bathroom, trying to get her brain to stop hearing the screaming clang of metal on metal.

When she returned to the bed, Dane had moved over onto her side, and she decided to go to the couch even though he wouldn't be happy if he found her there. She flipped on the TV and fell back to sleep to the hijinks of Corey Matthews and Topanga in Boy Meets World.

When Ellie woke up the following day, she quickly checked to make sure that Dane was still asleep before jumping into the shower. He was up when she came out of the bathroom.

"You slept on the couch again," Dane said. Crap, she thought he hadn't noticed.

"Yeah, sorry. I had another nightmare."

"Ellie, you need to get over this nonsense. Your accident was months ago. This is getting ridiculous." Dane brushed past her and into the bathroom, shutting the door behind him. She heard the water turn on a minute later and went into the closet to get dressed.

It wasn't that easy.

She could tell him about the girl. But she didn't want him to think she was crazy, and he already seemed to be thinking that, so if she added to it, he would definitely think she was nuts.

She got dressed in a nice skirt and a white button-down top, swiped mascara across her eyelashes, but that was it, and went to the kitchen to find breakfast. She decided on cereal, her new usual, and sat at the small bar counter to eat before Dane was ready to drive her to work.

Dane rarely ate breakfast, but Ellie couldn't live without it. After she finished her Raisin Bran and rinsed her bowl, she threw a quick lunch together, grabbed a thick sweater from the coat closet just in case Nancy had hot flashes again, and cranked the AC to arctic.

Dane came out of the room and walked straight for the door, grabbing his keys on the way. "Let's go," he said.

Speaking of the Arctic, Dane was bringing in a cold front. Ellie followed behind and thought maybe he was the one being ridiculous.

On the way to the library, Dane didn't say anything to Ellie, and even though she kept looking at him, he never glanced her way. He pulled to the corner, kissed her good-bye, and pulled back out into traffic as soon as she shut the door behind her.

Ellie watched him drive off and thought about the difference between his behavior a few weeks ago and now. Before he would have parked and gotten out of the car to walk her to the door, then he would have kissed her like he never wanted to let her go and would have lingered in the lobby while she walked in to make sure that she was settled and safe, but now he dropped her off with barely a goodbye.

She started walking to the door, and her phone rang. Stopping, she pulled out her phone and checked the id. It was Clara.

"Don't go inside! Come to the parking lot," Clara was talking fast when Ellie opened the line.

"Um, okay. Why?"

"Just come!"

Ellie walked to the parking lot and looked for Clara's Honda. She saw it several spaces down and walked to the driver's side door. Clara rolled the window down, "Get in!"

"What? I can't. I'm going to be late for work."

"You aren't going to work. You are going to Burbank with me to my audition. I need support. Now get in!"

"I'm going to get in trouble. I have missed work too much lately."

"Oh, just shut up and get in. They won't even care."

Ellie rolled her eyes and walked around to the passenger door. She pulled it open and hit the library on her speed dial. She told Ana she couldn't make it in and apologized for the late notice, but she said it was fine - to Ellie's surprise.

Clara had been right. They didn't care that she was missing work again. She processed that for a minute. It kind of stung, but then it felt good because she never missed work to have fun, and when she was with Clara, she inevitably always had fun.

"Ready?" Clara asked, looking over at her and handing her a bag of donuts.

"Ready," Ellie said. She looked out the window as Clara pulled out of the parking lot, and she pulled a donut out of the bag.

This was the first time she had left town without her parents, even though it wasn't that far, and she thought it would be nice to get away without anyone knowing for just one day. She sent Dane a quick message to tell him not to pick her up after work because she would be with Clara, it wasn't the total truth, but it wasn't a complete lie.

———

THEY MADE it to Burbank in an hour, practicing Clara's lines the entire drive, and when they pulled into the lot, Clara was ready to go. They walked around the building together, searching for the door to the suite she needed.

"Where should I wait for you?" Ellie asked.

"I'm sure they have a waiting room you can stay in." She found the door and pulled it open.

The room was sparsely decorated, with only a few

pictures hanging on the white walls and burgundy straight-backed chairs lining the walls surrounding the front desk and the young woman behind it. Clara went up to the woman and gave her name while Ellie found two seats for them in the corner of the room.

It was just a little past eight, and Clara's audition was set for eight thirty, so they had almost thirty minutes to waste in the little room. Another girl looked similar to Clara on the other side of the room, and Ellie was sure she was being auditioned for the same part.

A few minutes later, another girl that looked similar to Clara came in and checked in with the woman at the front, and a few minutes after that, the first Clara look-alike was called into the back section of the office.

"They will call me back after that girl comes out," Clara whispered. "I hope she sucks."

"Clara!" Ellie hissed. "That's so mean."

"Well, I want the part. If I hope she does well and I don't get it, I will be even more disappointed in myself." She winked at Ellie and stuck her tongue out.

Ellie stifled a laugh and shook her head at Clara. "What are we going to do after this?"

"I think we should make a day of it. There are some shops and ice cream places. We could even go to the movies."

Ellie thought that Clara liked shopping a little too much for someone with barely enough money to cover the rent, but she was a good friend, so she didn't say anything. Clara, look-alike number one, came out and walked out the front door with her head down and her body language reading dejected. Ellie felt bad for the girl, but Clara was starting to look panicked, so she remembered her function for the day was to support, and she gave Clara her best smile.

"You're next," Ellie said as she nudged Clara. "You got this."

"Thanks, Ellie," Clara said just as the door opened and her name was called. She stood up and looked back at Ellie before straightening her shoulders and walking through the door. She looked brave and composed, but Ellie could tell she was nervous.

There were magazines on the side table for people to look at as they waited, and Ellie thought about picking one up even though she hated the idea of germs. Everything from health and fitness to cooking and celebrity gossip spread out on the coffee table in the middle of the room. The other girl waiting was reading through a celebrity gossip magazine, probably envying everyone and hoping she would be like them one day.

Ellie finally picked up a cooking magazine despite not cooking much. She hated touching raw meat. It gave her the heebie-jeebies, so she had never mastered cooking. She could make a mean pasta dish with bread, though. Sometimes she thought she would make a great vegetarian, but she also thought she would miss bacon.

Ellie never liked to think about meat, though, and she could disassociate enough to believe that meat in a package just came that way, and she didn't picture a cute animal face along with it.

Two more Clara look-alike girls came in while Clara was in the back, and they were each assessing each other and then looking Ellie over like she didn't belong, which made Ellie squirm in her seat. She was about to go down and wait in the parking lot when Clara came out beaming from ear to ear. She motioned for Ellie to come on and jumped up, and followed Clara out the door.

"EEEEEEE! That was amazing!!" Clara squealed as soon as the door clicked behind them.

"That's great!"

"I think I might have a shot, Ellie! They said they had to see all the other auditions, but they liked me! I feel just like Franny in *Someday, Someday Maybe*, this could be my Someday." Clara was bouncing down the hall, and Ellie wouldn't have been surprised if she threw in a cartwheel or two.

"I'm so happy for you," Ellie was trying to keep up, but her personality was always more subdued than Clara's. "When will you find out?"

"They said they would call me by the end of the day. I have to call Jesse and let him know how it went." Clara called Jesse and filled him in on her audition as they made their way to her car. Ellie followed behind and listened to the half of the conversation she could hear, which started to make her nervous.

"Yeah, that would be awesome!" Clara was saying. "Where are you now?" She listened to where he was and said, "We'll be right there!"

"Where will we be?"

"We will meet Jesse at his office in the Warner Brothers studio. Remember I told you he is a writer? He is working but said he could take some time off to show us around the lot. Isn't that awesome?"

Ellie thought that sounded awesome, but she was also starting to worry about how Dane would feel about her ditching work and spending the day with Clara and now Clara's potential boyfriend.

They made it a few streets over to the studio lot, and the man at the gate asked for their names and checked his list, but they weren't on the list. Clara told him to check with Jesse Hall, and a minute later, the swinging arm swung up, and they drove onto the lot. They found parking on the side near the studio that the guard told them Jesse was in, and by the time Clara had reapplied her lipstick, Jesse was walking out the door.

"Hey, ladies," Jesse said. He kissed Clara on the cheek and put his arm around her waist. "How about a tour?"

The girls followed him to a golf cart parked on the side of the brick building and climbed in. Ellie sat in the back, and Clara and Jesse took up the front. They cruised around the lot, and Jesse pointed out studios and their importance. Clara ate it all up and knew almost all the shows and movies Jesse cited as being filmed on each lot. Clara was the movie and tv show buff to Ellie's book nerd.

After the tour, Jesse took them to an early lunch at a nice Italian restaurant near the studio. It was small and dimly lit, which made it feel like an excellent romantic spot, and that made Ellie feel like a third wheel, but it was worth it to see Clara so happy.

"So, Ellie, how did Clara convince you to ditch work today?" Jesse said with a grin at Clara.

"She didn't convince me so much as she ordered me."

"Hey! Don't tell me after our awesome day that you would rather be at work." Clara gave Ellie a playful shove.

"No, it was fun. I'm sure I will pay for it later, though."

"Was your work upset?" Jesse took a bite of his ravioli and licked the sauce off his lips which Clara watched intently.

"No, they seemed fine with it. I meant with Dane. He is always mad at me lately."

"What does he care?" Clara asked.

"He is protective," Ellie said.

"Protective or possessive?" Clara snarked.

"How long have you two been together?" Jesse asked while giving Ellie a kind look of concern.

"Oh, uh, about seven months." Ellie was always embarrassed when people asked that. She felt so sure about moving in with him at the time, but now she realized how crazy it seemed when they had been together for such a short amount of time.

"Who moves in with someone that quickly?" Clara asked Jesse, hoping for backup. She had been very vocal about the crazy timeline Ellie shared with her since their first friendship date.

"Well, I don't have a huge problem with moving fast as long as you know what you are getting into. Ellie, you didn't know what you were getting yourself into."

The look that Jesse gave her was even more than concerned now. It was pitiful. She squirmed in her seat and felt her cheeks growing red.

"Well, he is my first boyfriend, so I wouldn't know anything about what I was getting myself into. I love him, though. I know that." Her smile didn't have any confidence, though.

———

AFTER LUNCH, Jesse drove them all back to the lot and said goodbye to the girls so that he could get back to work. Jesse hadn't said anything else about Dane, but as Ellie watched how Jesse treated Clara, she realized something was missing between her and Dane. She just didn't know what exactly it was yet.

They drove off the lot, and Clara couldn't stop smiling.

"That was so much fun," Clara said.

"Yeah, it was. I like Jesse."

"He is sweet, right? And funny. Usually, the guys I date are either sweet and dull or funny but mean, so it is nice to meet a guy that can be both. And I get to see him again tonight!"

Ellie thought about that and wondered what other things people were and weren't at the same time.

"I have a grocery list for Lottie. You up for some shopping?" Clara pulled the list from the dash beside her and handed it to Ellie.

Clara headed back to the freeway. The whole way home, Clara told Ellie when to close her eyes. She had done the same thing the entire drive there, and it was unspoken as to why, but Ellie knew that Clara was protecting her from any roadkill and the anxiety that would surely come with it. It was only just past two when they pulled into the Target parking lot back home, and Clara jumped out of the car with Lottie's list in hand.

They walked through the doors, and the first thing Clara did was head to women's clothing. Ellie noticed no clothing items listed on Lottie's list, but she wasn't surprised when Clara walked right into the shoe section advertising a shoe sale.

"You can never have too many shoes," Clara said.

"Okay, but if I bring home more shoes, Dane will complain. He says I am taking over too much space in the closet."

"You can keep them at my apartment if you want. That way, I can borrow them if I want, and you can always borrow mine too." Clara was a problem solver, and Ellie thought her idea wasn't bad.

They started going through the shelves looking for shoes that they both liked. Ellie found a pair of low-heeled boots that she thought would go well with her dresses and slacks, making them a perfect everyday shoe. Clara found three pairs of shoes, red sling-backs, black pumps, and tan wedges, but she didn't have outfits that would go with two of them, so the next stop had to be dresses. They were halfway through the dress racks when Clara brought up Nick.

"Have you heard from the hottie?"

"Nick?"

"You knew exactly who I was talking about."

"I haven't heard from him."

"Well, that's a bummer. Maybe we should message him and see what he is up to. I want to know about this guy. Don't you?" Clara watched Ellie through the clothing rack; she had a t-shirt dress in one hand and a pencil skirt in the other.

"What would I say?"

"Just say hi and see what he says back."

Ellie pulled out her phone and stared at the screen. She typed out a shy *"Hi"* and then stared some more.

Clara walked up behind her and grabbed the phone out of her hand. She pressed a couple of buttons and handed it back to Ellie. She looked at the screen again and saw that Clara had sent a message to Nick for her, and her stomach clenched into a knot.

Clara had changed her message to *Hey* with a winking smiley face. That seemed a little too bold for Ellie, but she couldn't unsend the message, although now that she thought about it, they should create an unsend button for moments like this.

She locked her phone and put it back in her purse, out of sight, out of mind. Unfortunately, she felt her phone vibrate the second it touched the bottom of the bag. Ellie ignored it for the moment because she was holding a comfy-looking jumper and thought she might actually buy it.

"What do you think of this jumper?" Ellie asked Clara.

"I think it is cute, and I heard your phone vibrate, so stop pretending that you didn't notice and whip it out. I want to know what he said."

Clara walked back around to look over Ellie's shoulder. Ellie looked at the message, and the knot in her stomach twisted a little.

Nick: Hey! What are you up to? *Huge Smile Emoji*

Ellie didn't understand emojis and wasn't entirely sure what each meant. Safe to guess, he was happy to hear from her, though.

"Well, tell him what you are up to." Clara prompted after Ellie stared at the message for a few minutes.

"I am going to. I just don't think Dane will like me texting Nick. It's making my stomach hurt."

"What? Why would your stomach hurt from a text conversation? Maybe your lunch is coming back at you."

"It's guilt. I have guilt."

"Well, you don't need to have guilt. It's a message, not a date." Clara gave Ellie a little nudge with her elbow, and she chuckled.

"I know that... but Dane wouldn't like it."

"It's an innocent message, Ellie. A girl should always know her options until she finds the guy she loves." Clara stopped and looked at Ellie with a horrified look on her face, "Wait. Do you love him?"

"I... I don't know... I guess."

"No, Ellie," Clara was shaking her head vigorously. "You don't guess when it comes to love. If you love Dane and think he is "the one," then yeah, you shouldn't have options, but if you are still figuring it out, it doesn't hurt to just talk to someone as long as you don't do anything else."

Ellie didn't know all these rules and wasn't sure if they were universal or specific to Clara, so the knot wasn't going anywhere for now. She typed back a message answering Nick, then asked him what he was doing since that seemed polite, but she omitted any emojis. Those weren't her.

After a few more clothing item musts, they moved onto the grocery list from Lottie. It was mostly food, but there were a couple of toiletries, and she also needed food for Zeke. It took them over an hour total, and Ellie was shopped out.

They finally left Target and were headed home when Ellie got another text from Nick. She chose to ignore it for now. She didn't want to encourage him to write to her more when she was already on her way home.

And she wanted time to consider talking with him when she was with Dane. She didn't want to mess things up with him.

"I need to get home and get ready for my date with Jesse tonight. He is picking me up at six, and I need to be ready to knock his socks off." Clara said.

"You are always gorgeous, Clara."

"No, I mean, I want to literally knock his socks off. I hope he takes one look at me and decides that we should order in if you know what I mean." Clara smiled at Ellie and waggled her eyebrows. Ellie was shocked at first, but after the first wave of astonishment, they were both hit with the giggles.

Ellie wasn't one to talk about boys or sex, but she was starting to think that was only because she'd never had any girlfriends, and now she was thinking she had been missing out all this time. It was entertaining talking about boys,

Clara's abundance of boys and their problems, and Ellie's lack of boys and her issues. When they reached the apartment complex, it was almost four, and Ellie knew Dane would be home.

"You can help me up to Lottie's with the bags, right?" Clara asked when she saw Dane's truck.

"Yeah, but let's go carefully. I don't want Dane to see us because he will ask questions about me not going to work."

"Girl, if you are trying to sneak by your man and you haven't been together for over a year, you are not in love." Clara stifled a laugh when Ellie slapped her arm.

They grabbed all the shopping bags from the car and tip-toed up the stairs to Clara's apartment. When they made it inside, Ellie felt like she could breathe again. She didn't know why she wanted to avoid Dane, but she thought it had something to do with the look he gave her whenever she did something that he didn't agree with, and she knew he wouldn't agree that playing hooky was a good choice.

They dropped off all the bags that were just Clara and Ellie's stuff and then headed down the hall to Lottie's apartment. Ellie didn't know how Clara was carrying so many bags. She had half of what Clara did and was practically falling over. Clara's elbow knocked on the door. The plastic bags flapped with her arm and swayed precariously over her wrist.

"Lottie! Open up before I drop everything!"

"Coming, dears!" Lottie called from the other side of the gray door, and Clara and Ellie couldn't help but smile at each other.

The door opened with Lottie behind it, and Zeke bolted out the door sniffing and circling the two newcomers. He whined and wiggled around them as they brought in the numerous bags.

"Come on, Zeke! You silly pup, we don't have all day to dance around in the hallways." Lottie waited while Zeke danced and slid back into the apartment behind Ellie.

"They were out of the cookies you wanted, Lottie, so we got you a couple of different options, and whatever you don't want, I am willing to eat for you." Clara winked at her and started putting away the groceries. She knew her way around the kitchen, and Ellie was happy to jump in and pass her items to help the unloading move faster.

"You girls are such a help to an old broad like me. I don't know what I would do without you." Lottie sat nearby and rubbed Zeke's head, his tongue lolling out and his eyes sparkling as he supervised his owner's helpers.

Ellie felt honored to be included in the comment even though this was technically her first time helping out, and the statement was more about Clara. Still, she felt a joy well up in her that she had never felt before. She was needed.

After feeling like a massive burden for several years, she never thought anyone could ever rely on her for help.

"Alright, I will put the shampoo, soap, and toothpaste in the bathroom. Then we can head out." Clara said to Ellie. She walked down the hall and left Ellie alone with Lottie and Zeke.

Lottie's apartment was more extensive than hers and Dane's and Clara's too. This half of the building was all two-bedroom two bath apartments. The living room still looked over the kitchen, but it was more significant, and a hallway led away and past the kitchen into the bedrooms. Lottie's apartment was painted gray with white trim and paintings and pictures placed in threes and fives around each wall. She had a matching couch and loveseat facing the tv on the wall opposite which the short hall to the front door met in an L shape.

"Lottie, how old is Zeke?" Ellie courageously asked when the block-headed attention hog shoved his head under her hand to demand pets.

"He is about a year old. Some people said I was too old to adopt a dog but was so lonely. And I know he will outlive me, so I have everything planned for." She whispered the last part with a wink, like she was conspiring with Ellie.

Ellie blanched a little at the mention of death. She hated the idea of anyone dying, even someone she barely knew. "He is so cute. I wish I had a dog."

"Oh, everyone should have a dog, dear. My life has gotten so much better with him in it. In fact, I bet I live longer just to be with him. He is my best friend."

Ellie's eyes began to tear up at the thought of Zeke being Lottie's best friend. She didn't know if she thought that was the sweetest or the saddest thing she had heard, but she wanted to hug them both.

"Clara is my best friend," Ellie said without thinking.

"Awwwwwww, you are too sweet." Clara came up behind her and squeezed Ellie in her arms.

Ellie blushed and covered her face with her hands. "You weren't supposed to hear that." She groaned.

Lottie laughed as she stood up to walk them out. "Take my advice, dear. Tell your friends you love them when you can because before you know it, you won't have any left."

"Lottie, that's depressing. And besides, you have me and Zeke. And now Ellie." Clara started toward the door dragging Ellie along.

"Yeah, I can be your friend now too. You can call me if you ever need anything, and Clara isn't around." Ellie smiled. She usually wouldn't offer to help others because it might mean doing something she was scared of, but Lottie made her feel confident that she could be helpful.

"I will send you Ellie's number later. But now we gotta go 'cause I have a hot date!" Clara bounced a little as she pulled the door open. Before walking out, she swung around and gave Lottie a quick hug and Zeke a required pat. Ellie did the same.

Back in Clara's apartment, they tossed the remaining bags into the hall leading to her bedroom, and she grabbed the remote. The *Friends* theme song started up before Ellie's butt hit the couch. Clara almost always had *Friends* on in the background, even if she wasn't committed to watching whatever episode was on. She repeated the lines as the actors said them and put away her new clothes while Ellie watched from the living room.

Ellie was pretty sure that Clara didn't sit and watch the show because she could see it all in her head from watching the episodes so many times.

At four thirty, Ellie's phone was ringing, and she knew from the ringtone that it was Dane. She ran to her purse in the hallway and dug through her purse to find her phone, but she missed the call. She found it and called Dane back before he started to worry or got mad.

"Where are you?" Dane asked. Ellie could hear kitchen sounds in the background, and she knew that Dane must be making dinner.

"I'm at Clara's helping her get ready for her date."

"When are you coming home?"

"When do you want me to come home?" Ellie knew that Dane had a time in mind, so she figured it would save time for him just to tell her the time so she could get off the phone.

"Dinner will be ready at five."

"I'll be there."

Dane disconnected, and Ellie remembered that Nick had written her back a while ago. He said he was working and told her he hoped she had fun with Clara. His message had more emojis, and Ellie thought she needed to learn what they meant.

"Clara, what do the upside-down face and the wink face together mean?"

"Means he likes you, girl. He is being flirty. Let me see that."

Clara started typing, and Ellie was trying to object, but letting Clara take the reins on this one was a little easier. When Clara was done, she handed the phone back to Ellie, and she felt the knot twist tighter as she read the message that Clara sent this time.

Ellie: It was better than being stuck at work. It would have been better if we had run into you again. *Wink face* Where do you work anyway?

Ellie hoped that Clara would end the conversation, not keep it going. Maybe she just wouldn't write back this time when he answered. Of course, that would only work if she was no longer at Clara's place.

"What did Dane want?"

"He wants me to come home at five for dinner, so I will have to go soon." Ellie grabbed one of her bags with a few items of clothing and left the bag with the shoes.

"Wait, which outfit?" Clara held up a dress she had bought that day and the pencil skirt she held next to a white satin button-down.

"I say go with the dress."

"Okay, good, because that is what I would wear. I just wanted to make sure that you knew which one was better." Clara made a face at Ellie and laughed.

"You are a brat," Ellie said, but she was laughing too.

Ellie's phone vibrated, and they both stopped laughing and looked at it.

"That's probably Nick! Read it. I want to know where he works," Clara said.

"Okay, I'm reading it, but I don't think I will write back. I don't want to be texting him when I am home with Dane."

"Just read it."

Ellie opened the phone and looked at the message. Clara was back over her shoulder like a parrot.

Nick: I wish I could have been there. I own the used bookstore and coffee shop on Carter Road, Corner Bookstore, and Coffee.

Clara's mouth fell open, and she gave Ellie a look that held a lot of meaning but that Ellie didn't want to think about. She punched the lock button and saw that it was four fifty-five.

"I gotta go. Good luck knocking Jesse's socks off." She hugged Clara quickly and headed home to Dane with a million thoughts rumbling through her head, and happily, none were about the girl.

THIRTEEN

"How was work?" Dane asked when she walked in the door.

Ellie groaned internally. She hadn't decided whether to tell Dane about skipping work or not, and now she had to decide fast. She thought he would get mad if he knew she went out with Clara for the day, but she also felt it would be worse if he found out she lied.

"I didn't go to work, Clara called me before I went in and told me she wanted me to go with her to her audition, so I went with her for the day. I told you I was going to be with Clara."

"What?" Dane stopped working in the kitchen and furrowed his eyebrows at Ellie. "You didn't say anything about not going to work. You said that you didn't need me to pick you up."

"Right. I didn't need you to pick me up because I was with Clara." Ellie knew that she was giving a flimsy excuse because she was vague with her message to Dane for precisely this reason, deniability.

"Ellie, you shouldn't be ditching work and leaving town

without telling me! If I did the same thing, you would freak out!" Dane was shouting and waving his hands up and down.

He wasn't wrong in a way, but Ellie also thought that if he were to ditch work to go out of town, he probably wouldn't feel bad about not telling her, and she would never know. She watched him as he continued to yell about responsibilities and courtesy.

"I mean, I wouldn't be out checking the damn road before you got out of work if I had known you were off driving all over the place. And shit, if you can drive to Burbank and back and not have any problems, then why the hell am I even doing this stupid shit."

"What?" Ellie had no idea what he was talking about, but she was sure it wouldn't be a good thing. Dane stopped talking and looked at Ellie like a kid caught red-handed with his hand in the cookie jar.

"What?"

"What did you say? You check the road before I get off work? What are you talking about?" Ellie felt her throat tightening, and her palms started to sweat.

Dane blew out some air, "Alright fuck it, your dad and brother check the roads every day before you go to work and clean up any roadkill, and when you moved in, they gave me the after-work shift. It's stupid. They think if you see roadkill, you will freak out and turn into a crazy person that needs to be in a looney bin or something." He rolled his eyes to emphasize the idea of being completely bogus, but he continued to watch her as he went back to plating dinner.

Ellie felt lightheaded, and swallowing was all of a sudden very difficult. She focused on her breathing momentarily, and then it all came together. Her dad was always asking her to tell him if she was changing her route to or from work or if she was going to stop anywhere else. She thought he was just being a dad, but he was going beyond protective with this.

"How long have they been doing this?" Ellie felt numb. At some point, she had sat heavily on the stool by the counter and watched Dane without processing his movements.

"Like four years or something like that."

"They talked to you about this and told you to help? How does that even work?"

"So far, it has been pretty easy for me. Sometimes I skip it, and so far, it hasn't been a problem except for that one day that you saw the rabbit. But you didn't even freak out that bad."

Ellie thought back to that day and how she had hidden in the closet from Clara, Dane, and the girl in her mind. She felt her family must think she was crazy if they went behind her back to clean up roadkill on the streets to protect her from herself.

She knew she had problems with death, but she also thought they should have talked to her about it instead of telling her boyfriend how crazy she was and enlisting him to watch the streets for dead animals. The longer she thought about it, the angrier she felt toward everyone. Angry at her dad for orchestrating such a façade, angry at her brother for not telling her, and angry at Dane for keeping it up and not telling her himself.

Dane brought the plates of food over to the bar counter and set one in front of Ellie. He sat down with the other and started eating. He kept looking at Ellie from the corner of his eye, and she could feel him assessing her. She felt like he was waiting for her to explode in a fit of psycho rage.

"So, are you going to work tomorrow?" Dane asked after the silence had gone on into an uncomfortable amount of time.

Ellie knew that he was trying to change the subject because of the silence, but she also felt like she needed more time to process, and she didn't want just to pretend that it didn't happen. She nodded but didn't say anything. She wasn't ready to stand up for herself, but she also wasn't about to roll over, not entirely.

Ellie finished her food quickly and decided to take a shower. She locked herself in the bathroom, so it was clear to Dane that she wasn't looking for any help in the shower, and she turned the water to boiling lobster.

She removed her boot and clothes and carefully stepped into the water. Steam was curling up from the tile floor and filling the shower. She tried to relax under the water. She had been able to avoid thinking about the girl all day long while she was with Clara. But now that she was alone and had new information to consider, she was struggling against the thoughts rolling around in her head and clogging up her emotional drains.

When she was pruned and red from head to toe, Ellie finally decided to get out of the shower. She hadn't worked through anything, but she had placed it neatly in a box in her mind and decided she would deal with it later.

She dried her hair quickly, threw on an oversized ratty old t-shirt, and climbed into bed. Dane was still out watching tv, which was good because she wasn't ready to pretend everything was okay with him, even though she was with herself.

Her phone chimed as she fell asleep, and she pulled it out from under her pillow, hoping it was Clara telling her about her date. It was Nick. Ellie cringed and wasn't sure she even wanted to open the message. She liked Nick and wouldn't sue him for medical costs like Dane still wanted her to. He would bring it up occasionally, but she also didn't think she should be talking to him like Clara wanted her to.

Nick: I know you get your boot off in a few days, and I thought I could bring you a little gift as an apology. Where do you work?

He could have asked her where she worked earlier when he texted her, but he didn't. Maybe he assumed she would just give him the information, but his asking now with an excuse made her think he was just trying to get her to talk to him. She wasn't sure what that meant, but she felt the chances were good, which meant something she didn't want to consider.

Ellie: I work at Oak Valley Library. You don't have to bring me anything, though. When do you get your cast off?

She knew she probably shouldn't have asked the last question because it opened the conversation up to continue, but she couldn't help herself. She wanted to know and thought she was giving and asking for pretty basic information. Her heart jumped in her chest when the phone rang again, and she looked at the new message.

Nick: Oh, awesome! I go there all the time. I will try to stop by soon. I get my cast off in two weeks. Since you work at a library, I can safely assume you like books. What's your favorite?

She thought about his question for a while, not because she didn't know her favorite book, *Pride and Prejudice* by Jane Austen, but because she wasn't sure she wanted to tell him. She shoved her phone back under her pillow and decided she should sleep on it. If she tried to text him in the morning, she would, but she was too exhausted to keep up with a conversation after a day like today.

She fell asleep even though it was still early, and when she woke up at two am, Dane was beside her. She got up to go to the bathroom and thought she saw something move across the doorway by the dresser. She stopped and watched the spot for a minute, but nothing happened, so she moved into the bathroom.

The bathroom was quiet and felt safe, but she kept thinking about something moving in the bedroom, and the shadows started to feel like they were lurking behind the bathroom door, waiting for her to come out so they could pounce. She washed her hands and went to open the door, but she felt pinpricks in her fingertips, and panic shot up through her fingers and into her arm. The air felt thicker as she tried to breathe deeply, and it felt like she couldn't get enough in to satisfy her lungs.

What if there was someone else in the apartment? Was Dane really in the bed, or did she imagine that, and he was the one moving around outside the door?

She opened the door, and a triangle of light fell out of the bathroom and onto the bed where Dane was sleeping under the crumpled sheets. She tried to breathe in, but the air was too thick and came as short pants. She closed the door and sat on the bathtub ledge, putting her head between her knees. She continued to take shallow breaths and tried to talk herself out of panicking.

You are okay, Ellie. It was just a shadow.

There is nothing out there. You are alright.

Stop being scared of the dark and go back to bed.

It took her another twenty minutes, but she finally convinced herself to return to bed. She opened the door and ran back to bed as if the covers would protect her from whatever lurked in the darkness. She hopped into bed and covered herself with her blanket after tugging it out from under Dane.

Once she was covered and, in her mind, protected from the darkness, she tried to fall back to sleep. Unfortunately, she had spent too much time awake, and now it was hard to reverse. She tossed and turned until she finally fell back to sleep.

Tires were screeching, and metal was twisting in the dark misty air. Screams echoed through the air and slammed into her ears. Ellie twisted to see better, but no matter which way she turned, she couldn't see anything farther than a foot away. She reached out her hand to feel her way out of the hot steaming metal that encompassed her when she heard someone calling her name.

"Ellie! Help!"

"Where are you?" Ellie asked.

"Ellie! I can't breathe. Help me!"

Ellie pulled herself forward, trying to break through the misty blindfold blocking her vision. She was crawling on her hands and knees, and she could feel rocks and glass biting her palms.

"I'm coming!" She called out even though she didn't know where she was going. She didn't even know if she was going the right way.

"Hurry! I can't... I can't breathe!" The voice was struggling and gasping for air.

Ellie leaned forward, trying to get below the mist, and saw the girl. The girl was lying on the ground with twisted metal pinning her to the ground. Ellie tried to pull the metal off, but it wouldn't budge, and she felt her lungs tighten with anxiety.

"Help me, Ellie!" The girl was pleading. She reached her hand towards Ellie, and her mouth opened and closed like a fish

sucking in air instead of water. Ellie leaned forward, grabbed hold of the girl's hand, and pulled as hard as she could, but she still couldn't get the girl out from under the wreckage.

Tracks of tears ran down Ellie's cheeks in rivers that split and curved until they dripped off her chin and fell into the mist. The girl was still gasping and begging Ellie for help, but her voice was fading.

Ellie started to yell for help and continued until her voice was raw and fading. The girl's begging and gasping had stopped, and all that was left was salt on Ellie's cheeks.

She heard someone calling her name and the crunch of feet moving toward her in the misty darkness. A light swung over her and landed on her face blinding her.

"Ellie?" The voice called, it sounded familiar, but she couldn't place it. A hand grabbed her shoulder...

She woke up.

Ellie blinked into the dim morning light that filled the room. Dane was standing over her expectantly.

"Did you hear me?" Dane asked.

"No," Ellie's voice came out sleepy and coarse.

"We are going to be late if you don't get up and get ready," Dane looked annoyed. She checked her watch and realized she was already twenty minutes late.

"Why didn't you wake me up earlier?" She asked as she jumped out of bed and ran for the bathroom.

"Well, I didn't know if maybe you weren't going to work, and you just forgot to tell me."

Ellie rolled her eyes so hard she thought she saw her brain, but she kept moving and ignored Dane's sarcasm. She made it through her morning routine in record time, pulling on a bright sunflower midi dress that would be the perfect dress for twirling if she was into that kind of thing.

She ran into the kitchen and grabbed a blueberry muffin before grabbing her purse and following Dane out the door.

They drove silently to the library, and Ellie was surprised when Dane pulled into the parking lot instead of pulling up in front. He parked the car and got out. Ellie got out on her side and walked around to Dane.

"Why are you getting out?" She asked.

"I'm walking you into work because, apparently, you won't go to work otherwise." He gave her a side eye and started walking to the library's front door, with Ellie following him.

"I'm sorry, Dane. I was just being a good friend."

Dane sighed and finally put his arm around Ellie as they finished their walk to the door. "You are a great friend, babe. I'm sorry for being so hard on you."

Ellie smiled up at him as they stopped in front of the library building, and she felt glad she hadn't continued her conversation with Nick last night. She felt a stab of guilt as Dane pulled her close and leaned forward to kiss her.

"I will pick you up after work, and then we can go to the store to get stuff for dinner." He gave her the killer crooked smile and returned to his car.

Ellie walked into work, and her phone buzzed. She bit her lip as she pulled it out, hoping that it wasn't Clara texting her to tell her to run out the front door, mostly because she didn't want to miss another day but also because she would probably do it. It was Dane. She quickly read the message as she put her lunchbox in the fridge and walked to the time clock.

Dane: Send me a picture of you at your desk so I know you made it into the building.

Ellie read it twice more as she walked to her desk. She

didn't like that Dane was asking her to send him proof that she was at work.

He already walked her to the door, and asking for a picture made her feel like an object. She took a photo of her desk and all the work piled up around it and pressed send.

No one else was as good at doing book repairs, and no one else wanted to check books in, so all the books returned yesterday while she was out were stacked on and around her desk. She sighed and sat down to work on processing all the books so that Nancy could put them back on the shelves.

As she worked, she tried to sort through her dream last night and find some clue as to why she couldn't let this girl go back into the storage of her mind.

FOURTEEN

WHEN ELLIE LEFT WORK A WEEK LATER, DANE STOOD OUT FRONT waiting for her like he had every day since she ditched work with Clara. He smiled at her, but she couldn't muster much of a smile for him. He had been texting her all day to ask her about work and what she was doing. At lunch, he had offered to come over and have lunch with her if she wanted, but she declined.

"Hey babe," Dane said, putting an arm around her waist and steering her toward the parking lot.

Ellie stayed quiet. Dane didn't seem to mind because he didn't ask her what was wrong. He gave her a boost into the truck since she struggled with her boot, and then he hopped in after her.

"I bet you are excited about getting your boot off tomorrow."

"Yeah."

"Your mom is taking you?"

"No, Eric is taking me. My mom has to work."

"Oh, I thought your mom was taking you. What are you doing after your appointment?"

"He is taking me back home so he can return to work."

"Okay, well, you will have to text me when you get home and send me a picture of your bootless foot." He gave Ellie a nudge as if he was teasing her, but she knew he would again ask for a picture tomorrow.

"Okay," she said. "Don't forget we are having dinner at my parents' house this weekend." Ellie wanted to change the subject to something that didn't make her feel trapped.

When they stopped at the store, Ellie told Dane to go ahead without her because her foot was sore, and as soon as he passed through the sliding doors, she dialed Clara.

"Girl! I called you earlier. What are you doing?"

"I'm sitting in the truck outside the store waiting for Dane to get groceries for dinner."

"Well, I have big news!"

"Your date went well?"

"Yes, but this is better. I got the part!!"

"Wow! That's great!! Congratulations!" Ellie was excited for Clara, but she was also worried that if her only friend started working more in Hollywood, she would move and return to having no friends.

Clara went on and on about her part and when she would start filming. She told Ellie that she would take some time off work to film, and her job was being cool about it. Then she told her about her date with Jesse and how she knocked his socks off.

"He is so amazing, El," Clara said. "He is sweet and smart and fucking passionate. He has it all." She was giggling and gushing so much that Ellie felt herself blush. She didn't think she had ever felt that way about Dane. When Clara talked about Jesse, she turned into a whole new person.

"Did you even make it to the restaurant?"

"No," Clara laughed. "We ordered in and ate in my bed."

Ellie saw Dane walking toward the car, pushing a cart full of groceries. "Clara, I gotta go. Dane is coming back to the car."

"Okay, well, call me later!" Clara didn't sound happy, but she left it alone and disconnected. Ellie put her phone down in her lap. She watched Dane walk up and put the groceries in the back of the truck.

"Who were you talking to?" Dane asked.

"Clara. She got that acting job and called to tell me about it."

"Oh, good for her." He pulled out into traffic and put his hand on Ellie's thigh. It was a sweet move that felt more possessive now that he was so worried about where she was all the time.

He cares about you. Don't be stupid and ruin it.

No other man is going to put up with you and your craziness. You are overthinking things.

Ellie gave herself a mini pep talk and decided to change her attitude.

DANE MADE dinner after they made it home, and then he cleaned the kitchen while Ellie sat on the couch and worried about getting her boot off. To be cleared to no longer have to wear the boot, Ellie had to get an x-ray, and she was afraid she would have to keep wearing it. She looked at her ankle and flexed her toes, it felt better, but it was still achy, she wondered what that meant. Google was only helpful in freaking her out more and causing her anxiety to grow as she read about everything that could be wrong.

"Google says that if a broken bone doesn't heal, it could be a sign that the bone was compromised, to begin with, and could indicate bone cancer." Ellie read off her phone from the couch. Her heart was beating faster.

What if she had bone cancer? She heard stories about people walking around with cancer or a tumor and never knowing until an accident made it appear. She looked at Dane, and he was just shaking his head.

"Don't read that crap. You don't have bone cancer."

"But what if I do? This says symptoms are aching and pain in the bone or joint."

"Those are the same symptoms for a sprained ankle, trust me."

"What if they misdiagnosed me and it was really broken, so now it's not healing, right?"

"Fuck Ellie, stop. You are so annoying. You are fine." Dane slammed a cabinet under the sink closed and stomped over to the recliner to flip the TV on.

Ellie watched him for a minute, shocked that he had snapped at her, and then she slowly got up and walked into the bedroom. She got in her pajamas and crawled under the covers with a book. It was early, but she wasn't about to sit around with Dane if he would be a jerk just because she was a little worried. He didn't understand what it was like in her brain.

An hour later, Ellie's phone did a jive on the table, and she grabbed it as it was about to dive onto the floor. She read the name that popped up, and her heart jumped in her chest. It was Nick.

Nick: I just wanted to wish you luck getting your boot off tomorrow.

She looked at the door, thought about Dane, and locked her phone. She put it back on the table and returned to her book, but her mind didn't come with her, and after reading the same page three times and still not knowing what she read, she gave up and picked up her phone again. She opened it and typed out a quick message to Nick.

Ellie: Thanks. *Smiley face*

She got up and went into the kitchen to get a glass of water. Dane was asleep on the couch, and she grabbed her drink and went back into the room to call Clara.

"What are you doing tomorrow?"

"I'm working at the coffee house in the morning. What about you?"

"I'm going to get my ankle checked, remember?"

"Oh yeah, what are you doing after? Want me to pick you up? We could go and get a new book or something."

"Sounds good. Eric is taking me and bringing me home. I'll text you when I get home, and we can go."

"Oh, and Lottie asked if we could help her clean some stuff around her house."

"We should do that first. Maybe she will want a book too."

"She would probably love to join our little book club!" Clara laughed, and Ellie wished she could be with her right now.

Ellie tossed and turned, trying to sleep after getting off the phone with Clara. She missed Dane being next to her, and she thought about going out and waking him up. It wouldn't have been the end of the world, but she wanted to try and hold her ground.

She decided to leave it alone.

CHAPTER
FIFTEEN

Early the following day, Ellie stood under the scalding water, trying to shrink the bags under her eyes. She barely slept with all the emotions rolling around inside her head. When she slept, she dreamt about the girl and woke up sweaty.

Dane was knocking on the door to the bathroom and yelling something that she couldn't make out through the door and the water rushing past her ears. She figured he was trying to tell her to hurry up, but she knew she had some time and wasn't in the mood to hurry.

She was dressed and ready the next time Dane came banging on the door, and she opened it up while his fist was still posed for knocking, which caused her to flinch and duck to the side.

"I wasn't going to hit you, geez. It's time to go." Dane rolled his eyes at her and left the room.

Ellie followed behind and went through the motions of the previous day. Dane dropped her off, and she went to work feeling like she was under a microscope. She sat at her desk repairing books, answering phone calls, and helping clients find books. The day was taking forever even though she was only working a half day, and she found herself watching the clock, which was never her norm. She was repairing the last book on her desk when she felt eyes watching her.

"Hey, stranger," Eric said.

"Hey, you're early."

"I thought I could take you out to lunch first. Do you think your boss will mind if I steal you away a little early?"

"I can ask her." Ellie looked over her shoulder to find Ana. When that didn't work, she got up and looked for her. When she returned from talking to Ana, Eric stood at the counter.

"She said it's fine." Ellie had clocked out after talking to Ana, so she walked through the swinging door and followed Eric to his truck in the parking lot. Eric had a truck that was even bigger than Dane's, and he had to practically pick her up and throw her into the passenger side.

"Alright, step one, break out. Step two, eat. Where do you want to go?"

"I want a salad. Let's go to the deli on Magnolia Street." Ellie knew Eric loved the sandwiches there, and she could get a salad with all the fixings, which was basically a sandwich without bread. Eric smiled, knowing that Ellie chose that for him, but he was also unwilling to change it to anything else.

They ate outside on the little patio outside of the deli. Ellie watched as people went in and out of the cafe getting food and going about their day. Sometimes she wondered what it would be like to be someone else or at least be able to pop into someone else's mind and check things out. She wondered how many anxious, worried messes there would be, probably not as many as she needed to make her feel better about herself.

"How are Mom and Dad?" Ellie asked, trying to pull herself away from the people watching.

"They are good. You should go see them."

"I know, but I'm busy being independent." She gave Eric a smirk and stuck her tongue out at him.

Eric laughed and shook his head as he took another bite of his meatball sandwich. It was overflowing with meat and sauce, and he had to lean over his plate with every bite so he didn't drip red sauce on himself.

"Well, I will be there on Saturday for dinner and to meet your new girlfriend."

"Yeah, Mom said you were coming. She is great, so be nice, okay?"

"I'm always nice. What makes this one special?"

"What do you mean?"

"You never bring girls home. Why is this the girl you decided to bring home?"

"She is amazing. You are going to love her, Ellie. She is a pediatric nurse."

"But how do you know she is the one you want to introduce to Mom?"

"She is cool and fun. And Mom wouldn't let me say no. Something about dumping every girl I date before she can meet them, and I better not do that this time because she knows this one is different. She thinks I am in love because of how my eyes dilate when I talk about Jessica. Or something weird like that."

"You love her?"

"Uh, I don't know about love. I think I need a couple more months to figure that out. You will be the first to know, though. I can promise you that. Mom is the worst when she is right." His eyes twinkled as he gave her shoulder a slight nudge.

"How will you know if you love her?"

"Ellie, what the hell is with these questions?" Eric was frowning at her, and he had set his sandwich aside as if he couldn't occupy his mouth while his mind was occupied with all of Ellie's questions.

"I'm just curious how you know someone is the right one." Ellie paused and considered her words. "I just wondered if it's a feeling in your heart or your head."

"Are things not going well with Dane?"

"I don't know," Ellie pushed around the last pieces of lettuce on her plate.

Maybe she shouldn't have asked Eric so many questions because now he would worry about her.

"We are fine," she said. She wasn't sure who she was trying to convince. "I was just wondering. We should be going now. I don't want to be late for my appointment."

Eric watched her closely on the way back to his truck, and she knew she would hear about this conversation later.

———

ELLIE WALKED out of her appointment boot free and couldn't wait to tell Clara. She took out her phone and opened messages, finding a new message from Nick.

Nick: Did you get your boot off?

Ellie quickly typed out a reply.

Ellie: Yes! So happy!

She opened her ongoing message thread to Clara and typed a message out to her as well, and as she typed, Eric slowly moved in closer to her and put his hand on her shoulder to steer her toward the truck.

"People die doing this. You know that, right?"

"Doing what?"

"Walking and texting. You haven't heard about people walking into traffic or ponds?"

"No, I don't watch the news. It is always sad."

Eric shook his head at her, "You live under a rock."

Ellie put her phone away and quickly shoved Eric before they reached the truck. Eric laughed and opened the door for her. "Can you climb in now that you don't have the boot on, or do you still need a boost?"

"I think I can manage, thanks." Ellie stuck her tongue out at him and ungracefully clambered into the truck.

This brought another burst of laughter from Eric as he closed the door behind her. The door pushed her the rest of the way in, and she was up on the seat. The whole way back to her apartment, Eric joked with her and gave her playful little nudges. He was buttering her up, and she knew it, so she wasn't surprised when they parked in the parking lot, and Eric suddenly turned serious.

"So, seriously, is everything okay with you and Dane?"

"Of course," Ellie gave him her best- *I don't know why you would ask such a question*- look as she went for the door handle, but Eric stopped her.

"Are you sure? Because back at the deli, you were asking a lot of questions that didn't seem to be about me."

"Yeah, Eric. Everything is fine."

"Okay... If you say so." Eric definitely wasn't convinced, but he was letting her off the hook for now, and she was grateful because she just wasn't ready to talk about what was rolling around in the back of her mind.

She thought about bringing up the roadkill and the fact that she knew Eric and their dad had been cleaning up the roads and who knows what else to protect her. The only problem was that she couldn't decide if she was upset or grateful for it.

She remembered what happened the last time she saw a dead animal on the street near work. She had crashed her car and was hospitalized and didn't want to repeat that. Although she wasn't even driving, so they probably didn't need to keep it up.

Mostly she wanted to tell him she knew to see why they were hiding it from her, and if they were hiding that, then what else could they be hiding? She also wanted to know what they did with the animals. She thought it was nice that someone was looking out for them.

Eric walked Ellie to her apartment door and hugged her goodbye. She heard back from Clara while they were on their way, and she said she would be over in fifteen minutes which gave Ellie enough time for a snack and to text Dane letting him know what happened at the doctor and her plans with Clara. She had put it off until now because she figured he would be difficult about her going out with Clara. Because now, all of a sudden, he seemed marginally put out whenever she had plans with someone that wasn't him.

She was right in assuming that Dane wouldn't be thrilled with her plans because he wrote back right away and asked how long they would be, who they would be with, and what they would do. That was way too many questions.

Ellie wrote back and answered all his questions, hoping that would mean he wouldn't ask more but not get her wish. He wanted to know if they had any other plans after the bookstore and if she would be home for dinner.

Again, she wrote him back immediately and told him she would be home for dinner and there were no other plans. That seemed to work because he stopped texting her, and she could put her phone away while she got ready to go out with Clara.

Clara knocked a song rhythm on the door, which Ellie promptly cut off because she was standing in front of the door waiting to open it at the first sign of Clara. They walked down to Clara's little red car, but when they arrived, Clara didn't open the door.

"Ugh, I just remembered that I don't have gas. Let's take your car," Clara said.

Ellie froze. She didn't want to drive her car, and now it had been so long that she was even more afraid to drive it. What if she had a panic attack while driving? What if she accidentally made a mistake and Clara thought she was stupid or incompetent, or worst of all, what if she realized Ellie was crazy?

Ellie rolled the 'What ifs' around in her head for too long, and Clara stared at her with her eyebrows furrowed together into a giant caterpillar-shaped frown.

"Sorry, what happened?" Ellie tried to smile and pretend she hadn't heard what Clara said, like she was just off in dreamland rather than horror-vile.

"Can we go in your car to the bookstore?" Clara asked.

"Yeah, that's fine." Ellie was panicking and wasn't sure why her fingers were tingling, but she hoped it was just a coincidence. She walked over to her car and looked at the dirt that had accumulated on the hood and windows of the cute little Sentra. It looked like an abandoned home that no one touched or took care of.

She felt a stab of guilt over her neglect of the car, but her panic over driving it outweighed the guilt.

Clara jumped into the passenger seat and clicked her buckle before Ellie opened her door. She felt like she was moving through quicksand, and no matter how hard she tried, she couldn't get her body to move any faster. She slowly sank into the seat, feeling like she had stepped into the wrong shoes. She wiggled around and adjusted the settings in the car. Everything was still set to Dane's frame since he had driven the car last.

Ellie wondered what she knew about her dad and Eric and if she should call them and tell them she was out driving so that they could work their protective magic.

"Are you okay?" Clara asked, and her voice sounded miles away rather than half a foot.

"Yeah, I just haven't driven in a while." Ellie gave Clara a shaky smile and turned the key in the ignition.

What's the worst that could happen?

She started to back the car out of her assigned apartment complex, space number 116.

Ellie pulled out of the parking lot, going half the speed limit, and Clara was starting to notice that something was up. She kept giving Ellie little side glances and checking her side mirror every once in a while. When a man in the bike lane passed them, she said, "I know you haven't been driving much since your accident, but are you okay to drive? I could switch with you if you want?"

"Yeah, I haven't driven at all since my accident, actually," Ellie put her blinker on to get into the left lane, but since she was going a quarter of the speed the other drivers were doing, she wasn't able to get over until everyone had passed. She, in turn, had slowed down even more. "I think I can make it there, but maybe you should drive home."

"You haven't driven since your accident? Why not?"

"I have been too scared."

"Scared of what?"

"Mostly just getting in another accident."

"You will probably get in another accident because you won't speed up. You are going too slow, and someone is going to hit you. And what do you mean by mostly?"

"Well, I have nightmares about the accident, so I have been avoiding driving to avoid the dreams."

"Is it working?"

"No."

"Then I don't think it's worth it anymore. You need to get used to driving again, girl. You can't just rely on people to drive you everywhere. That's how you lose your freedom."

Ellie thought about what Clara was saying, and she knew that Clara was right, but she also felt comfortable with the way things were and didn't like change. She was watching the road carefully, and when they pulled into the mall parking lot, she realized she had been holding her breath. She exhaled heavily and closed her eyes for a second to remind herself that she was okay and to be happy that she had made it to the mall safely.

"Dude, you are so pale." Clara was chuckling a little when Ellie looked up, and she shook her head. "You would think that we just landed on Mars."

Ellie started to laugh. All the pent-up energy and anxiety from driving her car bubbled up inside her, and now it was overflowing out of her in uncontainable laughter. They laughed for a minute before pulling themselves out of the vehicle.

"I am surprised you came to the mall bookstore. I thought we were going to go to Nick's bookstore." Clara said, giving Ellie a side glance.

"Did you say that you wanted to go to that bookstore? I didn't even think of it." That wasn't entirely true. Ellie had been thinking about going to Nick's bookstore since she discovered he had one. But she knew Clara would treat it as a mission to check out Nick, not his store.

"Well, no.... But I just thought that you would want to go there. I see how your face lights up when you get his messages. It would be fun to see him again. Wouldn't it?"

"I'm with Dane."

"No, right now, you are with me." Clara winked at her sneakily, but she didn't say anything else. She grabbed Ellie's hand and steered them straight to the bookstore inside the mall. They already had a list of books that Lottie wanted, and they needed to get back to help her clean before Dane got home from work.

CHAPTER
SIXTEEN

THE TWO GIRLS SPENT AN HOUR IN THE BOOKSTORE BEFORE tackling Lottie's list. Once they had everything Lottie wanted and as much as they could justify for themselves. They walked out without a care and climbed back into Ellie's car.

"Are you good to drive home?" Clara asked.

"Yeah, I think I am." Ellie wasn't entirely sure, but she reminded herself again that she wasn't in any danger and felt okay, especially with Clara by her side.

They were driving down Rose Ave when all hell broke loose and ran up Ellie's windshield. She was behind a truck barreling down a forty-mph road, going somewhere near sixty, and Ellie saw a squirrel make a run for it across the street as the truck gained on him. The squirrel disappeared in front of the truck and rolled out from underneath the speeding vehicle.

As the squirrel was rolling toward Ellie's car, she saw the face of the girl flying at her through the windshield, and she yanked the steering wheel to the right. Clara screamed when the wheel hit the limit of its turn, and Ellie lost control of the car as the steering wheel pulled back. The car jumped the curb, and the back tires swung around, making it spin until a giant oak tree stopped it.

The car's metal crunched against a tree, and then all was silent. Ellie sat panting behind the wheel, looking frantic, and Clara had her head in between her hands. People were pulling to the side of the road and coming over to help the girls. Ellie took a shaky step out and looked at her car. She had heard the expression "wrapped around a tree," but she always thought that it was just that, an expression.

"What the fuck was that?" Clara was looking at Ellie.

"I... I was trying not to hit the-the squirrel." Ellie couldn't keep her voice steady. She didn't see the squirrel in the road, but she could still see the image of the girl's face flying toward her. She closed her eyes and kneeled close to the ground. She had just gotten her boot off, and now she had been in another accident. What kind of bad luck was that? She was never going to drive again. That was it. She was swearing off driving.

"You almost killed us for a squirrel!" Clara was yelling now. She was not her usual, laid-back self. Everything was great, and Ellie started worrying that she had just screwed up their friendship.

"I called 911," someone said from behind them. It was an older woman, probably around seventy, holding her phone. Every few seconds, she looked nervously back at her car.

Clara was on the phone sitting in the car, but Ellie couldn't make out what she was saying because her ears were ringing, and the girl's voice was talking in her head. She was begging Ellie to save her again. Ellie couldn't get her breath to fill her lungs. Every time she tried to take a breath, her lungs felt like they were filling with sand, and the next breath was even shallower than the first.

The EMT truck showed up, and the first paramedic out was the same one that helped Ellie when she was in her last accident. He went to her first and asked if she was okay. She struggled to breathe, so he put an oxygen mask on her and told her to sit on the curb. People were slowing to gawk at the car, and Ellie felt her face flush. She had really messed up this time.

The other paramedic was over helping Clara, and the police were talking to the witnesses that had stopped when Ellie lost control of the car, although she was starting to wonder if she had actually lost control of her mind.

The police officer walked past her and went to Clara. Ellie desperately wanted to know what he was asking her and what she was saying, but Sam was still trying to get her vitals to stabilize.

"Hey, Grant!" Sam yelled over to the officer and the paramedic near Clara. They both looked, so Ellie wasn't sure which one was Grant. "I need to take her back to the hospital. Does yours' need to go in the rig too?"

"I think she is good. She said her boyfriend is on his way, and he will drive her." Grant, who Ellie now knew was the other paramedic, started walking toward them.

"Alright, Ellie," Sam was talking to her in a friendly, calming voice. "We are going to take you to the hospital, alright?"

Ellie wasn't sure it was alright, but she also didn't want to stay here with Clara if she was mad at her and wouldn't be her friend anymore. She looked back up at Sam, and Clara stood beside him.

"Ellie, are you okay? I'm sorry I yelled at you. I was just

scared." Clara looked back at the car and shook her head. "But maybe you should take driving slow."

"I'm so sorry, Clara. And don't worry. I'm never going to drive again."

"Well, that's not true. At least, I hope it's not. You just can't go over correcting for a squirrel."

"Did anyone else see what happened to the squirrel?"

"Yeah, it untucked and ran away. It must have just gotten under the truck."

"Really!? So, the squirrel is okay?" Ellie felt so relieved that the squirrel made it. "I saved her. I was able to save her." Ellie closed her eyes and touched her heart to calm it.

"Yeah, but you almost killed us to save it. You realize that, right? We almost died so that a squirrel could live...." Clara was looking at Ellie like she had sprouted another head.

"I know. I'm sorry. I just couldn't have any more death on my hands."

Clara was shaking her head and sat heavily on the curb beside her. "Ellie, you need to figure this out. You should talk to someone."

Sam was shifting from foot to foot, waiting. Grant came up behind him with the gurney and leaned over to help Ellie onto it.

"Clara, I'm really sorry."

"It's okay, Ellie. I will call Dane now and tell him to meet you at the hospital."

Clara stood out of the way as Sam and Grant wheeled Ellie into the ambulance. As they loaded Ellie into the back, Clara gave her a small wave and pulled out her phone.

Ellie was dreading Dane knowing about this newest accident. She hadn't thought about that before because she was too busy worrying about the squirrel, but now that

Clara was going to call him, and she knew that the squirrel was okay, she could feel the lump in her stomach growing.

She tried to close her eyes, but when she did, the girl's face was behind her eyelids, so she kept them open and worried about Dane as she stared at the closed ambulance doors.

Sam helped distract her by asking her if he could call anyone for her, and she asked him to call her brother. He called Eric for her and put it on speakerphone as he talked. Ellie stayed quiet and only listened during the call because she was too embarrassed to talk to Eric. She felt like such a fuck up.

"Is she alright?" Eric asked Sam.

"She seems a little lightheaded and short of breath, so we are taking her to the hospital to get checked out." Sam looked at Ellie and pointed at the phone to see if Ellie wanted to talk to Eric, but she shook her head no.

"I will meet you there. Have you called her boyfriend yet?"

"I think the friend with her in the car was going to call him."

Eric asked Sam a few more questions, but Ellie stopped listening. She was taking stock of her life. She had been in three accidents in the last very few months and was worried there would be more. She was determined not to drive anymore, which probably wouldn't be an issue since she was pretty sure she had just totaled her car. No one would insure her even if she wanted to drive.

Sam and Grant unloaded Ellie into the emergency room, leaving her with the nursing staff and her thoughts. She was still struggling to keep the image of the girl out of her mind every time she closed her eyes, but she felt the adrenaline let down, pulling her under.

When she woke up, Eric, Dane, and her mom were in the curtained-off room with her. She felt so embarrassed that she immediately started to cry.

"I'm s-s-sorry. I don't know wh-what's wrong with me." Ellie sobbed.

"Ellie, it's okay. You are alright. The doctor was just in and said that you have a mild concussion but other than that, you are fine, and so is Clara." Her mom stroked her hair to comfort her, but Ellie couldn't stop crying.

"Ellie, what the hell happened? Clara said that you swerved to hit a tree instead of a squirrel. Why would you do that?" Eric was blunt, and that gave some normalcy to the family. Their mom was shooting him daggers, and she cleared her throat at him pointedly.

"I think Eric is just concerned that you could have been hurt badly and for a reason that doesn't make much sense." Her mom tried to smooth out her brother's criticism.

"No, Mom, she almost killed herself and her best friend for a damn squirrel. I know you love animals, Ellie, but this is too much. A squirrel is not worth your life."

Dane was standing quietly in the corner, watching them. Every time Ellie looked at him, he averted his eyes, and she was starting to worry about what he would say whenever he spoke up.

"I know, you're right, Eric. It was just instinct. I don't think I will be driving anymore for a while, though, so you don't need to worry." Ellie had pulled herself together and wished this day would end.

"You are right about that. Your car is trashed," Eric said.

"I figured it was totaled with how it was wrapped around that tree," Ellie sighed. "Where is Dad?"

"He is with the car waiting for it to get towed. He took a bunch of pictures for the insurance company, and he is having it towed to the house until they can come and declare it dead."

THE DOCTOR CAME in forty-five minutes later and told Ellie she could go home and what to look out for with a concussion. She knew that drill, so she didn't listen too carefully. She was still watching Dane, and he was still looking everywhere but at her.

Her dad was walking in as they were walking out and looked exhausted.

"You're okay?" He asked Ellie.

"Yeah, Dad, I'm alright. They said I just have a concussion."

"Well, that's good. The car didn't fare well, but at least it did its job, and you only have a few bumps and bruises. You got her from here, Dane?"

"Yes, sir, I will get her home."

Dane put his hand on Ellie's waist and led her to his truck. Her parents and Eric left with the reminder that they would see them on Saturday for dinner.

"Are you okay?" Ellie asked Dane.

"No, Ellie, you crashed your car to save a squirrel. That's fucking insane."

"I know. I don't know what I was thinking."

"You weren't thinking! Damn, Ellie. You get crazier and crazier."

Ellie felt like he had stabbed her in the gut. She kept thinking she was crazy, and the fact that Dane thought so was further proof that she must be.

She thought about the girl and the lengths her dad and

Eric went to protect her from triggers. She felt like she had insects crawling inside her veins.

When they entered the apartment, Ellie went straight to the closet and sat to think. An hour later, she was still sitting there when her phone rang, and Clara's picture popped up on the screen.

"Are you okay?" Clara asked.

"I don't know. I'm sitting in the closet."

"What happened?"

"Dane is mad, and he told me I'm crazy."

"I don't think you are crazy, Ellie, but you should talk to someone. At least talk to me. I know something more is going on, and maybe I could help if you just talk to me about it."

"You're right. I need to talk about it. I just don't know where to start."

"How about the beginning."

"Well, you know about my accident, right? When I hit the deer?"

"Yeah..."

"Well... I saw a girl's face on the deer as it died, and she was begging me to help her and saying that she couldn't breathe. I couldn't help her, and she died with the deer. Now I have nightmares about her all the time, and when the squirrel was rolling under the truck in front of us, I swear I saw the girl's face bounce off the ground and fly at me through the windshield." Ellie held her breath. That was the short version, but it was still more than she wanted to share.

"Wow," Clara said. "That is intense, Ellie."

Ellie agreed that it was intense. She didn't know what else to say about it, though, and she sat listening to the silence on the other end of the phone.

"Ellie, you need to talk to someone about this. Someone other than me. Talk to your mom or talk to a doctor, maybe. I'm happy to listen, but I don't think I will be much help. Not fixing it, at least."

Ellie sighed and leaned back against the wall. She could hear Dane in the kitchen making dinner, and she thought she should go out there, but she wasn't ready to face him. She also wasn't prepared to talk to anyone else about all this, it was hard enough to tell Clara, and she felt utterly dejected. She said her goodbyes to Clara after apologizing again for the accident and closed her eyes.

Dane pulled the door to the closet open. "Ellie... What are you doing?"

Ellie woke up with a start. She looked around the dark room and realized she must have fallen asleep in the closet. She blinked up at Dane, and he didn't look happy, so she quickly got to her feet and slid her phone into her pocket.

"Sorry, I didn't mean to fall asleep."

"Dinner is on the table." Dane turned and walked away. The shortness in his attitude left a burn on Ellie's cheeks. She felt like something was coming. Something big. And it was causing the lump in her stomach to roll and scratch at the walls of her core.

They ate dinner in silence. Ellie looked up at Dane occasionally, but he never looked at her, or at least she didn't see him if he did. He pushed away from the table first and placed his dish in the sink before going to sit on the couch.

Ellie was supposed to work tomorrow, but she was going to text Ana and tell her she was in an accident again and had a concussion, so she would have to miss work. She had a note from the doctor at the hospital, but she felt like this one might be the straw that got her fired. She hoped that wouldn't be the case because she loved her job, but she wouldn't blame Ana either.

The rest of the night was silent and weird. Ellie went to bed alone and woke up alone several times at night. She tip-toed out of the room at four a.m. when she had her third nightmare, but Dane was still sleeping on the couch.

He barely talked to her the night before, but they hadn't gotten into a fight, so she wasn't sure why he was acting the way he was. She felt the lump twist and flip, and she went back to bed, where she lay awake until she heard Dane get up and start getting ready for work.

Before he left, Dane came into the room and cleared his throat. He watched her for a minute and then sighed as he ran his hand over his face. "Listen, Ellie... I stayed up thinking about everything last night, and I can't do this anymore. You have issues. I mean all these accidents and hiding in the closet all the time... It's ridiculous. I don't know what else to do."

Ellie sat up and stared at him. Her mouth had fallen open, and she felt tears pricking her eyes. "You don't want to be with me anymore?"

"No, I just can't deal with all this.... I am sorry," Dane wasn't looking at her anymore, shifting from foot to foot. "I know you have today off, so I think you should use it to move out. You can leave the key under the mat."

Ellie didn't have a chance to say anything else because he turned and left after that. She stared at the door in shock for a minute, and then the tears she had been holding in flooded out onto the comforter. She had grown to love the apartment, along with the man who used to do everything for her. And now she was alone.

CHAPTER
SEVENTEEN

A<small>FTER A GOOD HOUR OF CRYING</small>, E<small>LLIE CALLED</small> C<small>LARA</small>, <small>BUT SHE</small> got her voicemail. She knew Clara was at work as an actress and didn't want to bother her, but she needed her best friend.

When Clara didn't answer the second time, Ellie felt claws of dread grasp her throat. The tears she thought had gone were back on her cheeks, and she gasped to catch her breath. She was pacing the floor, but she couldn't remember getting out of bed, and she was gasping in shallow breaths that couldn't have filled the lungs of a mouse. She clawed at her throat with her fingers, and her eyes looked wildly around the room. She needed something. She couldn't breathe. What was she going to do about getting out of her apartment, Dane's apartment, when she didn't even have a car?

Ellie went into the closet and closed the door, putting her head on her knees. Her mind was racing, and she felt panic vibrating through her veins, begging for a way out. Her skin was crawling, and she started to rub her arms and legs as she struggled to breathe and get her mind under control.

I need to get out of here. I need to leave. I can't breathe here. I need to get out. I can't be here anymore. He told me to go, and I can't leave because I don't have a car. Eric. I need Eric.

Ellie grabbed her phone from her pocket, and her fingers shook as she pressed his picture on her speed dial. She knew that he would come to her rescue, which was precisely what she needed, and yet she also knew that would somehow make her feel worse.

Eric answered on the third ring, and as soon as she heard his voice come through the phone, Ellie broke down into a new torrent of tears.

"Ellie? What is going on?" He tried to get some answers out of her, but when she couldn't breathe in enough to get words out, he gave up. "Don't move. I'm on my way."

She could hear the panic in his voice when he tried to find out what was wrong, and it rose as she continued sobbing. He stayed on the phone with her as he drove, even though that was against the law, and he would get a ticket if he were caught, but he was busy talking to her softly, telling her where he was turning and how close he was to her. He spoke to her the entire time he drove and as he walked up the stairs to the apartment door.

Ellie felt like she was finally pulling herself together, even though she was in the fetal position on the closet floor when she heard Eric open the door. She was afraid she would end up in tears again, so she blinked her eyes rapidly to dry them out while waiting for him to come to the closet where he always knew he could find her.

Ever since they were kids, Ellie hid in the closet whenever she was upset. She wouldn't know how to live in a house that didn't have one big enough to hide in. Eric opened the door and pulled Ellie up so he could look her over and ensure she was physically okay. After he pulled her up and held her away from him for a moment, she practically collapsed into his arms, and he let her silent tears soak into his shirt. So much for pulling it together, Ellie thought.

"Ellie, what happened? What's going on?" Eric was trying to pull her away from his shoulder far enough so that he could see her face, but Ellie was too far buried, and he eventually gave up and just held her as she cried again. They sank to the closet floor, and he stroked her hair as he waited for her emotional tidal wave to pass.

"I'm s-o-sorry." Ellie finally choked out after she had wiped off her freshly soaked cheeks.

"It's okay. I just want to know what's going on?"

"Dane dumped me." Ellie's lip trembled again, but she bit it to make it stop, and she didn't elaborate. Elaboration was a disaster for the newly dumped and anxiety-ridden.

Eric's jaw clenched against Ellie's ear, and she knew he was entering big brother mode. He let her go and pulled back to get a good look at her.

"Screw him, Ellie. I never liked him anyway. Let's get you home."

Eric moved away from Ellie and pulled out his phone. He hit a button on the speed dial and put the phone to his ear. Ellie looked into the bedroom and thought about all the things she had to get together to move out of Dane's apartment, and a new ache bloomed in her chest.

She doubled over and put her hand on her chest. She was trying so hard to breathe, and she was tired of making the effort. Maybe this will kill me, she thought, and then I won't have to deal with this anymore.

Ellie was trying to catch a good breath and get her heart to stop twisting around like a swing twisting its chains until it spun around and turned the other way, creaking and shaking. She felt Eric place his hand on her shoulder, and she tried to straighten up and act like an average person. She wasn't even sure how an ordinary person felt anymore.

"I called Dad," Eric said. "He is heading over. Do you have any boxes?"

Ellie thought about the boxes they had used to move her stuff to the apartment, and she couldn't remember why she thought they wouldn't ever need them again. She had seen enough romantic movies to know it doesn't always work out. It seemed like she could have kept at least a few, but she didn't.

"I don't have any boxes. I didn't think I would need them, so I recycled them."

"Alright, well, let's see what we can do with what we have, and maybe Mom can go get boxes to help out. I'm sure Dad will call her."

Eric walked into the bedroom; he knew that most of the stuff she had brought was in there. She hadn't brought any kitchen stuff because she knew as much about cooking and baking as she did about rocket science. She had a few little things in the bathroom and living room, but everything else was in the bedroom.

They packed up a good portion of her items by placing them inside the drawers to her dresser, tote bags of which she had several, and the only suitcase she owned.

By the time they finished gathering all her things into the living room, their dad knocked on the door. Ellie went to open the door, but she was resolved not to cry this time. She told herself she was okay and to pull it together. When the door opened, and she saw her dad, she was hit by the feeling of being five years old again and wanting her daddy to fix everything from her broken Barbies to her broken heart.

And the tears hit a second later. Her dad gathered her in his arms like when she was little and whispered in her ear. "He doesn't deserve a girl like you."

IT TOOK them an hour to collect all of Ellie's things. She was lucky to have only brought clothes, books, and some odd items. They carted everything down to Eric's truck, and she locked the door and left the key on the ledge above it. She felt her heart tug back as she walked away from the door, but she was determined to at least make it home before she started to cry again.

While her dad and Eric loaded the truck, she called her mom to tell her she was coming home. She knew that her dad had probably already talked to her mom, but she wanted her to hear it from her too.

Ellie rode with Eric because she knew from experience that he wouldn't make her talk about what happened. She wasn't ready to talk about Dane and what went wrong, mostly because she wasn't sure what went wrong.

She figured it could all be traced back to her crazy behavior and emotions that she let spill all over their relationship. The problem might have been the fact that she had gotten too comfortable. When they were dating and not living together, she could hide some of her genuine emotions and behaviors, the ones she was too embarrassed to share with him anyway, but then she moved in and got comfortable with him, letting her true colors show.

She thought about this until they pulled into the driveway, and she was snapped back to reality by Eric placing his hand on her shoulder. She looked at the house and felt a heavy weight sink onto her shoulders. She sat in Eric's truck and watched him and her dad carry her things back into the house. Soon it would be like she had never left. Everything would go back to the way it was, and she would return to how she was. Maybe the girl would go away now that she was home. That was a positive thought for Ellie because everything else made her feel as though she weighed a ton, and she couldn't lift her arm to open the door.

When all her things were back in the house, Eric came up and opened her door for her. He looked at her and held out his hand so she could use it to climb out of the cab.

"Come on, Ellie. Mom made your bed, and you can rest before dinner." He picked up her hand since she couldn't seem to lift it off her lap and gave her a gentle tug out the door.

He put his arm around her and guided her into the house and up the stairs to her room. As she climbed each step, she felt like water was rising around her. It rose steadily until she reached her room, covering her head, making it hard to breathe in the room she once felt the most comfortable in.

The feeling made her stomach clench and punch up into her lungs. She had never felt so lost at home.

CHAPTER
EIGHTEEN

ELLIE WAS LYING ON HER BED, STARING UP AT THE CEILING. SHE had already been home two hours, but the familiar comfort she remembered still hadn't returned.

Her phone buzzed, and she looked toward it, but she couldn't see it and didn't have enough energy to reach for it. She turned her head back to the ceiling. When she heard her mom at the door, she closed her eyes and pretended to be asleep.

Sarah slowly pushed the door open and peeked in at her. Ellie could feel her eyes assessing her, measuring her breaths, and determining if she was really asleep. She heard her mom sigh slightly and then her footsteps on the stairs as she walked away. She opened her eyes and noticed that the door was left open, and it was her turn to sigh.

Another hour went by, and Ellie's phone was buzzing again. She reached over and grabbed it. It was Clara.

"Where are you?"

"I'm at home."

"I just knocked on your door, and you didn't answer..."

"I'm back at my parents. Dane dumped me. And kicked me out."

"What!? He dumped you? I'm going to go down there and kick his ass. How dare he dump you. He is never going to find someone better than you."

"He thinks I am crazy."

"Girl, we are all crazy. You are not the only one that has crazy in you. He is crazy for dumping you."

"I guess."

"Why didn't you leave me a message when you called me earlier?"

"I didn't know what to say. I still don't, if I am being honest. I feel like a failure."

"Well yeah, you are probably depressed. If I just got dumped, I would be depressed. I would need some pizza and ice cream. Do you want me to bring you some of that? Yeah, I think you do. I'm on my way. I'm just going to tell Jesse that I can't see him tonight. This is a best friend emergency, after all. Text me the address."

Clara hung up so that Ellie couldn't tell her no, and she knew there was no point in arguing with her. She sent her address and laid back to wait for Clara to get there. It wasn't even thirty minutes later when she heard the doorbell chime and voices floating up the stairs. She sat up and moved to the door to meet Clara.

"Thanks a lot, Mrs. Finn," Clara said as she entered the room. "Your mom is going to bring us drinks 'cause I forgot that, and she put the ice cream in the freezer so it doesn't melt while we eat. I brought the Joey special."

The Joey special – *Friends*, of course – was two pizzas with the works, and Ellie felt hungry for the first time all day. They sat on the floor, opened the first pizza, and each grabbed a slice. Ellie leaned back against her bed, and Clara watched her as they ate.

"How was your acting job?" Ellie asked.

"It was perfect. Clark, one of the cameramen, is so nice and funny. He was making us laugh the whole time. I think I have one more day of shooting tomorrow, and then I'm done with my part. Then it is back to the coffee house."

"How are things with Jesse?"

"So great, he cooked me dinner last night while I was on the phone with you, and it was all set up on the table when I came out. He is so sweet. And he is amazing in bed." Clara waggled her eyebrows at Ellie to emphasize how amazing.

Ellie smiled and shook her head at Clara.

"No, girl, you don't get it. I mean, I saw stars. I think there was a light, and my toes literally curled."

Ellie thought about that for a bit and chewed her pizza. "Dane never made my toes curl."

"See! It just wasn't meant to be. You are better off without him."

That might be true, but she also felt like something wasn't right. Maybe she didn't get enough closure. She grabbed another slice of pizza, and before she knew it, they had finished both.

"How did we eat all that pizza?" Clara moaned as she leaned back against the purple wall.

"I don't have any idea, but I am stuffed."

"Good food is the best thing to bury your feelings with."

"That doesn't sound healthy."

"Healthy isn't what you need when you get dumped by a douchebag. What you need is greasy food and sweets. Which reminds me, I brought ice cream too."

"Ice cream sounds good."

They both went down to the kitchen, grabbed a pint of

ice cream and a spoon, and walked back up to Ellie's room. They didn't see anyone else on their way to or from the kitchen, and Ellie knew it was because her parents were trying to stay out of the way.

Any other time Ellie's mom would have been underfoot the entire time, but then Ellie didn't have friends over often. They were probably just in shock that she had a friend at home.

When they finished their pints of ice cream, they made a trash pile and put it all next to the door. Ellie felt a lot better now that she was stuffed fuller than she could ever remember and was having a good time with Clara. She laughed more with Clara than she ever did with anyone else.

"Thanks for coming over, Clara. I feel a lot better."

"Good, I knew you just needed some cheese grease and fattening sugar products to get over Dane. He did a lot for you but was jealous and controlling. You are better off without him if you ask me."

Ellie wasn't sure if that was true, but she felt better and wouldn't question it.

"So, did you talk to your parents about the girl you have been seeing?"

"No, not yet. I don't know how they will react. I don't want them thinking I am crazy too."

"Ellie, no one thinks you are crazy." Clara moaned as she rolled to her side and pushed her head up under her bent arm.

Ellie closed her eyes for a minute to try and visualize how that conversation would go with her parents. She thought she would rather just talk to her mom or just to Eric, maybe. Eric seemed to understand her the best, and he was never quick to judge as her mom could be. She sighed, and Clara was watching her when she opened her eyes.

"It's not like you need to jump up right now and talk to them, Ellie. Just think about it and wrap your head around the idea first."

Ellie nodded, and she could tell that Clara was getting ready to leave. She was checking her phone and pulled herself up into a fully seated position.

"Are you leaving?"

"Yeah, I blew Jesse off earlier, but he really wants to see me. He is already addicted." Clara winked at her and laughed lightly.

Ellie laughed a little too. "Well, thanks for coming over and bringing emotional eating supplies."

After she walked Clara to the door, she quickly ran back up the stairs and closed herself in her room to avoid her parents. She flopped onto her bed and forced herself to think about what she wanted out of life instead of Dane.

She should go to school now. She was older and wiser now. She still hadn't kicked the anxiety, but maybe she could manage it better now that she was older.

She also thought going back to school was a decision she should make later. She didn't want to make rash decisions just because she was dumped by a guy she drove away just by being herself.

Well, you have been more accident-prone lately. Ever since you started seeing that girl's face... maybe Clara is right, and Mom will know the answer. Or maybe she won't, and then she will think you are nuts too...

WHEN ELLIE WOKE UP, she looked around her room, and it hadn't changed much since she moved out, let alone since she was a kid. The walls were still light green, and there were book posters and posters of boy bands she used to like taped to the walls.

She looked at the bookshelves that lined the opposite wall and all the books that she had brought back and simply stacked them on the floor until she felt like playing librarian in her own room. Which she actually liked to do. She always thought owning her little bookshop one day would be nice.

There was a light knock on the door, and Ellie looked up as her mom cracked the door open and peered in at her.

"Are you awake, sweetie?"

"Yeah, I just woke up."

"Well, it is about time for dinner. Do you want to come help me set the table?"

Ellie looked around the room and noticed that it was much darker. She must have slept for a couple of hours, and while she thought the pizza might have moved down a smidge, she still wasn't ready to think about food or putting more of it into her body.

"I'm still full from all the food I ate with Clara. Do you mind if I skip dinner?"

Sarah looked surprised. In all Ellie's years living in this house, she didn't think she had ever told her mom she wouldn't come downstairs for dinner.

"Well, okay, sweetie. I guess if you aren't hungry." She did a little shrug and gave Ellie a small smile, and turned from the door, purposely leaving it open.

Ellie lay in bed and listened to the familiar sounds of dinner floating through the open door in the Finn house. Mom would set the table, bring out the food, and call "dinnertime." She was waiting to hear her mom call "dinner-time," but it never came.

Instead, she heard the next part of dinner, her parents' voices taking turns discussing their days as they ate their meal together. It was such a normal part of her life, yet it felt entirely foreign for some reason. She felt disconnected from her family; they were all she had. Well, her family and Clara, but that was it.

She was back home here, but it didn't feel like home. Back with her parents, but she was too afraid that they would think she was crazy to talk to them about the stuff that had driven her back home in many ways.

She heard the front door open, and Eric called out a greeting to the house. Her mom's chair scraped back against the hardwood floor, and she could hear the clinking of silverware as her mom set another place at the table. Ellie rolled over away from the door so the sounds of cheerful family conversations would float further through the house and possibly die on their way or at least be smothered by the air.

"Hey, El," Eric said. She jumped up a little before she rolled back over to face him. He was standing in the doorway.

She hadn't heard him sneak up the stairs, which wasn't surprising because he knew where all the creaky boards were, but she thought he would stay downstairs and eat dinner before coming up to find her.

"Sorry, I scared you. Why aren't you down at dinner?"

"I'm not hungry. Clara came over earlier and brought pizza and ice cream."

"Yeah, mom told me. She also said that was hours ago."

"Well, I'm still full. Why aren't you down at dinner?"

"I came to check on you, smarty pants, and I would be at the table if you were there."

Ellie managed a small smile, and Eric pushed her over and sat on her bed next to her. He leaned back against the headboard and sighed. When they were kids, whenever Ellie was upset, Eric would climb into her bed, closet, or under the dining room table to keep her company. And if she were distraught, like when she had nightmares and woke up screaming, her parents and Eric would all climb into her bed to comfort her. They sat side by side for a while in silence. There was a creak on the stairs, and a minute later, their parents were in the doorway.

Ellie looked at her parents and scooted closer to Eric, indicating they should join them. It was a little tighter than when they were small children, but they still all fit in the double bed.

"My ass is hanging off. Scoot in more." James said as he pushed his wife closer to Ellie.

"James!" Sarah's mouth gaped at him, and she gave him a little push back which caused him to lose his center and flop onto the floor with a thud.

The bed erupted with laughter, and tears streamed down Sarah's face as James struggled to get back on the bed. He made an extra show of it which made Ellie laugh even more. He made it back onto the bed but chose to lay across the foot of the bed away from Sarah's reach.

"You can't push me off from down here." He teased me.

"Yeah, but now you have to smell our feet." Sarah wiggled her toes at him. And Ellie and Eric joined in. They all laughed again, and Ellie felt like maybe coming home would be a good thing after all.

"Remember that night with the huge storm that

knocked out the power and the whole house shook?" Eric asked the bed.

"Yeah, that was a big one. Lightening hit the big tree in Mrs. Henson's front yard, and its splitting crack scared you both silly. You were nine, and Ellie was seven," Sarah said. She scooted closer to Ellie and laid her cheek on Ellie's head.

"I remember that night," James said from beyond the sea of toes. "El came into our room to wake us up, and right when I opened my eyes, the lightning flashed, and I thought there was a monster coming to get me."

"Well, I had to come wake you up because I thought a monster was coming to get me," Ellie said.

"Yeah, and I had to come in because I needed to protect you all from the monsters." Eric joked, and they leaned into him, jostling everyone as they laughed together.

They talked for hours about the times they shared a bed, during storms, movie nights, and every joy and heartbreak. Often, they were in Ellie's bed because she seemed to be the most heartbroken in the family. Still, at one time or another, they had all shared every bed in the house because they were a family, and family is like a soft, cozy blanket right out of the dryer; they wrap you up and protect you from the cold parts of life.

NINETEEN

ELLIE SPENT THE NEXT WEEK GETTING USED TO BEING HOME AND her new routine, which was just her old routine again.

She went to work at the same time and came home at the same time as she always had. She ate the same thing for breakfast every day and packed the same things for lunch that she always did.

When she was living with Dane, she would bring whatever leftovers they had in the house from the night before, but at her parent's house, they never had many leftovers, so she packed herself turkey and cheese sandwiches with fruit and crackers.

The only difference was that her dad was driving her to work while they waited for the insurance to pay for her car. She didn't mind her dad taking her to work, except she felt like a child when she stepped out of the car and had to wave goodbye to her daddy.

She was glad it was finally Friday, and she was sitting in the car listening to her dad talk about the insurance company. He had been talking about the insurance all week and was mad that they took so long to get the check to them. He wanted the check to be at the house waiting for them when they got home so they could go car shopping this weekend, but that was the last thing Ellie wanted. Whenever she thought about driving again, she felt the too-familiar tightening in her throat.

Everyone at work was treating Ellie like she was fragile. They knew about the accident, and they knew about Dane, and they were tiptoeing around her. Nancy or Ana were handling all the phone calls so that she didn't have to talk with anyone, and all she had to do was stay at her desk and check in and repair the books.

Ellie saw what they were doing, and, in a way, she was milking it. She was going through the books on her desk slowly so she wouldn't have to take on any more work than what was on her desk. Today was no different. There was a stack of books on her desk when she walked in that morning, and she thoroughly planned on making it last all day.

After lunch, Ellie still had a good number of books on her desk, and she was working on repairing some pages that had been ripped away from the spine of a book when Nick came in and stopped at the counter across from her desk.

She hadn't heard from Nick in a while, but that was because she had missed a couple of messages from him, and he hadn't written to her anymore. Well, she didn't miss them so much as she read them and thought about replying, but then she didn't because she felt anxious when she tried to think of what to say. Plus, she wasn't sure what type of relationship Nick was looking for, and she was still a little depressed over Dane.

"Hey, Ellie," Nick said, causing her to jump in her seat and hit her knees under her desk.

Ellie looked up at him and into his beautiful gray-blue eyes. She got lost in his smile for a minute before finding her voice and saying hello.

He wore a loose gray t-shirt that matched his eyes and jeans that didn't hang down but rode on the tops of his hips as they were supposed to. His dark wavy hair was longer than the last time she had seen him, curling around the back of his ears. He didn't have his cast any longer but held his arm awkwardly, indicating he wasn't entirely comfortable with it yet.

"I haven't heard from you in a while, and I hope you don't think I'm a stalker or something, but I was coming to pick up some books for the store and thought I would say hi." He was still smiling, and Ellie could feel her heart pounding in her chest. Her brain was screaming at her to say something, but her throat was closing up, and air was becoming scarce.

"Are you okay, Ellie?" Nick's smile was replaced with a concerned frown, and she realized how badly she wanted the smile back.

What is wrong with me?

Why can't I just be an average person and talk to this guy?

I could talk to Dane, and I can talk to Eric. This is no different. He is just a guy.

"Yeah, I'm good. Sorry, I was just in the work zone." She finally managed to rush some words out.

The smile was back. "Oh, I get it! How have you been?"

"I have been better. My boyfriend broke up with me, and I'm back home with my parents for now."

For the moment? Why did I say that?

I have no plans to move out. I am obviously ashamed of it.

Ugh, you are so pathetic, Ellie.

"Oh, bummer. It is nice that you have family close by,

though. I tried to move to Oregon a few years ago, but all my family was still here. I missed them so much that I ended up moving back. Do you have a big family?"

"No, it's just my parents, my brother and me. We are pretty tight, though. I don't know what I would do without them." Ellie was just starting to feel normal about this conversation when she saw Ana coming up from across the library. No doubt she was coming to rescue Ellie from human interactions.

"Hi, are you Nick?" Ana asked.

"Yes, I am here about the books." Nick had turned his attention to Ana, but Ellie noticed he wasn't smiling for Ana like he was for her, and she wondered what that meant. She made a mental note to tell Clara about it later. They had been texting and talking on the phone all week, and Ellie missed being closer to Clara.

"I'm Ana," she said as she stuck her hand out to greet Nick. "Your books are over here. We will probably need to make two trips to get everything to your car."

They walked off to the back of the library, where they collected the donated books. Usually, they tried to have a sale and sell the books themselves, but this year, they skipped it. Ellie didn't know that Ana had decided to donate them, but it was nice to see Nick, so she wasn't complaining.

She watched them as they made three trips back and forth from his car to the back storage room. After the last trip, Nick followed Ana back and stopped at Ellie's desk. Ana didn't stop but gave Ellie a little wink, making her heart jump into her throat.

Were they talking about her? What did that wink mean?
Shit, I need to call Clara...

"So, Ellie, I was wondering if we could get lunch next

week?" He was smiling again, and she probably had a stupid shocked look on her face. This was the second time a man had asked her out in the library. Maybe that thing Clara told her about men and librarians really was true.

"Sure." She smiled, trying to change her dumbfounded look to one that was mildly flirtatious. Even though she didn't know what that really looked like on her since she had never been able to accomplish the task. Clara had talked to her about it once at her apartment, and it was all she could think to do now. At least, she thought Clara would have told her to do that.

They set a lunch date for Tuesday, and Ellie immediately felt regret when the door shut behind Nick as he left the library.

She could barely get through the short conversation in the library, and she was awkward the entire time, so she had no idea how she would manage to get through a whole lunch. She started thinking up excuses to cancel, and the rest of the day passed quickly.

Clara's name and picture flashed across her phone screen as she was walking to check out. She picked up even though she was technically still on the clock.

"El, I need help. I have been putting off cleaning Lottie's apartment, and I need you to come with me. Please." Clara let a beat of silence pass between them. "Don't forget you owe me for trying to kill me."

"Okay, fine, I will head over right now. Are you ever going to let this go?"

"Absolutely not. See you soon!"

Ellie called her dad and told him she didn't need a ride yet because she was walking to Clara's and was met with little resistance.

Ellie walked up the stairs slowly, hoping she wouldn't

run into Dane. The beige carpet and walls bled together. Ellie didn't look at anything but the floor in front of her. At least if Dane saw her, she wouldn't see him.

She made it to Lottie's apartment and knocked tentatively. Clara must have been waiting on the other side of the door for it to fly open the way it did.

"Oh my god, girl. We have so much to do! Lottie has a whole freaking list like I am Cinderella or Mary freakin' Poppins."

"You said you would help a while ago, and the list kept growing. It's not my fault." Lottie called from across the room.

Zeke was looking between Ellie and Clara and whining occasionally to remind them that he was there and ready for love.

"Zeke, are you such a good boy? Yes, you are. Yes, you are a good boy." Ellie scratched his head behind his ears, and he looked up at her adoringly.

"Are you quite finished?" Clara had her hand on her hips, and the paper list was curled tight in her right hand, creasing the paper so Ellie couldn't see what it said.

"Let me see that?" Ellie reached out for the list and smoothed it out on the counter. She looked it over, and her brows furrowed the further down she got. "This is a long list."

"See?" Clara yelled toward the back room and presumably Lottie. "I told you it was long. Alright, El, pick your poison. If we split it up, we can get it done faster."

Ellie picked up dishes and headed to the kitchen while Clara grabbed out dusting rags and a handheld vacuum.

Lottie came out of the second bedroom with her walker and paused in the kitchen by Ellie.

"Thank you so much for coming, dear. You know, it is just so much harder for me to get around and do things. I used to have Hank to help me, but I have been so lost since he passed away three years ago. Then last year, I took a bad fall, and my doctor said I couldn't go anywhere without this damn thing. It was such a blessing to run into Clara. She has been such a help. And now you. If you ever need anything, just let me know."

Ellie smiled as the sweet old lady made her way to the living room, pausing to maneuver around Zeke, who was lying in the hallway.

Ellie turned back to the dishes and got back to the heaping mound so that she could clean the kitchen, which was the actual task.

It took a couple of hours, but Ellie and Clara cleaned the entire apartment, checking off each item as they went. They split up the rooms and bathrooms, which made Ellie's life way easier because she cleaned the guest room and bath, which were hardly used and barely dirty.

The window in the guest room overlooked the hillside and walking trails, which was much nicer than the other side of the apartment building, which overlooked office buildings. Ellie watched as some ground squirrels played along the base of the closest tree.

"Alright, Lottie, that's it for this time. Hope you enjoy those books, and I will come by during the week to check on you when I can." Clara said as she handed Ellie her purse and grabbed her own.

"Thank you, dears. If someone can take Zeke to his vet checkup with me, that would be so helpful. His appointment is on Wednesday." Lottie was already reading one of the books they brought, and she was struggling to find a bookmark and get up for proper goodbyes.

"Don't get up," Clara said. "We know the way out. I will be here on Wednesday then."

They both leaned over and hugged Lottie before heading out the door.

———

THE NEXT DAY WAS SATURDAY, which meant Ellie didn't have to work, so she stayed in bed late into the morning and thought about everything she had accomplished over the last several months. She moved out of her house and in with Dane, which was a massive step for her, especially since the last time she had moved out had ended in disaster. Although this time ended pretty badly, too, she thought, at least she lasted longer this time.

She was still in bed at eleven when Clara showed up with coffee and Ellie's favorite orange cranberry scones.

"You still in bed? Girl, the day started hours ago. I already worked the morning shift, and now I'm here to get you up and out of this bed." Clara handed Ellie the to-go mug and a scone.

"Thanks," Ellie held the warm cup between her hands and inhaled the scent of coffee.

"I have plans with Jesse later, but I wanted to talk to you about something really fast." Clara sat on the edge of Ellie's bed and pulled her legs up under her. "We would have to check and see if a two-bedroom is available, maybe next to Lottie, but what do you think about moving in with me?"

Ellie was shocked by the offer and didn't know what to say. She looked at her coffee and broke a piece off her scone to postpone answering the question. She couldn't move in with Clara.

That would be another significant change, and if it didn't work out, she would lose her friend and be right back where she was. On the other hand, she wondered what it would be like to live with a friend and not only that but her best friend.

After waiting a while, Clara cleared her throat, "Well, what do you think? We can share clothes, go shopping, and watch *Friends* constantly."

"That sounds like a lot of fun, but—"

"No but girl, you need to get out of your parent's house and be your own woman." Clara gave her a smile and a nudge, and Ellie was starting to think the idea might actually be perfect. She hated that this would mean another move, and her brother and dad were probably tired of hauling her stuff around. She looked around her room. She had just finished unpacking her books and hanging up her laundry.

"I feel bad that my brother and dad will have to move everything back to the apartment building."

"Is that a yes!? Cause I'm sure Jesse will be willing to help, and Eric seems super nice, so I don't think he will mind."

"First things first, we need to see if we can even get into a two-bedroom."

"Well, duh, I will find out Monday and let you know." Clara's eyes sparkled with excitement.

The more they talked about it, the more excited Ellie felt, but she dreaded telling her parents she would be moving out again.

But Clara was right; she needed to be more independent and stop living with her parents. Which reminded her of her conversation with Nick, and she had to swallow her panic over her lunch date because she needed to talk to

Clara about Nick and everything that had happened yesterday.

"I saw Nick yesterday."

Clara snapped to attention and turned her whole body towards Ellie, "And?"

"And he asked me out on a date..."

"Ahhhh! Wait, tell me everything!"

Ellie backed up to the beginning and told Clara everything, including how awkward she had been, the way she made it sound like she was going to move out of her parent's house, how nervous she was, and the weird flirty look that she didn't think had worked out. Then she told her she was already thinking about canceling the date, and Clara flipped.

"You are a hundred percent going on this date. I will not let you cancel. He is so cute, Ellie, and the way you talk about him, I can tell you really like him. The way you are feeling means something. He does something to you, and you have to see this date through. He could be the one! I'm so excited for you!" Clara was up and practically bouncing around the room.

Ellie couldn't help but smile at Clara's enthusiasm. She wanted to go on this date, too, but all the what-ifs were getting her down. She was nervous, and that was always her worst enemy. Nervous led to anxious, which led to panic, which inevitably led to her freaking out and in the closet.

"Come on, Ellie. I can see your wheels turning. Just stop overthinking and get happy. Nick is cute, and you like him. You should go on a date with him. You will have fun. I know you will."

"I know you're right. I just don't know how to get my

brain to stop spinning everything into a tangled web of darkness and disaster."

"Ellie, just stop. Think about what could go right and manifest the shit out of that. You get what you put out into the universe. If you are negative, bad things will happen to you, and if you are positive, good things will happen to you. It's pretty simple."

"I don't know how to stay positive. I can't control it. My mind just takes over and starts running away. I try to talk myself into being okay, and sometimes it works, but it also doesn't seem to ever work."

"Girl, you need to learn meditation. We should go to a yoga class. Better yet, we should go to a spa. Maybe that would help you relax. You are so tense." Clara was back leaning against Ellie's bed and looking at her closet.

"Are you already eyeing the outfits of mine that you want to borrow?" Ellie laughed at Clara's longing look.

"Yeah... I really like that red dress."

Ellie looked at the red dress and rolled her eyes. Of course, Clara wanted to borrow the red dress. She was the one that made Ellie buy it even though she told her that she would never wear it. "You should take it for your date tonight with Jesse. And then never give it back because I know what he will do when he sees you in that dress."

"Really?" Clara's eyes lit up, and she jumped up to pick the dress out of the closet. "I mean, we are going to live together, so you can still have it, and I will just borrow it."

"No, really, you should keep it. I told you it won't look good on me anyway."

"This is an amazing dress. It would make anyone look sexy." Clara held the dress against her body and did a twirl in the full-length mirror. "We should go shopping to get you a new outfit for your date! I bet that would make you feel better."

Besides work, Ellie hadn't left the house at all since the accident with Clara. She was an anxious mess, having nightmares all the time and constantly having to beat down the image of the girl popping into her head at various times per day. So, shopping didn't sound all that fun, but maybe she was wrong. Maybe going out into the world was precisely what she needed.

TWENTY

AFTER GOING SHOPPING FOR YET ANOTHER NEW OUTFIT SINCE meeting Clara, Ellie walked into the house with two bags full of new dresses, blouses, skirts, and shoes that Clara called "Wife-me-up pumps," but Ellie thought they were a broken ankle waiting to happen. Eric was already over and hanging out in the living room, watching TV with their dad.

"Hey, Eric! Can I talk to you for a minute?" Ellie called out to Eric and then started walking up the stairs to indicate to Eric that she wanted to go upstairs to talk in private.

She initially thought that she would talk to him in front of their parents about her moving back to the apartment building with Clara, but as she browsed through the fifth store, she decided that she would rather talk to him in private and see what he thought the best way to approach mom would be.

Eric followed her up the stairs as she walked into her room, and he stopped in the doorway. He watched as she removed each clothes item and placed it on a hanger and into her closet. She was stalling for more time.

"What's up?" He asked after she hung up her third item, an olive green fitted dress.

"I want to talk to you about something and see what you think."

"Okay... What?"

"Well, Clara asked me if I would be willing to move into the apartment building and live with her... If we can get into a two-bedroom."

"Okay, what's the question?" Eric was still watching her, but when she mentioned moving, he looked behind him down the hall as if making sure their parents didn't overhear. He stepped into the room and closed the door behind him.

"Well, do you think that I should? Do you think Mom and Dad will get mad?"

"Yeah, I do."

"To which?"

"To both."

Ellie groaned and sat on the edge of her bed with the new dress she was hanging up. It was black with a white lace pattern, and she thought it looked sophisticated and sexy in a way that she might be able to pull off, but she wasn't sure about the shoes.

"Ellie, you have to stop worrying about what Mom and Dad will think about every little decision you make. Yeah, they aren't going to like it, but they will get over it, and they will be supportive when it comes down to it. I think it is a great idea, and I will even help you move again." He gave her a playful shove on the shoulder and winked at her.

"Gee, thanks." She said with a hint of sarcasm and stuck her tongue out at him just a little to show that she was joking around too.

Eric looked around the room, "You will need everything

this time, right? Cause Clara doesn't have bedroom furniture for you, I am sure."

"Yeah, I will need everything. I will have my own empty room, so unless I want to sleep on a stack of books on the floor, I will need my bed."

"A stack of books on the floor doesn't sound so bad. You would probably like it."

Ellie laughed at how right he was. She had been a bookworm since they were kids, and he always teased her about wanting to live in an actual book with pages for pillows. There was a knock on the door, and their laughter caught in their throats.

Eric opened the door for their mom and stepped to the side so that she could come into the room with them. Ellie stepped as close to Eric as she could, elbowing him and shaking her head as she nodded toward their mom. She hoped he got her hint and didn't mention her moving idea.

"What are you two laughing about in here?"

"Nothing," Ellie said quickly. She wasn't scared of her mom, but she knew that moving again would disappoint her, and she wanted to put that off as long as possible.

"We were just talking about Ellie moving again. Clara asked Ellie if she would like to get a two-bedroom with her, and I told her she should do it." Even though Ellie was shooting daggers at him with her eyes, Eric kept talking, and Ellie turned almost entirely to face him to give the most effective death glare she could. "I think it is kind of fun being a pack mule anyway."

"Really, Ellie? Do you think you are ready to move out on your own again? You have only been home for a week, honey." The look she was giving Ellie was full of love and support but also begging for her little girl not to leave again, and Ellie felt it.

"Well, Clara asked me today if I would move in with her if we can get into a two-bedroom, and I think it might be fun to live with a friend. It isn't for sure until she finds out if an apartment is available."

"But you just moved out, and things didn't work out. What if things don't work out again in a few months, and you just start yo-yo-ing back and forth between home and wherever."

"Things didn't work out with Dane because he dumped me. I don't think that will be a problem with Clara."

"He was a douche," Eric added and was quickly smacked on the shoulder by their mom.

"Well, maybe we should talk to your dad and see what he thinks."

Ellie watched as her mom walked out the door before she turned on Eric and slapped him on the arms with both hands like a windmill. Eric put his hands up in surrender and covered his head with his arms in defense.

"Stop, Ellie, I am sorry!" He started laughing, and when she slowed her assault, he grabbed her wrists and held her at arm's length while she fumed.

"Eric, why did you say anything? I wasn't ready to talk to her about it!"

"What do you mean you weren't ready? What if Clara says you can move tomorrow, and you didn't want to tell Mom yet? Come on. I was helping you out."

"I was going to tell her tonight, but I was going to wait until she had a glass of wine first." She knew it was ridiculous to be upset with Eric, but she hated that Eric took away her moment and made their mom upset with her while doing it.

"Well, you can wait and bring it up again after she has had a glass of wine or two. Maybe she will have forgotten by then." He stuck his tongue out at her, and she slapped his arm again.

Ellie looked over at his outstretched hand and thought about a truce. Eric was her big brother, and she knew she should trust him. He had been looking out for her since she could remember, and even if he taunted or teased her, she always knew he had her back. She put her hand in his, and he pulled her in for a hug before pulling her toward the door.

They walked down to dinner side by side, and Ellie knew it wouldn't be fun talking about moving and all the reasons why she should stay, but she knew that Eric would be by her side both figuratively and literally.

CLARA ARRIVED early Sunday morning to pick up Ellie and take her back to her apartment. They hoped to hear back from the landlord even though it was the weekend. He was usually pretty good at getting back to people quickly about any apartment issues, and Clara figured even though this wasn't an apartment issue, it was still an issue.

"What is this?" Ellie was looking at a stack of what she could only describe as junk. It had a back massager minus attachments, a handheld vacuum and charger, some towels with stains and snags, and random clothing and books all in a mountain against the right wall of Clara's room.

"That's the giveaway. I started purging last night as soon as we decided to do this. I hate moving, so I wanted to get as much out beforehand."

"You still have to move it somewhere, though. What's the difference?"

"The difference is when I move that to the donation bin,

it will feel like a weight taken off my shoulders, and if I move it to our new apartment, it will feel like a weight is added."

Ellie nodded and looked around the rest of the room. Clara had lots of space in her room, and she suspected it was larger than Dane's apartment. The bed was pushed against the wall with the window, and the rest of the room was wide open until you got to the dresser and double bookshelves lining the walls. The closet was a large walk-in, just like Dane's. Tears pricked behind Ellie's eyes. She didn't want to think about Dane.

Luckily the phone started ringing, and Clara jumped out of the bathroom where she was fixing her hair to grab it off the bed.

"Danny! What's the word?" Clara listened to their land-lord on the other end of the line. Ellie couldn't hear what he was saying, but she stayed still and quiet just in case.

"Well, when do you think that spot will open?" Clara gave an annoyed look at the phone when she got the answer.

"Yeah, thanks, Danny. I guess just put our names down, and we will wait." Clara rolled her eyes at Ellie and shook her head. "Thanks."

Clara ended the call and sighed.

"So, I guess that was a no?" Ellie asked just to confirm.

"He said that he has a two-bedroom that will open in four months unless the tenants renew their lease, but he doesn't think they will. That's all he has."

"Well, I guess we'll just have to wait and see what happens." Ellie didn't want to wait for four months. That sounded like forever. In fact, she thought they should just find something somewhere else, but she would never suggest that unless Clara did first.

"Alright, well, you will still just move in here. We can share this apartment until another one opens up. You don't need your own room. Right?" Clara didn't pause to breathe or let Ellie respond before continuing her new plan. "This way, we can bond even more. This room is big enough for both beds. So, it will be a little tight. Who cares. And you can have a whole bookshelf 'cause I am going to give away a bunch of those anyway."

Clara looked very happy with this plan and was already pulling books off the shelf that she could donate so that Ellie would have space.

"What about when Jesse wants to stay over?" Ellie didn't know that this was going to work.

"I can just stay over there. And if Nick ever wants to stay over here with you or something, then we can schedule."

At the mention of Nick, a blush flared over Ellie's face. They hadn't even been on a date yet, and Clara was already planning sleepovers for them.

"Clara. We have to go on a date first." Ellie rolled her eyes and watched as Clara pulled more books and switched books to the shelf on her side of the room.

"Call Eric. We are doing this today!"

"What's the rush?" Ellie's eyes practically bugged out of her head at the idea of moving so quickly.

"What's the point in waiting? Besides, I need your help with Lottie this week anyway, so it will be easier if you are here."

A second later, Clara was on the phone with Jesse telling him the plan and asking him to come over and help.

Ellie pulled out her phone and dialed Eric.

Monday morning, Ellie's alarm went off, and she had to fight the urge to chuck her phone across the room. She hit snooze instead and drifted back to sleep even though the alarm loomed over her.

When it went off the second time, she still wasn't ready to face the world, but the third time her eyes finally opened to her new room with Clara. She looked around at the boxes and stacks of books. The furniture was all in place, but after all the packing and carrying of heavy boxes up three flights of stairs, she hadn't had the energy to put any of her things into their place. The most she had done was eat a couple of slices of pizza with Clara, Jesse, and Eric and then flop down on her bed.

When Ellie realized that she had hit snooze three times and was now almost a half hour behind on her schedule, she put getting ready into overtime. She grabbed her stuff and ran into the bathroom to catch a quick shower before work. She stood in the shower and let the warmth soak into her bones before she even lathered up her hair, and then the rest of her shower had to be done in double time.

"Ellie, you are going to be late for work!" Clara called to her from the kitchen. She promised to give Ellie a ride to work before working at the coffee shop a little later.

Ellie would have to find her own way home, and she thought thinking about a car might be a good idea. She didn't want to start driving again, and honestly, if she thought that she could just walk or roller skate everywhere, then she would do that, but she wanted to be more independent, which meant things like grocery shopping, and she didn't think that would work well on roller skates.

She brushed her teeth, threw her curly wet hair into an extremely messy bun, and ran out of the bathroom. She had no time to spare, so she grabbed a breakfast bar and her purse from the side counter.

"Okay, ready. Let's go!" She was breathing hard, and Clara was shaking her head as she walked toward the blue door with her keys in her hand.

"You should have gotten up the second time your alarm went off."

"I couldn't open my eyes. They refused."

"Yeah, right, blame your eyes." Clara laughed a little, and they walked down the stairs stopping at each level to peek around the corner and look for Dane.

Ellie didn't want to run into Dane, but she knew it was probably inevitable that she would see him around either in the apartment building or out in town at some point in time. She just wasn't ready today, so they were being extra careful. The most nerve-racking part of moving the day before was looking out for Dane, and Eric hadn't been as friendly and understanding as Clara.

Ellie worried about going home and walking to the apartment alone all day at work. She worried about it so much that the girl didn't pop into her head once for the entire workday. She walked home slowly after work, debating whether she should walk up the stairs slowly and cautiously or if she should run up them and get to the apartment as quickly as she could.

She decided to run up the stairs as fast as possible but stopped at each level to listen for footsteps. When she arrived at the apartment, she was huffing and puffing and considering getting a gym membership. The adrenaline was still rushing through her, so she went to their room and put things away. She thought getting her stuff together would make her feel at home and more comfortable in her new surroundings.

With the threat of running into Dane gone for the day, Ellie's mind wandered to the other worries that occupied its space. She worried about not being able to make it in this new home and having to move back with her parents. She worried about returning to college, which Clara was still trying to talk her into. And she was really worried about her date with Nick that was coming up quickly.

Why did you agree to a lunch date for tomorrow? What were you thinking?

You aren't going to know what to talk about, and then you'll get all weird and awkward, and then he won't be interested in you anymore, and it will all be because of this date.

If you fail, everyone already knows that you are going, and they will all want to talk about it and ask questions about it. That was stupid.

Ellie was so busy berating herself that she didn't hear the door open. She was still putting things away and talking shit to herself about herself when she heard a creak on the floors outside the door. She turned toward the door and jumped at the sight of Clara standing behind her.

"Clara, you scared me."

"Sorry, I got off a little early because I have an audition at four, and I wanted to see what you were up to. So, whatcha doing?"

"I'm trying to get my junk all put away. I want to feel like I'm home when I'm here. Maybe it will help with the anxiety that I am feeling."

"What are you anxious about?" Clara sat down on her bed and looked down at Ellie. Ellie was sitting on the floor organizing her books on the bookshelf that Clara cleared for her. She still had her bookshelves at home with all the books she didn't want to move, but she would move them once they got into a new place.

"Mostly, I am anxious about running into Dane in the halls and about my date with Nick tomorrow." She put another book on the third shelf and moved onto the fourth and bottom shelf, grabbing a book and sliding it all the way to the left.

"Well, you will probably run into Dane eventually unless he moves to another apartment building, so you should start wrapping your head around that as a possibility, and then you will be more prepared to handle it. And as for your date with Nick, you have nothing to worry about! He is going to love the outfit we picked out, and he already likes you, so I am sure he will be making an extra effort. You probably won't even have to think of conversation topics because he will keep the conversation going just to hear the sound of your voice."

Ellie thought that all sounded like a bunch of hogwash that romance movies try to sell you on, but she liked that Clara believed in it, so she thought she could give it a try. What's the worst that could happen?

He could hate your outfit and sit and stare at you in silence while you sweat like a dog and can't think of anything to say— way to stay positive, Ellie.

Clara was handing her books from the bed so Ellie didn't have to stand up to get fresh stacks, and her bookshelf was coming together quickly.

"Are you still having nightmares about that girl?" Clara asked as she handed her three more books.

"I didn't last night. I slept really well." Ellie put the books in order by author and then by title. She didn't want to think about the girl because she had been doing pretty well today at keeping her out of her mind, and she was afraid that talking about it would bring it back up to the front of her mind.

"That's good!" Clara seemed happy to hear that she wasn't having nightmares about the girl, and Ellie thought maybe Clara did believe she was a little crazy, but she pushed it down into her repressed emotions vault and moved on to the next books that Clara was passing to her.

The doorbell rang, and Clara jumped up. "That's Jesse! He is taking me to my audition. I'll see you in a few hours. It's not far!" She ran to the door and out of Ellie's sight.

She finished with the books and moved on to her next project. The clothes. Her goal for the day was to stay in their room and organize the madness.

Even though just about anything else sounded more appealing. She wanted to finish the room tonight so that she would feel like a put-together person tomorrow when she went out with Nick.

Three hours later, Ellie was done, and Clara was back. She peeked her head in and looked around at Ellie's progress.

"Wow! It looks like you are all settled in! Do you want to join us for some celebratory pizza?"

"Yeah, that would be great. Are you sure I won't be infringing on Jesse's time?" Ellie smiled at Clara and gave her a wink.

"No infringing at all. We have a date night out planned for tomorrow. And after you and Nick have been dating for a while, we can go on double dates!" Clara grabbed Ellie's hand and pulled her along behind her to the living room where Jesse was waiting, and Ellie felt the rise of panic from being the third wheel tonight and the pressure of making things work with Nick so that she could make good on the double date idea that Clara had in mind.

TWENTY-ONE

THE NIGHT WENT BY TOO FAST FOR ELLIE, AND BEFORE SHE KNEW it, she was waking up on Tuesday morning, earlier than she had ever set her alarm. She felt like when you are getting ready to go to Disneyland as a kid, you can't sleep from the excitement.

She got up and pulled her new outfit out of the closet, the one that Clara had helped her pick, but she wasn't sure she wanted to wear it out in public, let alone to work. She thought she could pull off the dress but knew she would look like Bambi learning to walk in the heels.

After a quick shower, Ellie shimmied into the olive-green dress. It said fitted on the tag; by that, it meant skintight and leaving nothing to the imagination. Ellie felt the tendrils of unease slide through her limbs.

She looked at the shoes she had brought into the bathroom and sighed at the thought of wearing them. Clara thought they would be perfect to impress Nick, but that was only if she could walk without falling on her face. She returned them to the closet and grabbed her trusty black flats instead. She looked in the mirror at the tight dress and returned to the closet to grab her oversized cream cardigan, which she quickly pulled over to hide the rest of her.

When she walked into the kitchen, Clara looked her up and down and sighed. She was pouring cereal into a bowl, and Ellie grabbed a bowl too.

"What happened to the shoes we picked? And don't even get me started on the cardigan. The thing is older than dirt. It should probably be buried because it is dead."

Ellie looked down at her comfy cardigan and pulled it tight around her. She loved this sweater. It covered her in a way that made her feel protected, and she needed that today.

"I can't walk in those shoes, and I'm cold."

"You are not cold. You just have no self-confidence. It's fine, I guess. I mean, he has seen you in worse, so I don't think your clothes will drive him away."

"What do you mean he has seen me in worse?" Ellie frowned as she spooned Frosted Flakes into her mouth.

"I have seen the way you dress. I'm sure he has noticed too."

"What is wrong with the way I dress?"

"Nothing, it's just really frumpy."

"Frumpy?" Ellie felt like a parrot, but she didn't understand why she was only just hearing this from her best friend.

"Well, you know what I mean. It's NOT sexy. Maybe frumpy isn't the right word, but I don't know. You are the word girl. Not me." Clara laughed at her joke as she put her dirty bowl in the sink and gathered her things.

She wore her "I'm an actress" clothes today because she had an audition. She wasn't dragging Ellie to this one because she had her lunch date, but she would have otherwise.

Ellie contemplated what other word for frumpy would describe her cardigan and was guessing most of her pre-Clara wardrobe.

Homely, uncomely, unattractive, dreadful....

She finished her cereal and put her bowl next to Clara's before grabbing her stuff and following Clara out to the car.

"When are you going car shopping? Didn't you say your dad was expecting a check this week?"

"Yeah, he is... the week just started, though. I'm guessing he will take me out to look for a new car this weekend. Why?" Ellie wasn't sure if Clara was just asking to change the subject from her bad wardrobe or if she was hinting that she didn't want the responsibility of driving her to work anymore.

"No reason. I was just curious because I might want to stay at a hotel in Burbank next week for another audition, and I was worried that you wouldn't have a way to get to work."

"Oh, yeah, I should have a car by then. Don't worry about me." Ellie didn't want Clara to start feeling like she needed to worry about her like Dane had.

She was going to show everyone that she was independent. She wasn't thinking about the girl. She was breathing through each new anxiety and pushing it down on top of the girl's image to become buried with all the other things that made her throat clench. She knew she would be okay if she buried it deep enough.

When they pulled up behind the library, Clara parked the car and turned her whole body toward Ellie. "Listen, please consider taking the cardigan off for lunch at least. It will be nice and warm, and you will look so pretty even if you aren't wearing the right shoes." She nudged Ellie with her elbow to show her she was teasing about the shoes.

"I will wear the shoes around the house, and then you will see..."

"I saw you when you tried them on, Bambi."

Laughter burst out of them at the thought of Ellie wobbling on the thin spiked heels at the store. Ellie still didn't know how Clara convinced her to buy them after she had walked with her knees knocking out of the dressing room and almost ended up on her face in front of Clara. The only thing that saved her was their plush seats in front of the dressing rooms.

"See! Could you imagine me walking like that on this date? Nick would have had to keep me from falling over the entire time."

This brought on a new wave of laughter for the two girls, and it took them a minute to compose themselves so that Ellie could get out of the car and go to work. She finally said goodbye to Clara and walked into work.

The day would go by in a blink, and she knew it would be full of anticipation and dread. She couldn't wait for her date with Nick, but she also could. It was an odd mix of emotions that kept her on her toes.

Work was the same as always, except for the air thick with apprehension and excitement. She repaired books and took phone calls as usual. If anyone called, that was too difficult, she knew she could pass it to Ana now, and Ellie felt more comfortable dealing with customers on the phone just knowing she had an escape route.

She was anxious for her date, and so were her coworkers. Nancy told Ellie that she looked lovely in her dress but that Clara was right and she should lose the cardigan before Nick came to pick her up. Jean told Ellie that the shoes were the right choice, and she thought the cardigan was cute. Jean was sixty-six years old and had the fashion sense to prove it, which had her doubting her cardigan choice.

She watched the clock for the next several hours, and when the time finally came for Nick to pick her up, she felt her stomach slide up into her throat, and she wasn't sure she would even be able to eat on this date. The anxiety sweats started when he walked in the door, and Ellie could feel her heart beating through her chest. She wiped her palms on her cardigan and remembered that she was supposed to take it off. She stood up and slipped her arms out of the chunky sweater letting it fall onto the chair.

"Hey," Nick's smile was so broad that Ellie could see his shiny white molars. "Are you ready to go?"

"Yeah, I just need to clock out." Ellie was focusing on her breathing so that her voice didn't quiver. She shouldn't be this nervous. She walked to the back room to slide her timecard through the clock, and she stopped for a minute and took a couple of deep breaths. She focused on the excitement and pushed the anxiety into the mind hole where she shoved everything else.

Ellie was walking back out to meet Nick when Ana came running up to catch her before she got back to Nick's earshot.

"Listen, if your date is going well, you can have the rest of the day off and don't worry about coming back in until tomorrow, but if it isn't, then use us as your reason to leave whenever you want to pull the cord. Okay?" Ana smiled and gave her a quick hug.

"Thanks, Ana," Ellie whispered, taking one more deep breath before returning to Nick.

He was still smiling at her, and his eyes twinkled as she walked toward him. He looked so relaxed, leaning against the counter with his hands in his front pockets and his button-down untucked from his jeans.

Nick crooked his arm and put it out for Ellie. It was such an old-time gesture, but she took it immediately and felt her heart soar. Her stomach unclenched and fell back into place.

They walked out into the sunlight, and Ellie waited for Nick to turn her toward the shopping center and down to one of the restaurants, but instead, he guided her to the parking lot and over to a shiny black Jeep Wrangler. He opened the passenger side door for her and gave her a hand up into the cab. She tugged at the hem of her dress as he walked around the car to ensure she was still covered.

"Where are we going?" She asked after Nick climbed into the driver's seat and turned the engine over.

"There is this little restaurant over by my shop called Jink's. Have you heard of it?"

"No, is it new?"

"It's been there since I moved into my shop almost two years ago. I'm surprised you haven't heard of it."

"I don't get out much. I like to stay home."

"Yeah, I get that. People are outside."

Ellie looked over and saw that Nick was smiling again. It was a contagious smile that oozed joy from every pearly white surface.

They talked comfortably the entire drive, and Ellie couldn't remember the last time she felt so relaxed with another person that wasn't Eric or her parents. Clara was hit and miss, sometimes she made her feel comfortable, and sometimes she brought a level of stress that Ellie couldn't quite put a finger on.

When they pulled up to the restaurant, Nick put the car in park and told Ellie to wait. He walked around the car and opened the passenger door for her, putting his hand out for her to take. He helped her out, and they walked arm-in-arm to the restaurant.

It was a small restaurant with one large open space filled wall to wall with mismatched tables and chairs spread from wall to wall. Pictures covered the walls so thick that you could barely tell what color was underneath. The closest waitress smiled at them when they came in and told them to seat themselves.

Nick led Ellie to a back table on the far-right side, close to a window but set back enough to avoid any direct glare. He pulled out her chair and pushed it in, and even though it was yet another old-school gesture, Ellie couldn't help but smile.

"This is probably going to sound super lame, but I have been wanting to take you on this date since I crashed into you." He folded his hands over the menu without even glancing at it. His attention was entirely on her.

Ellie didn't want to admit that she wanted the same thing. "I don't think that is lame. Sorry, I wasn't available until now."

"Did you just apologize for having a boyfriend?" Nick laughed, and Ellie quickly hid behind her menu.

"I didn't mean it like that."

"Sorry about that, by the way. Are you alright?"

"Yeah, we weren't right for each other." It was true. Even though it took hours of Clara talking her into believing it and not thinking it was all her.

"He wasn't right for you. You are perfect."

The waitress came then to take their order, and Ellie wasn't ready, so she said she would have what Nick had, which wasn't like her. They talked easily while waiting for their food, while they ate, and through dessert, Nick insisted upon. The conversation never ebbed. Ellie forgot to worry, and when she saw the check coming, she was desperate to extend their time together.

"Do you have to go back to work after lunch?" She asked.

"I was planning on it, but I don't have to... Do you have the rest of the afternoon off?"

"Yeah, I'm off. If you want to do something else. We don't have to. I just wanted to see what you were thinking."

"It's a done deal. I will call and let them know that I won't be back." Nick took the bill from the waitress, put his card in the slot, and handed it back.

As she walked away, he pulled out his cell and called in to let his employee know that he wouldn't be back for the day.

"What do you want to do?" He asked.

"I hadn't thought that far," Ellie said. "I just thought spending more time with you would be nice."

Nick was beaming at her, and she felt her cheeks blush. She was more forward than usual, and she liked seeing Nick smile. It made a tingle go through her core and into her toes.

"I think I have an idea. Let's go to the park around the corner. It is also a botanical garden so we can walk and see the flowers. Does that sound good?"

"It's perfect."

Nick placed his hand on the small of Ellie's back as they walked down the gravel path that weaved its way through the park. Along the trail were little signs with pictures next to each plant with its name and information about its origins.

Ellie was more interested in getting to know Nick than reading about the plants, but she tried to show interest anyway.

"How long have you worked at the library?" Nick asked as he slid his hand into Ellie's. Her heart leaped into her throat, and the tingling from his skin.

"I have been there a little over four years now. I love it there. I was thinking about going back to school to get my degree in Library Science so that I can move up and make it permanent." Ellie smiled at how comfortable she felt with Nick. They had already gone over childhood, siblings, and relationships. Nick had only been in one serious relationship with a girl named Lisa that lasted a year. He was twenty-five years old, he had an older brother who was married, and his parents, who were divorced but still liked each other well enough to hang out with their three grandchildren.

"I think going back to school is a great idea. I got my degree in English, but I am also thinking about going back to add an AA in Business. Might help with my bookstore."

"Seems like you are doing well, though. You have been open for two years?"

"Yeah, but if I have learned anything from opening my own business, it's that you need to know a lot more than just the product. I know the books, but I could be doing a lot better on my bottom line."

"There are books on business in the library. I can get you some. And I will get you a pamphlet for the community college."

Nick stopped walking beside a giant oak tree and looked down at her. She loved the way his golden-brown eyes caressed her. He leaned down closer, letting his hand come up and cup her cheek. She sucked in a breath, and his eyes melted over her face and down her body.

Ellie blinked, and his lips were on hers, taking her gasp and using her shock to delve deeper into her senses. She brought her hands up into his shirt and instinctively pulled him closer, which surprised them both. She was sure Nick was going for a sweet kiss, but she had never felt her nerves fire all at once in response to anything, and she wanted more.

Too soon, Nick was pulling away from her. "I have an idea." He said with a smile, grabbing her hand to drag her away from the park and back toward where they had come.

They walked past the restaurant and the parking lot and stopped outside the closed door to the Corner Bookstore and Coffee. The sign said, "Sorry, we're closed," but Nick pulled a key out and held the door open for Ellie.

She stepped under his arm and breathed in the smell of books. A happy sigh escaped her lips, and Nick closed the door behind them. The click of the lock echoed around the silent walls. She had been in the library while it was closed, but something about being in a dark closed bookstore with the owner sent anticipation shivering down her spine.

Nick stepped close behind her so that she could feel his warmth tinglingly across her back. The clock ticked past the four o'clock marker and chimed for no one but them. He placed his hands on her shoulders and leaned in to whisper in her ear.

"Ever dreamed about being loose in a bookstore after hours?" She looked over her shoulder to see the twinkle in his eyes. His jaw clenched at the sight of her as if it was hard not to kiss her again.

"That is my favorite dream."

"Mine too. Go crazy." He gave her an encouraging nod, and she walked around the little bookstore.

One whole side was dedicated to the Coffee side of the store's name, and there were little cafe tables with mix-matched chairs and comfy-looking stools. The menu was neatly written on a chalkboard above the counter, detailing the regular coffee flavors, add-ins, and specials. There was another little section with treats listed under it, but it was relatively short and had a disclaimer noting that treats had to be consumed in the cafe or taken to go, not eaten near the books in the stacks.

The rest of the store was wall-to-wall book stacks with labels telling you which section you were in and where you were alphabetically within those stacks. Ellie quickly found the Fiction section and then the Romance. She perused all the books and touched the spines of all her favorites and the ones that she wanted to make a mental note to return for.

"See anything you want? You can grab whatever you want. On me, of course." Nick was leaning against the Fantasy stacks nearby, watching her. His arms were crossed, and he leaned with the confidence of a man who knew he was providing the best first date ever.

Ellie's anxiety would have normally refused to let her take Nick up on his offer, but she was having so much fun and felt so comfortable with him that she found herself backtracking and pulling out three of the books that she already touched with longing.

"Is that all you want?" Nick asked when she walked back to him with her little stack. And for the first time, a dirty thought was the first thing to pop into her mind. No, this was not all she wanted, but she wasn't about to tell him that.

"Yep, I think this is good. For now." She added with a flirty smirk.

"I will keep that in mind. Now, dinner?" Nick held out his hand, and she didn't hesitate to grab it and follow him back to Alfredo's, the restaurant where they ran into each other after their accident. Their lucky place.

"Does this count as our second date?" Nick asked as they waited for the waiter to bring their angel hair pasta and shrimp scampi. Again, they both ordered the same meal. Ellie wasn't sure why, but this felt even more intimate. Going to a restaurant and sharing a meal was one thing. Going to a restaurant and sharing the same meal was a whole other type of companionable experience.

"Maybe even third, depending on what you count as a date."

"True, I was just counting meals, but if we can count locations, then we might actually be up to four." His eyes twinkled, and his bottom lip dived down, giving him a charming sideways smile that made Ellie weak in the knees. Good thing she was sitting.

"Shrimp scampi?" The waiter said as he delivered their food. They both smiled and leaned back. Ellie hadn't noticed how close they were leaning into each other. A blush hit her cheeks, and she saw Nick hold back a laugh.

The shrimp and pasta were delicious. Ellie groaned, thinking about all the times she had come to this restaurant and had only ordered one item off the menu because it was what she knew. Being with Nick felt so comfortable she was surprised at how willing she was to try new things and even more surprised by how much she enjoyed them. Now she was cursing at herself for missing out for so long.

Ellie's phone buzzed, bringing her back to reality.
Clara: How was your lunch date?

Ellie: Still going. *Wink face*

Clara: Oh really?? *Smirk face*

Ellie: We are at dinner now. How was your audition?

Clara: Not so great. But Jesse is making me feel better. I won't be home until late tonight.

Ellie: Have fun! Details later.

Clara: Don't do anything you would normally do! Channel your inner Clara.

"Everything good?" Nick asked, watching her.

Ellie felt herself smiling and knew that she had probably been grinning like an idiot while texting Clara, not to mention that it was rude to text while out to dinner.

"Sorry, my roommate was checking in to make sure I was okay." She smiled at him, hoping he wouldn't think she was too rude.

"Making sure your date didn't murder you?"

"Probably a little of that too. You met her, my friend I was out to lunch with when we ran into each other here. She has been a fan of yours since then."

Nick's head fell back into a laugh that came deep from his chest, and Ellie knew she wanted to make him laugh like that all the damn time.

After dinner, he drove her back to Ellie's apartment building, and Ellie still didn't want to leave him. She wasn't sure what feeling was holding her back until he leaned over the console and kissed her. Unlike their intense first kiss in the park, this kiss started light and whispery. He ran his fingers into her hair and pulled slightly so her head fell back into his hand and he could lean into her, his tongue touching hers as soon as her lips parted. Fireworks popped behind her eyelids, and she never wanted him to stop, but he eventually pulled away, leaving them both panting softly.

Ellie walked into the apartment that night feeling light and full of joy. She leaned back against the door to the quiet apartment and touched her fingers to her lips. She could still feel his mouth on hers and couldn't wait to kiss him again. She looked around the empty apartment and felt the loneliness seep into her.

ELLIE WAS SITTING in bed reading when Clara finally came home hours later. She heard her move through the apartment quietly, obviously trying not to wake Ellie. It was well past midnight, and Ellie couldn't sleep because the apartment felt too empty without Clara home.

She decided to peek out and see if Clara wanted to tell her about her night. And also because she really wanted to tell Clara about her date with Nick.

"Hey," Ellie whispered as she leaned out the bedroom door into the dark apartment. "Psssst, Clara."

"Yeah?" Clara whispered back.

"How was your date?" Ellie could see Clara now as she came closer to the door and away from the enveloping darkness of the living room.

"It was great," Clara whispered. Then she thought for a minute. "Why are we still whispering?"

"I don't know," Ellie whispered and then giggled.

"It was great," Clara said again in her regular voice. "Jesse took me to a really nice Italian restaurant, and then we went back to his place, and you know.... I wanted to stay the night, but I thought you might worry if you woke up and I wasn't here. I guess now I know you have the opposite problem. You won't be able to sleep until I am here."

"I probably would have fallen asleep eventually, but it was too quiet."

"I get it. When I first moved out on my own, it was always weird to be alone in the apartment."

"Yeah, it is weird."

"So, since you are still up, how was your date?"

They moved into the room, and Clara sat on Ellie's bed instead of her own so that they could be closer. They leaned back against the headboard, and Ellie gave a happy sigh.

"It was amazing. We went to lunch, and then he took me to the botanical gardens for a walk. It was so nice and peaceful, and we talked for hours. Then he took me to his bookstore to show me around, and then he took me to dinner at Alfredo's around the corner."

"Did anything else happen? Did you bring him home?" Clara was leaning in close with the excitement, and Ellie knew what she was asking.

"No, I didn't bring him home. He kissed me, though." Ellie paused for emphasis, and Clara's eyes went wide. "It was the best kiss of my life. I felt like I melted."

Clara squealed and bounced around from side to side. "I knew it! He is the one! I knew he was perfect for you!"

"The one?" Ellie blushed and couldn't help but smile, thinking about Nick being the one. She didn't want to get her hopes up, but she felt Clara's excitement oozing deep into her soul.

"Girl, he is so perfect for you. He is cute, sweet, a book nerd, and totally into you. You need to jump on that. We need to pick you a new outfit. Do you have your next date set up already? When are you seeing him again?"

"He asked me out for dinner tomorrow night."

"There you go! See? No guy would ask a girl out for basically two dates in one day and then a date the next day if he wasn't seriously into her!"

They talked for a while longer, eventually separating into their own beds but still facing each other and whispering into the night.

It would be hard for her to get up in the morning with so little sleep, but at least she wouldn't be tossing and turning all night. She slept better than she had in a long time, and when she woke up the next day, she was happy to get up and go to work—all the while counting the minutes until her date with Nick.

CHAPTER

TWENTY-TWO

THE REST OF THE WEEK WENT BY IN A FLASH. EVERY DAY AFTER work, Nick picked up Ellie and took her out for food or a movie. They talked about everything, and by Friday night, Ellie felt as though she knew Nick better than anyone else in the world.

And she knew she had shared more about herself with Nick than anyone else, except for the girl. She didn't talk about the girl, and she didn't think about the girl. She had buried it under all her other anxieties and hoped it would stay buried for good.

Nick picked Ellie up at the library's front door on Friday night after work. As they walked to Nick's jeep, he slipped his hand into hers, and she felt electricity zip between them. They got to the car, and Nick pulled Ellie's door open like he always did, but instead of letting go of her hand so she could climb into the car, he pulled her into his arms and brushed his lips against hers. She put her hands on his chest and curled into him as he deepened the pressure of his lips. When his tongue touched hers, she was surprised to hear a moan escape her lips, and Nick pulled away just a little. His eyes searched hers, asking a silent question, and they answered.

"What if we go back to my apartment and order in tonight?" Nick asked.

Ellie knew what that meant. She wasn't as naïve anymore and was absolutely ready to go back to Nick's apartment. After all, this was like their fifth or eighth date, depending on how you counted, and she was starting to think Clara was right about him being the one.

They didn't order in. They stumbled into the apartment, lips fused. Nick pushed the door closed with his foot, and Ellie threw her purse on the floor. She hadn't been to his apartment, so she had no idea where anything was.

"Welcome to my apartment," Nick said against her neck as he kissed his way down to her shoulder. "This is the living room, the kitchen is over there, and my bedroom is right through here."

They made it into his room, and Ellie looked around while he continued his kissing expedition south. The whole wall next to Nick's bed was built-in bookshelves full of books. There was a bed in the middle, which had a gray duvet cover. Ellie didn't think Dane even knew what a duvet was.

Nick didn't lead Ellie to the bed. He had stopped in the middle of the room, letting her choose to move forward if she was ready. She turned and moved backward until the backs of her knees hit the bed, and then she let them buckle, bringing Nick down on top of her.

THE FOLLOWING day Ellie woke up in Nick's bed with his warm solid arms around her, and she felt saner than she ever had. She felt him stir against her back, and she snuggled back into him. She heard a faint buzzing, her phone, she looked at the end table, but it wasn't there. She looked around the room and saw it on the floor next to the bed and her pile of clothes. She leaned forward to stand up, but Nick pulled her back.

"No, don't get up yet. Waking up next to you has been my dream for weeks." He nuzzled his face into her neck, where her pulse throbbed, and lightly kissed the delicate skin.

She thought the phone could wait, but she pulled her head up and looked back at it with a twinge of worry when it started buzzing again. She had messaged Clara the night before to let her know that she was staying at Nick's, so she knew it wasn't Clara worrying about her, and that made it more likely that it was one of her parents.

"Um, I think it might be important."

Nick leaned up on his elbow, pulled his arm away from her, and let her go. She got up and quickly walked to her phone, incredibly aware that she was naked in Nick's apartment in full daylight, and he was watching her. She bent over and picked her phone up off the floor. It was Clara.

"Your dad is here!" Clara hissed through the phone when Ellie said hello. For a minute, Ellie couldn't understand why her dad was at her apartment, but then it hit her that she had promised to go car shopping with him this morning, and she wasn't there.

She hit her head with the palm of her hand and pulled the phone away to look at the time. She had told him to pick her up at eight in the morning, and it was now eight-fifteen.

"I am so sorry, Clara. I totally forgot. Stall him, and I will be there in ten minutes!" She hung up the phone and turned back to Nick. Nick was already pulling on his pants from the night before as he made his way to the bathroom.

"I heard," Nick said. "Get dressed, and we can head over. I will stop and grab donuts on the way, and maybe he won't notice that his daughter just spent the night with a man." He winked at her before he closed the bathroom door, and she quickly grabbed her clothes and threw them back on.

They were wrinkled and didn't smell too fresh, but maybe her dad wouldn't notice. He would be so mad that she made him wait that he might not even think about why she was disheveled and with a man. Ellie groaned and sank into the bed with her head between her knees.

———

NICK STOPPED and grabbed donuts and coffee and still got Ellie to her apartment in ten minutes, a remarkable feat made possible only by a lead foot and light Saturday morning traffic.

When they pulled in, Ellie started to sweat. She was sure her dad would know she had spent the night with Nick, and she wasn't ready to face that reality.

She also wasn't ready to introduce her dad to her new boyfriend, if that's what he was, but she didn't feel like she could tell Nick to drop her off and run. It was better to introduce him to the man he knew she slept with rather than hide him. Somehow that seemed dirtier.

They went up the stairs quickly, and when Ellie walked through the door, she could hear her dad talking to Clara.

"So, she left this morning to get donuts, and it has taken her this long to get back? Are you sure she's okay?"

"Oh yeah. I talked to her just a little bit ago, and she is totally fine."

"Hey, I'm home!" Ellie called from the doorway. "I brought donuts and coffee."

Ellie's dad stepped out of the kitchen and looked at Nick. "What else did you bring?"

"Dad, this is Nick. He went with me to go get the coffee and donuts." She placed the square pink box on the kitchen counter, and Clara opened it and inhaled a donut in a couple of seconds.

"Well, someone had to drive you." Nick gave Ellie a reassuring wink and smiled at James.

Ellie's dad shook hands with Nick. There was a moment of silence while the two men assessed each other. Nick looked relaxed and utterly unworried about meeting the father of a girl he was dating, and that instilled some level of reassurance in Ellie, but not much.

"Yeah, that's why we need to get her a car. So, she can drive herself to get donuts." James emphasized "donuts" and narrowed his eyes at Ellie. She smiled back guiltily.

"So, what kind of a car are you two looking for?" Nick asked as he opened the cupboard for some coffee mugs. He poured a cup out for each of them and handed a mug to Ellie and Clara first before handing one over to Ellie's dad and pouring his own.

"We are looking for a small sedan. One that Ellie can feel comfortable in and get from home to work." James was still watching Nick as he moved comfortably around the kitchen. Nick was taking out small plates for donuts, and he picked Ellie's favorite out of the box without being told which one that was.

"That sounds good. Maybe you should look into a little Subaru or a Honda." Nick handed Ellie a donut, gesturing to the box as he looked at Mr. Finn. "Can I grab you a donut, sir?"

"I will grab one. I was thinking that a Honda would be good. She needs something reliable." He moved closer to the donut box and picked one out but refused a plate.

Clara was looking between everyone nervously and reaching for her third donut when her phone rang and gave her an excuse to leave the tense atmosphere.

Ellie heard her say hello as she walked out of the room, and she could tell it was Jesse. Clara's voice always did a high-pitched flip when she answered a Jesse call.

They all finished their donuts, and Clara didn't return for a fourth, so breakfast seemed to be officially over. Ellie wished she could shower and change but couldn't make her dad wait and act like she wasn't ready. She never even put her bag down, so she was ready to go the entire time they had been standing in the kitchen.

"Well, Nick, thank you for taking my daughter to get donuts and coffee for everyone. I think we should probably get going." He took a step toward Ellie and put a hand on her shoulder.

"Sure, I will walk out with you guys." Nick collected the dirty dishes and put them in the sink. He was comfortable in the apartment because he had spent a lot of time in it with Ellie the last week, and it showed. Ellie could see that her dad had noticed, and she clenched a little at the assumptions she could feel in his eyes.

"Clara, we are leaving!" Ellie called out as they turned toward the door.

Clara stuck her head out of her room. She still had the phone plastered to her cheek, "Bye! Have fun! Pick out something cute." She gave Ellie a wink and pulled her head back into the room.

"Does Clara want to come with you to make sure you get something cute?" Her dad chuckled.

"She probably wouldn't mind, but when she is on the phone with Jesse, it is hard to get her off." Ellie smiled, and her eyes drifted to Nick as she thought about their late-night phone calls.

She knew precisely why Clara didn't like to get off the phone with Jesse, she was in love, and every second with him, even if it was just on the phone, was not something she was willing to let go of.

The three walked down to the parking lot together, and Ellie worried about how she would say goodbye to Nick the whole time. Usually, she would kiss him goodbye, but she didn't feel like she could kiss him goodbye in front of her dad.

By the time they got to the parking lot, Ellie was so wrapped up in the anxiety her mind was spinning that she didn't have time to even make a choice on the matter. Nick grabbed her and gave her a quick kiss and a wink before he turned to walk away. She knew he wouldn't have left without saying goodbye to her dad, so she must have missed a lot while stuck in her head.

"Alright, El, already got a new guy, huh?" Her dad chuckled and shook his head a little as they walked to his car and climbed in. "I thought after Dane you were going to be a mess and swear off guys, and yet here you are with a new boyfriend not even two weeks later."

"I wasn't planning on it, but he came into the library and asked me out. He is charming and funny. He owns a bookstore."

"What is with guys asking you out in the library? Didn't Dane make that same move?"

"Probably because that is the only place they can find me." Ellie laughed.

Her dad laughed at that one too. "That's probably it. Your mom is going to be excited to hear about this. You should call her and tell her before I go home and tell her. Otherwise, she will get butt hurt that you didn't tell her." He gave her a playful nudge and turned the car toward the car dealership about six miles from her apartment building.

She had plenty of time to call her mom and get chewed out for not telling her about Nick before her dad knew; bonus, he got to meet him first. She was going to be in a tiff.

ELLIE GOT off the phone with her mom as they pulled into the car dealership and looked over at her dad. "Well, that was exhausting. Why did you make me do that?"

"It's better to get these things over with. Also, I didn't want to be the one to tell her." He chuckled a little.

They parked the car, and as soon as they got out, the car salespeople descended. They were coming from three directions, each trying to walk faster than the other to get to them first. Ellie moved closer to her dad and waited for him to pick a direction and, therefore, a salesman.

The salesman on the left made it to them first, and as soon as he stuck out his hand for James to shake, the other salespeople changed course, looking for fresher meat.

"Hiya, the name is Frank. How may I help you today, sir?"

James made a show of rolling his eyes at Ellie before smiling at Frank. "We are here to find a new car for my daughter. The most important feature would be impact safety."

Frank's eyes ticked over to assess Ellie, but he rolled with it and went right into his speech on the safety of the vehicles he could only sell to them. They followed him through the rows of cars as he spilled statistics and ratings.

It took them a while to find the perfect car, but they left with a new vehicle picked out and Ellie behind the wheel. It was a small champagne-colored Prius, and Ellie wasn't sure how her dad had been talked into a Toyota, but she was glad because she loved it.

She followed her dad back to her apartment and felt like she was finally getting her life back together. She wasn't living at home, she had a job that she loved, and now she had a car to get her to work so she didn't have to rely on others. She still didn't like driving, and the whole way back home, she worried but was holding it together with personal pep talks.

Her dad made sure that she made it home, and then he took off for home-home. Ellie couldn't help but still think about her childhood home as her true home. Maybe one day she would have a new permanent home that felt more like home than her parents, but she had no way of knowing.

Ellie was still thinking about the possibilities of a new heart home as she walked up the stairs, and she wasn't listening or watching where she was going. She shouldn't have been surprised when she turned the second-floor corner and walked right into Dane.

"Sorry." She said automatically. Her eyes were bugging out of their sockets, and she could feel her heart jumping around in her chest.

"What are you doing here?" Dane frowned at her. "I don't want to talk about us, Ellie. We broke up."

"Oh, um, well actually, I moved in with Clara upstairs about a week ago...."

"You moved in upstairs? Why would you do that??" Dane looked at her like she was utterly insane, and her heart was pounding so hard she could hardly hear over it.

"Clara is my best friend, and I didn't want to go back to living with my parents. I still want to be independent."

"You aren't independent. You probably just rely on Clara to do everything for you like you did with me. Is that why you are really here? Are you trying to be close to me so that you can try and win me back?" Dane had his hands on his hips, and his eyebrows were so creased that you would think he only had one angry eyebrow.

"No. I have been trying to avoid you. I promise." She shifted from foot to foot. She wanted Clara to save her from this awkward conversation.

"Well, you didn't do an outstanding job. I can't believe you live above me now." Dane was shaking his head and rubbing his hand across his face.

While he wasn't looking, Ellie quickly opened her phone and hit Clara's number on speed dial. She left the line open and hoped Clara would hear Dane's voice and rescue her.

"I'm sorry, I was thinking about something and forgot." Ellie looked around Dane longingly. She would really like to just walk around him. She could push him aside and stomp up the stairs if only she had that kind of confidence.

"You are like a stalker. I'm going to have to move. I mean, I can't believe this. I have had plenty of girlfriends, and none of them moved into my apartment building when we broke up." Dane was getting increasingly agitated, and Ellie was starting to think that retreat was a better option.

Just as Ellie was about to turn tail and run down the stairs, she heard Clara calling her name.

"Ellie? Where are you, Ellie?"

Ellie heard footsteps on the stairs, and she looked past Dane to see Clara bounding down the stairs. She closed her eyes in relief. Dane turned and looked at Clara too.

"Get the hell away from her," Clara said to Dane.

"Why did you let her move in with you? I dumped her so that I didn't have to see her anymore, and you just went ahead and brought her back into the building?"

Clara's eyes narrowed, and Ellie saw her clench her fists into tiny balls. "Excuse me, but do you own the damn building? No, I don't think you do. She has been here a week and hasn't given you any trouble. She doesn't want to see your ass either, so if you could kindly move it out of the way, we will go upstairs to our apartment and leave you alone. If you won't move, we will call the police and press charges on you for harassment."

Dane glared at Clara for a moment, then he huffed and turned back toward Ellie. "Excuse me." He said, and he moved around Ellie down the stairs.

When he was around the corner, Ellie and Clara turned and ran up the steps to their apartment, slamming the door behind them. They sank to the floor in front of the door and leaned back against it.

"Thank you so much for coming to get me. He blocked me, and I didn't know what to do." Ellie said after they had both caught their breath. They weren't winded from the run, but the confrontation adrenaline sucked the air right out of them.

"My pleasure, girl. I always wanted to tell that pinched-faced asshole off." Clara laughed and shifted to the side to lean against Ellie.

"I hope I never see him again," Ellie said.

She knew this probably wouldn't be possible, what with living in the same building, but a girl could dream. She heard that the elevator was finally working, and even though she didn't like to take it, she was starting to think that she might just to avoid Dane. She knew he wouldn't take it because he thought it was lazy.

TWENTY-THREE

ELLIE SPENT THE NEXT TWO WEEKS DRIVING HERSELF TO WORK every day and to the store nearly the same amount. She could have made the store a one-time-a-week trip, but she was trying to get used to being independent, and going to the store by herself was one of her small-term goals. Plus, she had completely taken over getting groceries for Lottie since Clara was so busy with Jesse and auditions.

Ellie and Clara had a schedule that worked out reasonably well. They had developed it throughout the week so that they could each spend time with their boyfriends in the apartment without it getting awkward. Monday and Wednesday, Clara would stay at Jesse's, and Ellie could have Nick over for the night. Tuesday and Thursday, Clara would have Jesse over to the apartment, and Ellie would stay with Nick.

The weekend wasn't entirely as set because plans were made on a day-by-day basis, and this weekend Ellie had the apartment all to herself because Clara was going to Las Vegas with Jesse.

Ellie was walking through the grocery store on Friday

night, thinking about her meal plans for the night and grabbing items off the shelves. She realized this was the first time she had felt comfortable at a store and was pretty proud of herself. But in a low-key way because how excited can you be about the ability to go to the store alone?

Ellie finished up and checked out in the self-checkout lane. People don't always like the self-checkout, but Ellie did because it was another way to avoid having to talk to people. And people were her least favorite thing, at least most of them were.

She got home in record time and turned on the oven. She was chopping the potatoes, and Brussels sprouts when the phone rang. Looking over at the caller id, she saw it was Eric and put it on speaker.

"Are you coming to dinner tomorrow night? Mom told me I should call you and invite you and Nick for Saturday night dinner. So, what do I tell her?"

"Yeah, I will be there. I'm not sure about Nick. I don't know if I am ready for that. We haven't been dating very long. I don't want to scare him away with Mom and Dad. Especially if Dad is going to enlist him in the campaign to keep Ellie sane."

"I think Dad learned his lesson with that." Eric chuckled. "Come on. It would be nice to have something to discuss other than the fact that I broke up with another girlfriend...."

"You broke up with Jessica? Why?"

"You know, she just wasn't the one."

"What does that even mean? Do you know what "the one" is?"

"Well, I don't know for sure what "the one" is, but I definitely know what "not the one" is, and that was Jessica. Plus, I think when it is the one you just know."

Ellie thought about that. She thought Dane had been the one, and then he quickly wasn't the one... Now she thought Nick was the one, and he was different from Dane, so he was more the one than Dane had ever been. But what if there was one even more than this one? How do you know when you have found the true one and not just one of the ones?

"Ellie? Did you hear me?" Eric's voice came back into focus.

"Yeah, sorry, what did you say?"

"I asked if you would please do me the extreme favor of bringing your boyfriend so that I don't have to have this "the one" conversation with Mom tomorrow night."

"Okay, fine, I will talk to him tonight, but I can't guarantee anything."

"He will come. He is a good guy like that."

"You haven't even met him."

"Well, yeah, but I can tell he is a good guy by the way he hit you with his bike and then fell in love."

Ellie laughed as she hung up the phone and returned to making dinner. She was excited about tonight. She hoped Nick would stay the whole weekend since Clara would be away. She knew he would stay the night, but asking him to stay day and night for multiple days felt like a different thing.

She was pulling roasted potatoes, veggies, and smothered chicken - her mom's recipe was called smothered because it was covered in thick creamy gravy - out of the oven just when Nick knocked on the door.

Ellie ran to get the door, taking a quick look at herself in the hallway mirror on her way to ensure her hair wasn't a mess and she had no food swiped across her forehead.

She wasn't the cleanest cook, but she was pretty good.

Nick's smile was disarming when she opened the door, it was wide and relaxed, and she felt her heart kick up a couple of beats as her eyes took all of him in.

He wore a gray long-sleeved knit sweater and relaxed jeans, his hair curled around his ears in a shaggy two-week past due look, and his eyes twinkled in the hallway light. Opening the door to him never got old.

"Smells good," Nick said as he walked in and kissed her lightly. He put his hands on her waist, and when she didn't pull away, he deepened the kiss and wrapped his arms around her.

"Oh boy! Aren't you two cute!" Lottie was walking down the hall with Zeke chuckling and shaking her head at them.

"Sorry, Lottie!" Ellie's cheeks flushed at being caught by the older woman.

Zeke pulled toward them, and Lottie stumbled a little. Nick jumped out of the doorway and placed his arm under Lottie's to stabilize her. It was hard for her to walk Zeke with her walker. Clara and Ellie took turns helping out with that, but Lottie couldn't rely on them to take him out whenever he needed to go.

"Thanks, dear," Lottie said. "He isn't usually any trouble but gets excited when he sees Ellie."

"Glad to help." Nick smiled at Lottie like she was his grandmother, and the protective look on his face made Ellie's uterus flutter.

"You, too, better get a room, as the kids say." Lottie shook her head, chuckling, and walked down the hall to her apartment.

They watched to ensure Lottie made it inside before they went to the kitchen. Nick helped plate the food and carry plates to the small dining room table. They ate and talked about the day, and it wasn't until the second glass of wine that Ellie felt brave enough to ask Nick about Saturday night dinner.

"So, Clara is gone for the weekend," Ellie said to feel him out.

"Oh yeah?" Nick pushed his plate away and looked up at Ellie.

"So, I was thinking, if you want to, maybe you could stay over." She didn't say for how long, wanting to see how he took it first.

"Tonight, or for the weekend?"

"Whatever you want."

"I could stay for the weekend, but I need to go home and get some clothes."

"Yeah, of course." Ellie took a deep breath before asking the next question. "The only thing is that I am supposed to go to dinner at my parent's house tomorrow."

"Is that an invitation?" Nick asked, laughing at Ellie's obvious hint.

"If you want to go, it is. But if you don't want to go, then no." Ellie smiled, hoping Nick was teasing her because he wanted to say yes.

"I would love to go. I already met your dad, so it will be nice to meet your mom too."

"And my brother."

Nick smiled, "And your brother.

The rest of the night was spent not talking about Ellie's family, and she was glad for it because it would have been a very uncomfortable night otherwise.

She wasn't thinking about the girl either, and she hadn't all week, but the image was still lurking in her mind, just waiting to come out. She could feel it when she relaxed too much, felt too happy, and wasn't focused on pushing her down into the dark corners; that is when she would creep forward.

Thankfully they "got a room," as Lottie suggested, and all thoughts were on Nick, his seductive lips, beautiful body, and the things he could do to her with both.

JAMES WATCHED his wife tell him about Ellie coming over and bringing her new boyfriend, Nick. He wasn't so sure how he felt about Nick. The guy met Ellie by hitting her with a bike, after all. And he wasn't so sure about her taste in guys after what happened with Dane.

He liked Dane. He thought he would be a good fit for Ellie, so he asked him to watch after her and take shifts helping with the road maintenance. That backfired on him, and now he was back to doing it all, along with a bit of help from Eric, and he didn't know if he would trust another boyfriend of Ellie's to help.

"Are you listening to me, James?" Sarah was scowling at him. He was busy thinking and forgot to listen to her sometimes, but it wasn't to be rude. It was just hard to concentrate sometimes.

"Sorry, what did you say?" He gave her his best "oops" smile, hoping it would be endearing and cute.

Sarah rolled her eyes at him and let out a huff. "I said, I don't want you talking to this boy about Ellie's anxiety. We don't want to scare another guy off."

"Hell, if a guy scares off that easily, he isn't worth having if you ask me." Like most dads, James didn't think anyone was good enough for his little girl, but you called his little girl crazy, and you weren't good enough for anyone.

"James, you better behave yourself tomorrow night. We have worked really hard for Ellie to be like the other girls, and I don't want you causing trouble."

It was James' turn to sigh and roll his eyes. They had worked hard, and he still worked hard every day for Ellie. But he also thought about what would happen if she got a new trigger.

What would he do then? Add another chore to his list of things to protect Ellie from. Well, that wouldn't go well because he still had to care for himself and had a job.

"I'm not going to drive him away, Sarah, if that is what you are implying. But a guy shouldn't be so damned sensitive to things. Dane mistreated our girl, and I don't want to see her in a relationship like that again."

"Fine. I just don't want Ellie to end up in and out of relationships. I don't know why Eric can't settle on a nice girl. I liked the last one he brought home; he already broke up with her. When we were young, you found someone you liked, and that was it. You made it work."

"So, you are saying you *just* make it work with me?" James chuckled and leaned forward to nuzzle Sarah's neck.

"Sometimes." She said, smiling coyly.

"Oh really? Well, let's see how hard you have to work tonight..." James shifted his weight closer to Sarah and kissed her the way no kid wanted to see their parents kiss.

CHAPTER
TWENTY-FOUR

SATURDAY NIGHT, DINNER WENT OFF WITHOUT A HITCH. ERIC AND Nick talked easily, and Ellie could see how happy her mom was that she was there. It was nice to have everyone she loved together in one room. And she was pretty sure she was falling in love with Nick, but it was too soon for her to say it out loud. Plus, she was waiting for him to say it first.

When it came time to clear the table, Ellie wasn't willing to let Nick go off with her dad and Eric, so she stayed with them. Usually, she helped her mom with the dishes, and when she followed the men into the living room instead of her mom into the kitchen, her dad and brother stared at her as if she had grown another head.

"You aren't going to help mom?" Eric asked.

"Well, I guess I should... Do you guys want to come back to the kitchen so we can all be together?"

Eric gave her a knowing look, but her dad and Nick weren't catching on.

"No honey, you go ahead and help your mom and let the boys hang out. There is a game on." Her dad was already flipping through the channels. He sat heavily in his favorite recliner, and the other two guys sat on the sofa nearby.

Ellie was worried about leaving Nick. She didn't want her dad and Eric planting seeds in his mind about her being crazy. But she also knew that he might think she was clingy if she hovered. She twisted her fingers nervously as she turned and returned to the kitchen, where her mom was already rinsing the dishes in the sink and placing them in the dishwasher.

Ellie walked to her place between her mom and the dishwasher to take up her job of placing the dishes in the racks while her mom rinsed. She was distracted by her worry over Nick. This felt too familiar, and she knew this exact situation was how things happened with Dane.

"Honey," her mom looked intently at her while holding out a glass she wasn't taking. "Are you alright over there?"

"Yeah. What do you think they are talking about?" She took the glass and placed it on the rack.

"Oh, I am sure they are just talking about some silly sport." Her mom continued with the dishes and handed a plate to Ellie.

"You don't think they are talking about me, do you?"

"Don't be so paranoid. I am sure they aren't talking about you."

Ellie leaned forward to see inside the sink. "How much do we have left?"

"Well, we barely just started, Ellie." There were a lot of dishes still in the sink, and she knew that was her mom's way of telling her to calm down. She always said something barely started when she was annoyed with Ellie's rushing to leave or stop anything as a kid.

Ellie placed another plate on the rack when Nick strolled into the room—and walked up behind her. He wrapped his arms around her gently and looked at Sarah Finn.

"You know, Mrs. Finn, you should take the night off and let me worry about the dishes. I will help Ellie so that it goes faster." He stepped in for Sarah nicely and took a dish from the sink.

"Are you sure? That is so nice of you. I never get just to sit and relax after dinner." She smiled at Nick, refilled her wine glass, and entered the living room.

"Alone at last," Nick whispered as he pulled Ellie into his arms. "I couldn't sit and watch any more Basketball while you were in here."

Ellie leaned back into his arms and let her head rest on his shoulder. She took a deep breath getting a whiff of the musky Italian bar soap he used that morning when they stopped at his apartment for some clothes and a shower.

He kissed her neck and took the plate that was still in her hands. He placed the plate in the dishwasher and took up rinsing the dishes in the sink.

"Your dad is nice. And I like Eric a lot. He is pretty protective of you. Exactly how a brother should be with his little sister." Nick's eyes twinkled as he gave Ellie a nudge.

"Oh yeah, I am sure you would be fiercely protective, too, if you had a little sister." She nudged him back and took the dish he was rinsing out of his hand.

"Yeah, if I had a sister. I am protective of my nieces and you." Nick had one older brother with three daughters, Nick's favorite little girls in the world. Ellie was hoping that she would get to meet them soon. Nick talked about them all the time and showed her pictures, but he hadn't invited her to go with him for a visit yet.

"You are the best uncle. I hope Eric gets married and has some babies someday so I can be an aunt."

"You will definitely be an awesome aunt one day. Probably not soon when it comes to Eric, though." Nick laughed shortly, and Ellie smiled at his contagious joy. He saw her smiling and flicked some water at her.

She gasped and stared at him open-mouthed, then leaned forward and grabbed some water from the faucet to flick back at him. Before she knew it, they were in a water fight, and their laughter carried down the halls to the rest of the family.

Eric cleared his throat in the doorway, and they stopped mid-water flick to look back at the family gathered in the kitchen entryway. Water dripped off Ellie's nose, and she had difficulty stifling her laughter.

"The dishes are done," Ellie said.

"And we will wipe up the water. Sorry about that." Nick was still grinning from ear to ear, which lessened the power of an apology, but he didn't mean that he was sorry that the water was there, just that it was in their kitchen.

A few minutes later, everyone was in the kitchen with rags helping to wipe up drops of water and laughing as they found water higher and higher up and further away.

CLARA RETURNED from Vegas Sunday night with Jesse, and they joined Ellie and Nick for dinner. They ordered Pizza and Chinese, ate everything out of the boxes, and watched the newest episode of *The Masked Singer*.

After the food was gone and the show was over, the guys decided to head out even though the girls tried to convince them both to stay.

As soon as the door closed behind them, Clara started gushing about Jesse, with good news on a new job that she would audition for during the week. She told Ellie that she planned to stay at a hotel in Burbank with Jesse the day before her audition until the day after so that she could be nearby if she needed to go back in to sign any paperwork. That is positive thinking at its best.

Ellie was going to have the apartment to herself again. She started thinking about inviting Nick over to stay while Clara was gone. They had a wonderful weekend, especially Sunday, because they didn't leave Ellie's bed the entire day.

"I don't think you should have Nick stay, though," Clara said.

"Why not?" Ellie stopped her thoughts and frowned at Clara. She hadn't been expecting that.

"I just think you should have some "me time," you know? You never just take time for yourself. I think it would be good for you."

Ellie thought about that for a minute. She hated the idea of being alone in the apartment. It felt so big when it was empty, and somehow it was creakier. She could tell that Clara was only trying to help her be more independent because of the way she made the suggestion. She didn't want to show her fear of being alone with her anxiety.

"Yeah, you are probably right. Maybe I'll see what Nick is up to and just have him over one night instead of both or something."

Clara was watching Ellie steadily. She knew Ellie would probably have Nick over for both nights or go to his place, and Ellie could see disappointment written all over her face. She decided that she would make sure to stay one night alone, and she told herself that it would be okay.

They continued to talk about the rest of Clara's trip. Ellie barely noticed the tendrils of anxiety creeping up her fingers while Clara talked about the steak dinner Jesse had taken her to the night before and how the room was filled with red roses when they returned. She pushed away the anxious thoughts whispering in her mind and tried to focus on Clara. She watched her lips move, and she smiled when Clara did and nodded when Clara paused.

Their group chat with Lottie went off, and both girls grabbed their phones. Ellie couldn't have been more grateful for the distraction.

Lottie: Could one of you come to take Zeke out? Bad day for the hips.

Clara: We will be right there!

They walked down the hall to Lottie's apartment and knocked. They heard Lottie call out that it was unlocked, and Clara pushed the door open. Zeke greeted them at the door with whole butt wiggles, squeaky whines, and a couple of jumps that he looked back to make sure his owner didn't notice.

Zeke loved Clara, but he especially loved Ellie. If they were both there, he was always by her side.

"Oh, thank you both so much. I got him out this afternoon, but it was rough. Thank goodness the elevator has been working, or I don't know that I would have been able to get him out." Lottie looked so relieved that Ellie felt terrible for not offering to take him out earlier.

Lottie looked about to cry, and Ellie ran to squat by her side. "What's the matter, Lottie?"

"I don't think I am going to be able to keep him. My hips are getting so bad that I don't think it's fair to him anymore." Tears were now freely streaming down her face and breaking Ellie's heart.

"Lottie, you don't have to give him away. We will just take him out for you."

"Yeah, between me and El, we can take him out whenever you need. And we can get him one of those grass potty spots for the balcony for emergencies." Clara said.

"I couldn't burden you both with that. He needs to go out several times a day. And the dog walker I hired only walks once a day." She sniffled again, and Zeke slid his head under her hand.

"Oh, look at him. Nope, no, he has to stay with you. The dog walker is mid-morning, right?" Clara was taking charge, and her eyes sparkled with confidence at Lottie's nod. "Perfect, Ellie will take him out early in the morning before her shift at the library, I will take him out in the afternoon after my coffee house shift and one or both of us will take him out twice between late afternoon and evening."

"See, we have a plan, Lottie, and we can adjust as we go. We will make sure Zeke can stay with you." Ellie squeezed her hand, and Zeke started to dance again.

"Starting now," Clara said with a laugh watching the dog.

They walked him around the block, and he did all his business, meaning he would be good for the night. When they dropped him back off at Lottie's, she had a spare key for them and thanked them again with tears threatening. She held it in, though, and settled for hugs for each of them.

TWENTY-FIVE

A MONTH LATER, ELLIE WAS TRYING TO PUSH AWAY THE ANXIOUS whispers that gathered when Clara told her she would be out of town for yet another audition, but they were becoming louder as she got ready for bed. She sat on the edge of her bed in the dark room. The silence was heavy on her ears.

Just go to sleep, and you will feel better in the morning.
You have been doing so well you can't go back.
You aren't crazy.
You are okay.

Ellie woke up at three, sweating and gasping for air. The girl was back. She saw her trapped under the twisted metal frame of the car and heard her crying out for Ellie to save her. She tried to calm her mind down enough to get back to sleep, but it wasn't working. She tried to push the girl's face down into the recesses of her mind, but the young face was burned into her eyelids, and every time she closed her eyes, she was there.

At five, Ellie gave up on the idea of sleep and decided just to get up and shower. She was ready for work before

Clara was even awake and cooking breakfast when her roomie finally staggered out of the room looking like a Monday morning.

"Morning," Ellie said more cheerfully than she felt. Fake it till you make it, right? "I made eggs, bacon, hash browns, and toast."

Clara stared at her with blurry eyes as she processed Ellie's words. Clara was so far from a morning person you wondered if she was even a real person in the morning.

Ellie grabbed a mug of coffee off the counter and put it in Clara's hand. This got a reaction, and Clara sat heavily on the bar stool at the kitchen counter and stuck her head down over the cup. She inhaled the coffee fumes first before bringing the cup to her mouth, and Ellie watched the routine with fascination.

After half the cup was gone, Clara seemed to come alive, and she got up to grab a plate of food.

Ellie was quietly eating the food on her plate and looking through the social media on her phone. She was doing an excellent job distracting herself from the anxiety, but she could feel it lurking like a monster in the dark corner of the room.

"You okay, El? You seem quiet this morning." Clara shoveled bacon into her mouth and washed it with more coffee, but she watched Ellie carefully.

"Yeah, I just didn't sleep very well." Ellie pushed the food still on her plate around in a circle and tried to convince her stomach that eating it was a good idea.

"Why not? You having nightmares again? You seemed good for a while there."

Ellie had been good for a while and was trying to figure out what triggered this newest episode of misery, but she couldn't think of anything during the four hours she had been awake that morning. She could still feel Clara's eyes on her, so she looked at her friend and tried her best reassuring smile.

It must not have worked because Clara frowned in response. She realized she was supposed to answer Clara's last question and not just smile. That was her mistake. Ellie sighed and nodded.

"So, you are having nightmares again. Girl, I am telling you, you should talk to someone. A therapist would totally help you out." Clara finished her coffee and went in search of more.

"I guess I should, but I don't know who to talk to, and it makes me anxious thinking about talking to someone about my anxiety."

Clara laughed out loud, and the sound breaking the silent kitchen air startled Ellie. She looked up at Clara. She was shaking her head at Ellie incredulously.

"You have anxiety about getting help for your anxiety!? That is your anxiety working double hard to ensure you don't get help, girl.... Your anxiety has fucking anxiety." She laughed again, but this time gently and in a way that begged Ellie to see the irony and laugh with her.

"My anxiety has anxiety," Ellie repeated, and she smiled at the ridiculousness of the idea. Soon, she was laughing with Clara, but when the laughter died, she was left with the idea that maybe she was crazy. After all, she let her anxiety control her, which seemed pretty crazy.

"You gotta go walk Zeke," Clara said, grabbing Lottie's key from the counter and tossing them to her. "I'm gonna send you the number for a therapist, and you are going to call. Today. Understand?"

Ellie nodded.

After walking and feeding Zeke, making Lottie some

tea, and throwing in a load of laundry, Ellie was on her way. She drove to work and was even a little early that morning.

She was happy to be in the comforting library before it began to vibrate with the activity of people. She clocked in and said good morning to Ana, who was in her office instead of out on the floor. She was relieved that the book stacks were thick and tall when she got to her desk. She had plenty of work to occupy her mind.

An hour into work, Ellie got a message from Nick saying that he would have to stay late at work that night and he would try to get over to her place later if it wasn't too late. She hoped she could ask to go to his place that night just to get out of the apartment, but she guessed that was out of the question now.

She didn't want to go home to an empty apartment, and Clara would be at Jesse's. Clara would be gone most of the week since she was leaving for Burbank with Jesse the next day and wouldn't be back until Thursday night. At least that meant that she would get to be the one taking Zeke out.

At lunch, she called Eric to see if he wanted to get together. She knew she should be facing her anxiety and not relying on Eric to save her, but she was tired of fighting off the fear, and she just wanted to feel safe for at least a night.

"What are you up to tonight?" She asked Eric when he answered the phone.

"Not much. I was just going to hang out at home. You okay?"

"Yeah, I just wanted to see if you wanted to do something tonight. Nick is working late, and Clara will be at Jesse's, so I thought it would be a good night for some brother time. If you aren't busy, that is." Ellie was trying her hardest not to sound desperate, but she knew she wasn't doing a great job when she heard a hint of brotherly concern in Eric's voice.

"Okay, sure. What do you want to do? Do you want to come over to my place? Or we could go out to a movie. Whatever you want, El."

The "whatever you want, El" was what gave it away. He was worried. And here she thought she was doing an excellent job at sounding nonchalant. She took a deep breath and tried to steady her voice.

"That would be great. Can you come over after I get off work, or what time are you off? I have to walk Charlotte's dog, or I would go to your place."

"I'll be off around five. I will come over after that."

"Okay, see you then."

"Alright. Are you sure everything is okay, Ellie?"

"Yeah. It's fine. I have to get back to work, so I'll see you tonight. Love you."

"Love you too, sis."

Ellie hated hearing Eric sound worried about her and didn't want to be a burden. She opened her messages from Clara and clicked on the first number she shared for a therapist near them.

Her thumb hovered over the call button. She took a deep breath and clicked.

ELLIE WENT HOME after work even though she feared being alone in the apartment while battling the anxiety demon in her mind. When she was feeling good, it didn't seem like such a challenging task, and she had even started to enjoy being home alone for short periods.

The therapist offered her an online appointment the following week, and she was anxious to start, but she also felt hopeful that it would be everything that Clara said. And it would fix all her problems.

She thought about going to the store to buy something to make for Eric, but she decided that braving the grocery store wasn't the best idea today. Crowds of people made her nervous, and she didn't need that extra jumpy energy rolling through her body today.

Even though she wasn't up to the store, she still wanted to make something for Eric. She searched the cupboards for ingredients and came up with Snickerdoodle cookies. She knew the recipe by heart because it was one of their childhood favorites to make together while they were home alone without their parents. Eric often "babysat" her even though they were only two years apart.

She made the snicker-doodles quickly, and it was time to take Zeke out for his walk.

He was happy to see her when she opened the door. Lottie was in her recliner watching Golden Girls and sipping tea.

"Thank you so much for taking him out, dear," Lottie called.

Zeke was dancing and crying around Ellie's legs. She could barely get him to contain himself long enough for her to clip his leash onto his collar. She giggled as he twisted to lick her face each time she bent over.

Finally, she got the leash on him, and they were off. The elevator was working again, but Ellie still wasn't willing to get on the thing. She took the stairs with Zeke, and when the cool evening air hit them, Ellie felt like she could finally breathe.

They walked down the sidewalk together, Ellie

watching the bounce of Zeke's ears, and she felt a tingle of peace. She didn't know how long they had been walking when she remembered that Eric was coming over.

She shook her head at herself and looked at her watch. It was about time that she headed back to meet Eric.

Ellie walked back into the apartment parking lot with Zeke, feeling better. She was excited to spend time with her brother, and she was sure Nick would be at her place when Eric went home.

He had sent her several messages throughout the day. The most recent promised he would be there by nine. Eric was waiting for her by his truck, and when she walked up, he pushed off the right fender to join her.

"How was your day?" He asked, and he watched her for an answer.

"It was good. Work was easy and quiet. After that, I went home, made some cookies, and walked with Zeke." Ellie reached down and scratched the dog behind his ears. Zeke looked back at Eric, judging him for not giving him any attention.

"Cookies and dog walking, my favorite." Eric chuckled. He reached over and patted Zeke. Zeke immediately moved his body to Eric for more. Eric looked back up at Ellie. "What kind of cookies?"

"Snicker-doodles."

"Are they inside?"

"Of course, what kind of sister would I be if I made snicker-doodles and didn't save any for my favorite big brother?"

"A crappy one. But I wouldn't want to say anything." Eric gave her a nudge, and they both laughed.

They dropped Zeke off, and Ellie promised to come back and take Zeke out again before bedtime. When they returned to Ellie's apartment, Eric ordered pizza, and they ate the cookies while waiting. Their mom wasn't around, so this was allowed.

Eric picked out a movie and put it on while Ellie was in the bathroom. She was feeling much better about life. She had beaten down her anxiety and locked it away. She was hanging out with her big brother instead of sitting at home alone worrying about an imaginary girl that she was convinced her mind had created to torture her.

When she exited the bathroom, she was ready to watch a movie and relax. She picked a spot on the couch and cuddled in for the film. Eric threw her a blanket and a pillow before he threw himself down on the sofa opposite her.

The movie started and was one of Ellie's favorites, *Secretariat*. She loved it because it was a simple feel-good type of movie. Ten minutes in, Eric declared they needed popcorn even though they were stuffed with cookies and pizza.

He got up to go into the kitchen, and Ellie itched the side of her eye. It kept itching, and then her ear felt itchy too. She was scratching her ear and worrying when she felt a heat flush into her cheeks and close her throat.

What if she was reacting to something? She had no idea what it could be, but she felt itchy and couldn't shake the feeling. She started texting Nick to calm her nerves, but she deleted it. She didn't want to start making him take care of her. It was her job to get her mind right. But she wished someone would tell her that she would be okay.

Ellie started searching her mind for answers to calm herself down, but everything she thought of only caused her throat to feel tighter and her breath shorter. Eric was still in the kitchen, and she was starting to feel dizzy.

Why are you panicking right now?

Calm down.

You're fine... Nothing happened.

I hate it inside my head.

She was sucking in air when Eric walked in from the kitchen with two steaming bowls of popcorn. He took one look at her and knew something wasn't right.

"What's the matter?"

"Nothing." Ellie tried to put on a smile.

"Bullshit. What happened?"

"I don't know. I just feel like I can't breathe."

"You look white as a sheet. Focus on taking in deep, steady breaths." Eric put the bowls down and sat on the edge of the couch next to her.

Ellie took a deep breath through her mouth.

"Not like that," Eric scolded. "In through your nose and count to five."

Ellie breathed in again through her nose and tried to focus on counting as she did.

"Now hold it for a count of three and then release on a count of seven."

Ellie was counting numbers in her mind and watching Eric as he matched her breaths. She felt the tension in her throat lessen and knew it was working. Her brain registered that she would be okay, and after a few more breaths, she closed her eyes and leaned back into the couch.

"You better?" Eric asked.

"Yeah, I think I'm good."

"Okay, good because we were about to miss the best part." He shoved her over so he could sit close and passed her a bowl of popcorn.

They finished the movie at five past nine, and Ellie immediately checked her phone. She was still hoping that

Nick would be able to come over so she wouldn't have to spend the night alone. She thought this was a sad comment on her independence, but she wouldn't try to change tonight, so fighting it was no use.

Just as she started worrying about Nick, her phone rang, and she saw his name on the id pop up. She felt relief run through her body as she answered the phone on the second ring.

"I'm just leaving work. Are you home?"

"Yes, Eric and I just finished a movie."

"Alright, well, I'm starving, so I'll probably stop for food, and then I will head over to you."

Ellie could hear Nick turn the engine over in his Jeep, and she was excited to see him, so she covered the phone with her hand and whispered to Eric, asking if she could give the rest of the pizza to Nick.

"Ellie? Are you still there?" Nick asked after she didn't reply.

"Yeah, I was just checking on something. I have some leftover pizza if you want to eat that?"

"Okay yeah, that sounds great." Nick sounded tired even through the phone, and Ellie felt the urge to take care of him, which was strange because sometimes she didn't even want to take care of herself.

Eric stood up to leave, and Ellie wrapped her arms around him. "Thank you for hanging out with me."

"Anytime, El. You are my favorite person." Eric kissed her on the top of her head.

She knew that Eric knew why she wanted to hang out tonight, but she didn't care because she would have been alone and hiding in her bedroom closet if she hadn't been with him when she had her panic attack.

TWENTY-SIX

Eric went with Ellie to pick up Zeke for the last time for the night, and they walked him to the large grassy area within the apartment grounds that also included a walking path. There were benches along the way, but there were very few lights, so Eric stayed with Ellie while she waited for Zeke to do his sniff, consider, then pee routine.

"Hurry up, dog, it's freezing out here," Eric grumbled.

"He probably knows this is his last time out, so he wants to make the most of it."

"I don't think dogs are that smart."

"They absolutely are! You don't have to wait. Nick will be here soon."

"What kind of brother would I be if I left you out in the dark?"

Ellie thought about insisting that he head home. But years of being a woman in American society made her hold her tongue.

A minute later, they watched Nick's Jeep turn into the parking lot, and Eric practically dragged Ellie and Zeke back to the parking lot. Zeke barely had time to finish peeing, and Ellie saw a few drips hit the sidewalk as they left the grass.

Nick parked next to Ellie's Prius and stepped out of the car, heading toward the building. He was surprised when Eric and Ellie appeared in front of him out of the shadows.

"Shit. You scared me." Nick feigned, putting his hand over his heart. But he smiled at Ellie.

"Sorry, man, I am freezing my ass off. You got her from here?" Eric was dancing in place, and Ellie thought he might want to rethink his clothing choices.

"Yeah, I got her." He wrapped the same arm around her and kissed her.

"Perfect. See ya later, El." Eric said, leaning over to kiss her cheek before patting Nick's arm. "Have a good night, man."

They watched Eric walk away, and Zeke whined to get the attention back on him. Ellie reached down and gave him a scratch, and so did Nick.

Nick's stomach growled against Ellie's arm.

"I think we should get upstairs so that you can eat." She chuckled as she moved out of his arm and grabbed his hand to tow along behind her.

"Probably a good idea. I'm half-starved. I had to manage the shop alone all day today cause Anne called out sick."

"That's a bummer. You know, I could have come in to help." Ellie tried to sound casual like she was just offering an idea she had only thought of as a helpful girlfriend, though she had thought about this idea a lot. What if she started working for Nick, and they could be this cute couple that worked at a bookstore together?

"Really? That would be awesome, babe. Thank you."

Nick gave her another kiss as they walked through the lobby.

Nick started for the stairs, but Ellie stopped and headed for the elevator instead.

"I thought you hated the elevator?"

"I do," Ellie said, reminding herself to breathe as the door squeaked shut and the elevator began to whir. "But I ran into Dane last week, and he was a total douche to me about living in the apartment building. So, I'm trying to take the elevator more to avoid him. When it is working, that is."

Zeke whined and pressed himself against Ellie's leg, and Nick quieted. It wasn't that he was one of those jealous types that hated hearing about other men in Ellie's life, not that there was a lot, but he hated how Dane had treated her and therefore hated Dane.

The elevator was old, and it shuddered its way up to the third floor. Ellie hated it for just that reason. It was old and unreliable in every way. It broke down often, and Ellie felt the tension of hoping it would work and the fear of being trapped in a confined space for any amount of time.

When the doors opened, Ellie realized she had been holding her breath and forcefully exhaled the stale air in her lungs. She could feel Nick watching her as they moved out of the elevator and down the hall to Lottie's apartment. She looked back at him and saw a flicker of concern leaving his face.

Lottie was already in bed, so Ellie unlocked the door and sent Zeke in alone. She patted him, and he trotted in tail wagging. She locked the door behind him and turned to head back to her apartment.

"You are staying the night, right?" She asked him as she unlocked another door, this one her own.

"Yep, I have big plans," Nick said with a twinkle in his eye.

"Pizza and beer?"

"Pizza, beer, maybe a show or two, and you." He grinned at Ellie, and she felt heat rush through her body.

THE NEXT MORNING Ellie woke up feeling relaxed and happy. Nick was by her side, and she felt like things couldn't get much better than this. If she could figure out how to get her anxiety to leave her alone entirely and never think about that girl again, then things would be perfect. Maybe the therapist would be able to help with that. The only problem was that then she would have to talk about it.

She rolled toward Nick, and he put his arm around her and pulled her into the crook of his arm. She snuggled into him and sighed. Sharing a room with Clara was a little weird, but how smoothly things worked out was amazing.

"Did you sleep well?" He whispered. It was early morning, and the light filtering through the curtains was flitting around like pixie dust.

"I slept great. How bout you?"

"Best night ever. I wish I could wake up next to you every morning." Nick kissed her on the head, and Ellie thought about waking up next to Nick every morning. It sounded like a dream. One that she was afraid to scare away.

"Me too." Was all she was willing to say, or rather, all she was brave enough to say.

Nick yawned and stretched his arms above their heads. "I guess we ought to get up and get ready for work. And you need to walk Zeke."

They both climbed out of bed, and Ellie thought about the day ahead. Clara would be out of town for her audition for the next couple of days, and she wondered how desperate she would sound if she asked Nick to stay the entire time Clara was gone. She decided to play things by ear, and a little of her Zen snuck away.

Nick's phone buzzed, and he grabbed it off the end table next to Ellie's bed. He looked at the readout and smiled.

"So, my mom just texted me. I guess there is a dinner at their house tonight, and they want me to come." Nick said.

"Oh, that is nice. Will your brother and nieces be there?" Ellie tried hard not to sound sad. She wanted Nick to go and have a good time with his family. She just didn't want to be alone.

"Yeah. It will be a lot of fun. Do you want to come?" Nick watched her; she could feel his eyes on her as he gave the invitation.

"I would love to go." That was the understatement of the year. Ellie could hardly wait to meet Nick's family. And she was excited until she remembered this was a big deal, and she didn't want to mess it up and have Nick's whole family hate her. If only she could swap bodies with Eric for the night. Parents always loved Eric.

"Great!" Nick kissed Ellie and looked back at his phone to give his mother the reply. And just like that, Ellie was signed up to go to Nick's parent's house and entertain a billion questions a new relationship brings.

Nick had to get to work to open, so he left almost an hour before Ellie needed to, but only when they had walked Zeke and brought him back to Lottie. He kissed her at her door, and Ellie felt the quiet wash over her in a comforting way. She didn't usually feel comfort in silence. In fact, silence had always been the enemy of her anxiety-riddled mind.

Ellie washed the dishes in the sink and grabbed a sweater from her closet because it was always cold in the library, even if it wasn't outside. She grabbed her purse and headed for the stairs until she remembered that she was taking the elevator and stopped short at the top with her foot dangling over the first step.

She contemplated just making a go for it since the elevator wasn't her favorite thing, and it always took forever, but she would rather wait for the elevator than run into Dane again. But just as she considered running down the stairs, Lottie came down the hallway.

"Hello dear," Lottie said as she shuffled over to her with her squeaky walker. She was wearing a bright pink track-suit that made Ellie smile.

"And just where do you think you're going?" Ellie was definitely going down the elevator now.

"I have a doctor's appointment. I already got a dial-a-ride on the way, too, so you don't need to worry about me either." Her eyes twinkled at Ellie, and she couldn't help but feel drawn to the older woman.

"Well, I would have been happy to take you too. Remember that for next time."

"Okay, dear, I will remember. Since I have you alone," Lottie leaned in conspiratorially. "I like that nice young man you have now."

"You do?" Ellie was happy with the approval, especially since she made such a lousy pick the last time.

"Yeah, he looks at you with love in his eyes. And he has a nice tushy too!"

"Lottie!' Ellie gasped and giggled at the bold talk of such a sweet old woman.

Lottie chuckled. "Gotta call it how I see it, dear."

The doors closed, and the elevator shook and shuddered as it moved along the wire. A minute later, the elevator jolted to a stop.

"Damn, elevator! This thing always goes on the fritz at the worst times. My ride is going to leave without me if I am late."

"Maybe it just stalled," Ellie said.

She wanted to be helpful, but she wasn't the best person to have around in a time of need. She pushed the button over and over in varying degrees of panic.

"Let's calm down," Lottie said, moving closer to Ellie. "Push the call button, dear."

Ellie looked back at the panel of buttons and reached out for the call button. Just as she was about to push the button, the elevator shook, and there was an ear-splitting snap before the tin box plummeted down, bouncing along the walls as gravity took over.

Ellie was thrown forward and hit her head on the panel of buttons before she could catch herself. She heard Lottie scream behind her, metal screeched, and the elevator hit the ground.

Ellie felt herself fly up to the top of the elevator box. Her body hit something, the force knocking the air out of her, and she crashed back down to the floor like a ping-pong ball.

CHAPTER
TWENTY-SEVEN

ELLIE LAY ON THE FLOOR OF THE ELEVATOR IN A DAZE. SHE couldn't remember passing out, but she couldn't be sure. She put her hand to her head and felt sticky blood oozing from a gash on her forehead. She landed on her left side, and everything hurt.

Lottie was moaning somewhere behind her, and Ellie tried to sit up to help her. The elevator seemed a little crumpled, and the lights were flickering, but other than that, it didn't seem like it had just fallen to the ground.

Lottie was tangled up in her walker, gasping and moaning. She put her hand to her chest, and her eyes were wide when they found Ellie's.

"Are you okay?" Ellie asked her.

"What happened?"

"The elevator just fell to the ground floor." Ellie crawled toward her and tried to pull the tangled walker off her.

Lottie cried out in pain. Ellie stopped trying to pull the walker off and took a closer look. One of the metal bars had broken off the frame and twisted around and into Lottie's thigh.

"What do I do?" Ellie felt panic gripping her.

"Nothing to do, dear. Just call for help." Lottie said as she continued to pant and gasp quietly.

Ellie pulled her sweater off and folded it to put it under Lottie's head. She smiled weakly at Ellie, and her face that had seemed so full of life earlier was pale and sunken. Her gasping for air was growing a knot in the pit of Ellie's stomach.

Ellie tried to stand again but couldn't get her left leg under her. She crawled to the elevator doors and tried to push the button for the doors to open, but nothing happened. She pulled on the door closest to her, but it wouldn't budge. Ellie could feel the panic rising within her.

She sat back on the floor, pulled her phone out of her pocket, and dialed 911 as she watched the woman's breathing slow.

"911, what's your emergency?"

"Um, the elevator in my building just fell, and we are trapped inside. I can't get the doors open." Ellie choked back a sob.

"Where are you located?" The calm voice on the other end asked.

"55 Klein Ave. The apartment building on the corner." Ellie tried to stay calm, but she was starting to hyperventilate. Short gasps of air barely made it past her lips.

"Okay, Ma'am, I need you to stay calm. Are there any injuries?"

"Yes. Uh, my friend, her walker is twisted around her, and she doesn't seem to be breathing very well."

There was a lot of clicking of computer keys, and Ellie's eyes flicked over to Lottie to see how she was doing. Her breathing was shallow, and her cheeks were pinched.

"Ma'am, can you tell if there is any bleeding? Can you tell me if you have any injuries as well?"

"The metal is in her leg, and there is blood, but I don't see much. I hit my head and side, but I think I am okay."

"Alright, Ma'am, I have responders on their way to you now. I am going to stay on the line with you."

Ellie was listening to the dispatcher's calm voice, but the calm wasn't doing anything to calm the hysteria in her mind. She was trapped in a metal box. She was in a metal box that had just plummeted to the ground level, and the door wouldn't open. She was replaying everything in her mind, and the more she did, the farther her brain went down a rabbit hole of panic.

"Ma'am...."

Ellie heard the voice and tried to answer, but all that came out was a squeak. One of her internal voices grabbed hold of her.

Pull it together, Ellie.

Listen to the woman on the phone; she can help you get through this.

Answer her. She keeps talking to you.

She probably thinks you are dead.

"Yeah," Ellie breathed.

"Are you okay?"

"No." Ellie didn't know if she could get more than one word out at a time, so she was just going for anything at this point.

"What is happening over there?"

"I can't breathe."

"Okay I need you to take some deep breaths with me. Breathe in and out slowly."

"Okay," Ellie remembered how Eric told her to breathe whenever she panicked, and she felt her body relax a little.

Her mind was still a tangled mess, but her body moved easier.

"Okay, Ma'am, can you tell me your name and the name of the woman with you?"

Ellie reached over to Lottie putting a hand on her arm in comfort and reassurance. But when she looked down at her, the eyes looking back at her were the little girl's eyes that screamed in pain in her nightmares. Ellie felt a shock run through her, and she pulled her hand away as if she had been electrocuted. The eyes changed to soft and kind in an instant, and the woman reached out to Ellie.

Lottie struggled to pull in more air; she gasped for the air with her mouth open wide. Ellie watched in horror as the woman's face flickered and morphed into the face of the little girl and then back again.

"Ma'am?" Came the dispatcher's voice again.

"Her name is Charlotte, uh, Lottie," Ellie said, trying to distract herself from what she had just seen. Her mind was playing tricks on her again.

"And yours?" The dispatcher asked again. Ever calm and collected.

"Ellie."

"Alright, Ellie, well, I have good news for you. My responders are arriving on the scene, and you should be hearing them on the other side of the door any moment now."

Ellie listened for noises on the other side of the door and could hear the faint murmur of people talking. She wasn't sure if that was from the tenants or the responders, but she hadn't noticed it before.

"I think I hear voices."

"Good, that means that people are coming up with a plan to get the two of you out of there." The dispatcher was clicking away at her computer keys, and Ellie wondered what she was typing and to whom.

Ellie looked back at Lottie and saw that she was barely breathing.

"Lottie?" Ellie shook her shoulder gently. "Lottie, look at me!" A moment ago, she wanted her to stop looking at her so she would stop seeing the girl, but now all she could see was Lottie.

She watched as she gasped lightly and then exhaled. She didn't take another breath, and Ellie couldn't hold back the floodgates in her mind any longer.

"What's going on? Talk to me, Ellie."

"She stopped breathing. What do I do!? I can't save her! She isn't breathing." Ellie gasped, dropping the phone, and pushed herself away from Lottie as quickly as possible. Unable to accept what she was watching. Her face had changed into the little girl's face again, and Ellie was transported back to the side of the road.

It smelled like burning tires, and metal creaked and groaned. She could hear voices, and she called out for help. She looked at the girl's face. She was gasping for air and reaching out to Ellie for help.

"Ellie, help me!" The girl cried as she reached out for Ellie.

"I can't. I don't know what to do." Ellie sobbed. She had watched this girl die in her mind and dreams for months, and she had never even thought to reach out to the girl.

"I can't breathe, Ellie. Don't leave me."

Ellie put her hand out and into the girl's outstretched hand. "I won't leave you, Maggie."

The voices grew as people approached the twisted metal, and Ellie could hear the grunts of adults as they pulled the twisted metal and debris off the two girls. She could hear other children crying and begging for help. They were all trapped together.

Ellie was against a window, and she turned to see the trees that lined the roadside.

"Ellie, it hurts," Maggie said. Tears were streaming down her face, and suddenly she was gasping in pain. Someone was pulling metal, and it was stuck in Maggie's side.

Ellie could see the metal being pulled away from Maggie's chest. She started to push it to help, thinking that getting the twisted yellow metal off her friend would make it easier for her to breathe, but instead, she was gasping more, and Ellie saw the glint of red oozing dark and ominous down the front of Maggie's shirt.

"Stop! Stop! You are hurting her!" Ellie yelled to the voices on the other side. She tried pulling the metal back, but the damage was done. Maggie was gasping for air, but it was all escaping with the blood coming out of her chest, and Ellie couldn't make it stop.

"I can't breathe." Maggie gasped. Her mouth opened and closed like a fish suffocating on a dock. Ellie cried as she watched her friend's gasping become shallower. She held Maggie's hand, and after a few minutes, the breaths stopped coming, and the hand went slack.

Ellie lay next to her best friend and waited for the voices to come for her. She listened to the children crying and stared at Maggie's face. Her face was relaxed and peaceful, and Ellie hated knowing that it was like that because she was dead, but when she closed her eyes, she saw the pain in her friend's eyes, and she would rather see her this way.

It took hours for the metal to be cleared and for the adults to find Ellie lying in the dark with Maggie in her arms. Someone picked her up, carried her out of the twisted metal of the yellow school bus, and placed her on a stretcher in the back of an ambulance.

CHAPTER
TWENTY-EIGHT

ELLIE WOKE UP IN THE HOSPITAL. HER ARMS WERE STRAPPED down, and she pulled at the restraints. Something was beeping, and its rise in tempo matched the pounding in her chest. She looked around the room and saw her mom asleep in a chair across the room. Eric was in the chair next to the bed, his feet propped up on the stark white hospital mattress.

"Eric?" Ellie's voice came out hoarse and weak. She cleared her throat and tried again.

Eric woke with a start and sat up to look at Ellie.

"El, you're awake." Eric sighed and wiped a hand across his face. "We were so worried."

"What happened?" Ellie pulled at her restraints again. "What's with these?"

"When they finally got the door open to the elevator, you were hysterical. They couldn't get you to calm down, and you were hitting everyone that came near you. You kept trying to pull out the iv, and they decided you were a danger to yourself, so they put you in restraints. Now that you are calm, they will take them off. Let me get a nurse."

"Wait, Eric. Before Mom wakes up. I remembered some-thing while I was in the elevator. I remember being trapped and watching Maggie die. I remembered Maggie, my best friend from third grade. Do you remember her? I have been having flashes of her for months, and I couldn't place her, and I finally remembered. She died. I can't remember every-thing that happened, though.... It feels like that time has been erased from my memory. Am I crazy?"

"Shit, uh, I can't believe you remembered that." Eric looked over at their mom to make sure she was still asleep. "Listen, El, that was a long time ago, and I promised Mom and Dad I would never talk about it. We all decided that it was best if you didn't remember... I promised I wouldn't ever say anything to you." Eric looked at Ellie and bit into his bottom lip. "I guess since you already remembered, that changes things a little."

"Yeah, I would say so. I remember watching her die, her name, and being trapped and taken into an ambulance, but I can't remember before or after. Please, Eric, just tell me what happened?"

Eric sighed heavily and rubbed his hand over his face. He looked at his mom again to be extra sure she was asleep and then leaned forward.

"You were on a school field trip. You guys were heading to some Museum. I don't remember the name. It was so long ago now. A motorcycle cut in front of the bus, and the driver swerved to miss it. He over-corrected. The bus was going downhill, and it rolled several times. Your entire class was on that bus. You and Maggie were trapped, and so were a couple of others. When they finally reached you, Maggie was dead, and you were catatonic. They couldn't get you to speak. They brought you to the hospital, and it took days for you to say a word finally. When you finally started talking, you couldn't remember what happened. The doctor said that children often repress traumatic experiences. Mom and Dad decided not to talk about it. Pretend it didn't happen. They thought that would be the best thing for you. We moved to Oaks Valley, and you went to a new school. It never came up again." Everything came out in a rushed hush. Eric's worried eyes roamed her face.

Ellie felt tears running down her cheeks, and she shook her head at Eric. "I can't believe you went along with that. I have been thinking I'm crazy for months. You guys just left me in the dark, and I went crazy trying to find my way out."

"You are not crazy, El. I am so sorry. I should have told you, but I watched you suffering in the hospital, and you wouldn't even talk to me. I thought you were going to starve yourself to death. We thought you were going to have to be committed. And then, one day, it was like your mind decided to survive, pushing everything into a box or something, and you were back. I didn't know you were seeing her face now, or I would have told you." Eric had his face in his hands again, and he looked sincerely distraught.

"I have been having nightmares for months. Since my accident with the deer. I have been seeing her face and listening to her scream, and I thought it was all in my mind." Ellie pulled at the restraints again. "I want out of these things. Get someone to take them off, now!"

When Ellie shouted, her mom jumped up. She looked around, suddenly awake and disoriented. "Elizabeth, darling, you are awake!"

"You should have told me about Maggie," Ellie shouted at her surprised mother. Sarah's open-mouthed shock turned her between Ellie and Eric. "They are treating me like I am crazy. They have me tied down. Why didn't you just tell me the truth? Why do you hide everything?"

"We don't hide everything. What are you talking about, Ellie? Darling, just calm down." Sarah was wringing her hands and reaching for her cell phone, which was still sitting on the chair where she slept.

"Dad and Eric picking up roadkill? Roping my boyfriend into doing it too? Thanks for that. By the way. I am sure that is part of why he dumped me. You let me think I am crazy."

"Eric, you told her!?"

"No, she remembered. She asked me about Maggie, and so I told her. I am done lying. We should have told her from the beginning. That doctor even told you that back when Maggie died. He said that it was normal for children to repress traumas but that we should get her help from a therapist so that she could work through the trauma. Well, this is why!"

A nurse stood in the doorway as the family yelled at each other. James was standing behind her with his eyes wide and darting back and forth between them.

"Is everything okay in here?" The nurse asked, looking between Sarah and Eric. Then she noticed Ellie, who had been quietly listening to her brother, stand up for her and went into nurse mode. "You're awake."

She walked to Ellie's bedside and started checking her vitals. "Can you tell me your name and where you are?"

"My name is Ellie Finn, and I'm in the hospital."

"Good. I think that we can take these restraints off then." She smiled at Ellie and started to undo the soft padded ties on her wrists. "I will page the doctor to come talk to you."

"Thank you," Ellie said. The nurse removed the soft restraints, and Ellie pulled her hands together to rub her wrists.

The family waited silently for the nurse to leave and

then continued until the silence pressed down on them, begging for someone to speak.

"You know?" Ellie's dad asked. His eyebrows were furrowed, and she could see the pain and concern in his eyes. Her dad had always tried to protect her, and she felt a tug of sympathy for him even though anger still rolled through her making her limbs shake uncontrollably.

"Yeah, Dad. I remembered."

"How did you know about the roadkill?"

"Dane told me."

"That jerk-off. I knew we couldn't trust him." James was talking to Eric now.

"Oh, that's the problem!? You guys have been lying to me for how long? Why didn't you tell me about Maggie? What else have you kept from me?" Ellie could feel her blood boiling. Her family had kept her in the dark for over half her life.

"Nothing. Honey, you repressed the accident on your own. We just thought it was better for you to forget. We didn't want you to be in pain." Ellie's mom talked softly and gently, but it had the opposite effect.

"Yeah, well, it didn't work. I want you to leave. All of you. Just get out." Ellie clenched her teeth and her fists; she couldn't remember a time that she had ever been as angry as she was at this moment.

Her parents both looked utterly shocked. Eric was the only one that moved toward the door at her request. He stopped when he was next to their mom and whispered something in her ear. He put his hand on her arm and guided her out the door.

Ellie closed her eyes and rolled to her side. She didn't want to watch them leave even though she had told them to go.

The doctor came in a few minutes later, and Ellie was ready with a handful of questions. The first was to ask about Lottie. She knew the answer already but needed to hear it from someone else.

"The woman I was with in the elevator, Charlotte, did she die?"

"Yes, unfortunately, she lost a lot of blood, and her heart was weak. There wasn't anything that you could have done." The doctor looked at Ellie with his best sympathetic doctor face. But she wasn't paying attention.

She had watched Lottie die. She had been there with her as she took her last breath. Her chest tightened, but the doctor was still talking, so she tried to pay attention.

"You have a slight concussion to go with your head laceration. While you were out, we put in twenty-one stitches and did a full-body CT. You have two broken ribs on the left side of your chest and a fracture in the wrist on that side. It seems you took most of the impact on that left side."

Ellie nodded, but she didn't know what to say. She was still stuck on the fact that she watched someone she cared about die. Another someone. And she finally knew who the girl's face belonged to.

She always thought that if she found out who it was, she would feel some relief, but it wasn't a relief at all. She struggled to remember her friend Maggie, but her head felt like it was searching through a fog.

"Can I have my phone?" Ellie felt numbness spreading through her, but she needed to get ahold of Clara. Someone needed to take Zeke out. Thinking about Zeke made her choke on tears.

The doctor got her phone and told her to page a nurse if

she needed anything else and that he would check in on her the next day before she was discharged.

Ellie wondered if Nick knew what had happened. She wanted to text him, but calling Clara would be hard enough.

The phone rang three times before Clara picked up. She sounded so happy.

Ellie gasped for air, trying to get the words out. Lottie popped into her mind. She squeezed her eyes shut. She thought that Maggie and Lottie would both haunt her now.

CHAPTER
TWENTY-NINE

Ellie woke up to a nurse in her room typing on the computer keyboard in the corner. She turned with a syringe in her hand, and when she saw that Ellie was awake, she smiled kindly.

"Hey honey, I'm glad to see you awake. My name is Charmaine. I'm your nurse for the night."

Ellie murmured a weak greeting and looked out the window to try and assess the time. She thought about Nick again and knew he would be worried about her by now.

"What time is it?" She asked Charmaine.

"It's four thirty, honey. I'm going to give you this medication for pain, which might make you a little drowsy. If you fall asleep, they will wake you when they bring dinner."

Ellie watched as Charmaine twisted the syringe onto the port from her iv and pushed the plunger down. She felt the cool liquid entering her veins and waited to feel drowsy and forget about Maggie and Lottie.

The forgetting never came, though, and her mind was

churning with the need to know what else she had repressed from her childhood.

Charmaine returned after a while, and Ellie was wringing her hands around her phone. She had called Clara again and made sure that Zeke was okay. They had cried for what felt like forever on the phone, but in reality, it was only ten minutes.

"How ya doin' honey?" Charmaine asked.

"I don't know. I want to write to my boyfriend, but I am scared." Tears pricked at the back of Ellie's eyes. She blinked to close the gates.

"Scared of your boyfriend?"

"I lost a boyfriend because of being accident-prone. I don't want to lose this one too."

"Honey, if you lose a guy over something like that, he is worth losing."

Ellie couldn't help but smile a little at that. She didn't tell Charmaine that. She also just didn't want to have to tell the story again. The story of Lottie, the woman she had come to love like the grandmother she had never had in just a few short weeks. The story of watching not one but two people die in her life.

All that aside, she just wanted to message Nick and tell him she was okay. If only her message could be that simple. Nick had called her twice and left her a voicemail and ten text messages. The last one was telling her that he was heading to the apartment to check on her because he didn't have any numbers for her family, and he was distraught that he hadn't heard from her.

"Looks like he really wants to hear from you," Charmaine said, looking over at her. "I'm gonna give you some space to call that worried boy back."

Charmaine gave Ellie an encouraging wink and left her

alone to stare at the call button. She took a deep breath and hit send.

AN HOUR LATER, Clara came rushing in, gushing hysterically. "Ellie! Oh my god! Are you okay?" Clara reached out and touched Ellie's shoulder lightly. She looked at the iv and the beeping machines and pulled her hand back cautiously.

"Yeah. I'm alright. How's Zeke?"

"He is fine. I brought his bed over to our place and left him with Jesse. He is going to come pick me up in a while. I know you said I didn't have to come, but that's ridiculous. I had to come." Clara choked on her emotions, and tears sprang from her eyes again, which brought Ellie down too.

Clara grabbed a handful of tissues and started wiping at her face. After she got the bulk of the snot and tears, she looked around as if for the first time.

"Where is your family? I thought they would all be here." This was not the first time she had been in a hospital room with Ellie, and she knew that her family never left her side during times of need.

"They were here, but they went home." Ellie felt herself shutting down. She didn't want to talk about her family. She didn't want to think about how betrayed she felt by them. She didn't want to think about the questions that were left unanswered. She just wanted to go home and pretend none of this ever happened. Now that she knew who the girl's face belonged to, she thought that would be enough to put it to rest.

"That's weird. I feel like your family is always here."

"Yeah, well, they have things to do, and like I said, I'm fine."

"You don't look fine. You look like you are turning into a walking bruise."

"Yeah. But Lottie is dead. So, it kind of puts bruises and stitches into perspective."

"I can't believe this happened. I can't believe she is gone." New tears threatened, and Ellie had to shake her head. She just couldn't cry anymore right now. She had been crying for hours.

"I don't want to talk about it, Clara. I'm more worried about the fact that you still have to get back to Burbank for your audition tomorrow. Who will take care of Zeke if they don't let me out of here?"

"When I heard my best friend and roomie got thrown around an elevator that crashed to the ground and another friend had died, I called and asked my agent to postpone my auditions. I have priorities, you know."

Ellie gave a weak smile. She felt the buzz of her phone before the sound reached her ears, and she picked it up right away. It was Nick. He said he was on his way to the hospital, and he asked what room number she was in. Ellie told him and put the phone back down. She wanted to see Nick but didn't want to see anyone.

Clara was watching her, "Who was that?"

"Nick. He is heading over." Ellie was starting to feel the drag of the drugs that Charmaine had given her, and she was trying to fight it off.

"Ellie, you don't seem alright. Are you sure you are okay?"

"Yeah, I'm fine. I just don't want to talk about it."

The two girls were silently staring at each other when Jesse came in. He looked between the two girls, and his eyes widened like he had walked into a bear's den, and he wanted to turn and make a run for it.

"Everything okay here?" Jesse asked.

"Yeah, everything is fine." Clara stood up and gave Jesse a quick kiss.

Ellie's eyes closed without her permission, and when she opened them again, she had to fight back the cotton film holding them shut. It felt as though she had only closed them for a minute, but she realized when she heard Nick's voice that it had been a little while. She tried to open her eyes, but her eyelids were too heavy to lift, so she just listened.

"When I got to the building to check on her, the elevator was taped off, but I had no idea what happened. I wish I had given her parents or brother my number so I could have been here earlier. I can't believe she was here alone all day," Nick said to Clara.

"Well, I texted Eric, and I guess they were here most of the day. But when she woke up, there was a "family issue," and she sent them away. He wouldn't tell me what the issue was."

"That's weird. They seem so close."

"I'm really worried. I don't know how much Ellie told you, but death freaks her out, and she watched Lottie die."

"She has told me a little, but there are a few times I felt like she was holding back. Like her car accident that happened right before Dane broke up with her, what happened then?"

"She saw an animal almost get hit by a car, and she swerved and hit a tree. It was awful. If she sees roadkill, it triggers her anxiety. And then there was the thing that happened with the deer."

"What happened with the deer?"

"She didn't tell you about her big accident? She hit a deer on that back road to the beach and couldn't get a hold of anyone. She watched the deer die. Then the deer's face changed, and she saw the face of a little girl dying. It has been haunting her and giving her nightmares ever since. It's been months. I'm surprised she didn't tell you that."

"She told me that she has been having nightmares, and she told me about the accident, but she didn't tell me about the thing with the deer."

"Probably because she didn't want you to think she was crazy."

"Crazy? I would never think that."

"Well, that's why Dane dumped her."

"He was an ass."

Jesse hadn't spoken up until then, "Yeah, he was. I never liked that guy."

"He was the worst," Ellie said finally.

"Ellie," Nick was at her side in an instant. Ellie opened her eyes to a thin slit and tried to give him a reassuring smile, but it was lacking.

"You scared me. You didn't answer my calls. I went to your apartment, and the elevator was all sectioned off as a crime scene. No one would tell me anything." Nick was starting to sound a little choked up, and the emotion in his voice made Ellie perk up a little. Her eyes widened to see him better, even though she felt like she was pulling sandpaper off them.

"I'm sorry. When they brought me in, I was out of it and didn't get my phone right away..." Ellie trailed off. She knew she didn't need to make excuses because that was not what Nick was implying. He wasn't trying to make her feel bad about anything, but she still did. She still felt guilty for making him worry.

"Don't worry about that, babe," Nick said, squeezing her hand. "I want to know why you sent your family away?"

Ellie stiffened. She looked at Nick and Clara. They were both watching her expectantly. She wasn't sure she wanted to talk about her family because she knew it would lead to talking about Maggie, and she didn't want to talk about that yet. She needed to wrap her head around it and figure out what else she was missing.

"I don't want to talk about it," Ellie said.

Clara frowned and started to speak, but Jesse put his hand on her shoulder. She clamped her mouth shut and sat back further in her chair. Nick looked from Ellie to Clara and sighed.

"Okay, if you aren't ready, that's fine."

He looked like he wanted to say something else, but Charmaine came in, and all attention went to her.

"Alright, honey, the doctor says you are staying the night with us. And visiting hours are almost up," She paused and looked around the room for emphasis. "But if you want someone to stay with you, the chair over there folds out."

"I'll stay with her," Nick said. He gave Ellie a wink, and she smiled a little. It was hard to feel happy at the moment, not with the loss of Lottie and all the thoughts churning in her mind, but Nick was helping.

Nick pulled the chair that was also a bed up alongside Ellie's hospital bed to show he was set for the night. He pulled and pushed on it until it opened up into something that resembled a bed but looked more like a broken chair. When it wouldn't unfold anymore, he took it for a test drive. The chair squeaked viciously under his weight. Nick got up and looked back at the ugly beige pleather.

"Well, I better not move while I'm sleeping."

Clara was wringing her hands and whispering to Jesse. Ellie couldn't determine what was being said but knew

Clara well enough to guess that she was worried about something.

"Clara, don't you guys need to start heading back to check on Zeke? He is probably anxious about not being with Lottie and being in a new place."

"Yeah, we will go," Clara was still eyeing her nervously. "Are you sure you will be okay?"

"I will be fine. Nick is here with me, and I will just be sitting around here. You go and take care of him. Animals grieve for their owners too, you know."

"Okay..." Clara smiled weakly. "I will call you tomorrow. Love ya."

Clara hugged Ellie, and then she turned to leave with Jesse, but on her way out the door, she whispered to Nick to text her if anything happened. They thought Ellie didn't hear, but she did, and she felt herself recede further at the thought of everyone watching her like she was about to break down.

"How are you, feelin' honey?" Charmaine asked, poking her head in the room.

"I'm alright. Do you know when I can go home?"

"They will probably release you tomorrow, but I have no way of knowing, hun. Not until they give me the order. You page me if your pain gets bad." She said as she walked out of the room as fast as she had come in.

An orderly came in with Ellie's dinner a moment later, and it didn't look bad. She was so hungry she probably would have eaten anything, though. Nick left to get food and a change of clothes, but he was back before Ellie had finished her potatoes and gravy.

"That was fast."

"I didn't want to leave you for too long. You might have gotten tempted to steal my awesome bed." Nick winked, and Ellie felt a twinge of pain in her side when she let a small laugh sneak out. She sucked in a breath, and her face went pale.

"Are you okay?" Nick hovered over her, "Should I page the nurse?"

Ellie nodded. It felt like someone was sitting on her chest. She could breathe shallowly, but any deep breaths were impossible. Her ribs were trying to hold tight with the pain, and her lungs were screaming for more air.

Charmaine came into the room as soon as Nick pushed the button and took one look at Ellie's face. "Looks like the pain came back. I'll get you something. Hold on, honey."

She was back almost instantly with a syringe full of clear liquid and some water. "These are pretty good, though, so you should be fine through the night. I was just waiting to see what your pain threshold was. You are a pretty tough cookie."

Ellie watched as the liquid flowed into her arm and thought about the "tough cookie" comment while she was swallowing the water Charmaine had brought.

Her mouth had suddenly gone dry when the pain started. She tried to take another sip of water, and it went down the wrong way making her splutter and cough. She thought momentarily that she might choke and die from water.

She didn't think thoughts like that were so challenging.

She had to repress the fact that her best friend had died in front of her to make it through life this long, and that felt weak too. She wondered what else she had forgotten from her past because she was too weak to deal with it. Tears pooled in the corners of her eyes, and she looked up at the ceiling to try and balance all the liquid. It would come spilling out if she blinked, and she didn't want that. She wanted to be a "tough cookie."

"Honey, it is okay to cry," Charmaine said, watching her. "You have been through a trauma, and you are hurtin', so you go ahead and let those tears out."

She gave Ellie a gentle pat on the shoulder, then turned and left the room. Ellie watched her go, and Nick came back to her side. He had moved away to give Charmaine room, and she could see the worried look on his face.

"Ellie, are you sure you don't want your family here? Or maybe just Eric? She is right, you just went through a trauma, and that is the best time to have family around."

"Not when they cause more trauma," Ellie grumbled. She knew it was the wrong thing to say. By the look on Nick's face, she had just made him even more worried.

"Okay, tell me what happened. Please?"

Ellie shook her head. She wasn't ready to talk about it with Nick even though she was pretty sure he wouldn't judge her. She still needed to get things figured out in her head first.

"Let's talk about it tomorrow. I think I can feel those drugs kicking in, and I want to get some rest." Ellie made a show of closing her eyes and wincing.

She didn't want Nick to press her for more information because if he did, she would talk just to keep him from feeling like she didn't want him around. She knew she couldn't avoid the questions forever but could at least avoid them for the night. Maybe this was how things started back when Maggie died, avoidance until mind numbness.

THIRTY

ELLIE HAD TO CONVINCE NICK TO GO TO WORK THE NEXT morning. He wanted to stay with her and call an employee to open the store, but she assured him she would be fine. She just wanted to be alone for a little while, and she hated the idea of Nick watching over her with a worried look all day.

It was almost lunchtime when the doctor returned and told her that she would be discharged. He wanted her to follow up with an orthopedist as soon as possible and her regular physician in a few days. He said it would take several weeks for the ribs to heal, so he gave her a prescription for the pain, which she wouldn't take because it would make her anxious. But he didn't need to know that.

"Do you have any other questions or concerns, Miss Finn?"

"Well, I have a question that is a little unrelated." Ellie had been building herself up to ask about her repressed trauma for hours.

She had told herself that she shouldn't ask because they might think she was crazy and commit her, but she had made herself feel better by thinking about all the ways that it could help. The doctor was looking at her expectantly.

"I just wonder about repressed memories. I guess I have repressed some stuff and wanted to know what that means and what I should do...." Ellie trailed off before an actual question came out. She lost her confidence as soon as she started speaking, and she felt foolish as the words tumbled out of her.

"Well, when stress or trauma is severe enough, the mind can repress the memories as a sort of survival technique. The mind goes into survival mode, and neurological adaptations develop to block the memories of trauma that are continuing to cause mental distress."

"So, what do I do if they are starting to come back up?"

"Are they causing you stress?"

"Well, I have been having nightmares."

"I would recommend seeing a therapist. Talking about the memories that are returning can help you start understanding them and make them less painful."

He was observing Ellie, and she thought he might be trying to decide his legal obligations to her mental state. She nodded and smiled but was afraid to say anything else. She didn't want to dig a deeper hole. And she already had an appointment for Monday, so there wasn't much else to say.

"I have a doctor that I would recommend for that if you are interested. I will have the nurse bring in her name and contact info with your discharge papers. Take care, Miss Finn." The doctor gave her a last cursory glance and left the room.

He must have decided that he had done his due diligence. Ellie wondered if the doctor who had seen her when she was eight and had just been in a bus accident had decided the same thing the day he discharged her all those years ago.

The morning nurse, who was not Charmaine, came in moments later with a smile and a stack of papers. She went over all the monotonous paperwork telling Ellie what to look for and where to go if she had any complications. It advised her everything she would ever need to know about broken ribs and fractured wrists. She was prescribed pills likely to cause addiction which scared Ellie more than pain. She signed every paper that asked for acknowledgment, and the last thing the nurse handed to her was a referral to Francine Weinberg, the therapist she had already called.

Ellie stared at the name and felt anxiety wave through her. She wanted to figure out what she was forgetting, but what if talking made her remember worse things? What if she felt worse about everything? What if her anxiety got worse?

"Miss. Finn?" The nurse said her name expectantly. Ellie knew she had missed something.

"I'm sorry. What did you ask me?"

"Do you have a ride home?"

Shit. Ellie forgot about that. She needed a ride home.... She would have to call Nick.

"I can call my boyfriend."

"Before we can release you, he will have to come up to check you out. We can't send you out of the hospital without a way home. Page me when he gets here." She turned and left the room, taking the giant stack of papers with her and leaving only a little pile behind for Ellie.

She sighed and pulled her phone out. Nick would have to leave work to come and pick her up. She knew he wouldn't mind, but it still made her feel like a burden. She dialed his number, and he answered immediately.

Ellie told Nick she needed a ride, and he promised to be there as quickly as possible. She thought he must be pretty worried about her if he was willing to drop everything to pick her up. It felt rather nice.

After they hung up, she looked at her other messages and saw that Eric and her mom had each sent her several messages. Her mom apologized and said she only did what she thought was best. She asked Ellie in each message to get back to her and let her know if she was okay and safe at home. The last message simply said: *I love you.*

Eric's messages were exactly his style; big - protective, indignant brother. He told her it wasn't his fault and that he was just going along with their parent's wishes. He said he should have told her, and he was sorry. His last message was: *Write me back, dude. I'm worried about you.* She thought about writing him back. She wanted to write him back. But something in her kept her from typing the words she wanted to say.

She was still staring at her phone when Nick walked in. He strode over and kissed her. It was a careful kiss that made her feel breakable.

"Let's bust you out of here, babe."

"I just have to call the nurse," Ellie said as she reached for the call button. She hit the button with the nurse icon, and like magic, the nurse appeared in the doorway.

"I see your boyfriend is here. You are free to leave," She smiled at Ellie and pulled a wheelchair up to the bed. She helped Ellie into the chair and had Nick sign one last paper acknowledging that he was responsible for getting Ellie home safely.

The nurse walked Ellie through the hospital halls in the chair. She felt like an invalid. She thought it was a little unnecessary, but it wasn't until they got to the elevator to go downstairs that Ellie felt like revolting.

Her nerves were crawling, her throat tightening, and her stomach flipped.

You are okay, Ellie.

Just breathe.

You don't want to freak out in front of Nick.

You are okay.

Breathe.

Breathe.

Breathe.

It didn't matter how much she told herself to breathe. She wasn't breathing. She was panting. She could barely take a full breath. As they wheeled into the elevator, Ellie clenched her hands tightly on the armrests of the wheelchair.

The doors closed, and she could hear the whirring of the elevator cords. She closed her eyes, and Lottie was there, bleeding on the floor. Ellie gasped, and her eyes flew open. She looked wildly around the elevator for a way out, and Nick was suddenly looking into her eyes.

"Ellie," Nick put his hands on either side of her face. "You are okay. Just breathe, honey."

Ellie nodded to let him know she could hear him but was still gasping for air. Every gasp was sharp, and her ribs were protesting the effort that was going into filling her lungs. When the door opened, Ellie felt the air hit her, and the coolness let her know that she had tears running down her cheeks. The nurse stopped the wheelchair before the lobby doors.

"Are you okay, sweetie?" She looked concerned as she watched Ellie and then looked to Nick for answers.

"Her accident was in an elevator. I think she was just afraid to be back in one. Right, babe?"

"Yeah," Ellie said breathlessly. "I'm okay."

The nurse looked skeptical, but she continued to wheel Ellie out into the sunshine and pulled her to a stop at the curb where Nick's Jeep was waiting for them.

Nick helped her out of the wheelchair and into the car's passenger side. He buckled her in so she wouldn't have to twist her chest or use her wrist. After she was safely inside, the nurse gave them a nod and a wave and walked back into the hospital.

Ellie was glad to be leaving but only felt it on the surface. Her soul felt cold and distant. She could feel herself shutting down and felt the pang of familiarity like she had been here once before.

IT HAD BEEN a week since Ellie was sent home from the hospital, and her life had quickly spiraled down a long dark drain dripping with denial and depression. She mostly slept in her bed and only left the room when the apartment was empty to watch TV to go to the bathroom.

"Ellie, I know you want to be left alone, but it has been days... I'm worried about you." Clara said, suddenly appearing in the doorway.

Ellie rolled over in her bed. She couldn't bring herself to face anyone. She wasn't eating or answering her phone, and she wasn't going to work.

"I am leaving for work! If you don't leave your bed by the time I get back today, I am having Jesse and Nick drag you out!"

She heard Clara's footsteps echoing down the hall and

squeezed her eyes shut. When her eyes closed, she saw Maggie's face, and when she opened her eyes and stared at the ceiling, she thought about Lotte. If it weren't for Zeke, she would be alone, which is what she wanted most of the time.

She had canceled her first therapy appointment with Dr. Weinberg. It was good that she hadn't told Clara about that, or she would have made her attend. She just couldn't bring herself to talk about everything that haunted her.

She felt a heaviness in her chest all day long. She only felt better when she was sleeping, and that was only if she wasn't dreaming.

Maggie wasn't the only one tormenting her dreams anymore. She would often start dreaming about Lottie in the elevator, and right when she was about to die, her face would morph into Maggie's gasping face. The pain on their faces as they died behind her eyes day after day made her want to die with them.

Her phone was so full that it was no longer accepting voicemails, and she had received hundreds of messages from her family and Nick. Everyone had tried stopping by but gave up after the first five days of no contact. She was given leave from work, but her time was ending, and she wasn't answering Ana's calls either.

After Clara left the apartment each day, Ellie would leave the room to watch trash TV, and she didn't move from the couch until Clara was due to be home. She didn't answer the door, and she didn't eat. She tried to eat at first, but she never felt hungry anymore. Only sad, lost, and, most of all, confused.

THIRTY-ONE

CLARA CAME HOME EARLY, AND ELLIE WAS STILL IN THE LIVING room watching TV. She tried to get up and go to the room, but Clara jumped on the opportunity to jump on Ellie and force her to talk.

Zeke jumped up in excitement and started bouncing around between them. He whined for the attention to be on him and rubbed against Ellie, who was quickly becoming his whole world. Ellie might be depressed and struggling, but she still made the effort to take him potty and cuddle with him.

"Ellie, you need to snap out of this. It's been weeks. Whatever this is, it isn't healthy. It isn't you." Clara scolded while reaching down to pat Zeke on the head. They learned that if you didn't give Zeke attention when he asked for it, you would never hear the end of it.

Ellie stayed quiet. Tears welled up in her eyes. She knew that Clara was right but didn't know what to do. She wanted to return to her usual self, the self she was before her accident with the deer. But now she knew that even then, she wasn't herself. She didn't know who she was anymore.

"I talked to Nick today. He said he messaged you to tell you he wants to take a break, but he asked me to tell you, too, since he doesn't know if you will read it. He said he didn't know what else to do since you won't see him or answer his calls or texts. You have completely pushed him away, and for what? Does that help you? I know he loves you, and maybe this is just an attempt to snap you out of it, but I think you might lose him. You have been home for a couple of weeks and have refused to see or talk to anyone. This isn't how people react to life. Okay? You need to woman up."

Clara was blocking the way to Ellie's bed now. Her arms were crossed, and the glare she was giving could have fried Ellie's skin off.

Ellie knew she needed to talk, but when she opened her mouth, all that came out was a sob. She couldn't eat, sleep, think straight, or sort her feelings. And she had pushed everyone who loved her away. She told her parents and Eric that she didn't want to talk to them or see them ever again, she barely spoke to Clara, and now Nick had lost his patience and dumped her. She thought his patience was limitless, but she had been wrong. She continued to sob as she thought all this through, and Clara stepped closer to put her arm around Ellie.

"Ellie? Talk to me?"

"I don't know who I am," Ellie said. She looked into Clara's eyes, needing something she couldn't comprehend.

"What do you mean?"

"I remembered who the face of the little girl belonged to, but I can't remember what happened before the memory of her dying. I can't remember being friends with her, but I can feel that she was my best friend. I can't remember anything about her. I can't remember anything about me before that point either."

"Maybe you will feel better if you find out more about her."

"No. I just want to forget about her and move on. Maybe I don't remember for a reason. Maybe my mind is making her out to be more than she is. I don't know." Ellie put her head in her hands and shook her face so her nose skimmed across her palms.

"So, your plan is just to repress the memory again and repress this new memory with it? How is that going to work?"

"I don't know. I don't remember how long it took last time. I assume I will wake up one day, and it won't hurt anymore. I want to forget Maggie and Lottie."

"Ellie, come on… There is no way that is going to work."

"It worked before. It will work again. Everything was fine for fourteen years. I had anxiety, sure, but it was never like this. I can't live like this. Every time I close my eyes, Maggie is dying right in front of me, and every time I open them, Lottie is bleeding to death on the elevator floor." Ellie choked on the words, and Clara finally allowed her to walk to her bed, but she followed.

"Well, I don't want to forget Lottie. I asked the landlord today if we could move into her apartment. It's bigger and has two bedrooms which would be great. Plus, it's close, and Zeke is already used to it."

Ellie stared at her mouth agape. How could she move into Lottie's apartment? She would never repress the memory of her if she were constantly reminded by where she lived. But she also couldn't very well not go with Clara if this was what she wanted. Where else would she go? Back to her parents? No way.

"He said yes," Clara added when Ellie didn't answer. "We move in next week. And I am going to need your help because I said we would help with Lottie's things. That's one of the reasons we were able to get in so fast."

Clara didn't seem to want an answer to that. It was an order, not a question. She turned and left the room, leaving Ellie to continue working through the heavy fog of thoughts in her mind.

Ellie couldn't believe that Nick had dumped her. And through Clara too. Although, she guessed she hadn't given him a choice.

She pulled out her phone and started looking through her messages. She had so many that she couldn't keep up with the numbers but everyone in her family had written to her several times, she had double the messages from Nick, and she had a few from Ana. She listened to the voicemails and deleted them one by one until her phone screen was free of red dots with numbers.

Nick had sent her a text telling her what Clara had already. He was so sorry he couldn't talk to her in person, but she wouldn't let him. He still wanted to be with her, but she seemed to need to focus on herself. And please let him know when she was ready to be in a relationship that leaned and trusted in one another.

She wanted to be mad. In fact, she tried to think about how rude and selfish Nick was for dumping her during such a hard time for her and for doing it through a text. But then a little voice in her mind pointed out that he probably wouldn't be dumping her if she leaned on him and included him in her struggle. And he probably wouldn't have sent a text if she would allow him to come over and speak to her.

She had frozen him out since he brought her home from the hospital.

Tears pricked behind her eyes. She had pushed away the people she loved the most. And what was worse was she was starting to think they were right. Her parents let her repress the memory of Maggie dying, and she was mad when she found out because she felt like they were controlling her life. But now she was starting to think that they were right. She couldn't have handled this pain. And she was doing fine before she started to remember. She wanted to forget again.

She rolled over and fell asleep with the sun beating through the window. The stream of sunlight brought the twinkle of dust and light particles floating in a ray over her. She wanted to go to sleep and wake up without Maggie and Lottie haunting her. She wanted to wake up with Nick and without the burden of memories holding her back.

———

A COUPLE OF DAYS LATER, Eric had woken her up by throwing boxes at her, and when she saw him, relief flooded through her, and she asked the question that had been burning in her head. Now she had the covers pulled over her head to hide at least her eyes from him. Clara had asked him to come over to help them get ready to move. And now Ellie felt foolish and embarrassed about blurting out crazy-sounding questions.

"So, let me get this straight," Eric said. "You want me to tell you how you repressed your memories? The ones that you yelled at me for letting you repress. The ones that you haven't talked to me in almost two weeks because of?"

"Yeah," Ellie mumbled. "I'm tired of feeling this way, Eric. Maybe Mom and Dad were right."

Eric looked at her incredulously. "Are you going to apologize to Mom and Dad for your reaction? Mom has been a mess since you kicked us out of the hospital. It's not fair for you to say they are right but not tell them. If Mom knew I was here right now, do you know how much trouble I would be in?"

"You're right. I will call Mom. But first, can you just tell me everything? Everything that you remember."

"Well, honestly, you look like you are on your way. We didn't even do anything to make you repress it. You did it all yourself. We watched you, but you did it."

"How, though? I need to know how Eric is. I don't want to feel this way anymore, and I want to go back to the way things were before."

"I don't know how to explain it. You just shut down. It was like you shut down, and then when you rebooted, you didn't remember what happened, and you never talked about it again. At first, we thought you just didn't want to talk about it, and you were pretending that it hadn't happened, but after a while, we realized that you really couldn't remember what happened."

Ellie stared at Eric for a moment. She felt like she had already shut down. How could she shut down more than she already had...?

"How long did that take? What are we talking about here?"

"Look, El, I was ten. I don't remember how long it took. I just remember being worried about you. We were all really worried. And we are all really worried now."

Eric had gravitated over to the bed and sat down on the edge. Zeke's tail thumped against the bed, and scooted closer to Eric for some pats. Talk about attention-seeking behavior.

Ellie contemplated what she needed to do to reboot her brain. She wished there was a reset button to which she could stick the back of an earring and restart her brain so she couldn't remember the pain and sadness.

"What if we go home? Maybe being home in your old room would help you feel better."

Ellie felt tears pooling behind her eyes. She tried to blink them away, but they didn't retreat. They stayed teetering on the edge, waiting for their friends to join so they could jump over. Her chest clenched, and she gasped for air as sobs started to work through her body, finally shaking her and allowing the tears to be free.

Eric put his arm around her and held her as she cried. Once her shoulders finished shaking and her tears had run out, he took her home.

CHAPTER
THIRTY-TWO

Ellie spent the night at her parents' house. Zeke came along because when Eric dragged her out of the apartment, he refused to let her leave without him. He was a loyal boy.

The whole Finn family talked into the night about Ellie's accident, the one that started it all and the one that brought it all back. They hugged and cried and ate pasta with thick creamy alfredo sauce.

And by the time Clara was calling, worried that she had disappeared from the apartment, she felt like she had a better grip on her world. Eric took her back to her place, and she went to bed with new hope. She was going to start doing all the things that she hadn't been able to manage before because of her anxiety.

She thought about the card with the therapist's number on it. It was on her dresser with the rest of her hospital paperwork. She was tired of letting anxiety run her life, and it felt like admitting failure to seek help from a professional, but she was going to do it anyway.

Maybe a therapist could help her go back to school. She needed to go back and finish what she had always regretted not finishing- college. Her anxiety kept her from going to school, and now that she knew her anxiety better, she could handle it better.

Ellie took a shower and went into the living room to sit on the couch with Clara for the first time in over a week. Clara looked slightly startled when she sat down, but she quickly grabbed the remote and flipped to *Friends*. As the theme song began playing, Clara leaned closer to Ellie and put her head on her best friend's shoulder.

"I missed you," Clara said.

"I missed you too," Ellie said back.

Zeke whined and jumped up onto the couch between them and curled up. He sighed as if to say he missed them too.

Three episodes in, Clara cleared her throat. And she picked her head up off Ellie's shoulder.

"So, I'm happy you have come out of seclusion. I need to talk to you about something."

"Are you dumping me too because I became an ugly recluse?"

"I am not dumping you. And I don't think Nick dumped you, either. I think he was trying to give you some motivation. To snap out of it."

"Well, I think it may have worked... Cause I am out here. And I am starting to think I need to make some changes. Like I was sort of thinking that I want to go back to school. And I am going to start therapy."

"Really!? That's a great idea! What would you go back to school for?"

"I started to go for English. I always wanted to be a writer. I am not sure that I still want to be a writer. Maybe I will get a degree in Library Science."

"Why aren't you sure about writing anymore?"

"Well, just because I would have to talk to a lot of people if I worked with a writing team. So, I don't know how well I would do. If I do library science, I can be a librarian like Ana."

"That sounds good. Maybe you should just play it by ear. Just start with English and then go from there. You know you love English and books, so that is a good way to go. This is so exciting. I'm so excited for you. Can I go with you to the school to sign up?"

"Yes, please! I would love you to come with me." Ellie was starting to perk up. She felt real joy for the first time since the elevator accident.

Clara was beaming at Ellie, listing off the things they needed to do to get her ready to go back to school. Ellie was listening to Clara when it hit her that she never heard Clara's news.

"Wait, what were you going to tell me?" Ellie asked.

"Oh, right, I was going to tell you... Ugh, this is hard," Clara cringed and shifted uncomfortably. "I wasn't going to tell you yet, but you just seem so much better tonight...."

"Well, just tell me," Ellie said. She was getting anxious and didn't want to wait any longer. She needed to rip the bandage off.

"This is the thing," Clara paused again and took a deep breath. "I know we are supposed to move into Lottie's old place, but Jesse asked me to move in with him."

"Wow," Ellie said. "Wow. That's great."

Her face must have said otherwise because Clara started going on about how she wasn't planning on saying anything and they would wait for Ellie to feel better, of course, but that she didn't want to wait, and when Ellie seemed better, she got excited. Plus, she had to tell her before they went and moved into Lottie's place anyway.

She apologized and chewed her bottom lip while she waited for Ellie to answer. It took a while, but eventually, Ellie started to blink again, and her brain processed enough to be able to answer.

"It's great, Clara. I'm happy for you, I really am. I'm going to miss living with you, though."

"Well, you can keep the apartment. We can switch it to just your name. Jesse and I are going to find a place of our own. So, it is still going to be a little while."

"Maybe you guys could move into Lottie's place."

"Yeah, maybe." Clara smiled, but she didn't sound sure about that.

Ellie nodded, and they both returned to watching the show as the punchline hit and the laughter burst into the room.

She wasn't sure she was ready to live alone but willing to try. She was going to go back to school and live alone. Like an independent woman. Just with a bit of extra panic mixed in.

MONDAY MORNING ELLIE called the library to see if she still had a job. Ana said yes, that she still had a job but that this would likely be her last chance. She knew this was fair, and something about the fear of having no income and, therefore, no way to live alone motivated her to get herself together. In order to show her seriousness, she got ready and went to work an hour later.

It was hard to leave Zeke, but she gave him an extra pat and left him with his new duck toy. It was hard to walk past the elevator with the "Out of Order" sign still hung on the door. It was harder to drive to the library. But the hardest of all was to walk through the door that once brought her comfort and now gave her palpitations.

She pushed back the thoughts about Maggie and Lottie and got to work on the massive stacks of books around her desk. Ana had tried mending some while she was away, but it hadn't gone well.

Whenever someone tried to ask about the accident, she told them she didn't want to discuss it. She stuck to her desk and didn't leave until it was time to clock out.

"Ellie," Ana called after her as she was walking out the door. "You never took a lunch."

"Oh, I know. I was late, so I thought I shouldn't take a lunch."

"Well, next time, please take a lunch. You are allowed a break. I'm so glad to see you back, you know. We really missed you. How are you feeling after your first day back?" She looked at Ellie's wrist, which was still in a splint as she asked, and Ellie felt the topic of the accident coming, so she tried to brush it off.

"Oh, I'm fine," She said with a smile. She wanted to brush off the questions and make herself seem okay because she knew that would bring fewer questions.

"I'm so glad. Well, welcome back." She looked skeptical, but she smiled anyway.

Ellie smiled and nodded at Ana before turning quickly and walking out to her car. Clara was waiting for her in the parking lot.

"Hey girl, I thought I would go with you to the college. Let's go check out school registration."

"I thought you would be at work?" Ellie asked. She had told Clara the night before that she was planning on going to the community college to register, but as the day passed, she had talked herself into going tomorrow. Now that Clara was there, she felt she had to follow through.

"I took off. I wanted to go with you, and I have some big news!" Clara was vibrating with excitement.

Ellie couldn't help but smile at her enthusiasm. "What's the news?"

"I got a call back from my last audition! I got the part!" She jumped up and down, clapping her hands like a girl in a chick flick. Maybe she was practicing for her part.

She grabbed Ellie and danced her around before coming to a stop. They were panting a little from the exercise and Ellie a little more from her still tender ribs.

"Alright, now that I got that out of my system, let's go to the college!" She pulled Ellie over to her car and jumped in. Ellie slid quietly into the seat and tried to push her anxiety back. It took a lot of effort and concentration to keep her mind off the things haunting her. The images and thoughts screamed through her head like a freight train if she let her attention slip.

The two girls made their way to the college and were able to quickly put in an application and get Ellie registered for classes all at the same time. Apparently, when you go to a community college rather than a state university, the turnover time is more expedited. Ellie registered for two classes to start. The last time she tried college out, she registered for four, which had been too much, so she decided to cut it in half this time.

They left Oaks Valley Community College a few hours later, and Ellie felt pretty proud of herself. She wanted to call Nick and tell him all about it, but she knew she should give him space.

Clara had already told her that he wanted space until she was ready to be all in, and she knew that until she figured out how to be independent, she would never be truly prepared. She would always question if she was with him because he made her feel safe or because she actually wanted to be with him because of love alone.

"I'm so excited for you, Ellie," Clara said as they drove back to Ellie's car. "This is a new start for you. I think this will be good."

Ellie nodded even though she knew that Clara couldn't see her. She was still thinking about Nick. She wondered what he was doing and if he was moving on or if he would wait for her to get herself put back together. She was trying to hurry. She was registered for school and working hard to push away her anxieties.

"You miss Nick?" Clara asked, reading Ellie's mind. "I know he said to wait until you were ready, but maybe you could just let him know you are working on it. Give him reason to have hope."

"I have thought about it but don't know if I should. I don't want to bother him..." Ellie trailed off as she thought about the different fears behind that thought.

"Do you want me to write him for you? I could feel him out."

"No. I need to figure things out on my own, and then I will call him." Ellie looked out the window and sighed. She knew she needed to be patient, but she just wanted to hit the fast-forward button and reach the next step.

THIRTY-THREE

ELLIE WAS BRUSHING HER TEETH A WEEK LATER WHEN CLARA CAME bouncing into the bathroom.

"We found a place! We found a place!"

Clara and Jesse had been looking for places to move since announcing their plans to live together. Neither wanted to move into the other's place, so they decided to move into neutral territory. Which meant Lottie's place was out too.

Ellie thought it would take them longer to find a place, but here she was with her toothbrush hanging out of her mouth, nodding her head while listening to Clara and the details of the new apartment as they tumbled out of her at warp speed.

"Isn't that great!? Are you sure you are going to be okay here by yourself?" Clara's eyes were shining bright with excitement, and even though Ellie didn't feel sure about the whole living on her own thing, she wouldn't bring Clara down.

"Yeah. It will be great. I will finally be completely independent."

"Are you sure? I know it's only been a few weeks since the accident."

Ellie knew all too well how long it had been since *the* accident. It still haunted her dreams. She was doing better during the day. That was when she could control her thoughts and push out the thoughts of Maggie and Lottie. She hoped that if she succeeded in pushing out the thoughts during the day for long enough, she could also rid herself of the dreams.

Clara continued talking about moving plans and everything she needed to do to get ready to move as they both got ready for work. Ellie was starting classes next week, and Clara would also be moving next week.

A knot was starting to grow in Ellie's stomach as she thought about the coming week. She hoped this week would go slowly and give her time to prepare and wrap her head around things.

A knock at the door pulled Clara out of her vocal list-making. She ran for it, and Ellie immediately knew it must be Jesse. Clara only ran to the door for three reasons: pizza, Chinese food, and Jesse. It was too early for the first two.

Jesse and Clara came into the kitchen while Ellie was making herself breakfast. They were continuing Clara's previous solo conversation about packing and moving. It was decided, Ellie heard, that they would begin packing during the week so that when the weekend came, they could focus only on moving into their new apartment.

They were discussing moving options when they brought Ellie back into the conversation. When Clara called out her name, she was about to walk out the door for work, trying her best to stick to her routine to avoid anxiety over the coming changes.

"Do you think Eric would be willing to use his truck to help us move? You will help, right?"

"Of course," Ellie said. "Can we talk more about this when I get home?"

"We will definitely talk more about this when you get home from work." Clara giggled and turned back to Jesse. Ellie was sure they would talk about nothing else until Clara moved out.

TIME DIDN'T GO SLOWLY as Ellie had hoped. In fact, it seemed that the week went by at super speed, and now Ellie was standing in front of the college, gripping the new bookbag that Clara helped her pick out along with the rest of her school supplies. She still hadn't made a therapy appointment, but she was starting to think maybe that could wait. Maybe College was enough of a step for now.

After getting Clara all moved into her new apartment with Jesse, she suddenly remembered that Ellie was starting school the next day, and she dragged her out to get pens, notebooks, paper, and a bunch of things Ellie was sure she would never need. She had everything in the book bag, and she was trying to remember to breathe as she walked onto campus to find her first class.

She wasn't looking where she was going and accidentally bumped into a girl walking in the opposite direction. Ellie muttered a quick sorry, but the girl just gave her a dirty look. All the buildings looked the same, and the map that she was holding in her shaky hand was giving her no help.

The map had tiny writing, and the names of the buildings were written on a legend along the side. She was looking for the building with an F on it when she bumped into someone else, and the map slipped out of her hand.

"Sorry about that," the boy said. He grabbed the map that was trying to run away on the wind, and Ellie wished it had managed to escape. "Here ya go."

"Thanks," Ellie said. She looked at the map again with a scowl.

"Do you need help?" The boy offered.

"I'm trying to find the Arts building."

"Oh, I'm headed that way. It's right over here." He started walking in the opposite direction. Ellie followed. They reached the building, and it was much easier to find her class, and she began to feel a little more relaxed.

She thanked the boy and walked into her first class. It was a Literature class, and she had picked it, thinking it would be the easiest to start with. Her other class was a sociology class, a general ed requirement that she thought would also be simpler.

As the professor began to talk about the different supplies that students would need and the list of required books, Ellie felt panic rising within her. She wrote down all the book titles and supplies, but her head was spinning by the second hour of the professor explaining his syllabi.

Ellie looked around the class at her classmates. Some were older than her. They sat straight, taking notes and smiling at everything the professor said. A few were staring off into space, looking bored and unconcerned. And the rest seemed as concerned as Ellie felt inside.

By the time the class was over, Ellie was beyond overwhelmed. The theme for the course was madness, and the idea of reading about crazy people while she was fighting off her own crazy was not entirely appealing. She already had homework, and she didn't even have the books. She looked at the title of the first book, *Fight Club*. Not really her type of book, but she was willing to try it out.

She would be back tomorrow after work for her second class. One class was Mondays and Wednesdays, and the other was Tuesdays and Thursdays after work from four to six.

She hoped this would give her enough distraction that she wouldn't even notice that Clara was gone, and she had only herself and Zeke to talk to now. Last night was her first night on her own, and luckily, she was exhausted from helping move Clara's things, and she had Zeke. Otherwise, the newly sparse apartment might have felt empty and lonely.

After class, she went home and was greeted by a jumping, whining, screeching Zeke. He was so excited to see Ellie she thought he would wiggle right out of his skin. She laughed and was instantly relaxed. They took a quick walk so Zeke could have a pee break, and then it was time for the worst part of the day. Figuring out dinner.

She looked in the fridge for something to call dinner, and when she didn't find anything, she decided to call for pizza. While waiting for the pizza man, she scrolled through every social media site she had and never posted on anymore. She hated the anxiety that came with notifications on her posts. It seemed that people on social media could find something to argue or comment on for anything.

The pizza finally came, and it helped to settle Ellie's nerves a little. Until she decided to go to bed, she suddenly felt very aware of all the noises in the quiet apartment.

The slightest sounds would bounce off the walls and echo through the apartment. Ellie hadn't finished turning the room she shared with Clara into hers yet. She would have time on the weekend.

Bedtime made anxiety rear its ugly head stronger than any other time of the day. It had been working its way up her throat, and she felt like it might choke her at any moment. Her phone dinged, and she was happy that Clara was checking on her.

Clara: How's independent life?

Ellie: It's quiet.

Clara: Are you trying to say I'm loud? LOL.

Ellie: Hahaha. No, but you definitely aren't quiet.

Clara: Well, I guess that's fair. I miss you and Zeke! Let's get lunch this week.

Ellie: We miss you too. Sounds good. Let me know when.

Ellie was glad to hear from Clara, and it helped to make her feel better but only for a couple of minutes while they talked. Once the messages stopped coming in, Ellie felt the weight of loneliness settle even heavier on her chest. She missed lying in bed talking to Clara at night.

Zeke must have felt her anxiety because he jumped onto the bed and put half his body over her chest. Weirdly enough, the actual weight helped lift the invisible one. Ellie sighed and put her arms around him.

She lay awake in her bed watching the shadows play on the ceiling, and when she finally fell asleep, she watched Maggie die again.

CHAPTER
THIRTY-FOUR

By Wednesday night, the knot in Ellie's throat was making it hard for her to eat. She tried to eat cereal for dinner, mostly because she was tired of ordering out, but she couldn't keep it down and ended up throwing up after a few bites.

She was having dinner with Clara tomorrow after class, and she couldn't wait, but she hadn't been sleeping well, and her classes were putting her nerves on edge. The only thing helping her sleep was Zeke's calm warmth, always next to her.

Too many people were in her sociology class, and the teacher talked like he was trying to talk over a jet plane. She sat near the door because she felt like she couldn't breathe. And tonight, when she went back to her literature class, the professor lectured for an hour about the insanity that the author was trying to portray within the novel.

When she switched to talking about the author's madness and how insanity can help inspire writers. Ellie thought about her anxiety and wondered if she was insane enough to be an author.

She had been down that road before, and now that she was faced with another sleepless night, she thought the chances of that being the case were growing. It was early for her to call it a night, but her stomach was in knots, her throat was spasming, and she felt like she might die, so sleep felt like a good way to escape all that.

She took Zeke out one last time and climbed into bed. He cuddled up next to her and huffed. He looked out the window and back at Ellie. She laughed, imagining his judgment was something like, "I can't believe you are going to bed before the sun has even set, loser."

She fell asleep quickly, but it didn't last. As Maggie screamed for Ellie to help her, a deer ran over her body, and an elevator dropped from the sky, landing on them both. Ellie woke up with a start and decided sleep was overrated. Another night of M.A.S.H. reruns it was. Zeke huffed another judgment.

The next day Ellie followed her daily routine and made it to work without a problem. She was back to taking the stairs since her accident, and the growing worry of running into Dane was always in the back of her mind. Work was nice mostly because it was the only predictable and comfortable time in Ellie's day.

It was the only time she didn't feel alone, the only time she could distract herself from her worry over classes and thoughts about Maggie, and the only time she felt like an average, sane individual.

Her sociology class was a disaster. The professor discussed an assignment they would have to present to the whole class. They would each have to research a topic and teach the class their findings. As Ellie listened to the research and presentation requirements, she felt a faint panic rise in her chest. When the professor finished explaining, she felt like she would throw up, and she broke out in a cold sweat.

She was trying to breathe. Her heart was pounding in her chest, and deep breaths were cut short by its rapid progress. Ellie felt wave after wave of dizziness slammed into her, and her head spun.

You are okay.

Just breathe.

I can't breathe.

I am going to die in front of all these people.

Calm down, Ellie.

Breathe.

Ellie felt a wildness inside of her. She needed to get out of the classroom. The walls felt like they were closing in.

She quickly gathered all her things, and half ran out of the room. She thought she saw the professor and students watching her as she left, but she didn't care. She was panting for air, and when she finally made it outside, she stood for a minute and let the cool air wash over her.

She sucked in the fresh air and waited for relief from the dizziness and panic, but it didn't come. She still couldn't breathe. Ellie sank to her knees, still gasping for air. Maggie's face flashed before her eyes, her arm outstretched, mouth open, and gasping for air right along with her.

The professor and some students from Ellie's class came out just in time to watch her pass out.

She fell forward, hitting her head on the sidewalk before lying still. Her breathing was still rapid but slowed as soon as she was unconscious.

ELLIE CAME to on the sidewalk. She was lying on her back facing the dark sky that was lit up by only the moon and a few random lights outside the building around the campus.

Sam, the paramedic, was crouched by her side, and she had an oxygen mask on. She could see her classmates and professor talking to a police officer closer to the building, and she closed her eyes in embarrassment. She was sure she would die, yet here she was, alive and mortified at how she must have looked.

"Ellie, we have to stop meeting like this," Sam said as he took the blood pressure cuff off her arm and folded it up.

Ellie knew that talking would be challenging with the mask on, and she didn't feel much like talking either, so she nodded and gave him a small smile. He had her phone next to him, and she figured he probably used it to call her emergency contact, her brother Eric. He saw her looking at it and handed it back to her.

"I called your emergency contact, Eric. He is on his way. How are you feeling?"

She held up a hand and wavered it to indicate that she was "so-so," then she tried to pull the mask off, but he stopped her.

"Nope, not so fast. You need to keep that on for a few minutes. Your teacher said you were struggling to breathe and acting strange when you passed out. You can tell me all about what happened after I get your oxygen levels back up."

Ellie's phone buzzed, and Clara's name scrolled across the top. They were supposed to meet for dinner, which she wouldn't make—another set of plans ruined by her damn anxiety.

Sam held out his hand, and she passed it over.

"Hi, this is Sam, a paramedic, and I'm here with your friend. She is okay, but she passed out and hit her head, so we are helping her out. Her brother is on his way. Yeah, we are outside the school. Okay, bye." Ellie could only hear Sam's side of the conversation, but she knew that Clara would be on her way as soon as he answered the phone.

Sam was helping her sit up when Eric got there. He looked worried, and Ellie hated that she was the reason he had his concerned big brother face on, as always. He stopped and talked with Sam's partner.

She could see much better now that she was sitting up, and the professor and students had all left. Sam took her mask off and retook her blood pressure. He listened to her breathing when Clara approached the pathway hot on Eric's heels. Luckily for both of them, the college was so close, and they could zoom over. Especially after this, she would probably need an escort to all her classes.

"What the hell, Ellie?" Clara was panting and bent at the waist with her hands on her knees to catch her breath. Apparently, she had run up the path from the parking lot.

"I'm fine," Ellie said. She was embarrassed that paramedics were once again treating her. She felt like such a mess.

"Well, I wouldn't say fine. But she is going to be okay," Sam said. He was writing down her vitals and gave her a quick smile before standing to go and talk to his partner.

"He said you aren't fine." Clara had her hands on her hips now. She looked at the two paramedics and noticed that Eric was next to her now.

"Looks like you will need to go to the hospital for a checkup and a couple of stitches, El."

"See! You need stitches!" Clara shook her head and

leaned closer to look at Ellie's head, which was covered with a gauze bandage but had blood seeping through.

Eric sat next to Ellie and pulled her close to him. She put her head on his shoulder and felt the letdown of adrenaline and a couple of tears slipping through. She squeezed her eyes shut to keep any others from following their friends.

"Ellie, what happened?" Eric asked softly.

"I don't know. I was sitting in class listening to the professor talking about a project we had to do, and as I thought about it and had to present it to the class, everything started spinning, and I couldn't breathe. I came outside to get some fresh air, and I guess I passed out and hit my head." Ellie's voice faded as she was talking. She was breathing better now, but she didn't feel quite right.

Eric pulled back a little to look at her. Her eyes had dark circles around them, her skin was paler than usual, and her eyes were red. She didn't look good. Add the head bandage and blood; she looked like an extra in a Halloween haunted mansion.

"Are you still seeing Maggie?" Eric asked.

"Yeah," Ellie said. "I haven't been sleeping very well."

Clara frowned, "Why not?"

"I don't know..." Ellie didn't want to say she wasn't sleeping well because it was just her and Zeke, but she wasn't sure how helpful he would be against an intruder, and she was afraid. She didn't want to look weak. Clara had lived alone for years before Ellie moved in with her, and now Ellie had been alone for less than a week, and she was already a mess.

Sam came back over as his partner packed up their things. "You are going to go to the hospital to get checked out with your brother, okay, Ellie?"

Ellie nodded. She looked at Eric, and he stood up to help her get to her feet. They all trudged down the short-sloping hill to the parking lot. Sam and his partner said goodbye and got into their rig to leave. Ellie liked Sam but hoped she didn't have to see him again for a while. Although it was nice to have a familiar face there when you woke up from passing out, so maybe it was nice that she knew the local paramedic.

Clara got in her car to follow them to the hospital, and when Eric had Ellie alone in the car, he was ready to cut the bull. "Alright, so tell the truth. Why aren't you sleeping well?"

Ellie sighed. She knew Eric wouldn't let that one go, "The apartment is so empty. I can feel it creeping up on me. And I have been having more nightmares. I feel like I have this knot of anxiety twisting around in my throat, and I don't know how to get rid of it. I think it is going to choke me to death one day. Like, this is how I die, anxiety."

Eric gave her a sideways look, and she knew she was being a little dramatic, but she couldn't help it. It was just how she felt.

"Okay, well, maybe you should move in with me or back in with Mom and Dad. I think it is too much for you to be on your own already."

The rest of the drive was silent as Ellie contemplated what Eric had said. She didn't want to move in with him or Mom and Dad. But she also didn't want to live alone anymore. They pulled up to the hospital, and Clara was already there. She was a faster driver than Eric, and she had parked and was waiting out front. Eric pulled through the drop-off zone and dropped Ellie off with Clara before pulling away to go and find parking for his truck.

"Okay, so listen before Eric comes back. I think this was all too much, too fast. There is an open apartment in the building that Jesse and I moved into, and it is right down the hall from ours. I think you should take it. That way, you are in your own place like you want, but you are close to me. And I think school was too big of a leap for you. A friend at the coffee shop has been doing all her classes online. We should look into that for you, and you should drop your on-campus classes. It is obviously too overwhelming right now. Don't argue with me right now because Eric will be coming back, but I want you to think about it. And I am staying with you tonight. I already told Jesse."

Ellie smiled at Clara. Her best friend had her back once again. She thought about what she wanted and needed, not just the latter, which she loved about her. And she knew that Ellie liked to think things through on her own, which is why she approached Ellie without Eric. However, that was the same reason that Eric waited for Clara not to be around. It was nice to feel this much love, Ellie thought.

She got three little stitches in her head in the emergency room and was out in no time. Eric tried to talk her into coming home with him, but she assured him she would be good at home with Clara.

The girls were on their second pizza and tenth episode of *Friends* when there was a knock on the door. It was Eric with two gallons of ice cream. He passed the bags over and gave Ellie a wink. "I just want you to be happy, Ellie. Let me know if you need me to stay over tomorrow night." He gave her a quick kiss and turned to leave.

"I love you too, Eric!" Ellie said.

Ellie brought the ice cream into the kitchen and put it in the freezer. After talking to Eric and Clara just a little about what was going on in her head, she thought about how much better she felt right now.

If talking just that little bit helped her feel better, then talking about everything would probably help her feel much better. Maybe Clara was right; she had just gone too big too soon. She went from a horrible accident and terrifying childhood realization to a debilitating depression to living alone and starting school all in a month.

She thought that Clara probably had a pretty good idea, but she was going to add something to that plan and see a therapist. Repressing and pushing away her anxiety wasn't helping her any. She just kept panicking and getting hurt.

Not to mention having a major mental setback and having to start her denial and repression again every time something traumatic happened.

"Hey! What was at the door?" Clara called from in front of the tv.

"Eric dropped off ice cream," Ellie said as she returned to the living room. "I figured we could eat it when we finish the pizza."

"Good idea." They each grabbed another slice of veggie lover pizza, it was the best way to get veggies in, after all, and it was a great way to chase the meat lover pizza they already consumed.

"I have been thinking about what you said. I think it's a good plan."

"You want that apartment?"

"Yeah, and I'm going to drop my classes at the college and enroll in online classes. I can't show my face to those people again anyway." They laughed at her pain but did it together, so it felt good.

"That's great! Especially since I already told Jesse to go

down and talk to the super when we were at the hospital."
She took a bite of pizza and smiled at Ellie.

"Well, that's good. I also decided that I am going to see a therapist. I think it is time for me to face these demons head-on. I have been hiding from them for far too long..."

"I think that's the best idea you've had yet."

THIRTY-FIVE

THREE WEEKS LATER, ELLIE WALKED OUT OF HER FOURTH THERAPY session. Thanks to Eric, she had moved into her new apartment, enrolled in online courses, and signed Zeke up for service dog training. He had researched the laws around service animals and how to get your dog trained and registered as an emotional support dog.

Her therapist, Francine, agreed that it was a great way to manage her anxiety since she had so many traumatic incidents that could have been helped by service animal support.

A lot can change in three weeks, and while therapy hadn't magically fixed everything, Ellie felt better.

Francine was helping her to work through what happened with Maggie. She was accessing memories from the accident each session. It was demanding and emotionally draining. She cried in every session and hated having to talk about things that made her so miserable, but as she spoke about them, little pieces of weight were chipped away from her shoulders, and she felt lighter every time she walked out the door.

Today they talked about her memories of the days right after the accident. The first few days after returning to school, the other children whispered when Ellie walked through the hall. She hadn't talked since the accident, and they all thought she was weird.

One particularly mean boy had made up a rumor that she had actually died in the accident with her friend and told everyone she was walking roadkill. Ellie felt the memory as if she was back in the halls of her elementary school. She remembered hearing their whispers calling her roadkill, and a week later, her parents moved her to a new school.

She knew she had moved schools in elementary school, but she had never remembered why. Francine explained how common repressing childhood trauma was, which helped Ellie feel like she was normal after all.

She wasn't the only person in the world that repressed memories and wasn't the only one that struggled with anxiety. She no longer felt like she was crazy and was starting to feel like true independence was within her reach.

When she recalled being called roadkill, Ellie felt another puzzle piece fall into place. No wonder roadkill had always been such a trigger for her. Her unconscious mind remembered the connection and triggered her panic; that and, of course, the simple fact that death itself was a significant trigger for her. She was terrified of dying, as many people are, but having come so close to it and watching it happen to her childhood best friend had left a permanent scar in her mind that she would probably always struggle with.

But the point of therapy, Francine told her, is not to fix you. It is not a cure. Therapy is a way to cope with and work through your pains and struggles to become stronger.

Taking classes online was going better than she had imagined, and she was getting straight A's in her classes. She still didn't like living alone all the time, but she had Zeke, and when that wasn't enough, she would walk down the hall to Clara's apartment.

The only thing missing was Nick. She hadn't talked to him since he texted her, telling her he needed space. She had talked about him in therapy today, and it made her realize that her whole relationship with him was on hold.

She needed to focus on herself and work through the traumas bubbling up to the surface after her elevator accident, but him dropping her at her most vulnerable time was a sore festering.

ELLIE AND ZEKE walked through Clara's door an hour later. They had walked to Francine's office and back to the apartments to get exercise which Francine promised was an excellent way to help with anxiety.

At first, Ellie thought that was a bunch of nonsense, but after three weeks of exercising regularly, she was feeling pretty good. Maybe it was just the therapy, maybe it was Zeke, or maybe it was all of it. Ellie wasn't sure, but she wasn't about to mess with a good thing, so exercise it was.

"Hey, girl!" Clara called when she heard Ellie come in. Zeke took off across the apartment and plowed into Clara's legs, almost knocking her off her feet. She laughed and scratched his ears, saying hi to him as well.

"It smells good in here," Ellie said.

"Thanks, I'm making Rigatoni with meatballs and red sauce. You want to stay for dinner?" Clara asked.

"Sure, that sounds good." Ellie sat on one of the bench seats and watched Clara as she checked the garlic bread in the oven. She went to stir the sauce and noticed that Ellie was staring at her.

"So, what's on your mind?"

"Well, I talked about Nick in therapy today and just realized how upset I am with him. He dumped me during a horrible time. I thought he would always be there for me, and he broke up with me when I needed him most. How could he do that to me? I thought he loved me. I feel so foolish."

Clara stopped stirring and gave Ellie a confused look. "You know, I think you remember what happened a little differently."

"What do you mean?" Ellie asked.

"I mean, you shut Nick out. You refused to talk to him. He would come to the apartment and bring you flowers and gifts. He would sit outside the bedroom door when you locked it and refused to talk to anyone. He begged you to talk to him through the door, through text, and through voicemail. He wanted to be there for you so badly, and you pushed him away. You broke his heart. And he has been hoping to hear from you ever since."

Ellie listened to Clara wide-eyed and slack-jawed. She couldn't believe she hadn't realized how horrible she had been to Nick. She looked down at Zeke, who was chewing on one of the toys he kept at Clara's place. And then it hit her, what Clara had said, that Nick had been hoping to hear from her ever since...

"Did you say he has been hoping to hear from me? Present tense?"

"Well, yeah. He has kept in touch with me a little. Mostly he just checks in to make sure you are doing okay. But Jesse and I ran into him a week ago, and he looked miserable. He misses you, Ellie. I think he thought you would get better and want him back, but now you sound like you are twisting the past to make him the bad guy, and he wasn't the bad guy."

"I was," Ellie whispered. She was shocked that she was the bad guy in the story of her and Nick and that she had complained almost her entire therapy session about how he had done her wrong.

Once again, she repressed and changed the story of what happened.

Clara was watching her again, and this time she smiled. "You were Ellie. But not on purpose. You went into survival mode. You were trying to make it through the hell going on in your head, and you can't change how you dealt. But now that you know that you are doing better, you can rethink how your story goes and how you deal with things in the future."

Ellie knew that Clara was right. She had changed the story, and she could change it again. She was still thinking about how to fix things when Jesse came home for dinner.

"Hey, Ellie. How are you today?" Jesse asked. He kissed Clara and peeked into the oven. "Smells good, babe. Are you staying for dinner, Ellie?"

"I was going to, but I think I'm going to go ahead and head home." Ellie stood up to leave, and Zeke jumped up and followed behind her as she gave Clara a quick hug and moved to the front door. "I will see you guys later."

Ellie walked down the hall with Zeke following behind her. She thought about school and work and how well things were going for her now.

She knew it had only been three weeks since she made all these changes, but she already felt so confident in herself and her ability to stick with it. She had finally found something that worked for her. If she had known how positive therapy would be on her life, she would have started it a lot sooner.

She had a new routine; work, therapy, walking Zeke, and school. She knew that as long as she stuck with it, she could continue to make positive changes in her life.

She pulled out her phone and scrolled back through her messages to the last one she had received from Nick. She hadn't read it since the day she dragged herself, kicking and internally screaming out of her funk.

Nick: Ellie, I know you probably won't read this, but I hope you will eventually. I told Clara to tell you I can't do this anymore. I have tried so hard, and I want to be there for you, but you won't let me. Maybe I am not the thing that you need right now. I think *you* are the thing that you really need right now. I'm not going to force you to be in my life, even though that is all I want. You are stronger than you think, Ellie. You just need to fight for yourself. Let me know when you are ready.

Ellie read the message twice. Zeke jumped on the couch beside her and snuck his head under her arm. She stroked his head gently as she dialed Nick's number. She held her breath as she waited for him to pick up, and for a minute, she didn't think he would, but his voice finally came through on the third ring.

"I'm ready," she said. And she was.

EPILOGUE

Five Years Later

"You ready, El?" Nick asked, and he adjusted his tie in the full-length hotel mirror.

"I don't know how I'm going to make it through this ceremony." Ellie's voice drifted out of the bathroom, where she sat on the floor in front of the toilet.

Ellie had become very well acquainted with every bathroom she was near the past four weeks while she navigated extreme morning sickness. The joke was that it was never just in the morning. They shouldn't lie about that when pressuring you to have a baby.

Nick peeked in and gave her his most sympathetic pouty face. "I'm sorry, honey. Are you sure you don't want to tell anyone yet?"

"If we tell them now, then it will be all about us, and I am not stealing my best friend's thunder. This is her day. If she had come to our wedding and announced that she was pregnant, I would have..." Ellie paused when Nick gave her a skeptical look.

They both knew she would have been perfectly fine if

Clara had come to their wedding and given any huge life news announcement. But she still didn't want to do that to Clara; attention was a much more important commodity to her.

"Yeah, you would have been fine, and Clara would too. But let's not worry about that until later. Now let's go. You know how you hate being late." He held out his hand to help her off the floor.

Nick put Zeke's leash on while he waited for Ellie to brush her teeth one last time before they left. He had his own matching bowtie attached to his collar and matched his emotional support dog tux vest.

When Ellie walked out of the bathroom, Nick's breath caught in his throat. She looked just as beautiful as the day of their wedding last summer. After a whole year married to the most beautiful woman in the world, he couldn't wait to spend the rest of his life showing her how strong and unique she was.

Ellie had completed her degree at Oak Valley Community College, doing almost all her classes online. When she had to go onto campus, she could take Zeke with her, which made college with anxiety manageable. It took double the average time to get her degree because she worked through it at her own pace and switched majors three times.

First, she declared English, then there was the early childhood development fiasco of year two, and finally, she landed on business. Now she was helping Nick with the bookstore, and they were moving locations to expand to new and used books along with a full cafe.

Ellie put her arm in Nick's and grabbed Zeke's leash from him. He looked up to her and whined. He knew she was anxious, so he attached himself to her leg, and Nick watched her from the corner of his eye. After so many years together, he knew every signal Zeke knew to watch for, and he could see just as quickly that she was a bundle of nerves.

"What's the worry?" Nick asked her. This had become the go-to saying whenever she was anxious, and it always made her smile, even if just faintly.

"What if I throw up in the middle of the ceremony?" Ellie used to ask these what-ifs in her head, but therapy with Francine over the last five years has taught her to verbalize her worries. This way, she could either hear how far-fetched and silly they were or get the support she needed from those around her.

"Okay, what if you do?"

"That would be mortifying!" She looked at him wide-eyed as they made their way down the hall. The wedding was in the hotel's garden venue downstairs, and Ellie dreaded the elevator ride downstairs. She had been working on this trigger for years, and it was the hardest one to shake, but she thought she could manage it with Nick and Zeke by her side.

"Well, if you feel like you will throw up, maybe just step out to the side."

"What if they stop the ceremony, and everyone thinks I object or something?"

"Whose opinion matters?"

"Clara's."

"So, this is why it would be good to at least, maybe, tell her. I know you want to wait till you are twelve weeks, but that is next week. I think it will be okay."

Ellie had heard horror stories, so she felt like she should wait, and her anxiety was playing with her emotions on the subject. Even with that hanging over her head, she generally felt so much better. She was excited to watch Clara, and Jesse get married.

Clara had done well with her acting career so far and was finally getting roles with characters that had names. Jesse proposed to Clara at the premiere of her first movie. She was finally an actress, and now she would be a wife too.

"Is Eric already downstairs?" Nick asked as they neared the elevator. He knew the answer, but it was best to distract Ellie whenever she had to face an elevator.

"Yeah, and Nadine is with him." She bit her lip as they stopped in front of the elevator. Nadine was Eric's girlfriend of three years now. Ellie liked her and hoped that Eric would pop the question soon. Their parents were equally hopeful. Sarah dropped hints at Eric about getting married as often as she dropped hints at Ellie about having a baby.

"Nadine wouldn't let them be late. What was I thinking?" Nick smiled at her mischievously. They had been late to the rehearsal dinner the night before. Ellie had been busy bent over the toilet, but she had been perfectly fine letting everyone assume they had been consumed in newlywed activities.

It had become a thing throughout the night, and Eric looked as queasy as she felt. Ellie was mortified initially, but seeing Eric so distraught had been fun.

"Don't you go encouraging people today."

"Are you sure about that?" Nick leaned down to kiss Ellie, his hand cradling her lower back. He pulled her close and deepened the kiss.

"We could make good on those rumors from last night," Nick whispered against her lips.

"We can make good all you want once we get back to the room. Right now, it's time for a wedding. And maybe even an announcement." Ellie smiled up at Nick. She always felt relaxed and safe when she was in his arms. Each new stage felt like a new hurdle for her anxiety to overcome. And since he came back into her life five years ago, he had made each one more manageable than the last.

Nick squeezed her hand with a dazzling smile, and Zeke leaned against her leg. She couldn't wait to have his baby, and right now, she couldn't wait to tell everyone she loved. She just had to take this one elevator to the wedding party waiting below.

She took a deep breath as the elevator dinged and the doors slid open. Zeke stood up and looked at the two of them expectantly.

"Ready?" Nick asked, his caramel eyes caressing her face. His gentleness with her told her it would all be okay, just like it always was with him.

"Ready." She said, and they all stepped on together.

ABOUT THE AUTHOR

I am a 35-year-old avid reader and writer. I started writing stories as a child and only wanted to put down a pen if my nose was in a book. I am also a mother, wife, animal lover, and teacher. I hope that you enjoyed my story. Mental health awareness has always been important to me, and with this story, I seek to give a voice to the internal battles that can cause external chaos.

Look out for more stories by me coming soon!